# Praise for
# *A Very Public Eye*
# and *Buyer's Remorse*

"The second installment in Lori L. Lake's newest series is a puzzler from the get-go with all the elements of a great mystery: plenty of intrigue, lots of suspense, and a fantastic setting (Duluth, Minnesota). With Leo's vision issues and the implosion of her relationship, Lake continues to stir the pot—providing a recipe for another winner."
**~Jessie Chandler, author of The Shay O'Hanlon Caper Series**

"It is no wonder that Lori Lake's books are best sellers. Her characters are deep-bodied, multidimensional, and convincing. Her plots unfold like pedals on a flower, coming to full bloom at just the right moment."
**~Foreword Magazine**

"This book is a page turner, as I've come to expect from any book Lori Lake writes. A well written story, with likeable characters, an exciting believable plot, and a comfortable easy read. I'm always confident when buying a Lori Lake book of an enjoyable read."
**~Terry's Lesfic Reviews**

"This was a very engaging mystery, and the character of Leo is someone you will want to follow into book 2 of the series. The writing is concise, and the pacing keeps you turning pages to find out what happens next. Well worth a read."
**~The Kindle Book Review**

"When it comes to plotting, Lake subscribes to the "one darn thing after another" school—something I like in a mystery. The protagonist, Leo (Leona) Reese leaped all the hurdles Lake set for her, along the way acquiring a terrific sidekick (I hope he's back in the next book) and dealing with co-workers who made me glad, once again, that I'm retired."
**~Carolyn J. Rose, author of the Catskill Mountain Mysteries**

"Considered one of the best authors of modern lesbian fiction, her work – part action, part drama, and part romance – gleefully defies categorization."
**~Lavender Magazine**

# Other Books by Lori L. Lake

=====================

### The Gun Series
Gun Shy: Book 1
Under The Gun: Book 2
Have Gun We'll Travel: Book 3
Jump The Gun: Book 4

### The Public Eye Series
Buyer's Remorse: Book 1
A Very Public Eye: Book 2

### Romances
Eight Dates
Like Lovers Do
Different Dress
Ricochet In Time

### Historical Fiction
Snow Moon Rising

### Short Story Collections
Shimmer & Other Stories
Stepping Out: Short Stories

### Anthologies Edited
Time's Rainbow: Writing Ourselves Back into American History

Lesbians on the Loose:
Crime Writers on the Lam

The Milk of Human Kindness:
Lesbian Authors Write about Mothers & Daughters

Romance for Life!

# A Very Public Eye

The Public Eye Mystery Series
Book Two

by

# Lori L. Lake

Launch Point Press
Portland, Oregon

**ISBN:**     978-1-63304-016-8
**E-Book:**  978-1-63304-017-5

**Editing:** Nann Dunne, Brenda Adcock
**Proofreading**: Carol Poynor,
Patty Schramm, Betty Crandall
**Cover and Book Design:** Lorelei

Portland, Oregon
www.LaunchPointPress.com

*Dedicated to Ruth Manning
with much appreciation for over
five decades of guidance, advice,
motherly wisdom, and love*

# Acknowledgments, 2012

The journey toward this finished book has been an odd and long one. When I first envisioned the Public Eye Mystery series way back in 2004, the plot of *this* book was where I started. I had gotten the idea of having my sleuth be a state investigator from Meg McAlister, who did a similar job for the State of Minnesota. But as I wrote, I came to realize the circumstances of Leona Reese's life called for a different debut book. I ended up setting aside this draft of *A Very Public Eye* and instead wrote *Buyer's Remorse*, which became the first book in the series.

Much time passed, and my life took many unexpected turns, but finally *Buyer's Remorse* came out in 2011. Unfortunately, I failed to give my old friend Meg a shout-out. So at long last, my first acknowledgment is to Meg McAlister for cheerfully encouraging me to write a different kind of detective than we usually see in crime fiction. I took many liberties with Leo's job description, and those changes are my responsibility and do not reflect the outstanding work Meg and her fellow investigators do.

I want to thank my editors, Nann Dunne and Brenda Adcock, for their patient guidance and sound advice. Jessie Chandler read early drafts, and Judy Kerr and Jessie (again!) read and commented on the later draft. I'm forever grateful for their time and ideas. Thanks to Carol Poyner, Patty Schramm, and Betty J. Crandall for their eagle eyes on the final proof.

I feel so much gratitude toward the smart medical women who assisted me. Dr. Lindsey C. Thomas, MD, forensic pathologist and Coroner/Medical Examiner for the seven-county region in SE Minnesota, spent an entire afternoon schooling me about poisons, strangulation, autopsies, and general information regarding homicide.

Patty Schramm gave me paramedic information, Sharon Carlson, RN/PHN, consulted with me about injuries, treatments, and medical procedures, and Joanne Middaugh, MSW, gave me lots of useful information about social work and treatment centers. Paula Offut took time out to talk about wheelchairs and van/car accessibility.

Thanks and cheers go to the usual suspects for ongoing moral support and encouragement: Betty Crandall, Lisa Boeving, MB Panichi, and Verda Foster. Very big kudos to Christina, Andrea, and

Samantha for keeping me focused by frequently asking why I *still* wasn't done with the book yet.

Gratitude for advice and inspiration goes to Ellen Hart, Lee Lynch, Elizabeth Sims, Pat & Gary at Once Upon a Crime Bookstore, and Marlene Howard and the Oregon Writers Colony.

**Lori L. Lake**
**Portland, Oregon**
**November, 2012**

# New Acknowledgments, 2022

At long last, it's time to get the print version of this book back out into the world. Thanks to all those who have written over the years to encourage me to get cracking on Book Three AND to reissue the first two books in print.

Going through this book again after over a decade has helped me discover quite a number of new plots to employ in this series. I'm excited to work on the next adventures of Leo and Thom.

Any "mistakes" you find may be because either procedures and technology have changed or the author messed something up. Any error you find should be attributed to me, and don't hesitate to write to explain where I may have gone wrong.

**Lori L. Lake**
**Portland, Oregon**
**April, 2022**

"Some things you cannot see or explain, but they are there, lurking.
Some things dwell in the dark: waiting . . . watching . . . haunting.
Sometimes evil takes on many forms, many faces.
And silence is the last thing you hear,
when it's already too late."
**~Barry K. Brickey**

# Chapter One

Eddie Bolton moved like a walking string of lit firecrackers. As he passed through the center's cafeteria, teenagers much bigger than him stepped aside. Those who were seated leaned in and looked away.

Yeah, Eddie thought, get outta my face. I could hurt you.

One of the more popular staff members rose to intercept him and raised a hand at the doorway. "Eddie—"

"Get out of my way." He pushed past and stomped out into the hallway.

"But wait, you can't . . ."

The man's voice drifted away as Eddie strode toward his room, the pulse in his head beating a staccato as fast as a stampede of wild ponies.

The part of the chemical dependency unit to which Eddie had access was shaped like a U, and he had to travel from one end all the way around to the other end to reach his assigned room. At the midpoint, he passed near the security station where an unarmed guard kept the general public from wandering in, while also assuring that Eddie and his peers were not allowed out. The guard was no taller than Eddie and much skinnier. With his worry-lined face and buckteeth, Eddie thought he resembled a rodent. He hated the guard on sight and wouldn't meet his eyes as he passed.

Each resident at the Benton Dowling Center was supposed to be considered a temporary "patient," but in Eddie's mind, *inmate* was the more appropriate term. No freedom. Locked up and the key taken away. He didn't ask to be here, and he wouldn't play their game. He couldn't get out until he was deemed emotionally ready—or until he reached the age of eighteen. After a quick mental count he mumbled, "Forty-six days. Just have to make it forty-six days."

He knew he wasn't supposed to leave his group at the table. They hadn't even been released to get their food yet. He would surely get in trouble for his angry departure, but there was no way he'd squeeze in, elbow to elbow, with that bunch of pathetic weasels. He considered himself a man while they were all stupid boys. He didn't want to deal with their shit.

After breakfast each morning, residents were allowed quiet time in their rooms until eight a.m. when school started. At eleven, they had athletic time in the gym. Today he would refuse to do either. All he wanted now was to curl up on his bed and convince himself not to beat the hell out of the pansy guard, escape, and run for the woods. He knew that wasn't a good plan. He looked down at his soft slippers and the baggy jeans and t-shirt he wore. No, he'd be found shivering within an hour.

When he reached his room, he grabbed both sides of the door frame and pulled, launching himself across the room and onto his assigned bed. He lay there panting, sweating, tense. He wanted a drink, some pot, anything—even just a cigarette. Some of the boys used behavior credits to buy candy for when they were jonesin' real bad. He'd only been at the place eleven days and hadn't yet earned any privileges. He was pretty sure that throwing a punch last week at Mike, the counselor, hadn't helped his cause. But, oh, it felt so good! The impact of fist on bone, the startled look in the counselor's eyes, the fear and anger as the bigger man went down. At once, Eddie felt calm—focused—as though the only objects existing in the world were the knuckles of his fist and Mike's scruffy, unshaven cheek. It was worth the night spent in isolation in a padded room with no toilet. He dreamed of slugging Mike all night long, though when he awoke the next day, stiff from lying on the thin padding, he agreed not to act out again. That was the phrase they used: act out. Like he was on stage somewhere. He wanted to tell them, "This is no act. You wanna see some real action? Gimme some crack or a few shots of Jack Daniels, and I'll show you an act!"

He was surprised no one came after him now, but breakfast would be over soon enough. He didn't want the lukewarm scrambled eggs or cold toast. Cheerios were for little kids, and the sausage looked like something from out of a dog's rear end. He contemplated going on a hunger strike and smiled grimly. He thought he could last forty-six days. Easy.

He swung his legs over the side of the bed and looked around the room: two twin beds, two chairs pushed up to small tables meant to serve as desks, and some open shelving near the doorway where he and his roommate kept jeans, plain white t-shirts, socks, and underwear. All of their personal clothing, shoes, and possessions were taken away. He wasn't allowed an iPod or even a watch in this unit. There was no door in the frame leading to the hallway. Anyone could look in. Worst of all, the bathroom door was cut out two-thirds up so staff could peek over. He hated that there was no privacy, that he couldn't even take a crap without worrying someone would come along and watch.

He stood and paced, but the room allowed him to take only six cribbed steps. He'd never liked enclosed places. Tightening his fists, he squeezed, tensing his forearms, and let out a growl. His breath quickened, and the panicky feeling welled up inside. The pale blue walls sported no pictures, no windows. It would take a year of Sundays and fifty jackknives to scratch his way through the cement block to the outside.

He stepped into the bathroom and whispered, "Gross!" under his breath. The room was, at most, seven by ten feet. To the right, the sink was built in an alcove. A sheet of high-gloss metal, screwed into the wall above the sink, served as a mirror. Two toothbrushes lay on the counter next to a plastic soap dish and one tiny tube of generic toothpaste. The area to the left sported a showerhead in one corner, and six feet away, in the other corner, a toilet stool. No curtain. He had to shower in the tiny space, and if the metal toilet got splashed, too bad. "Fucking gross. No fucking privacy . . . people watching you shit and shower . . . disgusting."

Eddie leaned over the counter surrounding the sink, his palms pressing hard. He could make out his reflection in the metal, but everything was fuzzy around the edges. In the past, he'd never understood when his Aunt Phyllis told him he was too intense, but obviously his level of intensity was too much for this hellhole. He knew nobody he could trust. His roommate, a fat kid two years younger named William, was closed off in his own mute world. Even after Eddie provoked him mercilessly, William pretended Eddie didn't exist.

The area under the sink was open. Beneath the water pipes was a rack made of plastic holding a stack of scruffy towels, washcloths, and a spare roll of toilet paper which had gotten speckled with water but was now dry and rippled. He kicked at the rack, and the shelf bounced up off the supports, then fell back in place. The roll of TP hit the floor, and so did something else.

Frowning, Eddie reached down for a flat metal container lying on its side. Liquid swished to and fro, gradually settling. He picked it up. The screw-on lid opened to reveal pungent-smelling liquid.

"Well, shit. What's this?"

He sneaked a look over the closed half-door. His roommate had not returned, and he heard no sounds in the hall.

"Oh, wow," Eddie whispered as he sniffed at the metal flask. "William, you little creep. How the hell did you keep this from me?"

He closed his eyes and took a tiny sip, just one touch on his tongue. He hadn't ever tasted anything quite like it. Jim Beam, Jack Richland, Johnny Walker Red, and Captain Morgan were familiar. He liked liquors with a man's name attached, but he'd been drunk plenty of times on Absolut, Cutty Sark, Bacardi, Wild Turkey, and every variation of cheap wine and beer. This tasted like bourbon—but not exactly like any bourbon he'd had before. He wasn't sure if it was of high quality—or perhaps only crap. He didn't care. He raised the flask to the makeshift mirror. "Bottom's up."

Relishing a mouthful, he swallowed in metered amounts, feeling the liquor burn its way down his throat. His eyes watered, and he wheezed for a moment, then let out a satisfied burp. With a deep sigh, he swirled the remaining liquid. A feeling of intense happiness threaded its way through him from the tips of his toes all the way up to his ears. He quaffed down another shot. This one tasted exceptionally bitter, and for a moment, his throat threatened to close up.

Eleven days and I'm already out of practice? He let out a snort, then turned and leaned back against the counter, holding the container in both hands. The next swig he intended to savor. He licked his lips and thought of his last binge, of how sweet the rum tasted and how cute the girl with him had been. He refused to think of the crash that put her in the hospital. Eddie's aunt's car was an older model with one air bag, on the driver's side only, so he'd been all right. His cousin Stevie in the back seat had only gotten banged up, but Kimberly went through the windshield. Aunt Phyllis hadn't known about the girl's medical condition when he'd seen her the day before. Oh, well, he thought. There'll be plenty of other girls.

At most now, there were two swigs left, and he had to choke down the first swallow. The dregs tasted grainy, and he decided against taking the last sip. He thought this booze was indeed the cheapest kind. Every sip turned progressively more bitter. He wiped his lips on the back of his hand and stuffed the empty flask under the plastic rack. Before he could stand up, his stomach felt tight and too full.

Eddie laughed, glad he hadn't eaten breakfast and knowing if he had, the liquor wouldn't have as much effect. He grinned to think how much he was going to enjoy the high.

He leaned back against the edge of the counter, arms crossed and eyes closed. As he rocked himself from side to side, he felt the power growing in his torso and upper arms. He didn't know how long he stood there, but when he opened the door and stepped into the room, William was entering from the hallway.

"Hey, Big Boy," Eddie said in a jovial voice.

William gaped at him, startled, then turned away and headed for his bed on the right.

"Your secret's out, Willie. It's out, out, out."

The chubby face appeared alarmed. William opened his mouth to speak, but then closed it and looked down.

"What's the matter? Cat got your tongue?"

William rose and strode toward the hallway. Eddie watched him leave, then stood swaying in the middle of the room, eyes closed. He hummed a Puddle of Mudd song and bobbed his head in concert with drumbeats only he could hear. Tipping his head back, he turned in a slow circle. His reverie was interrupted by William's return.

"Hey, the deaf-mute's back." Eddie giggled, and William ignored him.

The other kid lowered himself to his bed, scooted away until his back was against the wall, and crossed his arms over his chest.

"I want to thank you, Willie, m'boy. Your generosity is definitely appreciated."

The tight feeling in Eddie's stomach blossomed up his throat through the roof of his mouth, and into his head. Bam! He heard pounding, and then the sound gradually muffled as though someone had poked something into his ears. "Cut it out!" he shouted.

William gazed up at him, eyes wide. Eddie staggered over to his own bed and fell on his side. "Shut up," Eddie said. "You shut up. Shut . . . shut . . . shut . . ."

The pounding in his head increased, and with effort, he panted. His right hand came up and he pointed at William. "I'm a dog, Willie . . . like a dog . . ." He closed his eyes and let his tongue loll out as he strained to pull in a breath. "Doggie, doggie, dog, dog . . ."

A spasm rippled through Eddie's body. He tried to fight it, calling out, "No . . ."

Clenching his jaw, he struggled to control his arms, but they tightened up of their own accord. His legs spasmed. He jerked and thrashed. Fell off the bed. He felt himself falling and falling into darkness and pain.

"Take the fire away. No! Don't hurt me." His mid-section burned like it was on fire. He screamed.

Then it hurt too much to speak, to open his mouth, or to breathe. The hot hammer in his chest pounded, relentless, unyielding. A giant man—bigger than the scariest monster he had ever dreamed—let out a roar.

And Eddie Bolton stopped breathing forever.

# Chapter Two

Leon "Leo" Reese didn't need two eyes to see the emergency vehicle lights in the rearview mirror as they came up behind her on Highway 61. Even though the morning light was sparse, and the defrosters were working overtime to clear the windshield, she saw flashing red and yellow lights long before hearing the insistent sirens. She pulled her Lexus SUV to the right of the four-lane highway, stopped, and watched a police car go by followed by an ambulance. She craned her neck, checking for traffic, then hit the gas and picked up speed again. Gradually the ambulance pulled away, the ear-piercing whine fading.

Minnesota's November weather had taken a turn for the worse in the last two days. Sunday had been sunshine and fifty-eight degrees. On this dismal Tuesday morning, it wasn't quite forty. Fog rose up on either side of the road, and an occasional smattering of icy raindrops hit the damp windshield. For the first time in months, Leo dug out her lined raincoat. It smelled musty, like the bottom of the rarely used closet where she'd found it earlier.

The road narrowed from four lanes to two. She flipped on her turn signal, glanced over her left shoulder, and attempted to merge, only to hear the blare of a horn. She jerked the wheel back to the right, overcorrecting. A red Geo, sloppy wet, swept past, still honking.

"All right already! I get it."

Heart beating fast, she looked more carefully this time and saw nothing in her blind spot. The lane finally ran out, and she eased into it. Her vision was good on the left, so the near accident with the Geo surprised her. She thought perhaps only her right side was her Achilles heel, but now realized she felt less secure driving than she had hoped regardless of what direction she needed to observe.

Once again, she felt a disconcerting horror and hopelessness that almost made her gasp. Cancer. In her right eye. She still had a difficult time believing her eye had been surgically removed. She'd cried many tears about it, but now since she was back to work, she'd cry no more. She decided that no matter what, she'd focus on the job.

Ten minutes north of Duluth, at the very edge of the city limits, she slowed, squinting to find Lamont Lane, which led down a long, winding slope to the Benton Dowling Center. Named for a teenager who'd died of alcohol poisoning in 1970, the treatment center—or BDC, as Leo heard it called—was a rehab facility for young men and teens with alcohol and drug dependency problems. Whether their insurance paid or not, the BDC made room for any St. Louis County male, age fifteen to twenty, and the administrators went after county assistance funds with a vengeance. Leo was glad to see kids getting treatment and detox opportunities, but she wished there were more resources for adults and for girls.

One such teenager's complaint prompted her early morning call on the center. The previous afternoon, Leo had stopped by without an appointment, but Edward Bolton had just gone into group therapy, and she wasn't about to wait an entire hour. A disinterested receptionist assured her of an audience with Bolton at eight a.m. today.

Leo steered the SUV down the narrow lane toward the parking lot. Evergreens and nearly leafless birch and poplar lined both sides of the drive, and she hit three potholes in a row, reducing her speed with each jarring jounce until she was barely creeping along. She emerged from the lane and onto a much smoother blacktop lot.

The police car and ambulance that passed earlier sat at the entrance of the center, lights flashing. With a feeling of unease, she parked and took one last look at herself in the rearview mirror. She reached up to touch the dark blue patch on her right eye, which still felt foreign—like wearing a bathing suit on a wintry day—but every morning she found herself more resigned to it.

Leo extricated herself from the car. She leaned back in to reach for her leather valise on the passenger seat. A light rain fell as she headed toward the BDC entrance. She quickened her pace, glad to make it to the covered outdoor walkway. She'd almost worn a gray wool suit—but at the last moment, she'd switched to black slacks, a blue long-sleeved knit shirt, and her favorite toreador-style vest. The temperature was dropping. Maybe she should have gone with the wool.

Once inside the double doors and into the reception area, she found no one to greet her. The long counter, behind which a receptionist had been sitting the day before, wasn't staffed, and not a soul was in sight. A phone rang repeatedly, the sound echoing off the tall ceilings. Leo slipped off her raincoat and held it dripping over one arm as she strode down a short hall to the metal detector at the main junction. Passage through security led to the section of the BDC requiring an escort or permission to enter. With each step, she heard a rising din and shouts far off.

No one stood guard at the security station. She passed through the metal detector, and it went off, emitting a loud whooping noise. To the left, a security guard stood perhaps a hundred feet away with his back to her. He turned, caught sight of her, and raised a hand. "Hold it," he said in a nasally voice. He hesitated, poised between his post and a crowd congregated at the far end of the hall. With one look back over his shoulder, he rushed forward, walking with an over-exaggerated pumping of his arms. He looked like the scrawny cartoon turtle for a local casino, and Leo had to repress a smile.

"We've got a situation here," he shouted, frowning at her. He hit a button on the side of the machine, and the horrible whooping noise stopped. "I can't let you in, ma'am."

She was already in and didn't have any intention of leaving. "I'm Leona Reese and here on official state business."

He stared, not bothering to mask his apprehension. Because of the dark eye patch, Leo was getting used to people giving her odd looks. No matter how nicely she dressed or how attractive her hair style, nobody seemed to see anything but the patch.

She set the valise on the side table near the detector as his look of apprehension turned to suspicion.

"You got any ID there? And while we're at it, you did set off the machine, so I think we better check your bag." He peered again over his shoulder, obviously wanting to see what was going on down the hall. She slid the valise across the table. He fumbled with the clasp of the bag, which had been a special present from Leo's adoptive father many years earlier. It doubled as a purse and briefcase and also contained tape-recording equipment. She didn't like strangers touching it. She reached out, saying, "Here. Let me," and released the clasp to open the top.

He mumbled, "What . . . hmm . . . set it off . . ."

"It's probably the metal clasps on the bag. That usually gets me at the airport."

The guard poked around for a few more seconds then reluctantly pushed the bag away. "Who are you here to see? Mister Milford?"

"No, I'm here to interview a patient, Edward Bolton."

The guard bit his upper lip. His lower teeth stuck out as he chewed rhythmically, reminding her of a gerbil her foster brother once owned. With a toss of his head, he said, "Let me see your ID."

She reached into the valise, grabbed for a leather wallet, and held her identification in front of his face long enough to show the name and photo and the official seal for the State of Minnesota. With a quick motion she snapped it shut and returned it to the inner pocket in the valise.

Still biting his lip, he held up his hands, palms out. "Look, I don't want to get on your bad side or anything, Ms. Reese, but I don't know if I can let you in."

Far down the hall, she saw a knot of at least a dozen teenage boys hovering around a doorway. Someone in dark blue came out waving. He spoke sharply to the youths. They scattered to the other side of the hallway and leaned up against the wall.

Leo asked, "What's going on down there?"

"One of the patients is ill."

She heard a faint shout.

"Get back," a deep male voice responded.

As if of its own volition, the foot of a gurney shot out of a room followed six feet later by a paramedic who wheeled it around the corner of the door frame. Leo heard a creaking sound from the gurney's wheels. A second medic, two men in suits, a nurse, a cop, and the woman from the front desk followed in grim silence.

Leo stepped closer to the guard's table and out of the way as the empty gurney drew near.

The guard mumbled to himself. "Uh-oh. Not good. This isn't good."

"Make way," the EMT said. He and his partner negotiated the turn, and the gurney slipped through the metal detector with less than an inch to spare on either side. The machine went off, once again whooping loudly.

The two men in suits reached them, and one shouted, "Richland, turn that thing off!"

Leo frowned as she looked into the troubled face of Morton Milford, the center's assistant director. Over the scream of the detector, she hollered, "Mister Milford, is everybody okay? Who's the injured party?" Before she got out the whole question, the guard cut the alarm, and the last word of her shouted inquiry echoed in the hall.

Milford took out a handkerchief and mopped his brow. "One of the boys has died."

"Who?" Leo asked.

"His name was Edward Bolton."

➤■◄

Leo sat in a dim conference room sipping lukewarm coffee from a Styrofoam cup. The morning sun hid behind multiple layers of clouds, and the illumination shining in the window shed little light. When Morton Milford ushered her in to wait, he hadn't flicked on the overhead fluorescent lights, and she didn't bother to get up to do it herself.

Instead, she fumed a little because Milford hadn't been the slightest bit forthcoming. She found it strange and suspicious for him to be so unhelpful, especially considering that he and his boss could be found negligent in the death of the teenager. She'd asked him a few pointed questions: Did he know anything at all about the young man's death? Did he have any reasons to think other patients were unsafe? Had any staff person's background checks come back with anything suspicious? No, no, and no.

Wide-eyed and sweating, he had looked all around the hall, anywhere but at her face, acting as though speaking to her took every bit of effort he could muster. And then he put up a hand, backed away, and said she would have to interview him later. He turned on his heel and race-walked through the security stop, a handkerchief pressed to his forehead.

Now all Leo could do was wait.

She took a sip of coffee and sat for a few minutes with her eyes closed. Her right eye socket throbbed. She thought about how her life had changed since the surgery. In the weeks beforehand, two different men at work had given her copies of David Weber's Honor Harrington book—the one where the heroine loses her eye. Leo wasn't sure how that was supposed to make her feel better, especially since Honor Harrington received a new cybernetic eye that worked even better than her God-given one, something Leo wasn't ever going to get.

Strangely enough, most of the men were less ill at ease than the women. The day before, when she made a lame comment about how much time she saved each morning by not having to put eye makeup on both eyes, her cubicle neighbor, Thom, had laughed. The two women standing in the hallway had looked horrified and scurried off never to be seen again for days. She guessed that Thom, who used a wheelchair to get around and so also had a "disability," understood because he had to have a good sense of humor to get through every day, too.

She pulled out the Bolton complaint file. It lay flat and thin next to her Styrofoam coffee cup, a clean manila rectangle contrasting sharply with the dark blue table. The coffee would have been good if it were still warm. She craved another cup, but she didn't think she should leave the conference room to go in search of it. She took one last sip, set the remaining few ounces aside, and opened the file.

The records regarding Edward Bolton were not complex. Two sheets comprised the sum total of information about him. Before any on-site visit, Leo always pulled the arrest record for every complainant and alleged offender. Edward Benjamin Bolton was a seventeen-year-old, white male with four arrests: one for shoplifting three years previous, a second for setting fire to a neighbor's garage, another for suspected vandalism, and the most recent for driving while intoxicated. The latter offense landed him in BDC a week and a half earlier. No court date yet. No resolution of the charges.

Leo looked at the screening sheet the intake worker used to record complaint calls. Bolton must have been a lot more intelligent than the run-of-the-mill teenager. Somehow he'd had the smarts to find the phone number for the Department of Human Services' investigative unit and to call in a complaint. The intake worker's notes listed the kid's name, date of birth, approximate time of the offense, and a few other key details:

**Call Source:** BDC client
**Complaint:** caller alleges phys abuse, excessive force, incl. unnecessary restraint
**Complaint against:** "Mike" - counselor?
**Resp party:** aunt – Phyllis Bolton/ clt's parents deceased
**Assnmt:** Reese

A great deal more information could have been included, but intake had hit the highlights. Apparently Bolton didn't know the last name of the alleged offender, so Leo hadn't been able to pull up any information about him.

She heard the faint sound of voices in the hallway, then footsteps drawing closer. Detective Gary Clark stepped into the room and paused inside the doorway. She'd had occasion to work with him on two cases recently. She bit back a smile. Clark wore his typical outfit: black oxfords, mud-brown slacks, a shiny black belt, and a sickly, green-colored shirt. His sports jacket of tan corduroy came close to matching his pants—but not quite. The combination of odd colors marked him as a single man desperately in need of help from *Queer Eye for the Straight Guy.*

"Leona. Hi." He set an evidence bag on the table. The tag and writing on the side obscured the contents.

"Good morning, Gary."

He sighed as he pulled out a chair. "Cold enough for you?"

"Yeah. That's for sure."

"Where'd you get the coffee?"

"Lady at the front desk."

"Oh." He ran his hand through sandy hair and looked longingly at the cup.

"It's getting cold but take the rest if you need it."

With a grateful smile, he picked up the Styrofoam cup and tipped it to his lips, downing what was left in one swig. Compared to the rest of him, his hands were large. Laborer's hands. His father still worked in the taconite mine, and Leo had been around Gary Clark long enough to know he was glad to have avoided a laborer's occupation.

"So, what's the deal here?" she asked. "Edward Bolton is dead?"

"Yup." He took a memo book from his jacket pocket and opened it. "Medics knew he was dead when they left here. The M.E. and his people will be working the crime scene for a while longer."

"A beating?"

Clark frowned. "Now why would you say that?"

"Just a guess. I take it I'm wrong?"

"No sign of a fight." He pointed at the evidence bag. "But according to his roommate, he was drinking from a metal flask before he collapsed. Could be alcohol poisoning. What brings you here today?"

Leo filled him in about the complaint. He asked if she'd ever spoken to Edward Bolton.

"No, I didn't. Not in person or by phone."

"That's too bad. Would've been good if you'd gotten some facts out of the kid before he died."

His cell phone rang, and Clark rose. "Excuse me for a minute." He picked up the evidence bag and stepped out into the hall. She heard him as he made noncommittal grunts into the phone. "Okay, I'll let Bob know." He stepped back into the room, shaking his head. "Well, that tears it. Looks like a very bizarre accident—or maybe homicide. I've got to go shut down the kitchen."

"The kitchen?"

"Prelim report from the M.E. The kid was poisoned. That's what the paramedics thought, too. Could be something in here." He raised the evidence bag. "But just in case, gotta shut things down."

He turned to leave, and she was on her feet in an instant. "Uh, Gary?"

"Yeah, yeah," he said over his shoulder, "you can come along."

She grabbed up the file, stuffed it in her valise, and hustled out the door. She had to run to catch up with him. He rounded the corner and passed through the metal detector. Richland hit the button twice to keep it from going off as each of them passed through. She wanted to suggest that the facility administrators install an easy-exit gate to the side for departures, but who was she to tell them what to do. Maybe they didn't use one so they could get by with one guard instead of the two usually seen at those kinds of checkpoints.

Clark came to a stop at the front desk. The middle-aged receptionist sat there, pale and looking spooked, as though still shocked from the events of the morning. She was listening to some sort of nature program on the radio, and it sounded like an aviary behind the narrator's cool British voice. With the birds cawing harshly in the background like ravens, Leo was struck by the thought that the woman looked exactly like Edgar Allen Poe except her face was pockmarked from acne and her mustache was thinner. Her name tag read *Lizzie*.

Clark said, "Good morning, ma'am. You've got an intercom to the entire facility, right?"

"Yes, sir."

A door behind the receptionist opened, and Lizzie reached over and snapped off Jungle Kingdom or whatever it was. Leo got a brief glimpse of a sumptuous office decorated in dark wood and hues of yellow and blue before two men came hustling through. Morton Milford, at the rear, pulled the door shut.

Leaning down toward Lizzie, Clark asked, "Is there a room where all residents and staff can be convened?"

"Yes. The cafeteria."

"Get on the horn then. Instruct everyone to go there immediately."

"Now wait a minute here," the first man said. His voice was deep, authoritative. His light gray suit fit his physique perfectly. His silver hair was expertly cut and styled, as though he'd just come from the barber. Leo was sure the man was likely well over sixty, but he possessed the bearing and vitality of someone much younger. In her one other visit to the BDC, she'd only dealt with Morton Milford and had never seen this other man before. She figured he had to be some high-mucky-muck. In her experience, reptiles like him only came out when a disaster happened. Otherwise, she thought, you usually found them reposing comfortably under big, expensive rocks.

In an imperious voice, he asked, "Who are you, and why are you giving instructions to my staff?"

Morton Milford stood slightly behind him, grim-faced and twisting some rolled up papers in his hands. "Uh, Donald?" The man ignored him.

Gary Clark pulled aside his corduroy jacket to reveal the gold badge on his hip. He introduced himself. "And sir, you are?"

"Donald Robeson, owner and general manager of this facility. I understand we've had an unfortunate death, but I'll have you know I'm in charge of the staff here." Leo noticed how much extra emphasis he put on the word "I" each time it rolled off his tongue.

Clark nodded solicitously, but in a firm voice said, "Unless you want more deaths, Mister Robeson, then I suggest you allow me to quarantine your residents and staff."

"That's ridiculous! We've got a program to run here."

The man's face flushed red, as though he wasn't used to being challenged. She wondered why he didn't sound interested in getting to the bottom of Bolton's death. How odd. She glanced back at the assistant director. He was nervous as hell, with his breathing so labored she wondered if he was going to pass out.

Clark leaned against the counter. "Any minute now, this place'll be swarming with investigators and police, not to mention press, Mister Robeson."

"I'm telling you—" Robeson stopped and looked toward the entrance. The glass door clunked open, and a St. Louis County deputy strode in.

With one sweeping glance, the deputy took in the scene. He nodded to the detective and removed his hat. "Hey there, Clark. Got a call about a possible homicide?"

The two men stepped aside to confer. Unlike some other jurisdictions, the Duluth chief of police and the county sheriff had an excellent working relationship. Both had been in office for the better part of a decade, and their officers had long cooperated with one another. It only took a few moments before the two men turned, and the deputy announced, "This facility is in lockdown. Detective Clark will see you two managers privately, and I'll work with the secretary here."

Without a word, Robeson and Milford stomped back into the office behind them.

Leo met Clark's eyes, and she knew he'd update her when he could. As he moved away, he called out, "Catch up with you later, Leo," and disappeared into the office behind the reception desk.

The deputy pointed an index finger at Lizzie behind the tall counter. Her head was hunched down like a turtle trying to retract into his shell. "You!"

Her eyes widened, and she turned even whiter than she had been.

"Show me how the intercom works."

➤■◄

Although Leo hung around the BDC as long as she could, she didn't find out anything new and couldn't wait any longer. She stopped for a latté and croissant and headed back to the government building where she was temporarily assigned. Ever since her eye problems had emerged, she'd been working investigations for the State rather than serving as a police sergeant who patrolled the streets of Saint Paul and trained other officers. At first, she'd been upset by the assignment, but now she was grateful to be doing something to keep her mind occupied.

The fog had lifted, and the gloomy, gray sky spat out rain in steady bursts. She was sure it wouldn't quit any time soon, so with her valise tucked under her arm, she raced around puddles and made it to the covered walkway leading to the main entrance. One thing all her friends visiting from out of town liked about Minnesota was that snow and rain were well planned for. Skyways connecting some buildings in the downtown area, and with lots of extra canopies here and there, a person only had to get drenched in short bursts.

She slowed under the long awning and walked toward three men smoking cigarettes at the entrance. All were dressed in similar dark suits. One of them was her on-site boss, Paul Aitken, and he looked like he was conducting some sort of behind-the-scenes deal. "Leona," he called out in a falsely jovial voice, "how ya doing?"

She nodded. "Hi, Paul. I'm fine—a little wet, but fine." She didn't know the other two men, but so many people came and went through their building that she saw hordes of new faces each day. One of the men stepped over, grabbed the door handle, and pulled it open.

"Hey, thanks," she said.

"My pleasure."

Leo gave him a big smile, completely forgetting the eye patch until she splashed into the foyer. Then she remembered how odd her face looked. She flushed with embarrassment. Her foster sister had said, "Act like you're used to the patch and it's not slowing you down a bit. Nobody else will care. They'll look around it." Good advice, but Leo was well aware most of the world didn't love her like Kate did.

The entryway was painted a pale gray-green. In a living room, it might look like an inviting mint-green, but in a large, dim public building, she thought the shade came off as harsh, the color of a gaunt and denuded tree. She'd had her colors done, and this shade of green didn't look good on her. Or around her.

Leo exchanged greetings with Serena, the security guard at the metal detector. The heavy-set black woman possessed sympathetic brown eyes. Leo noticed people's eyes a lot now, and Serena's were shiny and clear. She waved Leo through saying, "Pretty shitty day, huh?"

Leo smiled. "You've definitely got that right."

Serena stood nodding, arms crossed over her white security shirt. "It's going to be wicked out there. They're predicting intense thunderstorms that may turn to freezing sleet and ice. We're going to have one hell of a winter if this keeps up. Who expects weather like this in early November?"

"Not me." Leo slipped out of her raincoat, shaking it in the process. "I may have visitors from the police or sheriff today."

"Alrighty then. I'll track you down."

"Thanks, Serena. Have a good morning." Leo didn't recognize the guard on the other side. She was new. In the few weeks before her surgery when Leo started working out of Rentreau Plaza, building management had gone through a couple of backup guards, though Serena was reliable. The new woman sat at a side table, studying a three-ring binder, her dark head bent low. She didn't look up as Leo went by toward the elevators.

The four-story building, officially called Rentreau Plaza, housed a number of state offices, some state/county collaborations, and a variety of boards and county satellite sites. She and Thom Thoreson were the lone investigators stationed at this office.

While she was primarily assigned to DHS, the Department of Human Services, Thom was allocated to DOH, the Department of Health. But for all practical purposes, they reported to both departments for many of the cases assigned in the northern part of

Minnesota. The main office in Saint Paul fielded all initial complaints and forwarded the appropriate referrals.

Before Leo's eye surgery, she'd worked in the Saint Paul office, but she'd run afoul of a lead worker, Fred Baldur, who had more juice with the brass than she'd expected. Baldur managed to get her exiled to Duluth, and now she was in a holding pattern as she waited to learn what would happen with her vision.

The elevator door opened on the fourth floor, and she used a magnetic security card to let herself into the suite. A narrow sea of cubicles stretched to the left. Beyond that, along the south wall, were two managers' offices with glass walls and a corner conference room that seated twelve comfortably around the table. If an announcement had to be made, as many as fifty could cram in with most standing packed like sardines.

She passed one long aisle, then another, before coming to the third aisle along the window where her cubicle was located. After hanging up her raincoat on a hook outside the entrance, she stepped in. Her work area sported a window on the west side, and she was truly grateful for the natural light. Looking out on a busy street gave her a feeling of more space than she actually had. With the cubicles a mere ten-by-ten-feet square, she'd feel seriously claustrophobic if she were stuck in the center section.

As usual, Thom Thoreson, in the cubicle to her left, was listening to metal music on his radio. "Hi, Thom," she called out over the wall. In cube-speak, that meant *I'm here—please modulate the volume.*

"G'morning, Leo." The station went off, and she heard a crinkling sound on the carpet as Thom backed up and rolled his wheelchair into the aisle and to her doorway. "Rumor has it one of our licensees is going to be under investigation in a big way."

"Yes, and it's apparently a puzzle, too." She set her valise on the desk and turned to face him. His brown eyes twinkled, and once again she was struck by how handsome he was. His gray-and-red tie was perfectly knotted, and his white, starched shirt didn't show a wrinkle. He wore expensive suits, all of which were tailored perfectly for him. With his black hair trimmed so tight against his head, his scalp was visible. His smiling eyes were his strongest feature, crinkly and bright, always ready with a joke. She thought he was more handsome than JFK Junior had been. His face still retained a touch of summer tan, and he looked strong from the waist up. Anyone would know he'd have been a formidable football player. Once, he told Leo he thought he'd taken a thousand hits from some of the biggest college tackles in the game—but all it took was one awkward fall down cement stairs, and he was paralyzed for life.

Now Thom was in his early thirties, and even in the short time she'd known him, she thought he would have been a kindred soul even if cancer hadn't taken her eye and made them "disabled" together.

He frowned. "Am I going to regret signing off on their license? You find anything we should have foreseen?"

"No, it's not like that. This is probably foul play—something hinky going on there." She pulled out the desk chair and sighed as she lowered herself into it. "The Bolton kid was court-ordered to BDC for drunk driving. Gary Clark says he apparently drank something laced with poison."

"And Bolton was our original complainant?"

"Yes. I showed up to interview him, and strange thing—he's dead. Looks mighty suspicious. The cops are grilling the administrators and at least one counselor is on the hot seat. Not much more I can find out today, though."

Thom brought his thumb and index finger to his bottom lip and stared at the carpet as he often did when he was thinking. When he looked up at Leo, his face was troubled. "If this kid had something on them and he was killed to keep him from talking, we need to shut them down, probably pull their license. Before you were on staff, I cited them for inadequate youth supervision. They beefed up their personnel, though, and have been right on top of things ever since."

"I don't know enough yet to say if they should be shut down." Leo pointed at her in-box, which was stacked to overflowing with new cases. "This kind of investigation is just what I need. Not. I've already got enough to keep me busy for a year."

"I'll help however I can."

Leo smiled. "I know you will, Thom, but you have your own workload."

He rolled back. "Let me know what I can do. While you're in the field, I can pull computer details. Give me a call me on your cell if you need anything. I'll run all the information I can on the owners and principals of the BDC right now, okay?"

"Thank you. I'll owe you another lunch."

"Don't worry. I'm keeping a tally. Say, do you know what you call a sexy guy in a wheelchair with a rope around him?

"No, what?"

"A pull toy."

She was so taken aback at the insensitivity of the joke that she blinked twice before she said, "That's lame, Thom."

He laughed. "Lame, huh?"

"Hell, you know what I mean. The joke's completely horrid. Where do you come up with this awful stuff?"

With a chuckle he rolled out of sight. She wasn't sure how he could be so cavalier. She imagined it took him a while to get to such a point of mocking humor. All she knew was that he managed to be much more lighthearted about his injury than Leo thought she could ever be about hers. So far, she hadn't ever been able to laugh about her misfortunes with any consistency. Yet. Maybe when she was old and gray. But probably not.

She turned to face the desk. She'd only been on staff since summer, and already the stacks of files and paper were out of hand. She needed a secretary. Who am I kidding? she thought. I need a backhoe.

She pulled out the desk's right-side bottom drawer, which contained thick phonebooks, and rested her heels on the drawer's edge. Leaning back in the chair, she crossed her legs at the ankle and looked out the window. A hard rain came down. People hurrying along the sidewalk all carried umbrellas. She didn't look forward to going out in the chill again any time soon, then realized she didn't have to. When she'd been sent up north to Duluth, her partner, Daria, stayed behind to take care of the house and continue with her attorney work in Minneapolis, so Leo didn't have anyone waiting at her temporary apartment. She could work as late as she wanted. Maybe by later tonight the rain would have stopped.

In a perfect world, Leo would receive an average of one new file a day or about twenty per month. As it stood, she was getting that many per week with no end in sight. Many of them could be resolved over the telephone, and occasionally an anonymous and unverifiable call came in requiring little follow-up, but nearly sixty percent of the cases warranted an in-person visit. Every case required a paper trail.

The unit door across the way clicked open. She didn't pay it much attention, but moments later Paul Aitken stood in her cubicle doorway. "Leona."

She hadn't expected him and jerked her feet off the drawer in surprise. Paul didn't come out on the floor much. When he did, usually it was for a big emergency—or at least an emergency in *his* world.

"Can you take a minute and come to my office?"

"Sure, Paul." She rose and followed him down the narrow walkway, glancing into Thom's cubicle as they passed. Thom looked at her askance, a smirk on his face, as he drew one forefinger across the other as though saying, "Naughty, naughty!"

Sometimes he was such a big kid. She suppressed a smile and followed the boss through the maze to his office. She had always wanted to tell Paul he ought to invest in a pair of regular, round-toe oxfords. He wore wingtips every day, and they pointed out and made him waddle more than walk. He also favored black suits. Give the guy a purple top hat, a monocle, and umbrella, and people would likely confuse him with Burgess Meredith's Penguin character on the old *Batman* TV show. His blond hair was fine and thinning, so he made up for that by pasting it into clumpy waves with a smelly gel always at odds with whatever cologne he wore.

They passed the reception area where Tonya, the administrative aide and transcriptionist, usually sat. She was away from her desk.

Paul went through the glass door into his obsessively neat office. He sat facing the unit, a credenza behind him and a computer workstation off to his left. He gestured toward one of the two visitor's seats in front of the desk and settled into a huge executive chair that dwarfed his small physique. Now, with his fingers laced together over a plump belly, he resembled a wild-eyed monk. "I got a call from Saint Paul earlier this morning on the BDC case."

Right. Something political. She should have known. He never called her into his office for any other reason. He went on. "I understand the complainant is dead."

"Yes. It changes the focus of the investigation. Preliminary report from the hospital on COD is poison."

"Poison! Jesus. Did you see any indication that we should pull their license and shut 'em down?" He leaned forward expectantly.

"Not offhand. I—"

"I thought that was what you'd find." He beamed at her. "They're good people up there. I'd like this wrapped up this week. Put everything else aside and get this one out the door. I want the report on my desk by Friday."

She tried not to frown. Or roll her one good eye. It wasn't possible to "wrap this up" by Friday. The interviews alone would take hours, and with the cooperation she was getting from the administration at the BDC, she figured she'd be looking at several weeks. "Paul, the autopsy report is unlikely to be finished before Friday. This one will be a lot of work, and I don't—"

"We don't have a choice." He leaned forward in his chair and raised a hand, as if in benediction. Behind his back many employees mocked Paul Aitken's extravagant hand and arm motions. If he was really worked up, he tended to look like a windmill—or a first base coach. "This comes from high up. I understand the autopsy has been flagged first priority, so get a move on with this, will you? I want answers by Friday."

"I'll do my best."

He smiled. "I know you will." With a flutter of his fingers he dismissed her. "Don't let me keep you. And if you need any extra help, please let me know. I've already emailed Thoreson. And Tonya. They'll give you a hand."

"Thanks, Paul." She rose, hoping he hadn't heard the sarcasm in her voice. She already had Thom's help, and what could Tonya do? The overworked transcriptionist was already bogged down with weeks' worth of tapes.

She tried not to stomp back to her little corner of the world. At Thom's doorway she paused, shaking her head. He rolled back from the computer and turned the screen toward her. "I see you're on a red ball here."

"What?"

"A red ball—you know, a big messy emergency." She knew she must be looking at him with a dopey expression on her face, because he went on to explain. "The Allies in Europe ran a massive convoy called the Red Ball Express in World War II so they could move supplies and defeat the Germans." He laughed. "I can see this is very meaningful to you. The name comes from the railroad phrase to 'red ball' or to ship it by express." He gestured at the screen.

"You read too many war thrillers."

"Not so many that I can't already predict your world for the next few days."

She moved into his cubicle and stood next to him to look at the e-mail on his screen. In typical official-ese, Paul Aitken had sent a stilted-sounding message instructing her to move the BDC case to number one priority. Thom and Tonya were both cc'd, and God only knows how many officials up the line were blind-copied. She couldn't hold back a sigh. "Lucky me."

"Political, right?"

"Yeah. How'd you know?"

Thom reached for a stack of papers next to the printer on the table behind him. "I pulled some records. Donald Robeson owns the BDC, incorporated with another principal."

"Morton Milford?"

"Nope." He handed me the documents. "Everett Robeson."

"Oh, my. You don't mean Everyday Everett?"

"The very one."

Everyday Everett sold used motor homes. His commercials came on late night TV, and the viewer never knew whether he'd be dressed as a clown or cowboy or a giant pickle. He was loud-mouthed, frenetic with energy, and used a lot of irritating puns, ending with his stupid tagline, "The best of previously owned motor homes, *every* day. Just ask for me, Everyday Everett!" Leo usually hit the mute button when his commercials came on. "What's he got to do with it, then, other than being a big-time businessman of such import?"

"He's married to Marilyn Robeson."

"And she is?"

"Governor McCarron's wife's sister, formerly named Marilyn Gowdy."

"This is confusing."

"The governor and Donald Robeson's brother, Everett, are married to the Gowdy sisters. The gov and Everett are brothers-in-law, which makes Donald a shirttail relative to the honcho in the state house."

"Oh, shit."

Thom laughed. "Yeah, shit is about right. Deep shit. Donald Robeson has easy access to the governor. Bad luck for us. Amazing how fast word came down from on high, and that's why I say we're on a red ball."

"Guess I'd better get to work on it, then, huh?"

"I'll keep digging, too." He turned the screen back toward him. "I'll work up background info on the BDC and the principals and clear out some of my stuff here by end of day tomorrow, then Thursday, how about I go to the BDC with you, and we'll crank through a million interviews?"

"Okay. Thank you, Thom. Tomorrow I'll try again to get the administrator's statements, and I'll go over to the courthouse and look at the records from Edward Bolton's hearing."

"Nah, let me handle the record collection so you can get right back to the BDC in the morning."

Tonya, their transcriptionist, appeared in the cubicle entrance. "I read a sort of bizarre e-mail from—"

"Yeah," Leo said, "from Aitken. Thom and I are talking about that now."

"What am I supposed to do?"

Leo said, "Keep on with your regular work but with two things in mind. First, please watch for the pre-autopsy summary Gary Clark will fax over, probably later this afternoon. If it comes in, get it right over here to us. Second, the minute I have any notes or tapes, I'll bring them to you. They'll have to be your first priority."

"You have any for me yet?"

Leo shook her head. "No. Wish I did. Let's just say everybody at Ye Olde BDC is being pretty close-mouthed at the moment."

Thom said, "Let's all meet back here before you go home, Tonya."

They agreed to meet at four p.m., and Tonya scurried off to get organized. Back in her cubicle, Leo moved the in-box off her desk and onto the table by the door. She didn't want to look at the thing. Not only was it depressing, but she'd need the space.

Her work area was tight—only three flat surfaces and the chair. The window took up all of the west wall. A gun-metal gray, government-issue desk was on the south wall, abutting Thom's wall. It was so old, she imagined WWII cryptographers probably used the metal monstrosity, but she liked it because of its size. The computer desk and keyboard were tucked into a corner along the north wall next to the window. Her printer sat on a narrow table near the door next to an alarmingly tall stack of paperwork that always accumulated when she wasn't looking. She couldn't deal with any of the other cases now. She turned a blind eye—literally—and set to work at her desk.

Leo goosed the gas pedal as she went up the incline of the driveway to her apartment. After the first snowfall, she wasn't looking forward to navigating the tight little lot in the clunky SUV. A few weeks earlier, Daria had surprised her with the new car. In place of her comfortable old Honda Accord, Daria picked out a Lexus that cost far more than Leo ever thought she'd spend on a vehicle. When things went wrong, Daria bought things. Ever since she'd lost a big case at the end of the summer, Daria had been on a bit of a spending tear. She'd also gotten involved with a colleague's political campaign and was busier than ever.

Sometimes Leo missed her old car, especially now with her vision causing problems. The rear side windows in the Lexus were unusually small. Her old Honda had much better sightlines.

She pulled into her regular spot and made her way to the apartment. She stuck her mittens in the sleeve of her jacket and hung it up, then stepped into the kitchen and dumped her valise on the kitchen counter. Though she shivered, the apartment was pleasantly warm and smelled faintly of the morning's coffee. She cut through the kitchen and went to check the blinking answering machine in the living room.

Daria's voice came through, deep and clear. "Leo, honey, I've got a political stop-off, then a late meeting, so this is my only chance to leave you a message before you're sleeping. It's likely things will run late tomorrow, too, so I'll try to catch you during the day. My cell will be off, but if you want to leave me a message, I'll get it late tonight after you've hit the hay. Hope your day has gone well. Love you."

The house was quiet. She stood for a moment looking at the machine, feeling lonely. Back to my case files, she thought, and headed to the kitchen.

# Chapter Three

Wednesday morning was a replay of Tuesday, only without the flashing lights of emergency vehicles. The drab weather shepherded Leo up Highway 61, and she arrived at the Benton Dowling Center a few moments after eight. Before Leo could get through the front door, Lizzie, the receptionist, was on the phone whispering frantically, her voice echoing with the sibilance of a snake. She dumped the phone back in its cradle and stared up, hostility radiating from her. "May I help you?"

Leo thought of the old joke, *I'd like to help you out—which way did you come in?* She smiled courteously and asked to speak to Mort Milford.

"Mister Milford is in conference and unavailable."

"Mister Robeson then?"

"He, too, is occupied."

Leo intended to follow the chain of command and be polite about arranging interviews, but if Lizzie were any indication of the level of cooperation she could expect to receive, she figured she'd be cooling her heels in the drafty lobby for a very long time. "I understand William Cattrall was Edward Bolton's roommate. I will require a conference room, and I'd like to speak to him now. After that, I'll also need to interview a counselor or male nurse named Mike."

She expected more flak from Lizzie, but the receptionist only sighed as she picked up the phone. "I'll call down to the unit and see what they want to do."

Twenty minutes later Leo sat at a table across from a nervous fifteen-year-old boy. He was tall and chubby, and his eyes were clear and bright, but he slumped as if fatigued.

Unlike police investigators, she was not required to notify his parents in advance. She had interviewed children as young as three years old, and afterwards she contacted the parents if necessary. Her department was allowed to sweep into any facility, take statements, and investigate fully. Sometimes this unearthed evidence of criminal wrongdoing, which Leo turned over to the police, but her main goal was always to determine whether the center or facility or residence should continue to operate and if any individuals needed to be cited or removed from their positions. In her brief tenure as a State investigator, she hadn't yet suspended a license or shut down a place, but Thom had. By the looks of things, the BDC might be the first place she cited.

She greeted William Cattrall, introduced herself, and turned on the tape recorder. She held her Cross pen at the ready to take hand-written notes about things she wanted to follow up on immediately.

"William, I'm here to find out from you what happened yester-day. I'm required to read a statement about your rights and responsibilities and the use of your witness statement. Give me a moment to do that, all right?"

William nodded and she launched into her reading. She wasn't sure how much of it the teenager would understand, but she couldn't omit it, even if she were talking to a small child.

Leo's position gave her the power to insist that witnesses speak to her, and if they refused, she had the option of turning them over to the police, removing them from the grounds, or closing the facility until she was sure it was safe. But the rules also contained a strange Catch-22. If any witness told her something incriminating, Leo was obligated to share it with the authorities. In advance, she was required by law to inform each interviewee of these facts. Surprisingly, it wasn't often someone took the Fifth with her. Most of the time they just lied.

As a cop, Leo often spoke to hardened kids: drug addicts, violent offenders, gangbangers, and those who were, quite simply, incor-rigible. They assumed tough, uncaring personas, and Leo usually couldn't break them. TV often portrayed these teenagers with a thin veneer that could be breached, but in Leo's experience, breaking through didn't happen very often. She had come to believe that kids have plenty of secrets—perhaps even more than adults—which they guarded with a ferocity most grown-ups weren't aware of.

William Cattrall, however, was an easy read. He wasn't tough. His reddish hair was cut very short, and the pale skin of his face was scattered with freckles. He had an old bruise along his jawline and dark circles under his blue eyes. If it weren't for his height and broad shoulders, he'd look like a chubby schoolboy. Instead, he was a hulking, scared kid who wasn't comfortable with his rapid growth and bulk. In another year or so, he'd lose the baby fat and become a solid, physically imposing man. But for now, only a boy faced her.

"William, why were you assigned to the BDC?"

He stared at the table, his hands in fists on the table edge, and the voice that came out of his mouth cracked. "Drugs. Alcohol. Got picked up at a party." William was obviously in the middle of voice-changing puberty.

She didn't laugh at the simple-minded answer. He wouldn't get himself into a residential treatment center any other way than by abusing chemicals. "What kind of drugs?"

"My mom's prescription drugs. For her pain."

"Her pain?"

"Yes, something's wrong with her arm muscle, so she has painkillers."

"Oxy?"

He nodded, still staring down at the table.

"Didn't she notice when you took her pills?"

He shrugged. "She doesn't care."

His mother must be a real piece of work. How could she not pay attention to her prescriptions? "Do you know why Edward Bolton was in here?"

Now he looked up. "I'm *nothing* like Eddie." A little slice of the man he would likely grow to be peeked out from behind William's blue eyes.

"How so?"

"I'll *never* be like him." His voice cracked again, going up an octave and dropping abruptly. Embarrassed, he looked down at the table again, and his fists went white. "Mean. Wait, he was cruel, not just mean. Lots of guys are mean, but he always took it a step farther."

"Is he responsible for the bruise on your face?"

Now the kid colored up, pink as a rare steak. "I don't like to fight. But he did."

Leo waited. Silence was often the best way to elicit information.

He opened his hands and flexed tense fingers, then ventured a glance up and looked away. "I could've probably beat the shit out of him. He wasn't as big as me, but . . . " His voice trailed off, and now he looked out the window behind her. "He was vicious. And you could never know how he'd hurt you. But I'm not a thug. I didn't want to cross him."

"I see."

"I didn't kill him." William met her gaze. "But I'm not sorry he's dead either."

"I think I understand." His shoulders dropped and he let out a sigh. She suspected he'd admitted the one thing of which he was most ashamed.

William had only been in the facility since the previous Thursday, so they went over the events of the last few days. On the first day, when assigned to Eddie Bolton's room, William told her they'd had a run-in almost immediately. "As soon as the counselor left, Eddie was on me. He got me in a headlock and made me tell him stuff."

She raised her eyebrows and waited.

He blushed again. "Stuff, you know. Like, was I a virgin or a queer, and did I have any crack with me."

He stared at her so defiantly that she hoped it wouldn't be important to know the details of those particular secrets. "Tell me more about his behavior toward you."

William sat back in his chair and let loose. "Believe me, I did everything I could to stay away from him. If he wanted something, I usually gave it up. I think right away he figured out I was no fun. Six of us are assigned to a team—and there's a bunch of teams. I don't know how many. It was all I could do to keep up with what was going on with my own team. Eddie spent any free time across the hall in Speed and Mouse's room."

She made a note to find out who Speed and Mouse were. "Tell me more about the fights that took place."

"He's been in lots—even punched a counselor. I wasn't there, but everyone says Eddie was picking on a kid from another team, and Mike, one of the counselors, tried to break it up. Everybody who talked to me said Eddie clipped Mike first, not the other way around."

"Who told you this?" He recited a list of names, and she made additional notes. "What happened yesterday at breakfast?"

"I don't know. I wasn't paying attention." His voice warbled, and he cleared his throat. "It was the other end of the table. I think Eddie got pissed at Mike. He got up and stomped out."

"Then what?"

"I don't know. When I came back to our room, he was standing near my bed swaying back and forth. And talking weird shit. He thanked me, said I was, um, generous. That was the word. Generous. Then it was something about a dog. He kept telling me to shut up, but I didn't say a word. I sat on my bed, ready in case it was a trick. He hadn't been like this before. His face was all red. I thought maybe he was high, but this place is picked clean."

"Do you know what he thanked you for?" William shook his head. "Where did the metal flask come from?"

"I don't know."

"You've never seen it before?"

"No."

She went over the details with him a few more times, came at him from different angles, but William's story never wavered. It didn't sound practiced or deceitful, and she believed him.

When he finally rose to leave, she asked him how long he was committed for.

He shrugged his shoulders. "My parents are on a cruise in the Bahamas. I'm not sure when they come back. I'm stuck here 'til then."

"Good luck, William."

"Thanks."

He shuffled out of the room, slumping enough to reduce his six-foot height considerably. For every kid like him, she'd interviewed dozens of others who didn't seem to have hearts. She wished him well. He looked like a miserable teenager with parents who simply weren't there for him. In Leo's mind, poor parenting was the real crime.

She made notes, then checked her watch. The first interview started close to nine a.m., and she'd asked them to bring the second an hour later. When the counselor, Mike—Seaver was his last name—hadn't shown up by ten, she walked out to the front desk and requested Lizzie Allan Poe page him over the intercom.

The man who entered the conference room at a quarter past ten was brown eyed with a full head of shiny dark brown hair. Though his looks were marred slightly by a bright purple bruise on his left cheekbone, it was clear he knew he was handsome. He strutted and preened, turning on the charm immediately as he reached across the table to take Leo's hand and compliment her on her blouse. She didn't fall for it. Instead she introduced herself and directed him to the chair across the table.

Seaver pressed his lips together and sat, obviously irritated she hadn't responded to his cheery bonhomie. He wore pale blue scrubs with his first name monogrammed in three-inch-tall letters on the breast pocket.

"This isn't a medical facility, right?" she asked.

"No, why?"

"Just wondering why so many of you who work here wear scrubs."

Seaver scowled. "We used to wear casual street clothes, but a couple of years ago the head honchos made us change. I guess they wanted us to look more medical—like wearing scrubs is going to fool the parents or the county. Obviously didn't fool you."

"I see." She clicked on the recorder and launched into the statement about rights and responsibilities and the use of his statement. Before she was half done, his scowl had deepened. She soldiered on. He crossed his arms, looking more antagonized by the moment.

When she finished, he shook his head. "Isn't this double jeopardy or something like that?"

"No, sir. Double jeopardy is when you have been tried for a crime and found not guilty for it. You can't be charged again for the same crime. I don't have the authority to charge you with anything."

"Jesus, if you don't mind my saying so, it sure seems like I could be jeopardizing my career by talking with you. It sure does feel like jeopardy."

"Mister Seaver, a young kid has died. You had an altercation with him. If you don't talk with me here in the comfort and privacy of the workplace, you'll be hauled down to the police station."

"But I've already talked to the cops."

"And you're required to talk to me, too."

He sat forward, elbows on the table, and narrowed his eyes. "You said you're what—an investigator?"

"Yes. For the State of Minnesota."

Now he sat back in his chair, arms crossed. "Oh, so you're not a private eye, you're a *public* eye."

Her face grew warm, but she said nothing. She felt extra-conscious of the edge of the scratchy eye patch against her temple. What a smart-ass. She knew plenty of guys like Mike Seaver. They thought they could control things with charm, but if that didn't work, they resorted to low-level nastiness. She'd seen worse patrolling the streets, and she always chose to ignore it. "Let's stay on topic here, Mister Seaver. I see the bruise on your cheekbone. Did Edward Bolton do that?"

"Yes. Eddie belted me. Out of the blue."

"Did you beat him for it?"

"What? Of course not. And I have witnesses. I did have to restrain him 'cause he went nuts, but I never struck him like he did me." Seaver launched into the same basic story William Cattrall had told her.

"What did you do to punish Bolton?"

"Three of us placed him overnight in solitary, which is a padded room. We keep an eye on a video feed and through gaps in the padding so we can see into the room. Eddie was monitored all night long. He calmed down after a couple hours and was docile by the next morning."

"Who were the youths involved in the scuffle?" Seaver listed five names, which Leo carefully wrote down. When she looked up, he was staring at her, his eyes small and hard. She met his gaze. "Are you aware Eddie Bolton called in an official complaint about you?"

He sighed. "I'm not surprised. Happens all the time. He's not the first and won't be the last."

"Why don't you go ahead and tell me your take on the young man."

For the next few minutes, Mike Seaver spilled out a stream of criticism about Bolton. Leo was amused that he was so willing to speak ill of the dead. He detailed three assaults on other kids he claimed were documented and finished by saying, "Eddie was one of the rottener of the rotten apples coming through here. He wasn't going to rehabilitate. He was biding his time to get out of here and go on his next rampage. The world is better off without him in it, but I swear, I'm not responsible for his death."

"You already know this about a seventeen-year-old kid?"

"He was seventeen going on thirty-five. I bet he'd already done more damage than anyone ever even knew."

"But you don't have proof of that?"

His chin went up in the air. "I've got several years of experience with kids like this. He was definitely a bad seed."

"I'll need copies of any reports you wrote about his bad behavior."

"Okay."

"Now tell me about how the alcohol got into his room."

Seaver uncrossed his arms and leaned on the table. "I had nothing to do with that."

She waited. An odd expression flitted across his face and then was gone. "But you do know something."

"No." He shook his head. "I have no idea. I didn't give him anything."

"Have you ever given drugs or alcohol to any of the youth?"

His hesitation was so fleeting that unless an investigator was watching closely, it would be missed. Surely it wouldn't be apparent on the audio tape.

"No, of course not. It's against the rules. Some of these kids are detoxing and drying out."

She looked into his dark eyes, searching for guile. He was hiding something, but she wasn't sure what. She asked a variety of other questions about his work relationships, other kids he'd had trouble with, and his impression of how the facility was run. Seaver clearly did not like the administrators, but he said he got along fine with his immediate supervisor, Shelley Clifton, who coordinated all social work in the building.

Leo consulted her rapidly growing list of interviewees, irritated that Robeson and Milford had made themselves scarce. She needed to get a list of all BDC employees. "Tell me about Clifton."

"That's my boss."

"Are there any other supervisors at that level?"

"Not on day shift."

"Clifton is a woman?"

"Yes. What does that have to do with it?" He bristled as if she were casting aspersion on Clifton's gender.

"Nothing. Sometimes men can be nicknamed Shelley, so I wondered. She reports directly to the assistant director?"

"Yes."

"How come I haven't seen Ms. Clifton here on-site?"

"She's away on vacation until Monday."

Leo examined the paper in front of her. She thought it bad luck that the supervisor wasn't available by Paul Aitken's Friday deadline. Clifton probably not only had access to useful records and information, but she, rather than Milford or Robeson, was likely to be the linchpin who kept the program going. Didn't it figure everything fell to pieces in Clifton's absence? And no wonder Milford was in such a snit. He was probably having to cover for her.

"I don't have any further questions at this time, Mister Seaver, but I may re-interview you later."

He rose, looking a lot less energetic than when he'd arrived. They stepped out into the hall and moved toward the security junction before he said anything further. "You people have to believe me. I had nothing to do with that kid or what happened to him. It's true I didn't like him, and he obviously didn't like me, but I didn't kill him."

Leo loved it when people called cops and investigators "you people." She wondered if anyone knew how condescending it sounded. In her politest voice, she said, "Thank you, Mister Seaver. I'll be in touch if I need further information."

"What about the information I need? Do I need a lawyer? Is the BDC staying open?"

"I can't comment at this time, Mister Seaver. It's an ongoing investigation."

"Just great. You haven't answered any of my questions or told me a damn thing." He stopped a few feet from the security station. Richland, the guard, sat behind his table with a crossword puzzle book in front of him. He was trying not to look interested, but if he'd been a hunting dog, his ears would be perked straight up.

Seaver said, "Tell me one thing. Are you going to write me up?"

"This investigation is only in the early stages. I don't know enough yet, so I can't tell you what the final outcome will be."

He grabbed at chest level of his scrubs and tightened the material into a fist. "Aw, crap. I can't afford to lose this job."

Leo nodded but didn't say anything. She learned long ago that empty assurances were never appropriate. She might cite this man—or the facility—but she couldn't predict the outcome. No matter how mad or distraught the person might be, she always refused to venture even a guess until she had all the facts.

A shout came from the front lobby, and she turned. Down the short hall, a woman pushed a something resembling a skinny two-wheeled handcart toward them. The receptionist was giving chase.

"No! Mrs. Bolton, stop! You're not allowed to go in." Leo moved toward the stocky older woman, and this time when she passed through the metal detector, it didn't go off. The plump woman's steps were slow and short, and she was close enough for Leo to hear labored breathing and see the clear oxygen tubes running to her nose from the tank she pushed in front of her.

"I want—answers!" Her words came out in hoarse gasps. "I want—to know—what happened—to my—nephew!"

"Ma'am. Ma'am, please." Lizzie reached the older woman and laid the flat of a hand on her shoulder.

"I want Robeson!" Mrs. Bolton stomped a foot, and the steel-gray bun on top of her head flopped and threatened to fall down.

Leo thought it might be none of her business, but then again, everything about the Bolton matter was her business, so she leaned down and said, "Mrs. Bolton?"

The woman turned and looked her in the eye. "Who are *you*?" Before Leo could answer, the woman's head rose, and her eyes focused somewhere behind Leo. "You! You're the one that killed my Eddie!" She lunged forward, dragging the tank along with her.

Seaver backed up, shaking his head. "Oh, no. No, no, no. I had nothing to do with—I didn't—" He turned on his heel and hastened away.

"Come—come—back here," Mrs. Bolton called out. Her voice was weak, and her eyes filled with tears. "My boy. My sweet boy." She trailed off, coughed weakly, and released her grasp on the oxygen cart's handle. The metal cart went from an angle to upright and thunked against the floor.

"Would you like to come talk with me, Mrs. Bolton?" Leo asked.

"It's *Ms.* Bolton. And who—" she drew a ragged breath "—who are you?"

"I'm an investigator with the State of Minnesota. Come around the corner here, and let's sit down." Lizzie opened her mouth to protest, but Leo frowned and shook her head. "Lizzie, perhaps you might be able to find Ms. Bolton a cup of coffee?"

The receptionist didn't answer. Leo didn't care if she brought coffee or not. She tucked a hand under the rotund woman's arm, grabbed the cart handle, and helped Eddie Bolton's aunt toward security.

The guard didn't even bother to search them when the metal detector went off. "Metal canister." He pointed at the oxygen tank and settled back in his chair to work on his crossword puzzle.

"You," Ms. Bolton said, her voice laced with accusation. "Some security guard you are. You did nothing to keep my nephew alive."

The guard smacked his puzzle page on the desk blotter. "Now see here—"

Leo interrupted the guard. "Never mind him. Let's go rest for a few minutes."

At the slow pace, by the time the two women reached the conference room down the hall, Lizzie had caught up. She preceded them into the room and placed two steaming Styrofoam cups on the table. In a prim voice she said, "I want you to know that the Powers That Be have been called." She rubbed her hands together, as if to wash her hands free of them, and left.

"She's a real piece of work," Ms. Bolton said.

Tell me about it, Leo thought. "Here, let me get that for you." She pulled out a chair.

Ms. Bolton shucked off a red-plaid wool jacket and hung it over the back of the chair. She lowered herself with difficulty. "It's hell getting old. Don't let anyone tell you different." She flared her nostrils and drew in a long breath.

"I am so very sorry about the death of your nephew, Ms. Bolton. If—"

"Yeah, yeah. Everybody's oh so sorry. Fat lot of good that does."

"You're right. All that's left for us to do is find out who did this and make them pay. Could you take a few minutes now to talk with me? I would very much like to take your statement. I know it may be a difficult time—"

"No, no, now is as good a time as any. Tomorrow'll be every bit as difficult as today." She lifted her coffee to her lips, closed her eyes, and took a sip.

"I have a little bureaucracy I must be sure to follow." Leo turned on her tape recorder and went on to explain Ms. Bolton's rights. All the while, the older woman concentrated on her Styrofoam cup. Leo finished, saying, "So shall we get started?"

"What do you do with dumb people who don't understand all the legal mumbo-jumbo?"

Leo smiled. "Whether people understand it or not, I'm required by agency rules to read it."

"Kind of takes the wind out of a person's sails having to hear all that."

"You should try having to read it over and over."

For the first time, Phyllis Bolton cracked the tiniest of smiles.

Leo said, "According to my records, you were Eddie's legal guardian for several years. This must be a terrible shock."

"Please, call me Phyllis. What did you say your name was again?"

"Leona Reese. You can call me Leona."

"Exactly how much do you know about this hellhole, Leona?"

"I reviewed past records for safety and adherence to state laws and local ordinances. My office has records about the BDC since its inception. I'm still learning, but on paper, I know the BDC moderately well."

"They killed my Eddie."

"It's my understanding Eddie died as a result of a fast-acting poison."

"He was supposed to be *safe* in here. Safe. They're responsible."

Leo wondered whether Phyllis Bolton referred to Robeson and Milford, or to the system in general, but she wasn't going to ask. "Could you take a few minutes, Phyllis, and tell me a little about Eddie?"

"What good will that do? He's dead now."

"I know, I'm sorry. But learning about his life and experiences might give hints about who would do this to him."

"All right then. He was a wonderful child. Bright. A good student. He won the fourth-grade spelling bee."

Leo nodded, urging her on with a look.

"Lately he's fallen in with some bad company. If it weren't for that, he'd probably be going on to college." Her eyes filled with tears, and she fumbled behind her in her coat, finally pulling out a single tissue.

"How did you come to be his guardian?"

"His mother died in a freak hang-gliding accident when he was two. Eddie's dad took care of him until he—Ed, Senior, he was my brother—died in a car accident. So I've raised Eddie ever since he was three. He and Stevie have grown up like brothers."

"Stevie?" Leo slid a legal pad and pen out of her valise.

"Yes, my grandson, Steven Bolton, who was my daughter's son. Technically Eddie is—was—Stevie's first cousin once removed, but like I say, I raised them as brothers. They're not even a year apart."

"This must be very hard for him, too."

Phyllis looked down at the table. "Stevie couldn't drive me over here. He was so upset."

Leo had been attempting to draw a genealogy chart, a circle for Phyllis and squares for Stevie and for Edward Junior and Senior. It wasn't connecting up. "Who are Stevie's parents?"

"My daughter, Kayla Bolton, died of a drug overdose when Stevie was four months old. As for the father, I used to be embarrassed to say Stevie was illegitimate just like Kayla was." She let out a little snort and crossed her arms in front of her. "Apple doesn't fall far from the tree, I suppose."

"Okay, so Stevie is your daughter's child, and Eddie was your brother's son?"

"Yes. I started real early, and my brother started late, so my grandson is nearly the same age as Ed Senior's son. Confusing as hell, isn't it?" She shook her head slowly.

"I understand. Let's talk about Eddie's time here at BDC. Did he mention any problems he experienced since he's been here? Any bullies? Anything unusual?"

At that, Phyllis Bolton's eyes took on a cold, steely look. "Damn right he did! He called me and told me what that counselor Mike did to him. Cruel so-and-so. And him acting like such a responsible man. It's all a front."

Leo waited for more. Phyllis Bolton threaded her fingers together and put her elbows on the table. With a deep breath she launched into the details. "After he got in the car crash, Eddie was either going from the hospital to jail or over here. I didn't want him sitting in a cell with a bunch of perverts and druggies. Everybody at the hospital told me residential treatment could turn him around, so I didn't fight the judge when he decided to send Eddie to this place. I thought this'd be better than juvie." She scowled. "I had no idea how wrong I was. He got here the Friday before last, and I didn't get to see him until this past Sunday. When he called me about that Mike fellow roughing him up, I came over right away." Tears rose in her eyes, and she struggled to compose herself.

Her single tissue looked all used up, so Leo grabbed a wad of them she kept in the side pocket of the valise and slid them across the table. Phyllis Bolton selected one and dabbed her eyes.

"Phyllis, your nephew called after work hours Friday night and left a voicemail at my office about his allegations. That's why I'm here."

"A day late and a dollar short."

Leo wasn't going to argue. Until the authorities found out exactly why he died and who did it, there was no way to know what might have happened if Eddie Bolton's interview had taken place twenty-four hours sooner. She steered the woman back on track. "What did he tell you happened between him and the counselor?"

"The man attacked him. Socked him in the gut and pushed him down on the floor with his knee in his back." She was indignant and warming up. "Eddie said some other kids cornered him, and that man, Mike, took the side of the wolf pack. He shoved Eddie and slammed him against the wall, knocked him to the ground. My poor boy hardly had a chance to defend himself. I was here Sunday, and I *saw* the bruise on his back—a big ol' round knee bruise. These people need to be shut down. I went and complained, and that weasel Milton Morland, Morley Morton—"

"Morton Milford?"

"Yes! That mealy-mouthed ass tried to shine me on. Didn't do a damn thing. Because Eddie was sent here by the law, I couldn't get him out on my say-so, could I? I tried. Believe me, I tried. If only I could've . . ."

She stopped, wheezing heavily, and struggled to inhale short breaths through her nose. Leo assumed she had emphysema, but she thought it would be rude to ask. She couldn't tell how old Phyllis was. Her face, unlined and clear-skinned, was a contrast to the unruly, prematurely gray mop she had attempted to corral in a bun. Her hands looked strong, the veins a little prominent as though she'd done some labor in her life.

"Have you always lived here in Duluth, Phyllis?"

"Nope. Grew up in Chicago. My parents moved to the Twin Cities in the early Sixties when I was in high school. They came up here once they retired. I had my daughter the summer after I graduated. At least I knew who the father was. But he split town. Never been heard from since. Never got a dime of child support either."

"What was his name?"

"Robby Parklin. Don't know why the heck I got hooked up with him. All the Parklins turned out to be useless."

"Did you go on to marry? Have other children?"

"Nope. Kayla damn near did me in."

"Must have been very tough raising the grandson and nephew, then."

"Yes. Luckily I inherited my parents' house when the boys were little, and we had some insurance money from Edward's death. We made ends meet." Her eyes filled with tears again, and she lifted a tissue to her brow. "I'm weary. I need to go home. But I wanted to talk to the stuffed shirt who runs the place. The big kahuna named Robeson. Leona," she said and looked up with pleading eyes, "can you get me in to see him?"

"To be honest, I'm also having a tough time arranging to speak with him. I've only seen him in passing, and that's it. When I do talk to Mister Robeson, I'll put in a request for him to contact you. Please give me your phone number and address."

As she rattled off the information, Phyllis pushed back her chair and rose slowly. "I'm telling you, the governor is going to hear about this. I'm calling my legislators. I'll call county services. I'll call the ACLU. I might be moving slow with this damn tank, but it sits real nice next to my phone. I won't rest until I get justice for my nephew."

"I understand what you're saying. I'm very sorry you have to go through this, Phyllis." Leo stood, came around the side of the table, and reached out a hand. The older woman shook with a strong grip, and for a moment she looked fierce, like someone to be reckoned with. Then she took a deep breath and deflated with the exhale. Leo helped her put on the plaid coat, and they headed toward the door, oxygen tank in tow.

Outside in the hall, Phyllis paused. "If I was a mafia wife, I'd have a hit put out on that counselor. Guys like him shouldn't be working in places where there's kids." With a grunt, she pulled the cart forward, stomping along with short steps at a surprisingly rapid rate.

Leo stood in the doorway watching her. Times like these she was glad not to have children. She didn't know much to speak of concerning Stevie Bolton, but if he was anything like his cousin Eddie, Phyllis Bolton must have her hands full.

She went back to the conference table, turned off the tape recorder, and wrote more notes, including a reminder to ask Mike Seaver some follow-up questions. She needed to make sure she got his behavior reports, if indeed there were any. Somehow, she wouldn't put it past him to have left the interview and run off to work up the paperwork today and backdate it.

With a sigh, she called Thom, and gave him details for further computer searches. After leaving a quick message on Gary Clark's voicemail, Leo decided it was time to find Messrs. Milford and Robeson. If they didn't agree to meet with her at some time in the next day or so, she'd get Detective Clark involved. She grinned, thinking how funny it would be to have the cops come and take Donald Robeson in a cruiser down to the Duluth police station. I'm wicked, she thought, but I hate pomposity and arrogance, and Robeson has both in spades.

➤■◄

Leo doubled back to Rentreau Plaza and hurried into the building, still irritated at her inability to track down either of the BDC managers. She'd never seen two administrators so intent on avoiding questions.

Leo's "official" work hours ran from nine to five, but she was usually in the office shortly after eight a.m. unless she went directly to an interview. When first assigned to the state office building, Leo attempted to keep Paul Aitken apprised of her comings and goings, but she soon learned he didn't care so long as she got results. And she did. She and Thom were closing cases almost twice as fast as their peers in Saint Paul, so she supposed their big reward was considerable independence. Anybody could track her down by cell phone. Other than giving Thom and Tonya a basic idea of what she was doing for the day, she came and went as she pleased. Today she was grateful for that freedom.

At her cubicle, the phone rang. She picked it up and heard the voice of Detective Gary Clark. "Leona, hey. Did you get a chance to review the autopsy findings?"

"Hang on, Gary."

She rose and checked the in-box over by the cubicle entrance. Sure enough, Tonya had delivered the report. "I've got it but haven't looked at it."

"Let me hit the high points for you. The M.E. is quite certain the Bolton kid was poisoned with potassium cyanide. Pitney tested for it when he did the autopsy, and he's certain. Like the medics, Pitney said he smelled almonds. And then the kid's skin was flushed pink—damn near red. The M.E. says only three other things can cause that sort of flushed reaction: sunburn, carbon monoxide poisoning, and extreme cold, none of which the victim experienced. The tox screens will further confirm it, but his stomach was full of what Pitney thinks was copious amounts of alcohol laced with cyanide."

"They called the ambulance immediately. How come the kid couldn't be saved?"

"I guess he had a seizure. I'm not sure how much cyanide he ingested or how much will kill a person that fast. We'll know after more extensive tests are done, but the doc says as little as fifty or seventy milligrams of it will cause immediate collapse and a very speedy death."

As Clark spoke, Leo scanned the report and read that cyanide impedes the cells of the body from using oxygen, which all cells need to survive. "This is awful. Sounds like drowning in the air. What a horrible way to die."

"Yeah," Clark said. "Whoever did this is some kind of twisted, messed up jerk."

"I guess that rules out suicide."

"No way would someone kill himself this way. It'd be less painful taking a header face-first off the roof. Besides, how would Bolton get the stuff in there? No, this one's on the books as a homicide."

"Now the key questions are where would anybody get cyanide these days and who brought it into the BDC? Ever since the Tylenol poisonings in the Eighties, aren't chemicals like this monitored?"

"Pretty much," he said, "but people who do electroplating or metal cleaning use it. And miners, I guess. The doc said it can be used to remove gold from its ore. This is a mining community, so maybe that makes it easier to get. I have to admit I've never investigated a cyanide killing. Strychnine, yes. Rat poison is somewhat common, and I've had a couple of those cases, but never a fatality. I'll be talking to the M.E. and doing a little research on cyanide. I'll find out where to get the stuff."

Leo took a couple minutes to give thumbnail sketches of her interviewees, all of whom Clark had also interviewed at length. He asked, "What's your take on Seaver?"

"I believed him when he said he had nothing to do with the poisoning, but it seems to me something else is going on there at the BDC. I'm not sure what, but he *is* hiding something. Maybe after I talk to more staff and administrators I'll get a read on it. Say, speaking of administration, I've not had any luck talking with the directors. You?"

"They're pretty close-mouthed, but of course they have to cooperate with me. If you don't nail them down before too long, let me know, and I'll put the fear of the Lord into them."

"I may have to do that. I've got an end-of-the-week deadline on this one."

"What? This is way too complicated for that kind of timeline. We won't even have all the autopsy information, much less witness interviews by then."

"I know. It's political. Didn't you hear Donald Robeson's brother is married to the sister of the governor's wife?"

"Damn! No wonder the chief called my lieutenant up to his office." He let out a whoosh of breath into the receiver. "Didn't have a clue about that. You know I'd like to help you out with your deadline, but—"

"Don't get me wrong, Gary. I know that. I just told you so you'd be aware. Come Friday, the fires of hell might be burning, and we should be prepared."

"Okay, then, I'll keep you posted."

"Likewise."

They rang off, and Leo sat perusing the last of the autopsy report: description of heart, lungs, liver, GI tract, other organs. Stomach contents, mostly bile, were in the airway, and there was pulmonary hemorrhage and edema present. The summary carefully spelled out that the pathologist suspected the cause of death was cyanide poisoning, pending final results of the toxicology screens.

She set the report aside and closed her eyes. The exhaustion she felt was nearly overpowering. After a moment, she took a deep breath and opened her eyes. The right eye still felt strange. The eyelid under the patch sometimes didn't want to open, and it felt weird to have one eye open and the other twitching. She blinked twice. Gradually her left eye brought the desk blotter into focus, and she found herself staring at the center where 1:PM DR GEST was written in bold red felt marker on a Wednesday. Today.

"Oh, crap." She looked at her watch, glad to see it wasn't quite noon. The day was already bad enough without having to go to the eye doctor. She thought perhaps she would cancel, then decided she shouldn't. She'd been waiting long enough for this particular date, hoping she was ready for the sizing of the prosthetic eye. She felt like hell, but this was one appointment she wasn't going to miss.

→■←

Doctor Gest reminded Leo of a bespectacled elf—or maybe Yoda from *Star Wars*. He was at least two inches shorter than she was, bowlegged, balding, and possessed extremely big ears. While his face was lined and craggy, his gaze was always kind. If she didn't know better, she would never guess one of his eyes was a prosthetic.

After a surgeon at the Mayo Clinic in Rochester removed her right eye, Dr. Gest, a Duluth ophthalmologist, took over her continued care. She felt comfortable with him. He was expert, both professionally and personally, in assisting the newly one-eyed with adapting to a non-binocular new world.

As far as Leo could say, there was only one advantage to the removal of her eye: she wasn't dead from cancer. Other than that, every other aspect was a big mess. She never even knew anything was wrong until the tumor inside her eye grew to a size that it interfered with the retina and obstructed her vision.

Removal of the eye is called enucleation, and what an excellent term that turned out to be. What occurred in her life since then had been almost like a nuclear reaction. She had an immediate meltdown, followed by a short period of such disbelief that she still couldn't properly recall three days of her life. She remembered all the times Daria held her late into the night, soothing her, keeping her from going crazy. She was there when they put Leo under for the surgery and still there—blurrily so—when Leo woke up with her right eye and forehead swathed in a mass of bandages.

The kind of cancer she'd had, choroidal melanoma, is malignant. She still found it hard to believe she malignant cancer had grown inside her so insidiously. The Big C—just like her mother—but her mother's form of cancer was ovarian, and she hadn't had any clue until it was too late.

Leo counted herself lucky. The eye tumor could have metastasized and spread to other parts of her body, but when her vision suddenly took a turn for the worse, she had eventually gone to an eye doctor. They found the tumor quickly. If they had discovered it sooner, the doctors might have been able to treat her with radiation and saved the eye. But the tumor was so large the amount of radiation needed would have wiped out the eye anyway. She'd asked repeatedly if they could operate only to remove the tumor, but there was no way to do so and keep the eye without spreading the cancer. Three different doctors confirmed that only complete removal could save her life. She hadn't believed the second opinion, but the third time she reluctantly accepted the course of treatment, and her eye went dark for good.

In a famous short story Leo once read, Somerset Maugham wrote, "In the land of the blind, the one-eyed man is king." Leo wasn't sure if that was true, but she'd since learned that in the land of the sighted, the one-eyed person is an anomaly. An oddity. She'd never known how much she used both eyes until she was without one of them. To top it off, her right eye was dominant. Now she had no idea how long it would take to achieve shooting accuracy, and until she did, she couldn't go back to work at the Saint Paul Police Department.

Dr. Gest removed the eye patch, gently pried open her upper and lower lid, and used a lighted magnifying glass to examine the temporary orbital implant and surrounding tissue.

He turned off the light and shifted back a few inches. "You haven't taken my advice about wearing protective glasses, Leo."

"No, I guess I haven't. The patch has been plenty to contend with. All I need now is clunky glasses to really doll me up."

Dr. Gest smiled. "I'm not suggesting you purchase glasses for a circus clown. Many lightweight, nearly invisible kinds are now on the market that you could wear. You'd hardly notice them."

"It's bad enough that my nose is curtailing my peripheral vision. Glasses would just add to that." She didn't see his hand coming so when he patted her on the right shoulder, she jumped.

"You're lucky to have a pert little nose. Imagine how much trouble somebody like Jimmy Durante would have had."

She wasn't sure who Jimmy Durante was, but she assumed his nose was the size of Pinocchio's.

He said, "Tell me you've been practicing the visual tricks I showed you."

She nodded. If she hadn't practiced the careful head movements and paid close attention to his instructions about improving depth perception and field of vision, she'd still be falling off curbs, missing hands when she went to shake, and generally teetering along through the world like a clumsy drunk. Nearly every night she stood in the basement laundry room at the apartment and bounced a handball against the wall. Trying to follow it with her eye, much less catch it, had been a comedy of errors for days on end. Dr. Gest insisted her brain would retrain itself, but that it took time. He was right. Her perception changed gradually, and some of the time her vision was almost normal. In fact, somewhere along the way, she felt like she had gotten back a semblance of 3-D vision, though how that happened she wasn't sure. At least now she wasn't scared to death to drive, though she'd had some close calls with cars on the right side.

Dr. Gest lowered himself into his rolling chair and pulled up to the side table to open her chart. "As we expected, the healing is complete, and you seem ready for a referral for the ocular prosthetic. I took the liberty of having my secretary check with the ocular specialist. They can fit you in on Friday. I thought you'd want to get in as soon as possible." He looked at her over his glasses. "Am I on track?"

"Yeah, Doc. You are." His words were the first welcome ones in the entire godforsaken day, and she actually found herself smiling.

# Chapter Four

At home, William Cattrall liked to be called Will. Not Willy, not Bill, and definitely not Billy. Just Will. Since Day One at the Benton Dowling Center, though, everyone called him William, and he didn't know how to change it. The two guys across the hall, Speed and Mouse, had cool names. How did they manage that? Even the counselors addressed them by their nicknames. Meanwhile, William was stuck.

A bell rang, and he rose from the bed on which he lay. He was supposed to make the bed, complete with military corners. Screw that, he thought. Ever since his roommate Eddie Bolton died so suddenly, nobody paid any attention to him. He wasn't toeing the party line until someone made an issue of it.

In jeans, scuff-slippers, and the standard white t-shirt, William shuffled out to the hall. As he turned and joined the flow toward the cafeteria, Mouse caught his eye. William stiffened. Mouse, a tough-looking sixteen-year-old, was mostly white, but also something else. William didn't know if perhaps one of his parents was Latino or Hawaiian or what, but Mouse's skin was a pale brown, and his glittering dark eyes reminded William of a Latino kid at school who was constantly getting beat up by other students. He wasn't sure where Mouse got his nickname. He wasn't particularly small, nor did he look rodent-like in any way. If not for the insolent swagger and tough-guy act, Mouse might be considered handsome. He had been friends with Eddie Bolton, though, so William kept a close eye on him. Mouse could be cruel, but nowhere near as awful as Eddie. William wasn't sure whether Mouse was ordinarily brutal and mean, or if Eddie managed to bring out the worst in everyone around him.

Mouse fell in step beside William. "So did they clean up the shitty smell in your room?"

William was surprised by this unexpected question. "Yeah, why?"

"Just wondering." Mouse glanced at him out of the corner of his eye, and William looked away. They turned the corner and trod down the long hallway to the cafeteria. "How can you sleep in there? I mean, shit, what if his ghost is in there?" Mouse let out a snort and put his head down.

William wondered the same thing himself, but he hadn't yet been visited by any spirits and didn't have any trouble sleeping. Through clenched teeth, he said, "I figure he went straight to hell, where he belongs."

Mouse let out a garbled laugh. "Dude, that's harsh."

They entered the cafeteria, and he followed Mouse to wait in line. William cast a quick look around, trying to locate Speed. Half-turned, holding his empty breakfast tray, he saw Speed burst into the room and fast walk toward the line. Without a second thought, William stepped back, and Speed cut in front of him.

Mouse said, "What the hell took so long?"

Speed rolled his broad shoulders and tipped his head down to stretch his neck. "Had me stuck in that fuckin' interview room forever. Bunch of bullshit. I don't know nothing, and I kept telling the bitch that, but it was one question, then another and another."

The line moved along, and William relaxed slightly, glad he was now invisible once more. He could listen in, and Speed and Mouse wouldn't pay any attention to him. They kept up a running patter of "I can top that" comments, none of which were worth noting. The cafeteria helper slid a plate of eggs and sausage to William, and he helped himself to some toast and a banana before grabbing two containers of milk. Completely ignoring William, Speed and Mouse started across the room, threading between full tables. William saw an open space ahead, near a kid who'd come into the BDC that week, and he moved to join him.

"Willy-O!"

William's head snapped up. Mouse made a jerking motion with his head. "Over here."

Uncertain and on edge again, William shuffled toward the two boys. They were already seating themselves at an empty table. Alarm bells rang in his head. He had a funny feeling he was making a bad move, but he couldn't figure out a way to refuse. He set his tray on the table across from Speed.

Mouse picked up a sausage with one hand and stuffed it in his mouth. In the midst of chewing, he said, "Tell the truth, Willy-O. You didn't off Eddie, didja?"

William shook his head. "No." He looked down at the tray full of food, suddenly feeling sick to his stomach. The memory of Eddie's final minutes bothered him. He hadn't liked the kid, but the convulsions, the screaming, and the froth coming out of his mouth was gross. "If I'd've killed him, it wouldn't have been by poison."

"Oh, yeah?" Speed said. He opened a carton of milk and eyed it. His voice was low, and his delivery slow, making him sound like a young Forrest Gump. "You were planning to put him down?"

"No." William jammed half a piece of toast into his mouth and chewed furiously. What did they want? Why were they suddenly being all buddy-buddy?

After shoveling in a mouthful of scrambled eggs, Mouse said, "We think we know who did it, and we're gonna make him pay."

William looked at them blankly. "Pay?"

"Yeah," Mouse said. "If you didn't do it, then who else would? Had to be that prick Seaver. We're gonna get him, and you're gonna help us."

Speed held his plastic fork in the air. "Eddie didn't deserve to die, and that ass-wipe is going to regret it. We may have lost Eddie, but you can be our new best friend and help us get revenge."

Oh, this is just great, William thought. Just what I need.

# Chapter Five

Leo stopped at her favorite sandwich shop on the way back to the office and picked up a foot-long sub, half for lunch, half for dinner. When she got back to Rentreau Plaza, Thom was rolling along the outer walk. A tall, knockout blonde strode next to him. As he propelled himself forward, he gazed up at her with a look of glee on his face. So this was Ashley, the girl he'd been dating for several months. Leo had never had the occasion to meet her.

Thom turned to face forward, a smile on his face, and caught sight of her. "Hey, Leo. How're you doing?"

She waved and smiled, and he slowed as she stepped up on the curb. The woman looked Leo up and down with an expression of disinterest on her face. Her cheekbones were to die for. Long, wavy blonde hair, much lighter than Leo's framed her face and cascaded down her back. The London Fog coat covered much of her top, but her legs, clad in tight-fitting jeans, were slim. She was around Leo's height, but she wore spike heels giving her an additional three inches.

"Ashley," Thom said, "this is the coworker I've told you about, Leona Reese. Leo, meet Ashley Johansson." Leo reached out, careful to gauge her hand's speed and trajectory. She always felt a sense of relief when she properly connected. Ashley's fingers were dry and wiry. No sooner had Leo given a brief squeeze than Ashley jerked back her hand and tucked it in her coat pocket.

"We're headed off for a late lunch. I might take an extra half hour, but I'll be back in plenty of time to update you on what I've found on the BDC case. Nothing all that helpful, unfortunately."

"Excellent. Thanks, Thom."

With a grin, he turned the chair and sent it down the sidewalk toward the handicap cutout. "Later," he called out over his shoulder.

Ashley looked uncomfortable, and Leo wondered why. Maybe it was the eye patch. Maybe she was one of those people who didn't like other women around their boyfriends. Or perhaps she was merely shy. Leo's stomach growled, so she headed into the office. She got on the elevator as two women from the Public Safety Department got off. She'd seen them around but didn't know their names.

"Oh, hi, Leona," one said as the other gave such a look of pity that no one could miss it.

As the doors shut, Leo heard her whisper, "She's the one who just had that terrible cancer . . ."

Leo's face burned. She leaned against the cold metal rail running along the walls of the elevator and felt grateful that very soon she'd have an artificial eye and put a stop to all the pity.

➤■◀

A quarter million people live near Lake Superior on the Minnesota side with 56,000 of them in Duluth, which is the fourth largest city in Minnesota. With a couple thousand licensed care homes, daycares, nursing homes, and other facilities across the state, a lot of work was generated for the state to investigate. Leo didn't think Duluth's residents in the harbor-side city always got their due because they were dwarfed by the needs of Minneapolis and Saint Paul.

Despite the burgeoning mound of paperwork, Leo wanted to believe she could make it home for dinner every once in a while, but no sooner had she gotten to her apartment with her leftover half-sandwich than a call came in on her cell phone. Tonya reported the city police called in another suspicious death, this time at a day program for ambulatory elderly Alzheimer's patients.

Oh, Lord, Leo thought, obviously this week is going to break all the records for stress.

Responsibility almost always won out over comfort. She had a deadline at work and a dead man with Alzheimer's who required her attention. Besides, as long as she was on the move with her work, she'd be less likely to crack. Less likely to break down and cry over frustrations with her vision. Less likely to do something rash. She put the sub sandwich in the fridge and grabbed a yogurt and a can of soda on the way out.

She was still getting to know the streets of Duluth, so she paged through her handy map book until she found the location of the adult care home. She drove south on Highway 61 for about a mile and went up the hill toward an older area where the houses were close together. They'd been built in the years after World War I, back when the ore boats were a major source of employment for returning soldiers. She parked the Lexus behind two police cars in front of a house on the right side of the one-way street.

Crossing the road, she paused for a moment to examine an oblong white chalk outline next to the road's center line. A figure-eight shape of dark stain was drying in the middle of the chalk. The body had been taken away, and she couldn't say she was unhappy about that. Tonya told her the elderly man had been hit by a car. The scene probably wasn't pretty.

Leo went to the house, which was being guarded by a patrolman who stood cross-armed by the front door. "Detective Clark here?" she asked.

The cop held open the screen door, grunted, and pointed inside. She went in and shut the heavy wood door behind her. A light on a metal box above the door handle blinked red, indicating the door alert was disabled. Most homes for patients with Alzheimer's or dementia used some sort of alarm system; otherwise, disoriented people would get out and perhaps come to harm. As one had today.

Straight ahead, she saw a hallway to the kitchen, and to the right was a community room with a television blaring what sounded like *SpongeBob SquarePants*. Two old men sat on the couch watching. To her left, at the bottom of a staircase, an elderly woman dressed in a pale pink pantsuit sat muttering to herself. She never looked up as she tugged at her wild, stark-white hair.

As Leo drew closer to the kitchen, she heard sobs.

Gary Clark sat at the kitchen table, a pad of paper open in front of him. His work partner, Ben Brandtson, leaned against the kitchen counter, his arms crossed. Clark always looked like an unkempt college professor in his tweedy, awkward-fitting sports coats. Ben wore nicer suits than Gary, but his physique was strangely proportioned, misshapen in odd ways. His arms and legs were too short and his chubby torso too long, giving him a Tyrannosaurus Rex look. His fine, sandy-blond hair barely covered his scalp. He wasn't smiling now, but when he did, his two rows of straight teeth were gapped, making him appear even more like a Jurassic Park escapee.

Across the table from Gary Clark sat a woman dressed in pale green slacks, a flowered top, and white tennis shoes. As Leo came further into the room, she identified the woman as an LPN or orderly.

"I couldn't stop him," she sobbed.

"I understand." Gary glanced up and caught Leo's eye. He said, "Nurse Linton, thank you very much for your cooperation. I'll get back to you soon."

The woman rose and stumbled from the kitchen without acknowledging Leo. Gary stood, too, and the two detectives huddled in the middle of the room with her.

"What's the scoop, guys?"

The two men exchanged a look. Brandtson gave a shrug. Clark nodded and met her gaze. "We don't think anything criminal happened here."

"But you called. Do we need to shut this place down?"

Quickly, the two men outlined the circumstances. Due to Alzheimer's, Oscar Leroy Holdenberg, age 77, six foot two, 171 pounds, had lived in this care home for four years. According to the nurses and attendants, he'd always been very sweet, but in the last few weeks he'd become more agitated. They had no warning he would become violent, but earlier in the day he said he wanted to leave. When the change of shift happened, he knocked down the woman attendant and the nurse, got through the open front door, and ran out. He made it to the middle of the street before being hit by a UPS truck.

"The UPS guy was under the speed limit as far as we can tell."

Brandtson said, "The attendant he attacked hit her head on the edge of the entryway table. Probably got a concussion. She's over at the hospital even as we speak." He consulted his notes and gave Leo the names of residents, owner, and the two staff on duty.

"Looks legit," Clark said. "By the way, I got some further background on the Bolton death." He thumbed through his memo book. "All the line staff are clean except Seaver has an old domestic abuse charge. Later dropped. 2005. And here's a good one on one of the administrators." He ripped a sheet of paper out of his notebook and handed it to her.

The front door opened, and there was a bustle of noise out front.

Brandtson said, "Wonder who we have here now? The owner, administrator, and another nurse have been called. My bet is on the administrator."

Clark said, "Name's Mark J. Johnson."

"Oh, good," Leo said. "Perhaps I can interview him then." But when she went out front, she found only a male attendant who'd arrived to fill in because of the emergency. Clark and Brandtson left, taking the patrolman with them, and she hung around a bit to get the feel of the home. Usually there were six occupants: three men and three women. Two or more staff were on duty at all times. The six patients had each been in residence for at least two years.

Leo spoke informally to Nurse Linton, and from the nurse's comments alone, it was clear the home was usually safe. While they were talking, the owner called on the phone. After speaking with him briefly and being assured he would personally appear at the state office Monday, Leo chose to follow Clark and Brandtson's lead. There was no hurry to investigate because her instincts told her nothing unlawful or inappropriate had occurred. Rather, Mister Holdenberg's escape was a dreadful accident. She would withhold further judgment on whether anyone needed to be cited, but this group home for elders had never had a whisper of a complaint previously.

She still held the sheet of paper Gary Clark had given her, and once she got in the Lexus, she took a closer look at it. What she read made her angry. She stuffed it in her valise, started the car, went down the hill to Highway 61, and turned north. It was after business hours, but she hoped she could get to the BDC in time to talk to either Milford or Robeson. If not, one of them would be seeing her or the police in the morning.

When she arrived at the front desk, the receptionist eyed her warily. With each visit, Leo became less enthusiastic about the woman's receptionist skills. Lizzie didn't even bother to greet her.

"You're working late, Lizzie."

"Personal favor to Mister Robeson since people are coming and going here after hours, even though we're supposed to lock up at five."

"I'd like to speak to Mister Milford or Mister Robeson."

"Mister Robeson is off-site. Mister Milford is busy."

"Is he in his office?"

"He's occupied with important matters." She held up both hands below the level of the chest-high counter and flexed them so she could examine her fingernails.

"Do you know what happens to your job if I shut down this facility?"

Lizzie stammered, "What—there won't be—you can't do that."

Leo let out a snort and grinned as maliciously as she could manage, all the while hoping the eye patch made her look rakish and dangerous. "You and your bosses don't seem to get it. One phone call from me, and the police and state health department walk in here, escort all your patients elsewhere, and close the doors. I hope you have a lot of vacation on the books since you'll be out of a job for however long it takes to fix things. If they ever get fixed, that is." Since Leo had no evidence of imminent danger to the current residents, she was exaggerating somewhat, casually neglecting to mention the citation process, hearing, and appeals that could take many days, if not weeks.

But Lizzie didn't know those facts. She turned pink and stumbled over her next words. "You wouldn't do that."

"If I don't get some cooperation around here, you bet I will."

She gave Leo a look of pure malevolence, but she picked up the phone and punched in some numbers. When Lizzie spoke into the receiver, she turned away so Leo only heard snatches of the conversation. The phone hadn't been returned to the cradle for more than ten seconds when an unmarked door on the other side of the front foyer opened, and Morton Milford poked out his head. "Well, come along then," he said impatiently.

Leo marched across the thin carpet and stepped through the door. He went down the hallway, and she followed, but not before miscalculating the doorway and scratching her left arm across the metal guard into which the latch fit. It didn't draw blood but did scrape away a strip of skin. One of the many drawbacks of losing her binocular vision was how her depth perception was unpredictable. She was constantly bumping into things.

Down the hall, Milford stood along the left wall and gestured for her to enter one of two open doors. The room appeared to be a break room for staff. Three chairs on each side were pushed up to an oblong table. The walls were bare except for a calendar tacked up next to the door. Leo started to put her valise on the table but shifted from one side to the other to avoid a not-quite-dry coffee spatter.

Milford lowered himself into a chair across from her. "How long do you think this will take?"

"Maybe an hour. Maybe less if you're one hundred percent forthcoming." She pulled out her recorder, not wanting to waste time getting it going. Milford had a lot of questions to answer, and she didn't want to miss taping any of it. After her regular spiel about rights and responsibilities, she asked some introductory questions about his job and his position, but then cut right to the key issue. "Mister Milford, on Tuesday the police asked you if you reviewed background checks for those who work here and if there was anything of a suspicious nature for us to monitor."

He dropped his chin slowly, then jerked up, looking for all the world like he was going to faint. His face was thin and lined. According to the information the detectives gave her, Milford was fifty-two, but with his sparse, salt-and-pepper hair and bloodshot eyes, he looked well into his sixties. He had been with the BDC for eleven years, first as a supervising social worker, then promoted to assistant director. Besides speeding tickets, he'd only committed one major offense, though he'd also been arrested once for something else. She had a hunch that was what he didn't want to talk about.

"Were you aware your employee Mike Seaver has previously been arrested?"

He let out a breath as though relieved. "Arrested? Or convicted? Many times people are falsely arrested."

She pulled a pen and notebook from the valise. "I believe an arrest occurred, and the charges were eventually dropped."

"That might have come to light in an initial screening. Prospective employees are given the chance to explain circumstances. Mister Seaver's employment here predates my assignment as administrator. However, I'm confident any arrest on his record was unrelated to his work here."

"And can you say the same for yourself?"

Milford sputtered, his eyes wide and blinking. He looked like a goggle-eyed fish. "What?"

"You were arrested in 1978 for suspicion of molesting a minor. A male minor at a pizza parlor."

Milford's hand went to the breast pocket of his gray suit. He pulled out a white handkerchief as if he planned to give up and toss it into the ring. His hand shook. She watched, fascinated, as beads of sweat formed on his forehead.

"That was an error. Inaccurate. I didn't, I wouldn't—" He sat back and blotted at his forehead. "I was a busboy then. I had nothing to do with what happened to that kid. I didn't even know him."

"What about Violet Lee Francisco? You were convicted of criminal sexual misconduct. What about her?"

He gulped. "You can leave her out of this. She has nothing to do with the death of Edward Bolton."

Leo folded open the sheet of paper containing Gary Clark's cramped writing. "I'm wondering about patterns, Mister Milford. First, it's a fifteen-year-old boy, then a fourteen-year-old girl about three years later."

"For God's sake! That's not how it was."

"I have verifiable proof that Violet Lee Francisco gave birth to a full-term, healthy baby girl two days after Violet turned fifteen. At the time, you were twenty-one-years old. You seem to like them young, Mister Milford. Was Eddie Bolton one of your conquests?"

"Oh, my God. No." Milford took short, sharp breaths of air and looked like he was having a heart attack. Shaking his head, he loosened the knot of his tie. "No, no, you've got it all wrong. I never even met this Bolton kid and didn't pay one iota of attention to him. I didn't match his face and name until he died." He daubed at his face and eyes with the handkerchief. "And there's no need to bring Violet or my daughter into this. That was years ago. Traci will be thirty in a few months—that's how long ago this happened. I pled guilty to getting Violet in trouble, and I got a suspended sentence so we could raise the child. I never missed a single child support payment. Not once!"

She wrote "Traci" on the legal pad and waited to see if he would say more.

With his elbows on the table he clutched the bit of white cloth in both hands, pulling at it as though it was the only thing keeping him from fainting. "I don't see what any of this has to do with what happened to Edward Bolton. I'd only just come in the building when they summoned me to his room." He paused. "The police didn't ask me about any of this. Why are you bringing it up?"

"Part of my job is to get all of the facts on the record. That's all."

"All the facts? What facts? You could ruin me if you deliver this information to the wrong people, Ms. Reese! It has nothing to do with Edward Bolton."

He was so panicked that she wondered if he was going to start crying. Leo didn't want him to lose it, so she steered him into other areas and asked him about procedures, staff habits, unruly youth, past infractions. He settled into the factual pieces, rising once to go across the hall to his office to get a stack of folders.

Imparting data, Milford settled into a groove. He was a wealth of information, and they were at it a lot longer than an hour. He had the kind of mind accountants tend to possess: heavy on monetary detail and organizational facts, though light on knowledge of human nature. "I didn't particularly like supervising," he said. "All that day-to-day complaining and handholding. I much prefer behind-the-scenes work."

"So you delegated the handholding?"

"Yes. Shelley Clifton has been a big help."

"And she's due back in the office when?"

"Monday." He swept his handkerchief from his lap and wiped his brow.

Leo ran out of questions and wrapped up the interview, at which point he got edgy again. "What will you do about the old information about my past?"

"Nothing at this time. If it has anything at all to do with this case, it may come out. Otherwise, it stays confidential with me until the investigation is over."

"I'm sure it has nothing to do with the young man's death."

"If that's the case, then you can relax."

And he did look like he was more at ease. He'd made a clean breast of things, and now he sat back in the chair and arranged the staff folders into a neat, squared-off stack. She packed away the recorder and legal pad and checked her watch. It was after seven p.m. "I know it's an imposition, Mister Milford, but would you mind giving me the nickel tour of the BDC?"

His eyebrows went up. "You haven't inspected the facility?"

"Not lately." She had seen most of it the one time she'd investigated a complaint, but she wanted him to show it to her now and give any background he could. The way he did the avoidance dance, she felt she might not get another chance. "How many kids are enrolled in the program now?"

"Hmm." He cleared his throat. "If I remember correctly, sixty-six."

"Is that normal?"

"Somewhat. We generally run between four and six dozen."

"Is there a typical age? Say, sixteen? Or older?"

"The median age is fifteen years, nine months. Over the last ten years, the number has dropped. When I began working here, the median age was closer to seventeen."

He sounded like a scientist, suddenly reminding Leo of her high school chemistry professor: precise, cold, and very dry.

On the walk-through, the rest of his comments were curt. He was obviously tired. There were a couple areas of the center she couldn't enter. She did, however, see several dozen youth and eight staff in the cafeteria eating hamburger hotdish for dinner. None of them looked like they were enjoying it much.

Fifteen minutes later, Leo was out in the parking lot, none the wiser for the tour. The sun had gone down and taken all semblance of warmth with it. She got in the car shivering.

She was supposed to wrap up this case by Friday, but how could she? Nobody had a clue as to who was responsible for the death of Edward Bolton.

# Chapter Six

Thom rolled into the building, shook a dusting of new-fallen snow from his hair, and hailed Serena and the new guard who sat at the desk on the other side of the screening area. As he went through the entrance, he disregarded the shrill beeping of the metal detector. Serena turned it off, saying, "You could be sitting on a load of C-4 or a pipe bomb, and I'd be letting your ass in."

"I like that about you, Serena. That you trust me so much. Lucky I'm such a stand-up guy." He choked back a laugh.

She rolled her eyes. "Bet you're the funniest person you know."

"Makes it easier to navigate my days knowing I can crack up in more than one way."

"Surprised you're wheeling around out in this snow."

"Couldn't be avoided. I needed to do some research at the courthouse. I planned on cutting across the street and getting a breath of fresh air, but now I'm glad I took the van. It's slick out there."

In all sincerity, she said, "You watch yourself, Thom. Traffic can be dangerous when the first snow falls."

"Speaking of watching yourself, did you hear about the blind man who walked into a store with his seeing eye dog?" He didn't pause to let Serena get a word in. "All of a sudden, the blind guy picks up the leash and begins swinging the dog over his head. The manager runs up to the man all freaked and asks, 'What are you doing?' The blind guy says, 'Just looking around.'"

Serena snickered, but then forced back the laughter. "I'm not laughing. I'm not laughing, Thoreson. You're a sick and twisted man. Simple, too!"

"You love me, I can tell."

"Now I know why they call you TNT: Terrible Nutcase Thom."

"I'm not copping to that!" He winked and continued on, nodding to the new guard as he drew near. The dark-haired woman looked up from her operating manual, her face passive and eyes expressionless. "Hey," Thom said, "I haven't met you yet." He squinted at her nametag. "Hi, Charlotte."

She blushed. "Call me Charley."

"I'm Thom." He reached to shake her hand. "How 'bout those Vikes?"

She frowned. "Sports, right?"

"You're not only new working here, but also new to Minnesota?"

"Yeah.

"The Vikings are a football team. Been here since before I was born, 1961 or thereabouts. Where you from?"

"Alaska. Never been much of a sports fan. It's not like we've got a lot of pro teams."

"Yeah, not with the size of your population. Or the weather. But wow, you've had some great skiers. How about that Hilary Lindh? Was she something or what?"

Charley's passive face suddenly became animated. "You know her?"

"Of her. I remember watching the Albertville Olympics. Pretty girl with great style."

"She was a year older than me in school. I didn't know her personally, but you can bet we all watched her ski on TV. I'm from a little town outside Juneau where she grew up."

"Cool. Well, the Vikings have a night game coming up next week. A bunch of people from the building watch games on the ginormous TV screen at the bar down the street." He glanced back. "You watching, Serena?"

"If we don't have a foot of snow," Serena said.

He looked back at Charley. "You should come and watch the game with us."

"I might." A gust of cold air blew into the lobby, and a crowd of people came to the security area. Charley rose. "I better help Serena. Nice talking to you."

Thom gave a salute and rolled to the elevator, hoping the new guard didn't think he was hitting on her. He had a hunch that if she did, Serena would set her straight. Ashley came to mind, and he decided he ought to call her. At his desk, he reached for the phone, but before he could pick it up, someone cleared his throat. Thom turned to see his boss in the doorway. "Hey, Paul. How's your day?"

"Not so good. What's going on with the Bolton mess?"

"Moving along faster than usual. Why?"

Paul worked his lips as though trying to unsuccessfully lubricate his teeth. For some time Thom had tried to figure out what exactly was wrong with Paul. He was a political animal through and through, so his behavior wasn't anything new. He was nice enough, smiled at the right things, behaved in a cheery manner, but his blue eyes were cold, and he wasn't particularly patient. He'd never blown up at Thom or Leo, but he was merciless with Tonya and many of the other support staff. The lower on the totem pole you went, the less respect Paul Aitken showed.

But it was more than that. All the cheesy smiles, the overreaching, the insincerity. Those were personality aspects Thom saw often in the majority of the people he'd ever known in power. Something else, some endless craving for power, buried deep and usually well disguised, was part of the problem. Right now it oozed from Aitken like something radioactive, smelling like desperation.

"Listen up, Thom. I've got to show some results. This department can't fail."

"Yes, sir. I think we all understand that, and we're doing our best."

"Your 'best' isn't good enough. Success is what's needed. The BDC needs to be cleared as soon as possible. You understand?"

Thom nodded and held his tongue. There was no success to be had in the Bolton murder. A kid was dead, and the culprit hadn't been brought to justice, might never even be arrested.

Paul stepped closer and leaned down. "What about Leona?"

"What about her?"

"Is she capable of clearing this case? Has she been affected?"

"Affected, sir?" Thom knew exactly what Aitken was getting at, but he wasn't about to stoop to his boss's level.

"You know. The eye thing. She up to par?"

"She seems fine. I can't tell any difference in her work at all."

His lips were pressed tightly together, and underneath them Aitken ran his tongue over his teeth. Thom was reminded of a horror movie he saw as a kid where a snake-like alien suddenly exploded from the mouth of a man. Aitken opened his mouth, and Thom almost expected a gray-green thing to burst out. Instead, Aitken said, "If she doesn't get this report cleared by Friday night, I'm pulling her off the case and putting you on it."

Thom managed not to let out the guffaw he felt rising. "I'm sure that won't be necessary. Nobody gets to the bottom of things better than a cop."

Aitken stepped back. He pulled at the black sleeve of his suit to expose his Rolex. "I'm late for a meeting." He spun on his heel and disappeared down the aisle.

Heartless bastard, Thom thought. He hasn't got a clue what kind of work Leo does, much less me. He only cares about the results, not the effort made. Aitken's facile posturing and fake concern never fooled Thom. He was the kind of guy Thom remembered from his college football days, all about himself and never about the team. If the team won, Aitken would be there to take the credit. If they lost, he'd make sure he was blame-proof.

Thom wanted to resolve the BDC case soon, like today, but he didn't have high hopes for it. Strictly speaking, he and Leo had nothing to do with determining formal guilt or legal culpability. They needed to find out whether a complaint or an incident at a licensed facility was supported by facts. Was the infraction, accident, or death the fault of employees or administration? Or chance? Or was it due to the actions of an outside party? In the BDC case, Thom wondered whether it might be a combination of all those factors.

All he knew for sure was that unless Paul Aitken contacted the State Human Services Department in Saint Paul and got approval to revoke their clearances, either he or Leo had the power to shut down the BDC facility for the safety of the residents. They could also cite any administrator or any employee, regardless of whether the infraction warranted criminal charges. Obviously, Aitken was afraid of that.

Thom reached for the phone, and once again he was interrupted.

"Psssst." Tonya poked her head around the corner into the cubicle. "You got a minute?"

"For you? Sure."

Tonya slid into the chair in the corner next to his side table. She'd often teased that "black girls don't blush," but if he didn't know better, she was. "What's the matter?"

"He's got his panties all in a wad again over this BDC case. He asked what I was transcribing, and when he found out it wasn't notes for you and Leo, he threatened to fire me for insubordination."

Thom could only shake his head.

"So give me some notes, Thoreson."

"You know I haven't got anything for you now."

"That's what I figured. So what am I supposed to do?"

"He'll be off your back for a while. He has a meeting with the bigwigs over at the courthouse, hobnobbing with the highest of the honchos. Probably won't be back for hours. If he gets on your case again, tell him you finished some BDC paperwork for me, and send him over. I'll cover for you."

"Thanks." She rose. "I don't need this shit today. I've got a Con Law exam tonight."

"Hope you ace it, Tonya."

"I hope I can manage a B."

Thom heard a noise in the hall, and someone said, "Anybody know where Leona is?"

Tonya peeked around the corner. "She's out on a case. What do you need?"

The floor receptionist came to stand outside the cubicle, a pink phone message fluttering in her hand. "I have an urgent message for her."

"Give it to me," Thom said. "I'll get ahold of her." Tonya passed it to him, and he saw it was from Detective Gary Clark. "Later, kid. Good luck with the test."

"Yeah," she said. "The sooner I get out of here the better." She flounced out of the office. Thom dialed the police station and waited for someone to get Gary Clark.

Without preamble, Clark said, "You just caught me. I'm on the way out the door. There's been another murder at the BDC."

"What?"

"I paged Leona. She's already there. I think you'll want to come up, too. I gotta go, Thom."

"I can be there in twenty min—" The phone went dead, and he hung it up. He grabbed his overcoat and wheeled his chair around. "Tonya!"

From a distance, he heard her answer. He headed down the hallway toward the back door as she came up behind him.

"What's the matter?" she called out.

He beckoned her close and whispered, "Another killing at the BDC."

"Holy shit."

"My sentiments exactly. I'll call in when I know more. Act like you know nada and zip if Aitken comes by."

→■←

For the second time in a week, Leo stood waiting in the BDC entryway holding her valise. The receptionist was nowhere to be seen, and not knowing where the crime scene was, she hesitated to head down the hall to the security officer's station. Perhaps Lizzie had stepped away to the restroom and would soon return.

The bay windows to the left of the front door were streaked with a sooty film, and the reflection off the new-fallen snow was so bright the window looked stippled, like old-fashioned isinglass. She saw a streak of white through the trees, and two police cars emerged from the long drive and pulled up to the front of the building, parking at opposite angles to the front walk next to the St. Louis County cruiser. Flashing red lights lit up the glass. For a moment, the window looked as though it were stained with blood.

The door behind the receptionist's counter opened. Leo wheeled around to see Donald Robeson and a deputy sheriff emerge. Robeson's face was red, and his usually sculpted hair was in disarray. Stooped over, he held a handkerchief to his forehead and blotted his brow with a shaky hand.

Leo moved to the counter and heard him say, ". . . couldn't happen here in my facility. I don't understand."

The deputy shook his head. "Don't look at me. We always get called in after the fact." He turned and inspected Leo.

She'd never seen this young officer before, but that didn't mean much. Plenty of law enforcers worked throughout St. Louis County whom she had yet to meet.

"Can I help you, ma'am?" the deputy asked.

Leo flashed her badge. "I'm with the state." He didn't answer. "Bad scene?" she asked.

"Something like that." He glared as if she were an impediment needing removal.

She recognized the insolence of youth and saw his name, Hampstead, sewn on his jacket. "Who's dead?"

Robeson took a deep breath to suck in some strength. He straightened up and met her gaze. "My second in command, Morton Milford."

"How?"

Neither man had time to answer. The front door opened. Two patrolmen came in followed by the detectives, Gary Clark and Ben Brandtson. Leo couldn't miss the relief in the young deputy's eyes as Clark and Brandtson paused to ask questions. Silently she listened to the men's excited conversation and learned Milford was dead in his office, discovered by the receptionist when he didn't answer phone calls and pages. Deputy Hampstead added that his partner was standing guard outside the office.

"Good work, Hampstead," Clark said. "We need to lock down the facility. Anybody leave?"

Robeson said, "I don't know. You can review the tapes from the waiting room and vestibule to see."

"The back is still secured, correct?"

"Yes," Robeson said. "The only way out the back sets off an alarm."

Leo said, "Gary, I've been standing here for ten minutes, and nobody has left since I got here, although I don't know where Lizzie is."

Robeson daubed at his brow again. "She's in the ladies' room. Indisposed."

Leo pointed toward the door leading to Milford's office, which was wide open. "Was that door closed and Lizzie unlocked it to look for Milford?"

An expression of annoyance flitted over Robeson's face. "How should I know? I didn't realize anything was going on until Lizzie started screaming."

"We're going to need to talk to her," Clark said. "Get her out here, while Ben and I go look at the scene. The rest of you, stay put."

Leo went back to the front window. The parking lot was filling up. Two sedans pulled in followed by a Channel 7 news van and the white truck from the medical examiner's office. Moments later Thom's van wheeled in. He parked away from other vehicles, no doubt to ensure he had room to enter and exit. Behind Leo, two patrolmen pushed through the glass doors and intercepted the news crew outside. She didn't even have to read lips to know exactly what the cops were telling them. The newsman and his camera guy got angry, but the officers were unyielding.

The county Medical Examiner, Jerome Pitney, had only a small staff of three investigators and a forensic pathologist who also served as a toxicologist, so Leo wasn't surprised to see the M.E. himself stroll in hauling a huge medical kit. She'd known him down in Saint Paul when he'd worked for the Ramsey County coroner several years earlier.

"Leona Reese, well, how good to see you. You're investigating the Bolton death?"

"Hello, Jerome. I guess so, though I don't know much at this point. Might be related to the other murder."

He nodded. "I'll let you know what I find out. Which way?"

She directed him through the door and waited for Thom to wheel in. She caught sight of the receptionist and Robeson tottering down the hall. He held his employee's arm under the elbow, but not in a supportive manner. If he could have gotten any farther from her, he probably would have.

Lizzie had been crying. Her face was pale and slightly gray, which accentuated her acne scars. When Leo met her eyes, Lizzie looked away. She pulled from Robeson's grip, strode behind the counter, and sat.

Robeson stopped ten feet from Leo. "What happens now?"

"I don't know yet, sir."

"When will you know?"

"The moment I can answer that question, I'll contact you."

He backed up, keeping his eyes on her. He raised one finger in the air and said, "You've been nothing but trouble. Every time you show up here, something bad happens." He turned and fled, the bottom of his suit coat flapping behind him.

She had to smile. The only time she'd ever visited the BDC was in response to a complaint. The man was grasping at straws.

Thom zipped through the front door and came to rest next to her. "Smells like shit in here. Literally. I've been in a whole lot better-smelling nursing homes."

"Yeah, it does. And it's getting too warm." Leo slipped out of her coat and set it on one of the chairs by the window.

"Who died?"

"The assistant administrator, Milford. Not sure how. Come on."

She met the scared eyes of the receptionist. "Lizzie, this is my work partner, Thom Thoreson."

"Nice to meet you, Lizzie." Thom stayed back from the counter so he could see her. Leo leaned an elbow on the counter.

"Lizzie, please tell us what happened."

Her voice came out low and raspy. "It was awful."

"He wasn't answering his phone, so you went looking for him."

"Yes." Lizzie closed her eyes. "I saw him come in at eight this morning, and then I never saw him again."

"Was the door over there open?"

"No. And neither was his office door." She shook her head and lifted up a key that hung around her neck on a lanyard. "I unlocked it. Oh, God, how I wish I hadn't. Why didn't I have security track him down? He was laying there dead!" She brought her hand up to cup her mouth and chin.

Leo gave her a moment to compose herself. She wasn't sure how to ask the next question. "When you found Mister Milford, how could you be sure he wasn't alive?"

"Oh, God." Lizzie looked like she was going to be sick. "His face was all swelled up and purple, and his tongue was . . . I threw up. I couldn't even get all the way out of the room without puking." She closed her eyes and dropped the key, then clutched her arms across her chest. "How will I ever get that picture out of my head? And him such a nice man. Always nice to me."

Thom said, "What a terrible thing, ma'am. I'm so sorry you experienced such an awful scene. I wish I could help."

Lizzie opened her eyes and stared at him. All of a sudden, it was like a switch popped on, and she was seeing him. Leo watched the process, as she often had, happy to note that even if Lizzie couldn't connect with her, she was able to focus on Thom.

Lizzie's eyes filled with tears. "I wish someone could help. I want to go home."

"I'm sure you do. I would, too. You have kids, a family?"

"I live with my mom."

Leo tuned out the small talk and let Thom work at calming down the receptionist. What Lizzie described sounded like another poisoning. Two deaths in two days. Not good. Whether Paul Aitken liked it or not, Leo had a hunch they were going to need to shut down the BDC and transfer all the patients to other facilities. It was one thing if one isolated kid got into something he shouldn't, but quite another when an administrator did the same.

Gary Clark came out then and interrupted Thom and Lizzie's small talk. "Miss," he said, "I want to talk with you, walk you through what happened."

She stiffened, eyes wide. "I'm not going back in there."

"I understand. I want to talk through every step, though. You can describe it, and we can do an actual walk-through when they've taken the body away. Please sit tight, and Detective Brandtson and I'll be right with you. Leo and Thom, might I have a word?" He backed up, so they followed.

Leo said, "She says the victim was bloated and purple. So it was poison?"

He shook his head. "Not this time. The ME says strangling."

"What?" Leo blurted out. She met Thom's puzzled gaze. "He was strangled?"

Clark said, "The ME will be positive after the autopsy, but he's seeing capillary rupture in the sclera, and anyone can see the bruising and edema around the neck."

"Holy shit," Thom said.

Clark pulled a notebook out of his jacket pocket. Brandtson came out of Morton's office entrance and joined them.

Thom said, "You think a man did it?"

"I don't know," Clark said. "Milford wasn't very big, so it could be a tall, strong woman. What do you think, Ben?"

"He put up a fight. The desk is a mess. I tend to agree with Thom. Probably male, but somebody a lot more imposing than the vic. Are there any women working here who look like WWE Superstars of Wrestling?"

Leo said, "Lizzie is the biggest woman here, but no way could she do it." She thought of the supervisor who was on vacation. "You'll want to check and see if Shelley Clifton is back. My understanding is she's on holiday and not due in until Monday. She's the only woman I haven't met, so I don't know if she's tiny or Xena-sized."

"Okay," Clark said. "What's your department's next move?"

"Can we let you know?" Leo asked.

Clark gave a curt nod. "Don't go far. We'll be back soon. We need to round up the usual suspects." He and Brandtson zoomed down the hall, setting off the metal detector.

"Jesus," Thom said, "this place is dangerous, Leo. I'm wishing I was packing a gun."

"I know exactly how you feel." She hadn't handled a gun during the workday since she got to Duluth. Her department-issued Glock was in her locker at the Saint Paul police station, and all but one of her other firearms were in the gun safe at home in Minneapolis. Her personal .38 was back at the apartment. Right now she wished she had it with her, but the folks who ran Rentreau Plaza disallowed staff from carrying firearms to the office. She could probably have overruled the practice because of her law enforcement credentials but hadn't felt the need to—until now.

She strode to the chairs by the window and sat level with Thom. "This makes no sense. First, it's a hotheaded seventeen-year-old degenerate, and now a quiet administrator. What do those two have in common?"

"Besides the BDC, you mean?"

"Yes, that's about it."

"I don't know if they have a thing in common," Thom said thoughtfully.

"I haven't noticed a single connection between Milford and Eddie Bolton. Milford told me last night he'd never even met the kid. I'd very nearly dismissed Milford as a suspect in Bolton's death. If he killed Eddie, then who killed Milford? And why?"

Thom shook his head slowly. "I don't understand it either. I guess the only thing that makes sense is maybe the two victims saw something here they weren't supposed to."

"But what?"

"I've been through this place plenty of other times and never found any hidden torture chambers, no obvious pockets of abuse. Same thing I found out when I did a wheelie-through yesterday." He grinned, and Leo rolled her eyes. "Too many people are coming and going all the time in the facility to have anything seriously nefarious going on. The only truly isolated spots are the employee changing rooms and the administration offices out here. Everything else is accessible."

Leo jumped, feeling like a hive of bees was attacking her hip. She whipped her cell off her belt and checked the number. "Uh-oh. Missed Aitken's call."

"He cornered me earlier. Wanted to know why you hadn't finished working the case. You better call him back and assuage his political shakes."

Aitken answered on the first ring. As soon as he heard her voice, he said, "Can you explain to me why I have to hear on the radio about the biggest boondoggle I've come up against!"

"I've only just found out myself. We—"

"I don't want excuses. I want to know what's going on."

"The assistant director at the BDC was found murdered a bit ago. I'll be—"

"I already know that," he shouted. "If you'd done your job in the first place, we'd have the other death squared away. Now there are two."

Leo wanted to mention she was perfectly capable of counting, but she kept her mouth shut. Paul Aitken hadn't yelled at her before, so this was a first. She wasn't quite sure how to take it. "Do you have specific instructions?"

"Do your job! That's my instructions. Figure out what's going on there and resolve it. Oh, shit . . ." His voice trailed off, and he must have been holding the phone away from his mouth. She heard him say, "Give me the message. Next time the governor's assistant calls, you damn well better interrupt me or I'll have your head. Leo!" His voice was strong now. "I'm sending Thom up ASAP."

"He's just arrived."

"Well, goddammit! My own people don't even check in with me."

Perhaps if you didn't take two-hour lunches, Leo thought. "We'll get right on it, sir."

"I want you back here before five to update me. I want that report put on high priority. I expect you to roll this case into the one from yesterday and clear them both immediately. Is that clear?"

"Yes, it is."

"I have to call the governor's assistant now. God knows what the hell I can tell him."

She heard a loud click, and the line went dead. Thom sat with his fingers threaded together in his lap. She met his eyes. "We are so screwed."

Thom said, "Yeah. The way I see it, we carry on, do what we can, and that's all we can manage. Aitken hasn't got a clue what our jobs really are, and he's not reasonable."

"No, he just proved that."

"This makes me realize the facts one more time. You know why men are like parking spaces?"

Leo frowned.

"All the good ones are taken, and the only ones left are handicapped." He went off into a gale of laughter.

She had no idea how he could be so merry at a time like this. "You want to do me a small favor, Thom?"

Smirking, he said, "Sure, what?"

"Don't tell me any more of those jokes until we wrap this up, okay?"

"Why? You still think I'm lame?" He slapped his leg, grinned like a crazy man, then sobered up. "Okay, I'll try to behave myself."

➤ ■ ◅

Leo and Thom waited for over an hour, anxious for the chance to talk to the detectives and to interview anyone the detectives allowed them access to. When Gary Clark finally emerged for some fresh air, she asked if she could view the crime scene.

Gary Clark turned to her, surprised. "The investigators will be at it for hours, and it's pretty gruesome in there."

It wasn't like Leo had never seen dead bodies before. In her time on the Saint Paul police force, she'd seen nine homicide victims, over a dozen elderly who had died of natural causes, and more dead and wounded car crash victims than she had kept track of. "I've seen dead people and autopsies on the job, Gary. I'm not squeamish and won't mess up your crime scene. SPPD trained us well."

Thom said, "I'd like to come along, too."

Clark winced. "You're going to hate me for this, Thom, but you can't enter the crime scene. Not in the chair. I'm real sorry. I can put booties on Leo but not on your wheels."

Thom very clearly arranged his face to hide disappointment. "You go, then," he said to her. "Come back and report every detail."

Clark said, "There'll be scores of photos. I'll let you see them if you like."

"Where's Brandtson?" Leo asked.

"He'll be here in a couple of hours. We had another major case call."

With her shoes covered in a pair of papery elasticized booties, Leo followed Gary Clark down the hall toward Milford's office. She glanced into the employee break room and found it empty. Though there was a keycard lock on both sides of the far door leading into the facility, the crime investigation team took no chances; a uniformed Duluth police officer stood in front of that door.

She turned to look into Milford's office. A wall of bookshelves on the left contained a number of leather-bound volumes artfully displayed in small clusters and held up with gold bookends. An oak desk was situated in the middle of the room. Peeking around Clark, Leo saw a swirl of papers and files atop the desk. An accountant's lamp lay on its side, the green glass broken. The lightbulb burned against the desktop, and she wondered if it would leave a mark. No overhead lights were on, but the room was well lit by the window behind the desk on the outside wall.

"Watch your step here," Clark warned as he moved aside.

She looked down and saw a puddle of vomit near the wall outside the doorway. A doughnut, she thought. And a lot of coffee. Lizzie's contribution to the scene.

Abruptly, the light was blocked by a man in a navy-blue coverall. The flash of the camera he held made Leo close her good eye for a brief instant. She blinked and squinted, then glanced down and saw the body. The head was turned away from the entrance so she couldn't see the face. His suit coat was bunched up underneath the torso, and the cuff of one pant leg was hiked up high enough to reveal a dark gray sock and an inch of pale white skin. The seat of the victim's pants was stained a wet, dark gray.

She looked around the room for blood or any other abnormalities.

Clark reached out toward Leo with Latex-gloved fingers, then apparently changed his mind and dropped the hand. "You sure you can take this?"

"Yup. Let's get on with it."

The photographer and evidence technician waited expectantly. Clark gave a toss of his head. "Guys, take five and grab a cuppa joe. We'll be out of here shortly." He stepped aside for them to pass, and Leo moved through the doorway.

Clark said, "Stay along the wall, will you?"

The room was warm and stuffy. As Thom had noted earlier, the odor in the air smelled worse than a long night at a nursing home. She moved closer to see that Morton Milford's corpse lay on its side, left leg stretched out, and the right pulled up so high his knee was near his chest. Though the forehead was pressed up against the base of the desk, Leo saw what the receptionist meant about Milford's face. It was a strange shade of purple, almost lavender in hue. His right hand was up near his neck, his fingers in a loose fist.

One side of his face lay against his shoulder, and that arm was stretched out above him, index finger pointing toward the bookcases as though he were trying to indicate something important. From the tip of his finger, Leo's gaze rose, and she saw four red leather books leaning to the side.

"The bookend there is missing."

"It's over there by the left side of the desk," Clark said. "Step in and see."

She took two cautious strides, closer to the gray-suited corpse. On the floor between the shelves and the side of the desk, an old-fashioned one-masted golden ship lay on its side. Its sails were unfurled, and the stern and bow curved up and in. To Leo, it looked exactly like the Argo she remembered Jason and The Argonauts navigated to seek the Golden Fleece. "Looks like blood on this bookend."

"Yes."

"I thought you said Milford was strangled."

A dark figure popped up from the other side of the oak desk, startling Leo. The light from the window behind him obscured all but his dark outline, and it took a moment for her to realize it was the M.E., Jerome Pitney. "I'm ninety-nine percent certain COD was strangulation. But someone hit him with the bookend first."

"I see." But she didn't see any blood at all.

"We haven't moved the body much," Pitney said, "Underneath his head he's bled a tiny bit from the wound. I'll see if it would have killed him eventually, but I'm pretty sure we'll find he died of asphyxia. And it would not have occurred in a fast manner. He's got some major bruising on his neck. He would have suffered."

To Leo's right, a computer table formed an L with the administrator's desk. Unlike the oaken surface, all of the files and papers there were neatly organized. The computer was on, and a password box was displayed.

"When I first got in here," Clark said, "the screen saver was bouncing around. I touched the space bar, and it went like that. Unless someone around here knows his password, we'll have to have the computer techs hack in."

Pitney slid open the middle drawer of Milford's desk and pulled something out. "This might help." Pinched between his white-gloved thumb and forefinger, he held a three-by-five-inch spiral-bound memo book. "Despite the current state of his office, the guy was nothing less than orderly. His files are alphabetized. His drawers are neatly arranged."

Clark took the book and leafed through it, careful to touch only the upper corners with his gloved fingers. "Several state passwords, Amazon.com, psychological sites, online medical dictionary, personnel policy manual. Was this guy an outdoor lover?"

Leo shrugged. "He seemed married to the job."

"He's got passwords for memberships to Ducks Unlimited and some British Birding Society. But I think this state password at the beginning is what we're looking for."

"I can input it," Pitney said. Clark read him eight letters and digits, and Pitney bent over the keyboard. The screen came up. Both Clark and Leo leaned in from across the desk to look. In large bold print, the document was titled "Written Reprimand," dated today, and it referenced Michael Louis Seaver.

"What's the line below say?" Clark asked. "It's too small for me to read from here."

Pitney said, "Please be advised that this is your official notice of. That's it. Stops there."

Clark rubbed his hands together. "I love it when criminals screw up. Seaver probably had a meeting with Milford and flew off the handle when he found out he was getting popped for bad behavior."

"You'll arrest him then?" Leo asked.

"Probably. We're certainly going to turn him inside out when we talk to him. He's not on my list of staff on duty today, though."

Leo heard a noise in the doorway. Detective Brandtson stood there, a flush rising in his face. He said, "Gary, can I have a word with you?"

"Don't touch anything," Clark said. "I'll be right back."

Leo wasn't sure why Brandtson didn't voice his objections right in front of her because with little trouble, she could hear most of his whispered argument in the hallway. He chastised Clark for allowing her in to see the murder scene.

Clark defended his decision. "She's the one who's going to have to close this place down. She deserves to know the facts."

"But this is a murder scene, dammit!"

"We've taken the pictures, dusted for prints. C'mon, Ben. She knows what not to do. She's a cop."

"Well, she's not one now. Get her out of here before she compromises the scene."

Pitney met Leo's eyes and shrugged. "Are you going to shut the place down, Leona?"

"I think I have to."

Clark appeared in the doorway. "We'll have the place crawling with cops and crime scene guys for the next few hours, but I'm thinking you're going to need to make arrangements with Robeson to move all these boys."

She glanced at Brandtson, who hovered behind Clark's shoulder. He avoided her gaze. "You don't think one of the kids did this, then?"

"We'll review the videotapes, but all the residents have been participating in the school program since Milford arrived this morning. Various staff have come and gone from the classrooms, and we'll look into that, but the kids have been locked down."

"What's the count?" she asked.

Clark opened his notebook. "Besides Robeson and Milford, there are fourteen staff, three kitchen attendants, and thirty-one youth."

Leo tried to recall her conversation with Milford the day before. "Thirty-one patients is all? I thought there were more like sixty-something."

"Nope. I have names, room assignments, and other details."

Leo said, "Maybe there were some discharges today. But even thirty-one is a lot of kids to reassign elsewhere in the snap of a finger. Any way you look at it, this is going to be a mess to shake out for the report."

Brandtson said, "That's your area of expertise, and we'll let you get to it."

Leo took the hint and moved toward the door. Both detectives stepped back, and Brandtson warned her about the puke on the floor. She pressed down her irritation at him, fully aware she had to watch her step. She strode toward the waiting room door, but before she reached it, Pitney's voice called out, "Call me if you need any information, Leona."

Without a glance back, she raised a hand in a wave. "Thanks." Even with her eye on the doorway ahead, she still managed to miscalculate, and once again she brushed too close to the metal latch guard and scraped her right arm. Ouch, she thought. Now she had a matched set of wounds.

At four p.m. Leo and Thom were still intermittently interviewing Donald Robeson. He'd been in and out of the conference room for the last two hours, and there was nothing they could do about it. While he spoke to them, they were constantly interrupted as he fielded questions from the staff about releasing boys to parents or ferrying them over to the Juvenile Detention Center or to other treatment facilities. He'd changed from his business suit into pale blue scrubs and white tennis shoes hours earlier. It made him look more approachable.

He came back in the room and settled into a chair. "That's a big bunch of paying customers out the door. Less than a dozen left." He glared at Leo. For some reason, he never gave the evil eye to Thom and hardly spoke to him. Leo thought that was strange. Usually men in power ignored the women and preferred to speak to other men. Leo wondered if Robeson was being disrespectful of Thom's mobility status. She had no way of confronting him about it, though, so she'd been handling the questions while Thom fell into the role of note-taker. He didn't seem to mind.

Leo said, "Let's talk about Morton Milford's work accomplishments, Mister Robeson."

"What's to talk about? He showed up every day, hardly took any sick leave. He ran the place while I focused on fundraising and the politics of keeping the BDC open."

"Did he win awards? Make anyone jealous?"

Robeson bit back a smile. "Who'd be jealous of Mort? He was a dried-up old sourpuss. Don't get me wrong. He did his job, and he did it well, but it's not like he was Mother Teresa."

"Were there many staff who didn't like him?"

Robeson let out a big sigh. "We've gone over this. I went over it with the police, too. Nobody likes their boss all the time. But people here mostly get along."

Thom looked up from his notes. "Mostly?"

"You betcha. Most of the time. Sure, people have occasional disagreements, but nothing worth murdering anybody over."

Leo watched Robeson's face closely. "You saw nothing out of the ordinary today?" He shook his head. "Nothing out of the ordinary this week?"

"Other than the last big brouhaha when the Bolton kid died, you mean?"

"Right. Other than that?"

"Nothing unusual."

"What about Mike Seaver's situation?"

He scowled at her, his blue eyes sparkling with intensity. "What situation?"

"Evidence was found that Mister Milford was in the process of reprimanding Seaver."

"For what?"

"That's what we'd like to know."

"If I remember correctly, Seaver took the next few days off."

"Was that a regular request?"

"No, I believe he asked Mort for time today. I think he was upset about the death of his charge, Edward Bolton."

"So he wasn't suspended or anything like that?"

"I don't know. As I said, I focus on the big picture. Mort handles the details. Handled, I mean." Robeson brought his palm to his face and covered his mouth for a moment. With a sigh, he dropped his hand into his lap. "If he was going to fire someone, he usually let me know, but if he was giving out a reprimand for tardiness or some other inconsequential thing, I didn't need to know. Maybe you should talk to Shelley Clifton on Monday."

Leo said, "Yes, we will. Is someone going to notify her about what's happened?"

"She can jolly well show up for work Monday, and she'll find out then."

"I'd like to try to reach her, if possible, in the next day or so. May I have her contact information?"

"Why don't you get that from the police?"

"I could, but they've got their hands full. I thought you might have it handy."

Robeson made a shooing wave. "Get that from Lizzie. Tell her I said it's okay. Look, are we able to reopen before the weekend?"

"I don't know. We'll be working hard to resolve the license and infraction issues, if there are any, as soon as possible."

Robeson closed his eyes. "All I've done for the last twenty-four hours is damage control, and I'll probably be doing it for the next twenty-four hours. Twenty-four weeks. Maybe twenty-four months." He opened his eyes and leaned forward. "What do I have to do to get my facility up and running again?" His eyes narrowed again, and his voice turned angry. "This is my business, my livelihood. And you're taking away help and much-needed guidance from youth who need it. How long are you going to persecute me, Ms. Reese?"

Leo didn't dare look at Thom. She forced herself not to roll her one good eye. Instead, she gave him her usual line. "We're in the early stages of the investigation, and we need a great deal more information from the police. I can't make any promises. At this time, Mister Thoreson and I are unable to predict the final outcome."

He let out a sigh. "You do know who I am, right?"

"Yes, sir, and every consideration is being given. We could have shut down the BDC on Tuesday, but we've been trying to work with you and the staff. This latest murder puts you in a difficult situation. At this point, if any of the youth or other staff were to be injured or killed, you could have a lawsuit on your hands, and so could the state."

Robeson's face went very red, and his eyes became small and pig-like. He looked away, an expression of distaste on his face like he'd choked on a chicken bone—or perhaps a ham hock.

There was a rap at the door, and one of the orderlies stood there. "Sorry to interrupt, Mister Robeson, but the van is back for the last of the boys for the JDC."

Robeson rose wearily. He leaned over the table, put his palms flat on it, and said, "Are we done yet?"

Leo looked at her watch. She and Thom only had enough time to debrief and get back to the office to update Paul Aitken. "Yes, sir. Thank you for your cooperation."

Robeson stood back, one hand in his silver hair. He opened his mouth to say something, then exhaled, spun around, and left.

"A real charmer," Thom said.

"Tell me about it."

➤ ◼ ◄

They arrived at Rentreau Plaza after regular work hours. Nearly all staff had departed for the day. Leo dropped off her coat and valise and followed Thom to the front of the office. One look at Aitken, and she could tell he was agitated. He stood at his file cabinet in shirtsleeves and hollered, "Am I losing my mind, or did I tell you to be back here by five to brief me?"

"Sorry, sir, but the investigation—"

He cut her off with a slam of the file cabinet. "You've got good news for me, right?"

Thom took the lead. "We worked with the police and the director of the BDC to close them down. It couldn't be avoided."

Aitken brought both palms up to his head and threaded his fingers through his hair as if to keep his skull from exploding. "That's just what we didn't want!"

"Look," Thom said, "even Robeson was amenable to the temporary closing."

"Amenable? If he's so damn amenable, why has he lodged a complaint with the governor? Jesus Christ, this will have terrible repercussions for us." He snatched up his suit jacket from the back of his chair, wormed his way into it, and slid into the seat behind his desk.

Thom rolled a little closer. "It's a murder investigation, Paul. The cops can't solve it overnight, and they can't leave a bunch of kids in the facility when we don't know who the killer is. It's not safe. One kid is already dead, and the Milford killing is probably not a coincidence. We had no choice."

Leo stood in the doorway behind Thom and watched Aitken. Slumped behind his desk, he moved his hand until it covered the lower half of his face. He sat for long seconds staring at his desk blotter. She got the impression Thom was holding his breath just as she was.

Aitken looked up. "If you don't resolve this case before the week is over, the governor will send in special investigators."

"What?" Leo said. "Aren't we the special investigators?"

"No, Governor McCarron has access to plenty of other law enforcement."

"What does that have to do with us?" Leo asked. "I thought DHS is tasked with the licensing."

"It makes us look bad!" Aitken shouted. He struggled to dial back his next comments. "We look bad if the governor has to bring in more people because we're incompetent or slow. Next thing we know, this place will be crawling with a bunch of feds or special prosecutors."

Thom said, "I'm sure Clark and Brandtson and the Duluth PD will be less than appreciative about that."

Aitken sneered. "If there's one thing you line staff never understand, it's the way politics works. This kind of thing can break a career."

Leo had a number of choice comments to make about whose career he was referencing, but she wisely withheld them.

Aitken slapped his blotter. "So here's what you're going to do. Get Tonya on the phone and have her come in. I don't care if you two have to work all night. You've got to resolve this by Friday afternoon so the BDC can get up and running before the weekend."

Leo checked her watch. "We can't reach Tonya. She's taking a Con Law exam up at the college."

"I don't care if she's having open heart surgery. Get her in here to type up your official reports."

Leo stepped around Thom and went to sit in the chair facing Aitken's desk. "Sir, we don't have any official reports. Everything has happened so fast we've hardly gotten a chance to interview a fraction of the people who need to be questioned."

"Why the hell not?"

In a soothing voice, she said, "We'll make every effort to be speedy and thorough. Thom and I will do all we can to fast-track this. You must understand, though, we have absolutely no control over the pace of a police investigation of this magnitude."

"I don't want to hear this."

"I know you don't. But you have to. We need you to back us up."

"Back you up? You've been incompetent! Derelict in your duties."

Thom sputtered. His face had gone red. He had a tight grip on the arms of his chair as though they were the only thing preventing him from launching up and tackling Aitken. "Have you ever looked at a single one of our reports for serious injury or death at a facility?"

Aitken blustered right back. "Of course I know all about your reports. I'm the goddamn boss here!"

"Good," Leo said. "Then you're well aware that the typical non-suspicious death in, say, a nursing home or treatment facility, takes a minimum of two weeks—usually four—to investigate and resolve."

"That's what I was getting at. I've always thought the timeline was inefficient."

"Come off it, Paul," Thom said, his voice rising. "You can't even write a personnel evaluation in two weeks."

Aitken turned on Thom, his eyes steely hard and his voice chilling. "I've made plenty of allowances for you, what with the chair and all. I know I have to accommodate your disabilities, but not yours, Leona. I may not be able to fire Thom because of all the ADA bullshit, but I can certainly send you back to Saint Paul and let your police department cronies decide where to assign you."

A silence hung over the room. Leo sat back in the chair. She reached up to finger her eye patch, then jerked her hand away. She wasn't sure how much power he had. If she couldn't be a cop right now, she preferred a challenging job in the BCA or elsewhere. Could Aitken send her back with a bad report and derail her chances at further investigative positions? She hoped he was all bluster, no backbone, but this swerve into disrespect made her despise him. She met Thom's eyes, expecting to see anger and hurt. Instead, there was a strange light in his eyes, and he seemed to be biting back a grin.

When she looked back at her boss, Aitken was blushing bright red, and Leo thought he was actually embarrassed. He broke the silence, speaking in a quieter voice. "I don't care if you have to work all weekend or how many hours of overtime you put in. I've got the budget for the extra hours. The BDC needs to reopen, if not by Friday, then Monday at the latest."

Small concession, Leo thought, but it was something. She hardly knew what to say now. She'd faced many hard-ass commanding officers, but because of their experience, they'd always garnered her respect. She understood, without a doubt, that Paul Aitken was a political hack, had never been in the field, and his expectations were beyond ridiculous.

Thom rolled back, spun the chair, and left the office without another word. Because it heightened the tension and made Aitken sweat, Leo continued to sit there, waiting.

"Leona, don't you have work to do?"

"Yes, sir. Any final instructions?"

Aitken's voice lost all edge. His words came out as if from a kid's toy running out of batteries. "Do your damn job."

Leo left the office. She found Thom in his cubicle shutting down his computer. "Holy crap. Is he always like that?"

Thom rolled his eyes. "He's a goddamn idiot and a hypocrite to boot."

Leo laughed and some of her tension dissipated. "Why don't you say what you really mean?" She got a half-smile back. "What's the plan then?"

"No plan. Not a damn thing we can do tonight. I'm going home. You?"

"I'm sure as hell not calling Tonya back from her exam. She really needs to pass it. We'll brief her in the morning."

He nodded. "You know, I had an assistant coach like him in high school. He didn't know jack-shit about people, much less about sports training. He was a slow-witted jerk who said he played offensive line in college. He acted like he'd been God's gift to quarterbacks. He ran the line to death. Never got off their cases verbally, either. It came time for the first big game, and the line ran out of gas in the fourth quarter. Our QB got mashed repeatedly in the final minutes. Asshole coach pushed them too hard, training for speed, not for endurance."

"What did you do about it?"

"The line stopped working for him. They went through the motions, but they didn't do much. He yelled all the more. Then some of us guys got together and called out to Washington State where the coach went to college and found out he never started a single game, never did much, never mattered in the scheme of things. He was a football wannabe, that's all."

"For the record, some of the wisest teachers I've had could teach the subject but not do it very well themselves."

"Not this guy. He couldn't coach and he couldn't play. We lost all respect."

"What did you do?"

"Had a sit-down with the head coach. Turns out he already had his own concerns. He took over the linemen and put the other guy in charge of scheduling, equipment, and the buses." Thom grinned like a mischievous little boy. "He was damn good at that."

"I'm not sure how his past applies to our current situation? It's not like we can have a sit-down with the governor."

"Exactly," Thom said. "But nobody's kicking *me* off the team, and they sure as hell aren't dumping you."

"He was just ranting. I don't think he'll fire you or me."

"But he can make us run and run until we don't have any endurance left."

"I'd love to see Mister Sedentary try to keep up with you when you get that chair going."

Thom laughed. "Sure wish he played wheelchair basketball. I'd cream his ass."

She looked both ways down the aisle, but there was no one in sight. "Don't worry about your job or mine. He's a typical bureaucrat with no endurance himself."

"I agree. He doesn't have the balls to can us. He damn well better not do a thing. I've been around here long enough to know where some of the bodies are buried, and if he thinks he can fire me, I've got news for him." Thom's computer finished powering down, and he picked up some files and stuffed them in the backpack behind his chair. "I'm out of here. I've got more important things to do. Later tonight I'll look through what little paperwork I have, but until we get the Milford autopsy report and talk at length with Clark and Brandtson, there's nothing we can do."

"We'll sort this out, Thom. We will."

"How can you be so sure?"

"I'm not, but we have to stay on it. This is exactly like police work. Lots of stress and unrealistic expectations."

"God, I wish Aitken would get promoted to a new level of incompetence. He's projecting his own shortcomings on us."

"You're right. So don't get mad, get even."

"Truer words were never said." He looked at his watch. "I'm late picking up Jeff and Mickey. We have basketball practice tonight, and I'm sorry, but I'm not missing it."

"Go take out your frustrations on your buddies."

"Exactly my intentions. Good night."

She stepped aside as he wheeled out. "I'll stay a while and organize my notes. See you tomorrow."

She went to the desk and sank into her chair. The day's events whirled in her mind, and for a few moments, she didn't know what to focus on first. The sun had long ago set, and she stared out her window at the damp street, illuminated by streetlamps. Someone had shoveled the bit of earlier snowfall, and a ragged pile of gray and white stretched along the edge of the walk. A man wearing a trench coat with the collar up walked along, hat-less and hunched over. She saw how the wind battered at him, and it made her shiver.

Thom's white van exited the parking lot. He passed in front of her window and traveled down the street into darkness, taillights growing smaller in the distance until she couldn't see them anymore.

➤■◄

Leo looked up from the mound of paperwork on her desk, suddenly weary. It was well after seven, and she hadn't heard from Daria. She never called Leo's cell all day as she'd promised, so perhaps she'd gotten hung up with work. One of the partners for whom Daria worked was running for election to a judgeship, so Daria was buried in extra duties and political responsibilities.

Leo was hungry and much preferred making a nice meal to slaving over reports, so she slipped into her coat, grabbed her valise, and left.

As she made her way to the parking lot, she thought about Paul Aitken's earlier comments. Her boss was so far out of line that she had a hard time believing he'd actually voiced his moronic point of view. Was that really all he thought of Thom, of her? What a buffoon.

Thom's responsibilities included inspecting and monitoring the huge number of nursing homes in the region. He handled the same kind of licensure, review, and action on complaints that she did, only she focused on the rest of the facilities: child-care centers, treatment facilities, group homes, residential chemical dependency facilities, day programs, adult foster care for elderly, outpatient chemical dependency facilities including detox, mental health halfway houses, and other placements for developmentally disabled people.

She knew the job responsibilities weren't originally planned for such a split, but with Thom in the chair, it worked out well for him to focus on the nursing homes and residences for the physically handicapped, especially since so many existed. With him handling that angle, it was more efficient, too, since the complaints tended to be similar. Even better, every single nursing facility—and the AIDS and hospice homes as well—was accessible by wheelchair.

Despite all the laws about access for the disabled, not all the monitored licensed facilities had ramps or elevators. So she and Thom split the workload based on that more than anything. They covered for each other at times, helping out with interviews when needed.

Maybe the time had come to change that, she thought. Maybe we ought to be citing these places for not being accessible to wheelchairs.

On the way home, she stopped at the grocery store, joining a flood of cranky shoppers. She came out a short time later with chicken and vegetables to make a stir-fry.

The first pulsing of a headache started in her right temple. She backed the Lexus out of the parking space and followed a string of cars to the stop sign. As she waited, she wondered if she and Thom should split the two murders and work them separately, or handle them as a team, focusing first on one, then the other.

She pulled up to the stop sign, glanced both ways, and accelerated. As she turned left, something smashed into the left rear quarter-panel. The back end of her car skidded. The airbags deployed, and the impact from the airbags took her breath away. A screeching sound rent the night. As the car tilted, she couldn't keep her hands on the wheel. She slammed on the brakes. As the airbags deflated, she tried to straighten her trajectory. The Lexus shook and moved sideways like a giant wheeled crab until it shuddered to a stop.

Headlights blinded her one good eye. Another car coming at her. She brought her left arm up in front of her face and leaned over the center armrest. The lights careened away, and the crash she expected didn't happen.

All was still for a moment, then she heard a strange clinking noise. Twisting in her seat, she looked toward the rear of the car. A gust of wind blew against the right rear window. Piece by tiny piece, the glass fell in.

She heard a muffled voice. "Lady! Lady, are you all right?" Someone banged on her window.

Dazed, she pressed the window button, and it rolled down automatically.

"Are you all right?" The man was beefy and swathed in a muffler and gloves. He wore an old-fashioned brimmed cap with an odd black-and-white pattern. She was reminded of a crazy MC Escher puzzle.

"Ma'am? Can you get out?"

She shook herself. The pulse in her right temple beat so hard that she could hear it. Cold air from behind her warred with wind blowing in the driver's window. I'm in a wind tunnel, she thought. She trembled as she opened the door.

Traffic was stopped behind and in front of her SUV. Several people got out of their vehicles and came over. Before she could even

get out of her car, a man in coveralls, work boots, and an unzipped
Carhartt jacket stomped up to her. "What the hell you think you're
doing, you idiot!" An unlit cigarette dangled from his mouth. "You
damn near hit me."

Leo learned from being a cop that sometimes the best tactic was
to back away, and that's what she did. But Mister MC Escher, the guy
with the puzzle on his cap, said, "Hey buddy, what've *you* got to be
pissed about? She actually hit me, and your truck is fine."

By then the guy with the cigarette was squinting at Leo. "I don't
believe it. You're driving around half blind on a snowy night?"

"I had some surgery, but I can see perfectly fine."

"Not according to this guy! Look at his truck."

Leo turned and made her way to the front of an old GMC pickup.
The grill was mashed in, the headlights on the left were broken, and
the paint along the left quarter-panel was scraped. She looked in the
truck door, which was ajar, and nearly laughed to see the orange
velour bench seat. "This is definitely an older truck."

"1984 GMC Sierra Classic 4x4. Pretty sturdy, but you did ding 'er
up a bit."

"I've got good insurance." She turned her attention to the back of
her own car. The truck's condition was nothing compared to the
damage to the Lexus. "Jesus," she said aloud. Other than a pounding
headache, she didn't feel any bumps or bruises, so despite her car
resembling half a doughnut, she hadn't been hurt at all. "How fast
were you going?"

MC Escher said, "Dunno. Maybe thirty-five. But I saw you in
time to hit the brakes. I hit you going slower than that."

Someone honked a horn at least a block away, and Leo saw the
accident aftermath was fast becoming a major obstruction. Her cop
training kicked in. "Hey, you!"

The workman with the cigarette looked her way. "What?"

"Give me a hand here. Let's push the car out of the way and get
this road opened back up."

He scowled. "You're supposed to wait for the police."

"The hell with that," she said. "Everybody saw what happened,
and I'm sure you'll be eager to tell the cops this is my fault."

"It's a crime scene."

"You watch too much TV." What a dolt, she thought to herself.
God save me from men who think they know everything.

She smiled and tried her best to look pleasant. "Your car is
blocking traffic. You really need to move it."

He threw the cigarette down and strode off. Two young men, probably high schoolers, sidled up. "We'll help you, ma'am."

Before she could get to her car, the two boys and another man were pushing it out of the way, and some guy in a leather jacket and jeans was hanging out of the car, steering. She was relieved to see it rolling, though there was a loud scraping sound she wondered about.

MC Escher pulled his truck out of the way and leaned out the window as she made it to the sidewalk. "You want your car towed, lady? I can call a tow truck on my cell."

"I was hoping to drive it to the shop myself tomorrow."

"I'm sorry, ma'am, but what about the airbags?"

"Oh, yeah." The Lexus wouldn't be operational. "Please do call a tow truck. Thanks."

Traffic resumed, though very slowly. The guy with the cigarette was gone. All that remained was to exchange information with the truck driver. Would the Duluth police show up? She didn't know for sure.

She looked up toward the streetlamp, high in the air. For a moment, her vision seemed fuzzy. Then she noticed it was snowing again.

→■←

Hours seemed to pass before Leo arrived home, but it was actually only nine when a taxi dropped her off at the apartment. She wrestled her grocery bag out and paid the driver. The nice thing about vegetables was their hardiness. The bag ended up on the floor of the Lexus with carrots, green peppers, and mushrooms rolling around. She'd gathered them up without too much difficulty. She put the groceries away and called for pizza delivery.

As she sat at the kitchen table, half-asleep over her reports and paperwork, the phone rang. Head pounding, she rose and answered the kitchen portable.

"Got any snow yet?"

"Kate. How are you?"

"Not bad. Got the kids down, and Susie is in the shower, so I thought I'd touch base."

"No policing for you tonight?"

"Not scheduled for a shift again 'til Sunday."

"Woo hoo. Nice break. How are the mean streets of Saint Paul?"

"Quiet. We got a couple inches of snow, and that drives a lot of thugs indoors, at least temporarily. Arrests are way down. Bunch of fender-benders today, though."

"Speaking of that, I crashed the Lexus tonight."

"Oh, shit. What happened? You all right?"

"Emotionally, I feel like I've been dragged backwards through a keyhole, but I'm okay. I got nothing more than a bad headache out of it. I'm so thankful nobody was hurt." Leo described the accident and said, "I really hate the damn car. I always hated it, even before the surgery. The sightlines are awful."

"But it's got GPS."

"Lot of good that did me tonight. I could have had a GPS expert advising me and still wouldn't have seen the truck that hit me. As soon as the damn thing's repaired, I'm buying something different. I never liked this car anyway."

"Daria will be disappointed. She was so excited to get the Lexus for you."

"I'd be much happier with something simpler."

"I've got a terrific Chrysler Le Baron here in mint condition I'd gladly trade you for."

Leo laughed. "That old olive-green piece of junk? It's a rear-wheel-drive tank. I could be mowing over small children and puppy dogs and never know it."

"Great sightlines though."

"I'm sure I wouldn't feel anybody hitting me."

"See, it offers peace of mind as well."

"Oh, yeah. Kind of like the GMC truck that crunched me tonight. It was so old it still had some metal parts. I think the grill was made of honest-to-goodness steel. I'll bet it costs less than five hundred bucks to repair his truck, and I can't even imagine how many thousands mine will run."

"Trade with me. Think of the money you'll save on your next accident."

"I'll pass this time, sis."

"Your loss."

"And there isn't going to be any next accident. I feel bad enough about this one happening."

Kate laughed, the sound warm in Leo's ear. For a moment she wished she was down at Kate and Susie's house, stepping over Duplos and Tonka Trucks, making peanut butter sandwiches, and soaking up the energy of two rambunctious kids. "I'd like to drive down soon, but I'm in the middle of a horrid murder case, and I don't know how long it will take to resolve it. I may not even be able to get home this weekend to be with Daria."

"Murder? That job doesn't get homicides very often, does it?"

"No, and we've actually got two related ones this week. Believe me, they're doozies."

Leo went on to describe the poisoning and strangling. She often conferred with her foster sister and shared insights regarding the crimes they each encountered, but this time Kate was as stumped about motive and opportunity as Leo.

"Sounds like you have a lot of interviewing to do."

"Yup." Leo heard Susie's voice in the background.

"I've got to go, Leo. The kids are asleep, and for the first time in a week, Susie and I apparently have a few adult moments to take advantage of."

"Don't do anything I wouldn't do."

Kate cackled. "I bet we'll be asleep in half an hour. Or less."

"Sweet dreams."

Leo hung up the phone and went back to the paperwork arranged across the kitchen table. She wondered what approach to take in the morning. The removal of all the boys from the BDC had curtailed what she could find out from them, though she didn't think she'd have any trouble discovering where each kid had been sent. That reminded her she'd never gotten a chance to talk further with William Cattrall or the two boys, Speed and Mouse, who claimed they hardly knew Eddie Bolton. William had said they were Eddie Bolton's friends. She made a note of that. Depending on where the kids were placed, she might have to drive all over the countryside in a rental car. The thought didn't appeal to her at all.

Donald Robeson had yet to sit down and give them a thorough and uninterrupted interview, and there were a number of counselors like Mike Seaver she wanted to talk to as well. She made a list of interviews related to the Bolton murder. As an afterthought, she included Phyllis Bolton and her grandson, Steven Bolton. Perhaps she'd gotten all she could get from Eddie's aunt, but Steven might know a lot more about his cousin's habits and enemies than anybody gave him credit for. She decided to talk further with Detective Clark in the morning to see if he'd turned up anything else on that case.

She had little information on the Milford murder. Pitney had told her one of his deputy medical examiners would do the autopsy in the morning, so until then, she didn't have any official documentation.

She pulled out an Initial Report Form and began filling it in, then stopped. Who would want Morton Milford dead? Who would be so angry or so threatened by the man that they'd clonk him on the head, then follow that up with a deadly throttling? The crime seemed to her to be one of rage. Rage over a written reprimand? Over the Bolton murder? Or did this have to do with something completely outside the BDC?

Thom had told her he'd been to the BDC many times in the past, and he remembered that sometimes the hallway door from the waiting room to Milford's office was left ajar. Could robbery be a motive? She'd never asked if Milford's wallet was taken. Could it be possible someone wandered in and killed him for his cash?

That was worth checking on. She was anxious to find out what the video cameras would reveal. Was it too much to hope that the tapes would show the murderer tiptoeing stealthily in, then coming out flustered, sweaty, and with clothes in disarray? Nah, it only happened on TV. But Milford *had* put up a fight. Would he have left marks on his attacker?

Those were other details to ask Gary Clark about.

At what point could she authorize the reopening of the Benton Dowling Center? Until the cops caught the murderer—or at least identified him—she wasn't sure she could do a single thing. She let out a sigh, knowing that would be the first question she'd be asked in the morning. She wasn't looking forward to Paul Aitken. He was sure to be in attack-dog mode.

# Chapter Seven

The sunlight pouring in the window next to Leo's desk belied the grimness of her day. She hadn't slept well, and fatigue hung off her like a sagging overcoat. After the snow of the last twenty-four hours, suddenly the weather took a turn for the better, and the skies were clear. The sun was so bright it made her squint. Forecasters were predicting clouds would roll in by midday, though, so more snow was on the way.

Today it sounded like Thom was listening to Counting Crows, and the melancholy tone of the lead singer's voice suited her mood. Thom's voice drifted over the wall. "Yo, Leo."

"Mornin' Thom."

"You're a bit later than usual."

She shucked off her coat and went around to his doorway. "Had to arrange for a rental car. My car's in the shop."

"I hate having car trouble in the winter."

"Uh-huh." She didn't want to go into the accident details. She already felt foolish enough.

He turned slightly and looked over his shoulder at her. "What's the plan of attack?"

"Funny you should use that term."

"I'm all about the war. We're the Brits in the late 1930s, and our awe-inspiring boss, Neville Chamberlain, is rallying the troops."

"It's not that bad," Leo said.

"Yeah, at least we haven't been assigned to Auschwitz yet."

"Holy hell! Let's avoid that. But since we're in the middle of a red ball, I'm thinking we ought to split interviews and check back with each other later."

"Aha, now you're getting the drift, Leo. Red ball it is."

"I already called the M.E.'s office. Milford's post is scheduled for ten a.m."

"This is one of the few we should both probably attend. Who's doing it?"

Leo said, "Chrisanne Summers. You know her?"

"She's good. You'll like her. She's great at keeping us in the loop."

"One of us needs to check things out at the BDC."

"I hate to admit it, but you'll make tracks faster than I will. Do you mind going to the center?"

"Not at all," she said. "I've already called over to see who's on duty today."

"How about I roll over to the JDC and talk to some of the kids, then I'll catch up with you at the autopsy and get whatever updates we can from Clark and Brandtson." He reached down, backed a bit, and turned the wheelchair so he faced her.

She squinted, unsure if her mono vision was playing tricks on her. "Is that a black eye there?"

"Battle scar. Got it routing one of Mussolini's troops last night."

"What?" His smirk was infectious, and she smiled in spite of her weariness.

"I took an elbow in the eye from an Italian guy who scrimmaged with us." He reached up and touched his brow tenderly. "His elbow must have been made of the same stuff they use for police batons. I saw stars for ten seconds, and I still have a headache."

"Ouch. Next thing you know, you'll need a military helmet with extra padding."

"I already feel like I need one around here when dealing with Our Cheerless Leader." He looked toward Aitken's office and shook his head. "Back to business, Leo. You want to get Robeson officially on the record, so we have something for the report Tonya is supposed to have already typed up?"

"I suppose I'll have to. Why do I get the feeling that everything the guy says is a lie?"

"Because he's a liar?"

"You're only saying that to humor me, right?"

"No, he's all about me, me, me. Selfish guy to the core. You'd think he'd show a lot more remorse about his assistant director being brutally murdered."

"Some people do handle death oddly."

"The guy is odd, that's for sure."

"Don't forget he's got to maintain a level of decorum in his role there. Who knows what he feels like when he's alone."

Thom shrugged and didn't look convinced.

Leo said, "I'll see if I can track down the vacationing BDC supervisor Shelley Clifton, and I want another crack at Mike Seaver. Then I'll go to the BDC and either see you back here or at the autopsy. Call me on the cell if you'll be late, and I'll do the same."

She went to her cubicle and phoned her insurance agent's office. The claims person promised to get someone over to the auto shop and assess the damages for her car. Delighted she could put that out of her mind, she grabbed her coat and valise and left.

Leo didn't care if she was late for the autopsy, her least favorite aspect of a murder investigation. Over the summer, she and Thom had investigated a string of murders in an independent living community in Minneapolis as well as a couple of run-of-the-mill nursing home deaths. Unless a death was clearly a homicide, they worked from the M.E.'s reports. But this case was different. Even though the M.E. was very quick to turn around preliminary findings, they couldn't wait another twenty-four hours for the information.

She took off in the rental car, a late-model Toyota Corolla. The hatchback's rear window sloped, and the glass and corner supports afforded decent sightlines. The car was also nowhere near as long or as tall as her Lexus, which made it easier to see over her right shoulder. She was determined to be extra cautious and drove under the speed limit, constantly checking all around her.

No one was home at the address she'd gotten for Shelley Clifton, so maybe the Cliftons really were on vacation. Leo navigated back to Highway 53 and made her way to Interstate 35 to Mike Seaver's home address.

The tan duplex she arrived at was shabby and desperately needed work. Even from the street she saw cracks in the house's stucco. Three inches of snow had fallen in the last twenty-four hours and covered the grass to make everything look clean and white. The snow on the sidewalks and driveway was thinner, evaporating faster than the blanket on the lawn and bushes.

Her footsteps were the first to traverse the new-fallen snow on the walk. At the front door, the flip-up mailbox was full. That gave her a bad feeling. Leo checked her watch. 8:50. Plenty late enough to awaken him. She rapped on the door and waited. A minute passed, and she rapped again. Far off, she heard a shuffling sound that gradually grew louder. At least another minute passed before she heard the deadbolt opening. The door cracked an inch, but she couldn't see into the depths.

"Hello? Mister Seaver?"

The door swung open. In the darkness of the foyer, a pudgy grandmotherly woman stood frowning. She wore a purple housecoat and pink scuffs and had old-fashioned black rollers in her hair. Puffy eyes squinted into the morning light, spending an inordinate amount of time staring at Leo's eye patch. Finally she rasped out, "Mike's not home."

"Do you know where he is?"

"Never came home last night. Probably pulled a double shift at his job."

"Actually, I checked there, and he wasn't scheduled for work yesterday or today."

The woman groaned. "Why don't you come in out of the cold, and I'll look on the fridge for a note."

Leo stepped inside, closed the door, and was assaulted immediately by the odor of stale cigarette smoke. The woman shuffled her way across the hardwood floor, never lifting her slippers. She looked like she was skating but sounded as though she had sandpaper on her skates. She lurched to the left through an arched door and disappeared into a dark hallway.

The living room gradually came into focus as Leo got accustomed to the low light. On her right, the drapes at the bay window were closed completely. Not one ray of light permeated them. What little illumination there was came from a window in a far alcove, but it, too, was obscured. A mass of vines, their leaves cascading from above, hung down over the un-curtained window. The arch between the two rooms prevented Leo from seeing where the plants originated—in baskets hung high and near the ceiling? She'd seen walls at the university with fewer vines and wasn't sure why anyone would cultivate them indoors. It gave her the impression someone had transported an exterior wall inside.

The living room walls were a dark olive, stained from years of cigarette smoke, and the one reprint hanging over the television set was a cheesy-looking picture of a medieval sailing warship being tossed about on roiling seas. A saggy brown davenport, circa 1980, slouched under the bay window next to a light blue recliner that had seen better days. Both faced the TV, a three-foot-tall ancient model sitting on an end table that looked none too stable.

The sandpaper sound preceded the woman. She scuffed around the corner with a sheet of paper in her hand. "He didn't leave a message or anything. I don't know where Mike is."

Leo said, "I apologize if I awakened you."

"I needed to get up anyway. Today my shift starts at ten." When Leo didn't speak, the woman said, "I usually work the dinner shift at Fitger's, but we have a special party for a lunch banquet today, so I have to go in early. They gave me last night off to balance it out."

"I see."

"Here's Mike's schedule. They don't make too many changes from it, but sometimes he does stay over for a late shift. Wonder where he's got himself off to?"

Leo perused the schedule, a simple calendar page for November. Seaver's shifts for all but Thanksgiving week were Tuesday through Saturday. Over the holiday weekend he'd been scheduled for two four-hour overtime shifts. She handed it back to the woman and saw her once again peering intently, staring at the eye patch. Leo took a deep breath and tried to stand tall. "Thank you. I take it you're his mother?"

"Oh, goodness, no. He's my grandson. Been with me since high school when my son-in-law down in Rochester tossed him out for smoking pot. I took Mike in and got him on the straight and narrow, and he's lived with me ever since." She smiled, and it transformed her face from grumpy to glowing. Her brown eyes were warm, and suddenly Leo could see she might be a friendly waitress, someone people would tip. "I'm awfully proud of him. He worked so hard to get certified, and he's never failed to help with rent and utilities. Some girl's going to snap him up one of these days, though, and it'll be my loss. Is that why you're looking for him?"

"No, ma'am. My name is Leona Reese, and I'm investigating some problems at the BDC."

"Nice to meet you. I'm Dorothy Hardaway. I'm sure Mike will be happy to help you. He told me about the poor kid who died of alcohol poisoning. That's the problem you mean?"

"Yes. Once he comes home or calls in, will you give him my card?"

She said, "Will do," as she accepted Leo's business card.

Leo opened the door and stepped out. She pointed at the batch of letters sticking out of the postbox. "You've got a full mailbox."

"Mike always drags the mail in and sorts it. All I ever get is bills."

"I know what you mean, Mrs. Hardaway. My postman doesn't come until practically five o'clock though. Yours is here early."

"Actually, ours comes at noon, so that's yesterday's mail. Here, I'll take it."

Leo scooped out the envelopes and handed them off. "There you go. Please greet Mike for me and tell him to call right away."

Dorothy Hardaway smiled and brushed her hand over her rollers. Leo got the distinct impression Mrs. Hardaway was appraising her as girlfriend material.

Back in the car, Leo sat for a moment to let the Toyota warm up. The bucket seat was cold through her slacks, and unlike the Lexus, there was no heat mechanism to turn on. She decided the Lexus had spoiled her and wondered if Hondas offered heated seats. She might have to check that out.

She dug her cell phone out of her valise and rang Gary Clark, but he wasn't in. She asked for Ben Brandtson, but he was gone, too. She didn't leave a message but instead tried Thom's cell.

"What's happening?" she asked.

"I've talked to four boys from Bolton's wing, but none of them knew anything helpful. Now I'm waiting for William Cattrall."

"I'll be curious what you think of him."

"In what way?"

"I don't want to prejudice you. I'll ask you later."

"Where are you?"

"I'm leaving Seaver's house now." She described what she'd learned from Dorothy Hardaway, then said, "I've got a bad feeling about this. The mail hasn't been picked up since yesterday at noon, and since it snowed, nobody has approached the house or driveway."

"You think Seaver skipped the other night?"

"Either that or something's happened to him. What if whoever killed Bolton and Milford also got rid of Seaver? What if they all saw or knew something, and the killer responded by murdering Seaver, too?"

"Could be. Look, I hear them coming with the kid. Anything else I need to know?"

"We didn't see Seaver's criminal record yet."

"Nope, haven't had a chance to ask for it from the detectives."

"Let's do that this afternoon. With pot-smoking in his past, maybe Granny doesn't know her favorite grandson might still be in the business. Maybe this has something to do with drug use or human trafficking."

"Okay, I'll pull up the records while I wait."

"They let you bring a laptop in there?"

"Nope, my iPhone. I can check all kinds of stuff with it. You ought to dump your boring old phone and scale up to 4G. Makes a huge difference. I'll find out what I can. Later."

The connection went dead, and Leo sat for a moment thinking. If Mike Seaver was a drug dealer, why would he live in a dumpy duplex with his grandmother? She thought back to the time she'd spent with him on Wednesday. He acted suspicious and also like a jerk, but she hadn't gotten a criminal feeling from him. He *had* known something he didn't share, but she had a strong feeling he didn't kill Eddie Bolton.

She put the rental car in gear and looked all around before pulling away from the curb. At the stop sign at the end of the block, an empty school bus, glaring bright yellow, paused to her left. The driver waved her on. She went right and headed back to I-35, her thoughts returning to Seaver. It wasn't always possible to tell when people were lying. If Mike Seaver had a long history of practice, he may have fooled her. He'd been adamant he didn't want to lose his job. Then again, if he sold drugs, he had a captive customer group to sell to at the BDC. She'd try out the scenario on Donald Robeson. For all she knew, he could be in on it, too.

➤ ■ ◄

Thom made notes on a legal pad as he sat waiting at a scarred wooden table near the entrance to an interview room. The juveniles ushered in couldn't have anything sharp, so he wondered how they'd managed to scrape up the table so much. He was glad to have his own padded wheelchair seat. The plastic chairs were low and guaranteed to give a guy a painful case of scoliosis. Contrary to popular belief, paraplegics lost motor function, but a great many still had feeling in their legs. He felt every bump, every bruise, every soft touch to his legs and feet. He couldn't rise up and walk or run, but he could feel everything.

His upper body was strong. In a fair fight, he could give as good as he got, but seldom were fights fair. The minute his wheelchair tipped over, he was in trouble unless he could get the other fighter down on the floor with him. If his opponent stayed on his feet and Thom got dumped over, he was dead meat, so for interviews he always situated his chair near the open door in case he had to make a fast exit.

A deputy brought William Cattrall into the room and directed him to the seat against the far wall. "No funny business, pal. Got it?"

The boy nodded. With a sigh of resignation, lowered himself into the seat across from Thom. In baggy jeans and a too-tight white t-shirt, he looked like a pudgy giant. His hands were bigger than Thom's, and though the boy sloped his shoulders forward, he was broad like a football lineman. Thom estimated his weight at two-twenty. With some physical training, the kid could trim the fat and be an imposing force on the gridiron.

William opened his mouth wide and yawned, perfect teeth gleaming white. The freckles scattered across his cheeks were noticeable against his stark white skin. Thom looked a little closer and saw that freckles were interspersed with a five o'clock shadow from the beginnings of a red-brown beard. The youth stared at the table, his hands in his lap, and yawned once more.

"Man, you're making me tired," Thom said. All this got was a grunt. "My name's Thom Thoreson, and I need to talk to you about what happened at the BDC earlier this week." Still no response. "They treating you okay here?"

William shrugged.

"Can I get you anything? A candy bar? Some caffeine."

William looked up. "I could use a Coke."

Thom called for the deputy, gave him instructions and pocket change, and turned back to his interviewee. "I know you've probably gone over this repeatedly, but I haven't heard it from you."

William yawned again, sat up, and put his forearms on the table. He launched into a rambling account about the death of Eddie Bolton. In the middle of it, the deputy came in and smacked the can of soda on the middle of the table. William paused to open it and take a long pull. He neared the end of his story, then trailed off.

Thom held his pen poised over the legal pad. William hadn't told him anything new. "Looking back now, can you think of anything else unusual that happened while Eddie was your roommate? Drugs? Odd behavior?"

"He was all about odd behavior. What do they call people who like being cruel?"

"Sadists?"

"Yeah, he was one of those. He liked being mean."

"Besides the altercation with Mike Seaver, what other fights or problems did he have with staff or the other boys?"

"I don't really know. He already staked himself as a tough guy by the time I got there."

"What about these other kids he hung around with? Guys named Mouse and Speedy?"

"Speed. Mouse and Speed." He sat back, his face flushing, and he wouldn't look Thom in the eye.

"Something funny was going on with those two. What was it?"

William crossed his arms and shook his head. He tipped the chair back on the rear legs and sat rocking with his eyes closed.

"What do you know, kiddo? I get the sense you want to tell me something." Thom waited, but William didn't answer. "Are you afraid of what they'll do to you if you talk?"

The kid's eyes popped open, and he sat forward with a clunk. "I'm not afraid anymore."

"But they did scare you?"

"Maybe. But nothing like this shithole. The guys in here are, like, criminals."

"Your stay shouldn't last too long. Can you gut it out?"

William looked away. "You ever been in lockup?"

"Not in a place like this, unless you count the four months I spent in rehab after I broke my back."

Biting his lip, William's blue eyes scanned Thom's physique—or as much of it as he could see. He picked up the can of soda but didn't drink from it. "What happened to you?"

"Had a freak fall down a flight of stairs at college and damaged my spinal cord."

"Is there anything they can do so you can walk?"

Thom didn't answer for a moment. He'd spent the first few years out of rehab insisting he'd recover, that one day he'd walk again, run, play football. Lately he hadn't thought about it as much. "I don't know. So far, science and medicine haven't come up with a treatment or a way to heal the spinal cord. They're working on it."

William's face gradually turned red, and Thom knew what was coming next. "Can you—you know?"

Thom grinned. He was amazed at how many people wondered about his sex life and even more amazed how they actually had the balls to ask. "My injury is low on my spine, William. The higher up the damage to your back, the more of your body is affected. In some ways, I'm lucky. I can actually move my upper legs, but not from about mid-thigh down. So I can't run around like you can, but I can still feel. Except for not being able to get up and walk, I do pretty well with the ladies."

William blushed an even deeper red and crossed his arms over his chest. Thom waited to see if he had any more questions, but after a count to ten, William hadn't spoken. Thom said, "I guess that's enough about me. Let's get back to these friends of Eddie's. What's the deal with them?"

For the first time, William's gaze met Thom's and held it. "If I tell you, I'm screwed. But shit, if I don't tell you, it's gonna bother me forever."

Thom didn't speak, didn't make promises. Until he knew what "it" was, he couldn't assure the boy about anything. All he could hope was that his own willingness to share information about himself would inspire William Cattrall to unburden himself.

"Jeez. Well, it's like this. Speed and Mouse hated the damn counselor. They thought he offed Eddie. So they came up with a plan." William stopped.

The silence extended for so long Thom finally said, "Go ahead. Tell me about the plan."

"They went to that one guy—the dork in charge. They called him The Weasel."

"Morton Milford?"

"Yeah, whatever. They told him Mike Seaver gave them drugs and alcohol in return for, you know. Sex games."

Thom scooted the wheelchair closer to the table and picked up his pen. "Was this true?"

William shook his head. "Nah. The boss guy didn't believe it either."

"But then Speed and Mouse roped you in."

He exhaled and shook his head. "I don't know why I did it. They sort of pushed me. Threatened me. God, my parents are gonna kill me."

"Wait a minute. Let's not go there yet. What happened next? How did it all go down?"

"We got called into the interview room, and Mike the counselor was there looking like shit. Speed and Mouse did all the talking to The Weasel. All I had to do was nod every once in a while. But when it came to the sex part, I couldn't go along with it. No way. Speed laughed and told The Weasel he'd made up that part to make him listen, but he swore the rest was true."

"What did Seaver say?"

"That it was only the cigarettes."

"Then Seaver *did* do something against the rules?"

"Sometimes if a guy was having a bitch of a time and he opened up during our circle discussions, Mike would let him step outside for a cigarette with him. But that was it."

"You ever go?"

"Nah, I don't smoke. Besides, I'm not gonna sit there in front of the group and tell my secrets."

"But Speed and Mouse did?"

"No, see, that's the thing. They didn't. But some of the other guys told them about the cigs."

"Did the administrator believe you boys or Mike Seaver?"

William bit his lip. "I think maybe Mike."

"Why?"

"The guy sent us out of the interview room. Told us to go back to class. I stopped at the restroom." He colored. "I was in there for a couple minutes. When I came out, everything was quiet. I passed by a doorway there in the main hall where you need a special credit card to get in."

"By the front entrance?"

"No, near the security guy's area. Suddenly the door blasted open, and Mike came out. He didn't see me. He went the other way, toward the cafeteria. But then The Weasel practically fell out the doorway. He had a white cloth up to his forehead, and there was blood. Kind of a lot, I think."

"You think?"

"It was red, like blood. He was stopping the bleeding with a cloth."

"Show me how—left hand? Right?"

William closed his eyes and did a little shift in his chair as though he was envisioning the scene. He opened his eyes and brought a meaty paw up to the left side of his head. "He had his right hand on the door frame. So he was holding his left to his forehead."

"Okay, then what?"

"He yelled 'Seaver,' but Mike went around the corner."

"Where was the guard?"

"I don't know. Nobody was there. Nobody at all."

"What did Mister Milford say to you?"

"Nothing. He looked at me like I was a ghost, then he stepped back and slammed the door."

"What time was this?"

"I don't know. Shortly after eight-thirty? We'd only been in math class a little while when Milford came walking in all nervous and weird and jerked us out of there. We talked in the interview room for a while. Maybe twenty minutes?"

"All right, so he shut the door, and then what?"

"Then nothing. I went back to class and didn't think about it much until a few hours later when The Weasel was dead, and pretty soon we were all getting transferred to this shitty place."

"How come your parents didn't take custody of you?"

William's voice was quiet, almost defeated. "They're not back from the Bahamas yet."

"What are they doing there?"

The kid closed his eyes and went back to the near-catatonic state he'd been in when he first arrived.

"William, I wish I could get you out of here. You don't seem to belong. Have you got a record of offenses?"

After a moment, he said softly, "No."

"What's the deal? Tell me."

William leaned forward and hunched over the table like an old man. He yawned again. "I've never gotten arrested before. I got busted at a party. I was high, so I got sent to detox, and since I'm not sixteen yet, they sent me here for treatment until my parents get home."

"Who were you staying with—a family member?"

"I was supposed to be with my best friend's parents. They can't get me out."

"Didn't anybody call your folks on their trip?"

"Couldn't find 'em. They don't even know about this yet."

"Isn't there anyone else in the family nearby?" The kid shook his head.

"Oh, man. Sorry about that." Thom reached into his pants pocket and extracted his wallet. "Here, take my business card. Call me if you need a stand-up guy to talk to your parents with you."

William's eyes widened.

"What? You think I'm not a stand-up guy? Just because I'm stuck in this chair?"

Despite Thom's smile and the lightheartedness he thought he was displaying, William's face turned pale, like he was feeling sick. His mouth opened but nothing came out.

"William! I'm kidding with the wheelchair joke. I kid around a lot, and you should, too. Someday very soon, all of this is going to pass, and the whole experience will be like one great big, odd dream. Someday it'll strike you as bizarre and maybe even funny. You'll see."

"I don't think so."

"Keep my card. Call me when you get phone privileges. I'll help you if I can."

# Chapter Eight

Leo left the BDC interview room in a huff. She had grilled two of the social workers, the infirmary nurse, and all three of the kitchen workers. Only the kitchen staff offered anything useful. Despite statements from Robeson to the contrary about the outstanding level of security, staff *were* able to exit the building through a door at the back of the kitchen leading out to the garbage bins. Beyond the trash area was open space leading to a forested area. So long as someone had a pass-card to get through the locked door from the cafeteria eating area, they could access that door. The BDC was classified smoke-free, so some of the smokers, including Mike Seaver, went out back on their breaks. One of the cooks told Leo they all turned a blind eye to staff coming and going, and none of them knew what happened after seven p.m. No kitchen workers were on duty after supper ended.

Now all the staff had cleared out, and if she needed to talk to any of them again, she'd have to track them down at their homes. Nobody was any too pleased to be temporarily off work.

Twenty minutes of putting questions to Donald Robeson yielded nothing. He pleaded ignorance about the staff using the kitchen entrance and stated he was pretty sure no pass-cards were unaccounted for. He had purposely been less than helpful, refusing to allow her to tour the empty facility with him and failing to answer questions fully. He looked tired and had been argumentative. Maybe she'd have to try another angle. She decided to suggest Thom come up to talk to him.

She stomped down the hallway, toward the security entrance. Even though the BDC was shut down, the guard was scheduled to be on duty. Though he hadn't been there earlier, now Richland sat at the side table reading a shabby paperback she was unable to identify.

"You all through, ma'am?" he asked.

"For today. By the way, where were you when Milford died?"

The scrawny guard set down the book and gave her a hard stare. "I was here that morning."

"But not at your post some of the time."

"Look, a guy has to use the restroom periodically. I told that to the police."

"How in the world does the BDC keep these kids from taking off if someone's not consistently minding the exit here?"

"I'll have you know not a single camper's left the park on my watch."

Really, she thought. He was damn lucky—and the worse camping guide ever.

"If you want to know more, you can touch base with the cops, ma'am." Richland rose to deactivate the alarm which went off as she passed through the metal detector.

"Have a nice day," he said. The words sounded like they came through gritted teeth. She made tracks for the front door. Nobody sat at the receptionist's desk, and the doorway leading to Morton Milford's office was closed.

Out at the rental car, she stood in three inches of snow in the unplowed lot. She had to insert the key to unlock the Corolla. She had no clue why the hell the rental agency couldn't find the keyless remote. Why wouldn't they keep that together with the keys? She settled in the front seat and waited for the car to warm up. When she looked into the rearview mirror, she let out a gasp and frowned even more deeply. Her face was pale, she was having a bad hair day, and the eye patch made her look even more rakish than usual. Her left eye reminded her of a Christmas candy cane. The white was shot through with red capillaries leading to her blue iris. She ran her fingers through her blonde hair, looking for gray, but didn't find any. "At least that's one good thing," she said aloud.

The dash clock showed 10:38. The autopsy was now under way, so she put the car in gear and headed to the medical examiner's office.

When Leo finally reached the morgue, it was nearly eleven. She signed in and composed herself. She'd seen a half-dozen autopsies in the past, but she didn't think she'd ever get used to the indignity of it all. With a deep breath, she pushed open the double doors.

The metal table sat in the middle of the room with the forensic pathologist, Chrisanne Summers, at the far side of the body and facing the door. Leo could only see the back of Chrisanne's assistant. Thom sat in his wheelchair, against the wall, at the head of the exam table. Gary Clark and Ben Brandtson were hunched over on a pair of bar-type stools a half-dozen feet back from the corpse's feet.

Summers stopped her recitation, and everyone looked up when Leo entered. The pathologists both wore blue scrubs covered with pale blue plasticized aprons. Each sported latex gloves, cloth face-masks, and glass shields to protect their faces from fluid or matter.

Between the shields and the bright light streaming down from above, Leo had a hard time making out Summers' face. "Good morning. I'm Leona Reese, investigator for the Department of Human Services. With your permission, Doctor, I'd like to join Thom and the detectives."

"Be my guest."

"Hey, Leona," Clark said, rising from the stool. "You can have my chair."

"That's okay, Gary. I need to touch base with Thom over here anyway."

In a low, conspiratorial voice, Thom said, "I'd offer you my chair, you know—"

"Oh, shut up."

He smiled up at her. "Boy, do I have a lot of news to share with you."

"Likewise, partner." She leaned against the wall, slid down to a squat, and set her valise on the floor. "Anything worthwhile to report here?"

"She's not done fishing around in the innards, so no, not yet. She said the probable cause of death is strangulation, but she wants to look more closely at the neck and examine the head wound."

"Okay." Leo closed her eyes and let out a breath. She felt like she'd been on the run for days on end, and yet, she hadn't even completed a week's work since she'd come back from medical leave. This temporary job hadn't seemed this stressful before—before what? Prior to the surgery, back when she worked in Saint Paul, she couldn't ever recall feeling so harried. Everything had been simpler, even with all the criminal activity she encountered. She thought of Daria, whom she hadn't seen since Sunday. She always felt out of sorts when they were apart and thought her discomfort had a lot to do with her current feelings of relationship frustration.

She took a deep breath, aware of pungent odors that made her slightly queasy. A ventilating exhaust hood hung down from the ceiling, but it helped only so much. The dank smell of the autopsy room reminded her of other deaths, other postmortem examinations. Every morgue smelled basically the same: a layer of something vaguely putrefied covered over with formaldehyde and strong antiseptic cleanser.

The pathologist droned on, weighing organs, making observations, instructing the assistant. The room was warm. Perspiration beaded on Leo's forehead. She rose, slipped out of her coat, and hung it on a hook on the wall near the entrance. She strolled back to stand next to Thom.

The pathologist stepped away, scalpel held close to her chest, to allow the assistant to adjust an overhead camera and take a photo. She looked toward Leo and said, "I don't usually have such a large audience. Of course we don't have a lot of murders either. Why are there four of you?"

Clark answered before Leo could. "This man was killed at the Benton Dowling Center which is a CD treatment place for youth. You know of it?" When she nodded, he went on. "Besides this murder, we had another one there earlier in the week."

"The poisoned kid? I heard about that one. Wasn't my post though. The M.E. did that one himself."

"Thom and Leona are in charge of determining if and when the center can be opened, and of course Ben and I have to find the murderer."

The assistant finished with the photos and pushed the camera along its track and out of their way. Summers set down the scalpel she held. "What's the catch?"

"Catch, ma'am?" Clark asked.

"Uh-huh. Catch. I got called in on my day off to do a rush post. What's that all about?"

Leo exchanged a glance with Thom and wondered how Clark would address the question.

"The public is outraged about these murders, and a lot of kids in treatment have had to be sent home or transferred to the juvenile detention center. The JDC is over-full now. The state is anxious to get the treatment center reopened as soon as possible, and the chief wants this case solved soon."

"Nice try, Clark," Summers said as she leaned over the body. Leo imagined that under the mask, the pathologist was laughing at him. "Give me the low-down, boys. What's really going on?"

"That's about it. Really."

"Oh, come on! This has politics written all over it. You can share with me. I always keep the juicy stuff confidential."

Thom let out a guffaw. "Juicy stuff, huh? Well, our esteemed colleagues in blue probably have to be cautious with the facts, but maybe I can give you some background that won't get anyone in trouble."

Summers didn't speak for a moment. Leo had a view of the upper half of Milford's body. She watched Summers replace peeled-away skin and fascia over the body's chest. She smoothed it with a gloved hand. With the exception of the thinning, steel-gray hair on his head, his upper body was hairless and appeared stark white under the bright lights. Leo had only ever seen him in suits, and their padded shoulders hid the narrowness of his shoulders. He was slender and lean for a man his age, so trim, he could have been mistaken for a teenager.

Summers stepped back a half-step. "Go on, Mister Thoreson. You were saying?"

"Call me Thom. Here's the deal. If you were to do a search of the ownership of the BDC, you would find one of the principals is related to the governor and to a famous local personality."

"Ahhh, I'm beginning to see. Which personality?"

"Everyday Everett."

"The obnoxious RV dork?"

Leo laughed out loud. She was starting to like this woman.

Thom said, "The one and the same."

Summers leaned over the head of the corpse, dug the scalpel in over one ear and made a steady cut across the top of the head to the other ear. "So the faster you get results here, the faster the politicians and advertising hacks are off your back."

"Pretty much. Leo and I are on the hot seat because the BDC is closed down, and everyone who's anyone wants it reopened. Like yesterday."

Leo looked away slightly when Summers started peeling the skin away from the skull. No matter how many times Leo had been at autopsies, she'd never been able to watch this part. It went beyond gross, reminding her of creepy old Halloween movies like *Night of the Living Dead* or of the part in *Silence of the Lambs* when Hannibal Lector put on someone else's face. She didn't think she would ever get over the horridness of it. The insult of having one's face pulled away and the top of the skull removed was too great.

The assistant helped hold the head, and the examiner held out her right hand. "Saw, Danny." He reached under a nearby counter and pulled out an autopsy saw for her. When turned on, the saw emitted a high-pitched whir that slowed and glugged when she touched it to the head. In seconds, she turned it off and handed it back to the assistant, then removed what looked like a dish of bone. "Hmm. This fellow definitely took a blow to the head. It left a small mark, but it didn't crack his skull. The skull would have healed itself. He'd have had a tender bruise here for days, but this didn't kill him."

Brandtson said, "We found an awful lot of blood, though."

"Yes, there would be. The face and head bleed like a son of a gun. The crease in the skin wasn't sealed up when he was strangled, so blood was forced out."

Leo said, "But if the airway and blood vessels were cut off, why was there so much blood? Shouldn't it only have been what little blood was in the scalp?"

"Give me a few minutes, and I can tell you more about that."

The pathologist set to work below Milford's chin. Leo couldn't see what she was doing, and she wasn't about to move any closer. The clock on the wall ticked slowly. When Summers finally spoke again, Leo saw it was 11:50.

"His larynx was crushed. Possibly the hyoideal bone as well. We'll take some X-rays here in a minute to verify. But here's what happened. In a matter of seconds, certainly less than a minute, he was brought to near death. You probably can't see it from there, but this man was strangled from behind. We've got thumb marks at the back of his neck and multiple bruises at the front from some very strong fingers. The victim was bent forward against the edge of something, maybe a table, a sharp railing, a desk, some hard surface along those lines. He's got uniform bruising to the tops of his thighs, so the killer used his own body to wedge him against a surface parallel to the ground. So much force was used that the eyes exhibit evidence of petechial hemorrhaging in the conjunctival surfaces. Our victim was strangled quickly and with great force."

"Definitely a male assailant," Thom said.

"Yes," Summers replied. "Very likely a man, and probably someone much bigger than him. The victim is slight, only five-foot-seven, weighing a hundred-forty-eight pounds. When he stopped breathing and quit fighting, the killer probably let loose of him. But Mister Milford here wasn't dead yet. His heart still beat for a very short while. Wherever he came to rest—which was where? The floor?"

Clark nodded. "Right in front of a desk, as a matter of fact."

"Okay, he came to rest there and continued to bleed from the head wound for perhaps a minute or so until his brain finished dying from lack of oxygen and stopped telling his heart to beat. People die by strangulation for three reasons: the brain is deprived of oxygen for too long, deoxygenated blood can't exit from the brain, or the airway is closed off so the victim can't breathe. In his case, his airway is obliterated, and the asphyxia is very obvious, characterized by the closure of blood vessels and air passages. When I examine his brain matter, I'm guaranteed to find more verification of strangulation."

"Jesus," Brandtson said. "Why would anyone do that to this guy?"

Summers shook her head slowly. "I'll give you the 'what' and 'how.' You have to figure out the 'why' on your own."

"So it was painful?" Clark asked.

"At first, probably. Likely he became unconscious fairly quickly though. After the throttling he took, his heart would have beat for a bit, and he bled, then died. Based on the report of body temperature, stomach contents, rigor and liver mortis, the approximate time of death is shortly before he was found. And unless something very unusual crops up, which I highly doubt, the immediate cause of death is manual strangulation."

Brandtson rose from the bar stool. "If he hadn't been strangled, would the head wound have killed him?"

"Nope," Summers said. "Not a chance. Slight headache might have been the only thing he dealt with." She leaned back down. "All I've got left here is the brain, and I'll withdraw cerebrospinal fluid, get the vitreous fluid from the eyes, take blood and bile samples, and assemble a few other odds and ends. I doubt I'll come up with anything else interesting for you, except perhaps in toxicology and drug screening, and those results won't be back for a couple of weeks."

Clark slid off the bar stool and stood next to his partner. "You'll call us then if anything unusual pops up?"

"Definitely."

The detectives ambled to the door, both of them looking calm and composed. Leo, on the other hand, felt sick to her stomach. After the door closed behind them, she said, "Thom, did you get a full report from Clark and Brandtson?" He nodded. "Do you want to stay?"

"Not if the doc thinks we've got all there is to get."

Summers flipped up the shield covering her face and pulled the face mask down to reveal blue eyes and a heart-shaped face. "It's pretty cut and dried."

"No pun intended," Thom replied, laughing.

"Now there's some appropriate morgue humor. You've got the right attitude for this. We try hard to be professional when we've got visitors. Danny and I were very restrained today, weren't we?"

The assistant shook his head. "Makes for a rather dull post."

"Thom, I'm curious," the doctor said. "You've got a spinal cord injury?"

"Unfortunately."

"I did a year's residency in the SCI and traumatic brain injury department at Craig Hospital in Denver, so I've always been interested. You navigate well and look like you're in great shape."

"I stay very active."

"It's not a recent injury?"

"Nope. Happened while I was in college. I've had a lot of time to adjust."

Leo said, "Doctor Summers, you didn't stay in that field. What made you go into forensic pathology instead?"

Summers pulled her shield back down. "Dead people don't talk back."

→ ■ ←

Leo burst out of the building. The fresh air helped to clear her head a little, but not enough. The slight pounding in her temples didn't bode well. She still smelled formaldehyde as though it were wafting off her clothing. She shivered in the cold. When she was a small child being shuttled from car to house, her birth mother used to say, "Run from the North Wind Monster or we'll be caught in the teeth of his breath!" The breeze today had exactly that quality.

She stood on the landing a few feet from stairs leading down to the street. The snow had stopped. Far beyond the two buildings across the way she saw Lake Superior, cold, flat, and gray. Not a single tanker or freighter was anywhere in sight.

Thom rolled up behind her. "Hey, Leo, did you hear about the two vultures sitting in a tree? One vulture sees a man in a wheelchair going down a hill. He taps the other vulture and says, 'Look, Fred! Meals on Wheels!'"

Leo turned around, unsure how to respond.

"Ah, jeez. You never seem to enjoy my jokes." He shrugged like a naughty kid caught with his hand in the cookie jar. "I'm merely a storyteller on wheels giving you all the very best tales from the crip."

"Why do you do that?"

"Do what?"

"Put yourself down?"

"I'm not putting myself down. I'm laughing at the absurdity of the world I find myself in. You ought to do the same."

"Not like that."

She pivoted toward the stairs, but he reached out, and his hand, warm and strong, grasped her chilled fingers. "You're not yourself at all, Leo. Maybe you came back to work too early."

"I'm fine." She pulled her hand away.

"No, you're not. You're unusually upset."

"I'm not. I just want to get this case resolved."

"How do you propose to make that happen?"

"Keep working it. What else?"

His face took on a thoughtful expression. "I see. And what's your plan of attack?"

"It's after noon. We meet back at the office, compare notes, and keep at it until the BDC can be reopened."

"Yes, good plan, but why go back to the office?"

She shivered. "Because it's too cold to spend any time giving you all the details out here."

"We both need coffee. Food. A break somewhere warm. Let's go up the hill to the café."

"We don't have time for that."

"Of course we do. You're cold, and you must be as hungry as I am. Let's go. I'll take the ramp. Meet me around the corner. I parked the van there."

She was torn. What she really wanted to do was give him a quick rundown of her morning discoveries, then get back to her interviewing. She could eat later.

He didn't give her a chance to speak. "You owe me lunch, Leo. I'm claiming it now."

With a sigh, she said, "Only if you promise not to dredge up any more cornball crip jokes. Not for the rest of the investigation."

He hesitated. "All right. It might be a deal."

$$\rightarrow\blacksquare\twoheadleftarrow$$

The air in the café was so warm and humid Leo wondered if they had a hidden sauna in the back. She and Thom sat at a table off to the side, beside a wall painted in swirls of rainbow colors. Steam from a bowl of corn chowder tickled her nose, and the cup of coffee at her right-hand emanated heat. She hadn't thought she'd be able to eat after the autopsy, but the moment they entered the restaurant, her stomach started doing flips of joy. After the chowder, she planned to order a piece of apple pie.

Across the table Thom was tucking into a giant bowl of beef stew, and he'd ordered a roast beef sandwich as well. As he chewed, his face was happy and relaxed. Leo wished she were so content. She'd told him about her morning before their food arrived, but she wasn't going to ask about his until they'd both had a chance to eat.

He was through half the sandwich and most of his stew when he sat back and wiped his mouth with a napkin. "Here's the important stuff I learned from the cops."

She put down her spoon and slurped a sip of the steaming coffee.

"Around eleven o'clock on Tuesday morning, apparently after all the hoopla wound down surrounding Eddie Bolton's death, someone turned off the video cameras for a little over three minutes. When they came back on, the camera angle had changed. Have you noticed where the camera is in the waiting room?"

"It's up to the right, in the corner above the entrance to the Milford hallway. I assume it's pointing toward the front door."

"Right. That's where it's supposed to be. Clark was quite de-scriptive." Thom reached into the breast pocket of his shirt, pulled out a notebook, and thumbed through. "The video previous to eleven a.m. on Tuesday shows a nice panorama of the waiting area, front door, and a lot of the reception counter. Starting shortly before six a.m., various staff come straggling in. The receptionist arrives. A while later, the paramedics come busting in. Eleven minutes after their arrival, there's a nice shot of you coming in, wiping your feet on the mat, and looking around for someone. Then you walk forward and pass out of camera range. People come and go like crazy for the next couple of hours. Then at eleven, the picture goes dead. When it comes back on, somebody had scooted the lens far enough to the side so all you can see in the videos is the front window and the chairs in the waiting room. The first row of parking spaces can be seen through the windows, and that's about it. No shot of the front door or most of the waiting room and reception area."

"And nobody noticed until when?"

"Today."

"Good God, it's been three days."

"It's taken this long for the police to realize it. Clark said they looked at the footage around the Bolton kid's death, but they hadn't rolled ahead that far. When they looked at the tapes for the times around Milford's murder, they discovered the change. It's been corrected now, locking the barn up after all the horses have escaped."

"Where are the master controls for the video equipment?"

"Remember when you step into that hallway leading to the break room and Milford's office?"

Leo imagined the doorway, but her strongest memory was of the metal latch guard she kept getting hung up on.

Thom said, "There's a closet on the left past the break room. Clark said it's hardly big enough for one person to step into, but that's where all the equipment for the front entrance is. Other cameras are located throughout the BDC, but all of those are run on a couple of different systems elsewhere in the facility."

"Someone had to get in there, turn the thing off, adjust the camera angle, and turn it back on in three minutes. How did they do it?"

"Clark had someone bring him a broom, and he was able to stretch up and tap the camera back into place." He grinned mischievously. "Obviously, I'm not a suspect."

"Hey, watch the jokes."

"No joke. My whereabouts are accounted for at the times of both murders, so I'm pretty safe. Yours, on the other hand, haven't been verified."

"Very funny. I'll keep my whereabouts to myself, thank you very much."

"I'm wounded by your cavalier attitude. What'll I do if you're tossed in the clink, and I'm stuck running this red ball on my own?"

"I'm sure you they'll let you see me during visiting hours. I could read case files and provide snappy questions and comebacks. For instance, did someone move the camera angles so they could sneak out after killing Eddie Bolton? Or were they preparing to kill Milford?"

Thom shook his head. "Great question. I don't know. The cops don't know either. Brandtson put the screws to Richland, the security guard. Said he scared the crap out of him. The video system is old and runs on some sort of overlapping sequential program on four different VCRs on racks in the closet. The tapes are pulled every shift, and each Friday, they archive the week's cassettes and rotate old videotapes back in. They're using a hundred tapes, so they've got an archive going back about twenty-five days."

She did a quick calculation in her head. "Maybe six hundred hours."

"You think they'll watch all that?"

"Somebody has to. It's two homicides."

"It'll take some poor chump forever even in fast-forward mode."

Leo was once stuck watching surveillance tapes when she did a temporary rotation into investigations. She could attest to how boring the process was. "They'll prioritize the time frames and focus on viewing the taped events since Eddie Bolton came onsite first."

"That makes sense. Brandtson asked Richland how often he and the other security guards checked the cameras. Richland was evasive."

"Anybody think he's a suspect? He seems like a doofus. I can tell you right now that when I got to the BDC this morning, nobody was at the security station. I don't know where he was. I could have walked right in, set off the alarm, hit the reset switch myself, and kept right on trucking. Richland was there when I left though."

"Speaking of not being at his station, your favorite kid, William Cattrall, reports Richland was nowhere to be seen Tuesday, early morning." He explained the scam Speed, Mouse, and William tried to pull to get Mike Seaver in trouble. "When William came out of the restroom, he saw Milford with blood on his forehead and on a handkerchief which he was holding to the left side of his head."

"Consistent with the M.E.'s findings."

"Exactly."

"You told Clark?"

"Oh, yeah. He was interested to hear that. They've got Seaver's fingerprints on file from a previous arrest, and they're rushing the processing of the bloody bookend."

"If I had to bet on who might lose his cool and strike out, Seaver would fit the bill. It's possible he clonked Milford with the bookend, which didn't kill him, and fled. The question is whether he came back to finish the job."

Thom took a bite of stew and chewed thoughtfully. Leo signaled for the waitress so she could order pie. She turned back to Thom and said, "You know, I never saw Seaver on Tuesday after Eddie Bolton died. I was there more than two hours. Seaver didn't pop up until Wednesday. You'd think if he killed Bolton and his boss figured it out, Milford would have been a lot more careful in confronting him yesterday." She took a long sip of coffee. "So the boys tried to pull their shenanigans, and after they left, Seaver and Milford must have gotten into it in a big way. Seaver got up to leave, was upset, grabbed the bookend, and hit his boss."

"While William was in the can, Seaver would probably have had time to leave."

Leo said, "Maybe Milford heard William in the hall and came out, thinking it was Seaver. Then he saw William instead and returned to his office. But that would mean either Seaver came back to strangle him, or else someone else did the deed."

"Maybe someone else was in on the meeting. It's possible the assailant wasn't Seaver at all. What if someone else clobbered Milford, and that mystery man hadn't left Milford's office? Hell, maybe it was Robeson."

"Robeson is certainly withholding information."

Thom said, "Look up uncooperative in the dictionary, and Donny Boy's photo is the illustration."

"But something's still off. Think what a timid character Milford was. My questions alone nearly gave him a coronary. He didn't strike me as being a very courageous person at all. He would have run for help, maybe even said something to the kid in the hall, not gone back in there like a lamb to slaughter if someone was still waiting. If that person hit him, he would have made a big stink and gotten away."

"That may be. But based on what William Cattrall had to say, my bet is on Seaver, and that's what the police are pursuing. They're staking out his house, looking for him in a big way."

"I think we should both attend the funerals."

Thom said, "The cops will be there, I'm sure, but yeah, I agree. Never know what will turn up. Bolton's is on Saturday. Milford's is today."

"So fast for Milford?"

"He's Jewish. That's the custom. I'm sure his people probably wanted to bury him a lot sooner, but with the autopsy, it wasn't possible."

Leo took the last spoonful of her chowder, which was now only lukewarm. She swallowed, pushed the bowl off to the side, and set to work eating her pie. She thought about her meeting with Seaver. He was slightly taller than she was, perhaps five-nine, maybe five-ten. His hands were strong, and he looked to be in good shape, as though he worked out periodically. He was bigger than Milford and probably outweighed him by twenty pounds, but that wasn't all that much. "I've got a bad feeling about Seaver. My gut says he didn't kill Eddie, that he wouldn't kill Milford, but he's going to turn up dead."

"Who the hell instigated this mess then, Leo?"

"Wish I knew. We're missing something. You sure the cops aren't holding something back from us?"

Thom shrugged. "Let's go back to the office and pull the facility reports for the BDC. We can take a look at any patterns we can find. I bet we'll discover more than one disgruntled employee."

# Chapter Nine

"Hey, doll," Serena said as Leo passed through the metal detector at Rentreau Plaza. "Did you have a good lunch?"

Leo nodded.

Serena peered at her, a quizzical expression on her face. "Is it just me or are you not well?"

Leo felt like she was wading through knee-high water. "Didn't sleep much last night. I'm whipped today." She set her valise on the side table for Serena to inspect. "You want to take a look here?"

"You're not packing military ordnance today, are you?"

"No. Not my style."

"Yeah, you'd probably use your bare hands." Serena waved the valise away as Leo cracked her first smile in hours. "If I can't trust you," the guard said, "who can I trust?"

Leo picked up the valise, thinking it felt like it weighed thirty pounds. "Speaking of style, you braided your hair differently. It's nice." Serena's shoulder-length hair sported cornrows interwoven with bright-colored beads. When she moved her head, her hair made soft clicking noises.

"What it is, I tell you, is a shitload of work. If I'd known I'd have to sit there for four hours for my sister to do this, I might have considered cutting it all off."

"It looks lovely."

"Thanks. Nice of you to notice. Now if I could only get my husband away from that damn TV so he'd catch a clue." She rolled her eyes. "Oh, a heads up. Thom—Mister TNT, I mean—isn't here yet, so he doesn't know, but a few minutes ago I checked through two guys from the BCA who asked for your boss."

Leo frowned. "From the Duluth office?"

"No. I know those guys. These were strangers—I think from Saint Paul. Both of them juggling jumbo lattés and whining about how long it took to drive up from the Cities."

The front door opened to let in two of the surveyor's staff and the receptionist from the second floor. Thom scooted in behind them. He wore a sky-blue down jacket, unzipped, over a dark gray business suit. The fingers of his gloves were cut off at the halfway mark prompting Leo to ask how they kept his hands warm.

"I don't wear these for warmth. I need 'em more for traction. I've got some lined leather chopper-type ones in the van if my hands get really cold." He came through the metal detector, setting it off, and Serena waved him on.

In a grouchy voice, Thom said, "Are you going up now or loitering around here for a while? 'Cause if you're loitering, I'm joining you. I have no desire to meet up with Aitken, not any more than you do."

"Serena told me two BCA guys arrived asking for him."

A line creased the center of his forehead. "Why? I don't have any calls out to Bemidji. Do you?"

"Not from Bemidji—Saint Paul."

"I definitely have no lines in the water there."

"Me, neither, so I've got a bad feeling about this."

"You don't think Aitken, that son of a—"

"Thom. Don't jump to conclusions. Let's go up and see."

"Do we have to?"

When they reached their cubicles, Leo ducked in and left her valise and coat, then stood on tiptoe in her doorway to get a good view over the cubicle walls. She saw the backs of two heads in Aitken's office.

Thom came out of his cubicle. "Wish I had a periscope. That's one of the biggest disadvantages of this damn chair. Living life at fart level, I can't see a thing."

Leo laughed.

"Oh, so you think reality is funny, but not any of my actual jokes."

"I've got a special place in my heart for scatological humor. Come on. Let's go face the music."

He guided the chair away with decisive strokes. Leo took a moment to smooth her hands over her black wool pants, straightened the matching jacket, and tweaked the black eye patch which she suddenly noticed matched her outfit. She'd worn a red blouse hoping it would help disguise how pale and wrung out she looked. With Serena's comments, Leo understood color coordination didn't help much.

As she drew close to Aitken's office, she bit back a smile of amusement. The two men sitting with their backs to her looked like textbook cops. Hair trimmed three inches above their collars, ultra-erect posture, and bad suits. She followed Thom to the office.

"Thom. Leona," Aitken said in a falsely hearty voice, "I've just been telling these fellows about you. I want you to meet Special Agents Mel Kryzinski and Adam Finn from the BCA."

Kryzinski grunted, but Finn, in a very precise voice, said, "Pleased to meet you both."

"Hi, guys," Thom said. He didn't move, and neither did Leo. She stood in the doorway behind him, crossed her arms, and leaned against the door frame.

From the front, the two men were polar opposites. Kryzinski was in his late fifties, gray suit, dark hair graying salt and pepper, face and nose the florid red of a man who enjoys more than his share of alcohol. His face was craggy, probably pockmarked when he was younger, but now it was rugged, like a slab of pitted granite. He looked Leo over as through she were a prime rib at The Best Little Steakhouse in Duluth, pausing longest to stare at her eye patch. She resisted the urge to reach up and adjust it.

Finn, on the other hand, was clear-skinned, brown-eyed, and very young. Leo didn't put him over mid-twenties. His light-brown hair, gelled into submission, matched the color of his corduroy suit. The tan of the jacket was interspersed with tiny white lines. She squinted, trying to make out what the lines were and decided maybe cat or dog hair. He looked tweedy, like a shy version of the English professor from whom Leo took a class in college. Finn nodded at her, somehow managing to seem respectful, and then looked back to Aitken.

"We are blessed to have help here now," Aitken said, "thanks to the kindness and foresight of the governor. He's freed up some manpower to assist us with the BDC case. Kryzinski had seventeen years' experience in Saint Paul homicide before joining the Bureau of Criminal Apprehension many years ago. Finn is a computer and accounting expert."

Thom said, "Why aren't they working with Brandtson and Clark?"

"The governor made special provisions to assign them to help us."

Thom wheeled his chair a few inches closer. "How come these guys came all the way from the Cities? Why didn't the Bemidji office send over Wiggins or Eigert? They're stationed right here in town."

Aitken's face darkened. He didn't speak for a few seconds, so Leo knew he was struggling to keep from shouting at them. But she thought it a fair question. The Bemidji Regional Office was supposed to provide investigative assistance to the northern half of the state, and in order to accomplish that, field offices in Duluth, Thief River Falls, Grand Rapids, Brainerd, and Moorhead served the public. So why had these Twin Cities Special Agents been sent all the way up north in the middle of the winter?

Kryzinski's voice came out in a low growl. Leo thought he must have smoked a million cigarettes—this year. "BCA's shorthanded everywhere. Finn and me got pulled from leave, so we'd appreciate it if we could get to work. Sooner we resolve this case, sooner we get to go home and back to our vacations."

"Yes, good idea," Aitken said. "So here's the plan. First, I'm putting Thom in charge of coordination."

A flare of concern shot off in Leo's mind.

"Finn is going to sift through the BDC's records and files, cross-reference details with the police, and build a database we can use. Kryzinski will work with Thom to cooperate with Mister Robeson, finish off the last of the interviews, make a determination, and report to me ASAP so the BDC can be reopened."

The flare of concern exploded into bright lights. Leo was so stunned she didn't know what to say.

"Thom, I understand the Milford burial is later today. Please skip it. Special Agent Kryzinski can go, just in case."

Thom said, "Leo and I planned to attend the service together."

"No. We're stretched too thin. I hate to even send Kryzinski."

"But—"

"No 'buts' about it, you hear me? You two seem to have forgotten something critical. It's not your job to *solve* the case. You only have to determine if and when the BDC is up to professional standards, and if anyone needs to be cited, you write 'em up. Leave the rest to the police. Got it?"

Neither Leo nor Thom answered. Leo became aware that she was holding her breath. She held herself still, feeling a chill rising from the floor, and still she didn't move or give assent.

Aitken went on. "Now, Thom, first thing is getting Finn set up at an empty cubicle. Give him some stuff to research."

Stuff to research? Gathering the materials together would take as much time for either Thom or Leo as the actual research. She resisted shaking her head, instead biting her upper lip. What a poor use of time. It took all the energy she could muster not to scream at her boss.

Thom spoke up and saved her the trouble of choking out a protest. "Paul, the case is Leo's. I don't feel right about this arrangement."

"I've got other important tasks for Leona."

She dug her fingers into arms held tight to her chest and kept her voice level. "Like what?"

He sifted through some papers on his desk. "I've got . . . ah, let's see . . . yes, right here." He held up a single sheet. "Oscar Leroy Holdenberg."

The name sounded familiar, then it dawned on her. "The accidental death at the adult care home."

"The very one."

"Yes, sir. I've conferred with the police, the prelim notes are complete, and by all accounts, it was an accident. It's not a priority like—"

"I'll be the judge of that, Leona. I want the case wrapped up. The press gets hold of it, and we're on the hot seat. I understand a number of other complaints have been received as well, and I want someone on top of them. Even though we have a difficult matter in this BDC case, we cannot eclipse the high level of service the department provides. Now that we have these two ultra-competent detectives at our disposal, I'm exercising my authority. You understand?"

Leo nodded, but she didn't understand. Her face burned, though she wasn't sure if she should be embarrassed. Something was hinky, and she couldn't help but think it was about her. She was the investigator on this one, not Thom. She didn't have anything against Thom, but this was her case. Being pulled off of it stung, not because she wanted credit, but because she was invested in seeing it to a conclusion and ensuring justice was done.

Why would Aitken make this change? He couldn't have a problem with her paperwork. She turned it in like clockwork, and though she and Thom hadn't been able to provide many of the official BDC case reports yet, the delay was to be expected since they'd interviewed so many people so fast. Had Aitkin heard about her car accident? If so, wouldn't he have been more polite and called her on the carpet to discuss it one-on-one instead of publicly revoking her lead status on the case? It wasn't like him to interfere this way.

She didn't believe it was his style to ever get involved in the specifics of the work, so if this wasn't personal, then it was political, and if it was all about politics, the trail of dog-doo on the shoe led from her weasel of a boss to those in power. Now she got it and wanted to kick herself for being so dense. Did she dare ask about how explicit the governor had been? Was Aitken specifically told to remove her from the case? The only person who had that kind of access to the powers that be and a motive for such a request was Donald Robeson. She wouldn't put it past him to get her pulled from the case. She'd hammered at him mercilessly each time she talked to him. She thought of his shifty blue eyes, his sense of entitlement. She not only disliked the guy, but now she wondered what he was covering up.

Thom spun his wheelchair around, and Leo realized she'd missed the final comments. He looked up at her and winked, raising a single finger to his lips.

The two agents rose, and both of them shook hands with Paul Aitken.

Their boss stood beaming as though he'd just won a free ski trip to Lutsen. "Do us proud, men. Let's wrap this up today if we can."

With that sexist remark, Leo turned on her heel and marched out of the office and down the hall. She was so angry she miscalculated the corner of the front cubicle and banged her right shoulder into it. Shoulder smarting nearly as much as her pride, she flounced into her office, threw herself into her office chair, and wheeled around to face the window.

Lacy flakes of snow drifted past the pane, coating the outer stone sill. She wondered if she had, indeed, come back to work too soon after her surgery. Everything was out of order. This unexpected turn of events stank to high heaven, and she felt that if she'd been on top of things, she could have prevented its occurrence. She didn't feel efficient, wasn't enjoying the work at all. In the time she'd been working with DHS, she'd been surprised at how much satisfaction she felt when she got to the bottom of issues and disposed of cases. For the first time, she wondered if maybe, just maybe, if she had no other choices, she might want to stay in the investigation role if police work was out of the picture. But now Paul Aitken had become an albatross around her neck. The victims of the BDC case and the horror of their deaths seemed lost in the Machiavellian maneuverings of men in power.

I will not cry or lose my cool over this, she thought. She took a deep breath. No tears over this. It's not worth it.

She heard the low murmur of Thom's voice across the aisle and understood he was getting one of the agents settled in the empty cubicle across from him. She rose and stepped out in time to hear a sneeze.

"Jeez, you got a herd of cats or what?" Thom asked.

Finn stuttered before saying, "Two. Only two. Persians."

Leo stopped behind Thom's wheelchair. She didn't know where Kryzinski was, but she didn't care. She'd taken an instant dislike to him. She looked at the misery etched into Finn's face and decided he might be different.

"Hey, man," Thom said, his voice annoyed, "a word from the wise: Buy men's suits that match your pet hair not your eye color. And while you're at it, get a lint brush. I'm allergic."

Finn looked down at his corduroy jacket, his face flaming. Leo thought most guys would flip the bird or growl back to hear a comment like Thom's, but Finn merely blushed. He might be okay after all.

➤■◀

Leo sat in a reclinable exam chair at the ocularist's office. The morning had been so stressful that her feelings of anger and helplessness carried right over to the appointment. She closed her eyes and tried to breathe regularly, but still, she felt anxious. She couldn't even begin to guess what this doctor would tell her. She almost didn't want to know.

Dr. LaVoie was nothing like Dr. Gest. Tall, thin, and full of energy, Dr. LaVoie looked to be no more than forty. He told her he'd recently moved his ophthalmology and ocular practice to Duluth because his wife got a job at the University. He beamed at her as he plopped onto a doctor's wheeled stool.

"There aren't all that many of us across the country. I belong to the American Society of Ocularists." He gestured at a certificate on the wall. "Some states, like Nevada, don't even have ocularists. So when you go off gambling there, make sure you only lose an arm and a leg." He winked and literally gave her a nudge. He looked nothing like Thom, but his gleeful telling of the joke reminded her of him. "You're lucky you don't have to travel very far to see an ocularist."

He took a thin flashlight from the pocket of his white doctor's coat and asked her to remove the eye patch. He kept up a patter about the accomplishments of his two kids as he removed the temporary prosthetic and examined her. She held herself very still and focused on a poster of the Badlands hanging on the wall. Though empty, her stomach was roiling.

"Excellent work by the surgeon, Ms. Reese. The socket looks fine, the muscles are healthy, and you're ready for the first prosthetic. I'll be able to connect it to the muscle tissue, and it's highly likely it will function in concert with your other eye."

This had been one of her worst fears: having an eye sitting dead in her head while the other eye moved indiscriminately. It was almost too much to expect that an artificial device would look normal, but he'd raised her hopes.

He sat back. "Here's how this works. First off, everyone calls prosthetics glass eyes, but they're not. We make them out of a plastic substance called methyl methacrylate which is much sturdier and will last. The longer they hold up, the better, because they aren't cheap, and your particular insurance company only pays fifty percent."

"I wondered about that. Is it thousands of dollars for the eye?"

"Nowhere near that. Don't worry. I'll set you up with an affordable payment plan."

Leo didn't tell him that wouldn't be necessary. She was thankful she and Daria possessed a healthy bank account. She wondered what people did when they couldn't afford treatments and prosthetics. She supposed they were stuck wearing an eye patch forever.

"I'm going to take a wax impression, and I'll need your help to create a perfect fit for your eyelids and for blinking. I'm getting pretty good at ballparking not only for a comfortable fit, but also for a natural look."

"Pretty good?"

"Yeah, I'm not perfect yet, sorry to say. The nice thing is even though some trial and error is necessary, you'll know the moment when it feels right. Then we'll reinsert the temporary for a few more days, and I'll take photos of your left eye to use as a guide for the iris."

"So you won't be done today?"

"No, early next week. I need to use the impression to create the plastic eye, and I have to paint the iris. Here, let me show you. He whirled on the chair, opened a drawer in the counter behind him, and whirled back. "See this?"

He handed her something that looked like a glass button. "This piece is embedded in the eyeball, and I'll make it look almost exactly like your other eye. Even the small red veins in your eye are duplicated. I take micro-thin strands of fabric and place them on the plastic, then it's all sealed. When completed, your new eye will look so much like the other one nobody will even know."

"Somebody told me standard eye units were used."

"In the olden days. But the human eye is such an individual thing, not just blue or brown or green. The subtle gradations of color are remarkable. For instance, people probably call your eyes blue, but they're a most remarkable combination of bright blue along with green, brown, dark specks, and flecks of gold. Very pretty. No way can standard colors exist for such variation, so we paint on the proper markings."

Her face flamed hot, and at the same time she felt such a sense of loss that her stomach clenched. Fighting to maintain her composure, she said, "Care and maintenance?"

"It's easy. You'll hardly ever need to remove it. But you should know this first prosthesis will only be good for four to six months. Your eye socket is still adjusting. The muscles tend to recede for a time, and before too long, the eye will likely fit badly. So the more permanent eye will be fashioned next spring. Thereafter, we wing it. You come see me every six to twelve months, whenever needed, and we keep on adjusting. All right?"

She nodded.

"Good. Then let's get going here with the wax impression."

Back at the office, Leo opened the door leading into her work area. A shaft of gray light crept in the top half of the window over her cubicle wall. Since she'd entered the building, the snow had stopped. She was strolling toward the windows when it hit her: there was a strange electricity in the air. Was everyone in the room holding his or her breath?

She looked down the aisle toward Paul Aitken's office as she approached her doorway. He stood at his desk, index finger in the air, talking to Tonya. Tonya sat in one of the chairs in front of his desk, hunched down, as though she were trying to minimize the abuse raining down upon her.

Aitken looked up and caught sight of Leo. His features twisted, and even from behind the glass she heard him shout, "Leona Reese!"

He passed from her angle of vision and came out of his office, ranting as he moved along the far side of the cubicles. He emerged at the end of the aisle and stomped toward her. "Do you listen to nothing I have to say? Am I not the boss? What the hell is wrong with you?"

She stood in her cubicle doorway, her valise in one hand and her coat half off one shoulder. She knew she must be looking at him with a puzzled expression because as when stopped before her, he said, "Don't give me that goddamn innocent look!"

Leo had no idea what set him off and didn't know what to say. She heard a squeaking sound from over the cubicle wall. Thom was there and had moved in his wheelchair.

Aitken's face was suffused with color. He'd obviously run his hands through his hair, and it looked like he had a bizarre cowlick in front. "Did I not make myself clear?"

"In what regard, sir?"

He actually stamped his foot. "In regard to the BDC cases."

"What about them?"

"I hate it when you people play dumb. You know what I mean!"

"I have no clue." His behavior was becoming tiresome, she thought. What on God's green earth was his malfunction?

"You were specifically instructed to stay away from today's funeral, and yet you went anyway. Against my express orders. That's insubordination! I'll write you up."

"I'm sorry but you're badly mistaken. I did not attend the Milford funeral."

"Don't you lie to me. I've got it on good authority."

"I think you better check again." She moved closer to her desk. From the out-box she picked up a Time Usage slip and handed it to him. "I haven't had a chance to fill in the hours used yet, but I was at a doctor's appointment."

"The hell you were."

"Excuse me for taking exception to your tone and accusations, *sir!* I didn't travel anywhere except to the office of Doctor Peter LaVoie where I was fitted for a prosthetic eye. You can call him to confirm. Would you like to see the replacement orb he inserted for me until the new eye is complete?" She reached for her eye patch.

"No!" He backed up a step, a look of horror on his face. "No, no, that's fine. I—I—must have gotten bad information." He leaned forward and thrust the time slip at her. "My mistake."

Before she could get proper hold of the paper, he raced back toward his office, duck-footed, his black suit tails flapping behind him. The sheet wafted to the floor. She bent to pick it up, and when she rose, Adam Finn stood in the entrance to his cubicle.

"That was mighty unpleasant, ma'am. Is it always so contentious here?"

"No, it's not."

"That's for damn sure," Thom's voice called out.

She slipped out of her coat, threw it into the visitor's chair, and smacked the time slip back into the out-box.

What was going on around here? Had everyone gone nuts? She sat in her chair and waited for her heartbeat to return to normal. After a moment, she understood what she'd done. She'd very nearly ripped off her eye patch to scare him! She'd never considered that he'd freak out over her eye, but in the rush of anger, she'd used the knowledge without giving it conscious thought.

At heart, Paul Aitken was a petty little man. He made a big deal about the paperwork he ushered through his office, but he'd never last out in the real world. He was made for ivory towers, for purely intellectual thinking, not for the guts and grit of an investigator's day-to-day life.

A bubble of laughter rose up. She'd been so angry, she'd almost wanted to reach right into the eye socket, take the temporary prosthetic out, and throw it at him. He would have fainted! She laughed, holding it in quietly. It wouldn't do any good for her current situation if someone came by and heard her giggling maniacally.

When she stopped chortling, a thought occurred to her. She had just used her "disability" as a defense against somebody and something offensive. Was that what Thom did?

She didn't care what Aitken said about the Bolton case or the Milford case or the BDC. Maybe she couldn't be involved with it during work hours, but her time off was her own, and she would do as she pleased, whether Aitken liked it or not.

➤ ■ ◄

Thom sat in his cubicle, debating what to do next. Finn had called it quits at five and retired to his hotel. Kryzinski never came back from Morton Milford's funeral. The service had been set to begin at two o'clock, and it irritated Thom that now, nearly four hours later, Kryzinski had neither phoned in nor stopped by to provide an update.

It had been bad enough that Thom and Leo spent most of the day wasting valuable time updating the two agents about the case, but now Kryzinski didn't even have enough class to check in? Thom could smell nothing but trouble.

Meanwhile, Leo worked on, still shuffling papers on the other side of the wall. Thom shut down his computer, and he wanted to leave. But he also wanted to talk with Leo and didn't know how to go about it, so he sat with his coat in his lap, chewing on his thumbnail.

He thought back to high school when a well-to-do member of the Booster's Club gave a big donation to the high school football program, with the unspoken expectation that his son would get significant minutes at the quarterback slot. The only problem was his kid, Fitz Fuller, was worse than mediocre. Only one thing saved the coach from an unpleasant row with the booster. Fitz got smeared by the opposing team in the second game, and a broken tibia kept him out for the rest of the season.

Thom remembered what a relief that had been. They'd lost their first game due to Fitz's weak play and poor skills. His failure to see the field and the receivers during the eight minutes he played completely sank the team. Thom hadn't wished any harm to come to Fitz, but they won all but one of their remaining games, and Richie Stahl, the starting quarterback, went on to play for USC.

Aitken was like the crappy quarterback. He couldn't see the field or identify his skilled players. His head wasn't in the game, and all he cared about was the Boosters—or the politicians. He didn't have respect for those on the line and in the game. He wanted to strut on the sidelines, make a few stunning substitutions, and drink a lot of beer after the game while claiming the victory for himself.

Meanwhile, that moron had sidelined his best investigator. Thom knew he possessed many useful skills, but nobody questioned people quite like Leo. With her police background, she had an interesting way of putting one and one together and coming up with seven. Or thirteen. He enjoyed watching her work, listening to the way she interviewed people in a crisis. She got more than basic information from even the most recalcitrant jerks, often finding out things people hadn't intended to divulge. He wasn't a fool; he'd watched her closely in the short time they'd worked together and learned a lot from her.

As he sat there twisting his coat in his lap, he recalled he hadn't thanked her for all the times she helped him streamline cases. Before her surgery, she'd gone to facilities and homes not accessible to him, and she never complained about any requests for help. While she was out on medical leave in October, he missed her can-do attitude and their good rapport, and they hadn't even worked together all that long. He knew they both believed in "you scratch my back, I'll scratch yours" and went out of their way to help one another whenever they could.

And now this.

God, he hoped she didn't think he had any part in it. What if she thought he'd manipulated to get the big political case? He wished

Paul Aitken played wheelchair basketball so he could run him over and knock him on his ass.

On the other side of the wall, he heard Leo sigh. Her chair smacked into her desk. Click. Out went her desk light.

He rolled into the hallway as she came out. Her face looked slack from fatigue, and her normally cheery expression was missing. She peered at him with a tired eye. "Hey."

"Hey yourself. Leaving for the night?"

"Finally. I got the Holdenberg case knocked out."

"Tonya got everything transcribed that we gave her, and Finn is busily reviewing BDC financial records."

She held the door to the hallway, and he rolled through. "I noticed the big lunkhead never came back."

"No, he didn't. Concerns me."

They got on the elevator alone, and as the doors closed, he said, "Leo, it's important you know—"

The elevator dinged and before the doors closed, they reopened to let in a state worker who made small talk with them until the main floor. Leo stepped out behind him, and Thom followed.

"You were saying?" she tossed over her shoulder.

He strong-armed the wheelchair to catch up. "Yeah, I just wanted to—"

"Good night," one of the night guards said.

Thom nodded and went through the security area and into the foyer. Two businessmen in suits stood inside the door carrying on a clandestine conversation. They kept looking around as though they were suspicious of everybody and everything. Thom followed Leo out into a sharp wind. The parking lot's lights shone down upon them. He hastened to slip into his coat, shivering as tendrils of chill wind tickled at the back of his neck. "Whoa, it's cold out."

Leo stopped at the edge of the sidewalk. "Let's talk in your van."

"It takes forever to warm up."

"So does the piece of crap I'm driving. Never have liked economy cars much."

"Who could hate a Toyota?"

"I do, right now. Although the sightlines aren't bad."

He headed to the sidewalk cutout and maneuvered into the lot. Clots of snow and unexpected ice got in his way. He had to muscle along to reach the Toyota van, and by the time he got there, his fingers were wet and half-frozen. He clicked the remote to unlock the van, opened his driver's door, and removed his backpack from behind him to drop between the front seats. He reached up for two special handles inside the van. In a fluid motion, he pulled himself up and out of the chair, slid onto the leather seat, and reached back to manhandle his wheelchair through the sliding back door. The chair collapsed and fit snugly into a floor rack behind his seat and within arm's reach.

By then Leo was in and slamming her door shut. She said, "I'm always amazed how easy you make that look."

"Helps to have a strong upper body and I'm lucky my hip flexors aren't paralyzed." He started the engine.

"I've never been nosy enough to ask this, but why do you drive a van but not have a lift in the back?"

"I do, but I don't use it much. It's called an Infloor ramp. I'll show you sometime when it's not so damn cold. It's under the flooring and slides out like a giant tongue."

"I see. So if you don't need a ramp, why do you have one?"

"I can cram four or five guys in here and all their gear. That's why I don't have the middle seats in. It's a lot more convenient for traveling to basketball games than all of us trying to take different cars. I know the van's not sexy. I take shit from my friends all the time." He rolled his eyes. "Three of my crip friends have trucks and think I drive an old lady vehicle. They call me Soccer Mom Thom," he said with a grin. "But you don't hear 'em complaining when I'm chauffeuring them down to Bloomington or Greenfield or some other game location two hundred miles away."

He saw her shiver. "I've got a pair of choppers here. Want 'em?"

"That's okay. You must need them more than I do. What did you want to talk to me about?"

He took a moment to adjust the heater which was spitting out tepid air. The interior wasn't going to get any warmer until the engine ran another couple of minutes. He sat back and examined her face. The eye patch stood out in bold relief next to the pallid skin. She had a dark circle under her good eye. "Man, you look whipped."

"Thank God it's Friday."

"Look, I need to make sure you know I had nothing to do with what Aitken decided today."

She cocked her head and frowned. "Of course I know that."

"Good. I think he's the biggest dumbass on the planet, and I wanted you to know I'd gladly hand the case right back over to you. I know it's yours."

"Why would you think I'd blame you?"

"I don't know."

"Don't ever worry about that. You and Tonya are the only people in the whole department I trust. The rest of them are only out for themselves."

"My sentiments exactly." He let out a sigh of relief. "I can't believe what an ass Aitken was. He was out of control. I'll give that Finn guy credit. You probably saw I set him up in the cube straight across from mine, and when our Clueless Leader lit into you, he and I looked across the aisle, and Finn was seriously concerned. He got up and hovered."

"Hovered?"

"Yes, he did. He looked like he wanted to take Aitken out. He doesn't know yet that Paul is all yippy barks, no teeth to bite with."

"Now you get it," she said. "He couldn't fire me. Or you. Or really, any of us. We'd have to be grossly incompetent or commit some sort of remarkable malfeasance."

"I'm still smarting over the crack about the American Disabilities Act he made the other day. Asshole."

"Thom, we'll get through this case and through whatever comes our way. Don't give it another thought. I've already let it go."

"You have, huh? So what are you doing tomorrow morning at eleven?"

A tiny grin pulled at the corners of her lips. "Maybe the same thing you're doing?"

"You bet. Want me to pick you up? The van will be nice and warm then."

"Yeah, sure. Come about half an hour early and we can get there and scope things out. Who's assigned to go to the Bolton funeral? Kryzinski?"

He said, "Finn."

"He doesn't seem like such a bad guy. How about we buttonhole him afterwards and see if we can pump him for information?"

"Exactly my plan."

➤ ■ ◄

Leo snuggled under a patchwork quilt in the apartment living room, her stocking-clad feet poking off the end of a far-too-short loveseat. She looked around the furnished place. Somebody with a flower fetish had once lived here. A wallpaper border along the ceiling sported bluebells and green leaves. All of the cheaply framed pictures on the walls were of wildflowers. The loveseat was covered in a light brown material with roses on it. Even the tan wall-to-wall carpet had a tulip theme going around the edges. Despite the flower motif, the room didn't feel warm or like a garden. It was the coldest room in the apartment.

She picked up the cordless phone and dialed long distance. Daria didn't pick up, so she left a message, then dialed her sister's cell.

"Wallace."

"Kate, you got a minute?"

"I'm cruising University, looking for a ho."

Leo laughed. "You do know how raunchy that sounds, especially coming from a lesbian."

In a mock-offended voice, Kate said, "What? You don't think I have needs?"

"Yeah, what do you *need* to find her for?"

"Material witness to a drive-by shooting from last week. Happened on her corner. I think she's laying low, though, worried about her safety. But she'll pop up before too long."

"I see. I've got a question for you."

"Shoot."

"Did you ever work with a guy named Mel Kryzinski? I remember his name, but that's it."

"Oh, boy."

"What do you know about him?"

"Prick."

"Such language. Your mother would be so appalled."

"You asked, I answered. He closed some big cases and got lots of notoriety. He's a lone wolf. Likes to get all the credit. Thank God he left for the BCA. He's the stereotypical asshole cop. He moved on a few months after I made probation. I actually went to his going away party at the bar because I was so glad he was leaving. Why?"

"Your poor sister is now stuck with him."

"What?"

"You know the case I was telling you about—at the treatment center? The governor has seen fit to drop a couple of BCA special agents on us, and Kryzinski is one of them."

"My sympathies, Leo. I remember he could be a jerk."

"Can he do his job?"

"I suppose, if you can keep him from pissing off all the people he talks to. He's got some kind of attitude. And if you notice, he's not too pretty above the neck. He always acted like the ladies flocked to him, but in my opinion, they were bunching up together for protection so they could escape as a group."

Leo laughed. "Okay, you've confirmed my initial impression. What about another guy named Adam Finn?"

"Small world. He was at the Metro University program with me."

"He was? I got the impression he majored in other fields."

"He did. He's some kind of brilliant. He was enrolled in my Law Enforcement program at the same time he was completing an undergrad degree at the U of M. I saw him around some, but we traveled in different circles. I was in one class with him, Crim Justice Ethics. Walk in the park for him. I'm lucky I got out of there with a B-minus."

"He seems decent, but young."

"He's a couple years older than me, more like your advanced age."

"Oh, thanks. You're not such a spring chicken yourself anymore."

Kate laughed. "I don't think Finn would be too bad. I never worked with him, but he was smart and pretty nice. Is he over at the BCA now?"

"Yes, and I can't reconcile the description of these two guys and see them working together."

"You know how it is. Sometimes you get stuck with your polar opposite or someone who's hell to work with. It's a blessing I'm in one-man cars so often."

"Thanks for the lowdown on these two, and good luck with your ho."

"Any time. Over and out."

# Chapter Ten

Near the end of the previous school year, two popular students from a Saint Paul high school were killed by a drunk driver who crossed the center line and crashed into them head-on. Leo still remembered coming upon a funeral procession of a couple hundred cars, and the news stories showed over a thousand grief-stricken people at the service for the two girls.

She was prepared for a repeat of this. Whenever a young person died, especially a high school kid, the funeral was a zoo.

But when she and Thom pulled up to the Catholic church Saturday morning, she didn't find the madhouse she expected. They entered the church to find perhaps four dozen people sitting there, somber and quiet.

"Let's split up," she whispered to Thom as they waited in the narthex.

"I'll go hang by the choir area so I can keep an eye on the congregation."

A deep voice behind Leo said, "Uh, hello."

Leo turned to see Finn. He was dressed in the same suit as the day before, but his shirt was different. The pale blue hue didn't exactly go with the brown of his suit, but she noted his jacket was swept clean of cat hair.

"Hey, Finn," Thom said.

"I would appreciate it if you guys would just call me Adam."

Leo nodded. "How about you plant yourself on the right side near that group of young people." She pointed, and he nodded assent. "I'll camp out right behind the family. Looks like the gang's all here. I see our friendly police officers are already present." Brandtson stood near the left rear of the church while Clark stood halfway up the right side next to a large pillar where he had a nice view of the proceedings.

Leo settled into a seat in the fourth pew. She turned at one point and noticed a handful of young people, mostly girls, filing in. Some of them sat sniffling into tissues. She examined each person, one by one. Nobody stuck out as unusual.

The organist began to play, something from Bach. Leo recognized it as a Prelude, but she didn't know which one.

The family filed in slowly. Phyllis Bolton, without her oxygen tank, was draped in a black veil and a black wool dress that made her look lumpy. She clutched the arm of a young man Leo assumed to be Stevie Bolton. He was tall and slender with long hair that fell into his eyes. He wore a brand-new gray suit. They were followed by a short man who took mincing little steps. When he turned to file into the pew, it was clear he was quite elderly. He sat a good arm's length from Phyllis, his shoulders straight.

The service that followed was grim. In a flat monotone the priest trotted out platitudes and insincerity. Was it her imagination or did the priest dislike the deceased? She wondered whether Mike Seaver's assessment of Eddie Bolton was accurate. Was he merely a hotheaded, spirited young man? Or was Eddie the sociopath Seaver and William Cattrall painted him to be?

As she rose for the final benediction, she glanced behind her and estimated there were only about sixty people in the church, the majority of them high school-aged girls. The congregation remained standing while the pallbearers maneuvered the casket down the aisle. As Leo turned, Gary Clark caught her eye. He smiled, hopefully, his face pink and happy. Oh, geez, she thought, looking away. She'd seen that look before. He was interested in her. Didn't he realize she was gay? She brought her hand up to the patch over her eye and filed out behind the rest of the mourners.

Outside the church, the wind was an icy blast of moist particles. Hard pellets of snow blew off the church roof and swirled in the air. As the casket was lifted down the stairs to the waiting hearse, she caught a glimpse of Stevie Bolton, his face pale and eyes red-rimmed. He looked dazed. He and his aunt and the elderly man got in a sedan for the ride to the cemetery.

Interment was deferred until the ground thawed. The priest's final words were said over the coffin outside a marble building where Eddie Bolton's remains would wait until spring thaw. As Leo stood there, she couldn't help but recall the snowy morning when her mother's funeral service was held. She remembered almost nothing about the day except for being cold through and through. Nothing she did could warm her. She never wore dresses to winter funerals or memorials now. Even in her lined wool pants, she shivered.

The priest finished, and the two-dozen people dispersed. Leo found Thom waiting on the concrete walkway, his face philosophical. In a quiet voice he said, "I want a good old-fashioned Irish wake when I go. None of this dark and dire stuff for me."

"Right," she answered. "We'll have the priest tell un-PC crip jokes."

He snickered. "Works for me." He rolled along the icy sidewalk, and Leo followed. They were near Thom's van when she became aware of a gradually rising torrent of words. At first, she couldn't make it out, but she turned and saw Phyllis Bolton standing with Clark and Brandtson, her arm raised in front of her.

She pointed her index finger and jabbed it into the front of Clark's chest. ". . . now. Get to work. I want to see some results from your useless investigation. Who killed my boy? You need to find out!"

Clark bent and spoke softly, and Phyllis turned away, crying. Stevie stood next to her, his shoulders slumped and head bowed. The elderly man was nowhere to be seen.

"For Clark's sake," Thom said, "I sure hope we catch the person who did this. I'd hate to have her dogging my office week after week, year after year."

"No kidding," Leo said.

They waited respectfully at a distance until Clark and Brandtson finished with Phyllis Bolton. Leo watched a half-dozen sobbing young girls surround Phyllis's grandson. One girl, in particular, came close to him, her arm around his waist. She was a head shorter and stood on tiptoes speaking urgently. After a moment he leaned down so she could talk to him.

Clark stepped into Leo's line of sight, Brandtson following. "Afternoon, folks." He smiled at Leo, and she nodded back. He came to stand at an angle in front of her, close to her left side.

Thom said, "Anything new?"

Clark shook his head. "Not really."

Thom crossed his arms and let out a sigh. "Nothing really interesting at the funeral either. You find Seaver?"

"No. We're looking. No luck yet."

"Who was the older gent with the family?" Leo asked.

Clark reached inside his coat and took his notebook from the breast pocket of his suit. "Nathan Duffin, age seventy-nine. He's Phyllis Bolton's one surviving relative, her mother's brother. Retired clock and watch repairman." He snapped the notebook shut and returned it to his pocket.

Brandtson looked at his wristwatch. "Nothing new to report on our end. Anything from you people?"

Adam Finn appeared then, his hair windswept. "I talked to the priest. He was reluctant to speak of the deceased, but he did finally say the boy had been a handful. Eddie Bolton went to the Catholic grade school here until he moved on to the high school for his freshman year."

Brandtson said, "Handful, huh? Cops tend to call kids like Bolton juvenile delinquents."

Clark put his hand on Leo's shoulder. "Well, if Ben and I are going to have any weekend at all, we'd better get back to the office. Let us know if anything turns up, and we'll do the same." After a brief squeeze, he removed his hand, nodded to the group, and turned and strode off with Brandtson.

Leo was glad she was wearing a thick coat. Gary Clark's gesture didn't feel quite as forward or invasive that way. She hoped he wasn't going to be a problem. It was just her luck he probably would be.

>■<

Leo pulled into St. Luke's Hospital parking lot and killed the engine. She had met up with Thom and Finn in a coffee shop to eat a snack and decide on a course of action. Finn was going back to the office to continue to research, and Thom would check in later in the afternoon after his basketball practice. They'd all agreed she should interview Eddie Bolton's girlfriend, Kimberly Nichols.

She grabbed her valise from the passenger seat and cut across the street to the hospital's main entrance. The complex consisted of five buildings connected by skywalks, but she was fairly certain the Nichols girl would be in a trauma bay somewhere in the main facility. If she'd been released elsewhere, Leo hoped the hospital would inform her where the girl had been sent.

When she finally found the correct area, it was part of an intensive care unit, and Leo's spirits dropped. She hoped Eddie Bolton's girlfriend was on the road to recovery, but if she was still in ICU after more than two weeks, her condition must be very serious.

She went to the nurses' station and interrupted a woman entering data into the computer. "Can you tell me how to locate the physician for Miss Kimberly Nichols?"

"Dr. Francis is on call today, however, he's not due to make rounds until sometime around three."

"I see. Who can I speak to about—"

Someone gripped Leo's elbow. She turned to find a thin, dark-eyed woman, her face haggard. She looked like she hadn't slept for days. Her jeans and sweater were rumpled, as though when she did sleep, she didn't change out of her clothes.

"Why are you asking about my daughter?"

"Mrs. Nichols?"

"Yes."

Leo introduced herself. "Is there somewhere we could talk?"

The woman spun and moved out of the bay and a short way down the hall. Leo thanked the nurse at the computer and followed Mrs. Nichols. She went through a doorway into a family waiting area containing four freestanding chairs and three matching navy-blue couches pushed up against three of the four walls. Coffee tables in front of the couches were heaped with well-thumbed magazines. The blinds on the far windows were closed, so the room was dim. The only other occupant sat leaning into the arm of a sofa, his head resting in the palm of his hand.

"Jed."

The man jerked awake and sat up, eyes wide. Like Mrs. Nichols, he appeared to be in his late thirties, and if she looked haggard, he looked even worse. His thinning blond hair stood on end, and if she didn't know better, Leo would have thought he was on a three-day drunk.

"This woman from the State wants to talk to us about Kimberly."

The man rose, and Leo went through introductions once more, ending by saying, "I am so sorry about your daughter's condition. Can we sit for a few minutes and talk?"

Mister Nichols lowered himself back into his seat, and his wife sat next to him. Leo set her valise atop the magazine pile, slipped out of her coat, and sat across from them.

"I'm investigating the death of Edward Bolton."

Jed Nichols face twisted into a half-smile. With a gleam in his eye, he said, "That little bastard. Eddie. I never met an Eddie who wasn't a complete asshole. I can't tell you how glad I am he's dead."

His wife put her hand on his knee, and said, "Now, Jed . . ."

But this only served to anger him. With clenched fists he said, "If he wasn't already dead, I'd have beaten him within an inch of his life."

Leo was used to angry reactions, but even she was taken aback by his vicious tone. Maybe the police missed a possible suspect. "I take it you didn't like the kid."

Mrs. Nichols removed her hand from her husband's knee and said, "He seemed all right. Such a handsome boy. The blond hair and those big blue eyes. Kimberly was wild about him. She'll be crushed that he's dead, that is, if she ever wakes up."

"Please tell me about her condition. What happened to her?"

Before his wife could answer, Nichols sat forward. "No, Betty, let me." His face turned red, and he took a deep breath. "That little asshole crashed his car on the highway with Kimberly in the front seat. The cops say he spun out before he went into the trees, but they think he was going over eighty, maybe even a hundred miles an hour. He had an airbag. Kimberly didn't. I'd like to kill the little fucker—"

"Jed!" Mrs. Nichols turned to Leo. "We're just so angry, so upset, so—"

"We haven't slept for days!" he yelled. "We don't know if she's going to live!"

"Oh, God." Mrs. Nichols hunched over, her shoulders shaking.

Leo gave her a moment. She felt awful for upsetting the girl's parents, but it had to be done. "So she's had a head injury?"

Mrs. Nichols sniffed and raised a tear-stained face. "Yes, brain trauma."

"Skull fracture," he said, angrily ticking off items on his fingers. "Fractures to the collarbone, right leg, ulna, and radius." Gathering steam, he said, "Almost every one of her ribs were cracked, and you've never seen so much bruising in your life. It's amazing she lived long enough for the paramedics to get there. I didn't even recognize my own daughter when I saw her for the first time." He brought his hands up to his face and sat for a moment, breathing fast.

"Ms. Reese, you'll have to forgive us," Mrs. Nichols said. "Jed's right. We haven't really slept for days, and it's all so upsetting."

"Kimberly has been in a coma then?"

Mrs. Nichols nodded. "The doctors keep telling us there's a good chance she'll wake up soon, but it's been so long now. Yesterday she thrashed around quite a bit. They've had to restrain her to keep her from pulling out the tubes and IVs."

Leo didn't want to give false hope, but she said, "That sounds very promising. I hope she comes out of it very quickly."

"Thank you," Jed Nichols said. He ran a hand across his mouth and sat up taller. "What is it you need from us?"

"I was hoping you could give me some information about Eddie Bolton and about your daughter. Had they dated long?"

He deferred to his wife. She said, "No. It's only been a couple of weeks. We didn't know anything about him, but last week Britney told us Eddie was out of control. She told Kimberly he went through girls like Kleenex, but Kimberly was walking on Cloud Nine."

"Frankly, I don't know what Kimberly saw in him," Jed Nichols said.

"Britney didn't like him. I heard her warn Kimberly one day when they were watching TV."

"Britney?" Leo asked.

"Yes," she said, "Kimberly's best friend, Britney Gallagher."

"I'd like to find out more about Eddie Bolton. Would it be all right if I talked to Britney?"

"Hell, yeah," Mister Nichols said. "Find out all you want. I want to know who killed the kid so I can congratulate them."

His wife gasped. "Jed! Cut it out. Next thing you know you'll be arrested!"

"We've hardly left here," he said. "I don't know when exactly that little fucker died, but I'm pretty sure I was either at work or here."

Mrs. Nichols shook her head and looked away, embarrassed. When she turned back, she said, "Britney's phone number is in the book under her dad's name, Lucas Gallagher."

"Where do you work, Mister Nichols?" Leo asked.

"At the DECC." She must have been looking at him blankly because he went on. "You know, the Duluth Entertainment Convention Center. That great big convention place down near the harbor?"

Leo blushed. "Oh, yeah. I've only lived here a short while. I know where it is but have never been there."

"I coordinate conventions."

"And you, Mrs. Nichols? Do you work outside the home?"

"You can't tell from my hair today, but I'm a stylist at the Brandywine Salon. I haven't been working since this happened to Kim."

"I understand. Is there anything else you think I need to know? Anything about Eddie Bolton or your daughter?"

They shook their heads.

She rose. "If you think of anything, will you let me know?"

"Of course," Mrs. Nichols said.

They wearily hefted themselves up from the couch, and Leo took a business card from her valise to hand over. "I'll keep you and your daughter in my thoughts and prayers."

The other woman's eyes filled with tears. "Thank you so much. She reached across the coffee table and grasped Leo's hand. "Please come back anytime."

Jed Nichols followed her out to the hallway. He stopped and ran his hands through his short, thinning hair. "I think I ought to apologize for being so callous."

"It's all right, Mister Nichols. I can't even begin to imagine how terrible this is for you."

"Still," he said, "I'm not—not usually so mean-spirited."

"You'll feel better when Kimberly is back up and around and you can get some rest." She reached out, and he enclosed her hand in a dry, leathery grip.

"Thank you, ma'am."

She moved away. When she reached a T in the hallway, she looked back. Jed Nichols still stood there, his head bowed, his fingers pressed into his brow. She wasn't sure, but it looked like he was crying. She hadn't been entirely honest. She *could* imagine how difficult the situation was for them. Not only had she experienced the same stress of waiting when her mother was dying, but also, on the job she often dealt with people on the worst day of their lives. Most of the time she felt helpless to do anything to spare them the pain of her questions. She wished she could comfort them, but her job was to get answers. Sometimes the process felt far too bleak.

➤ ■ ◄

"Daria, I'm so glad to finally catch you."

"Leo, when're you comin' home? Are you in the car?" From the cell phone, Daria's voice sounded extra far away, as though the 160 miles between them were ten times farther.

"I'm in the car, idling in a hospital parking lot. I'm working on a case, and I'm probably not going to get out of town this weekend after all."

"Oh? What's up?"

Leo gave her a quick rundown of the case, and Daria responded with a sigh. "I came up against Aitken once, way back before he went into administration. Let me think. He was a junior prosecutor then and my firm cleaned his clock. I can't say I remember the case details, but I don't recall being very impressed by him."

"That makes two of us." She sighed. "I'm sorry about this. I want to see you. I miss you."

"Well, hon, miss you, too, but I've got a lot of work to do here anyway, and you know how it goes with the candidate. Somebody or other is calling me every twenty minutes. Let's both focus on our work burdens, and maybe next weekend we can be couch potatoes."

They said their goodbyes, and Leo hung up, feeling forlorn. A wave of homesickness passed over her and brought tears to her eyes. Nothing had been right for so long. Daria was distant, but not only in time and space. She also seemed so disengaged. Why didn't she ever take a day off and drive the 160 miles? Granted, Leo hadn't been stationed in Duluth very long, but not once had Daria even suggested plans for such a trip.

Their relationship had always been one where their two little planets spun in alignment for periods of time, then gradually shifted away. Leo wasn't sure whether there was a cycle to it, but always in the past, after a few weeks at most, they managed to line back up again. Not this time. Since before her cancer diagnosis, they'd been spinning out of one another's orbits. Sometimes she felt like she was the only one trying to get realigned.

She put the car in gear and drove out of the lot. Over six months had elapsed with things not being right. Was it her fault? Going through the diagnoses and initial treatments had been hellish. She tried not to think about the surgery and its immediate aftermath, the way her hopes were dashed, her sense of helplessness.

With a wince, she thought back to the day she first learned she might possibly never wear a badge and gun again. She'd devoted so many years of work to moving ahead, careful not to cross anyone in the Old Boy Network. She'd been on the verge of another promotion. Within a year, she had fully expected to get her gold shield and work investigations permanently. But now, she had no way of guessing what would happen. Could she rehabilitate her vision sufficiently? The worry was so heavy, so painful, that she'd forced herself to stop thinking about it.

Daria had been supportive, but she was busy with her court cases and the judge's race. Ever since summer, when Daria lost an important trial, the partners had shut down her fast track to promotion. All she did now was work even longer hours and struggle to make up for her failures.

They both worked long hours before the eye problems emerged, and when Leo went on disability for treatments, she'd had a lot of time on her hands. She'd missed Daria terribly and never got used to spending the tedious days and most evenings alone.

Being posted in Duluth seemed like a good idea at the time. It got Leo away from familiar streets and memories of loss while giving her a chance to learn something new. She liked investigating, though the Bolton and Milford deaths would have been much more interesting if she were assigned to them as a police officer. Better this than nothing, she thought. She recognized she wanted to do more than look into one aspect of suspicious deaths. She wanted to *solve* the cases. As Paul Aitken said, seeing a case to the end couldn't be her goal most of the time. No matter what the rules or expectations were, it was in her nature to want to get to the bottom of both of the killings.

Up until she returned to duty after medical leave, she had gone through the motions at the job. Nobody could fault her or the work she did. She prided herself on being thorough, fast, and efficient, so the State was definitely getting its money's worth, but her heart wasn't in it. She saw clearly now how major crimes like murder, while sad and depressing, were also exhilarating to explore and examine. While on patrol, she'd always been interested in bringing criminals to justice, to answer for their crimes against the community. That wasn't the same goal in her State Investigator role. In matters of life and death, she dealt most often in this new job with life, but the foray into the Bolton and Milford killings provoked a different feeling. The two deaths were an assault against law and order, and as such, she wanted to bring the killer in.

She knew now that eventually she needed to find a job where her efforts led to the arrest and conviction of wrongdoers. The work she did now was new, and, for the most part, kept her interest. She was still learning, and she couldn't say for certain yet, but she had a hunch she wasn't going to find satisfaction in it for too long.

Things would go much better when there was an opening at the main office in Saint Paul. Once she was back down in the Twin Cities there was a lot more variety, and other opportunities were likely to open up. Despite her eye problems, she had high hopes she would qualify with a handgun again, and when she did, she might also qualify for an investigator's position at the Bureau of Criminal Apprehension. Even a civilian role at the BCA might be better than working for DHS, especially if Paul Aitken was her superior.

She turned into the Rentreau Plaza parking lot and pulled into the first row next to Thom's white van. There were only two other cars in the lot, and one of them likely belonged to the security guard. Nobody else was driven enough to show up to work on a Saturday.

As she got out of the car, a thought suddenly stunned her. She stood, one foot in the snow, the other still on the carpeted floor. Finn and Kryzinski were from the BCA. What if they carried back tales about her attitude or investigative methods? She wasn't one to suck up to people for her own advantage, but it might be a good idea to attempt to develop a rapport.

Rentreau Plaza was L-shaped, but the side entrance at one end of the L had been rendered inaccessible except by keycard for the hours the main entrance was closed. Ever since 9/11, people were funneled in and out the main entrance, sent through the metal detector, and searched as necessary. An inconvenience, for sure, but she thought the previous inattention to security in most public buildings was alarmingly lax. One time she rode on the elevator next to a woman carrying a purse from which an unusual wood handle stuck out. Leo had politely asked, "Say, what have you got there?"

"Oh, this?" The woman unzipped her leather bag and pulled out a mean-looking hatchet. "See here?" She'd turned and, with the head of the hatchet, gestured toward her own face. Lavender- and yellow-colored bruises mottled her jaw, cheekbone, and around one eye. "That sonuvabitch I divorced did this to me on the street. I was on my way to work last Friday, and he stops and beats the hell outta me." She stuffed the hatchet back in her bag. "Won't happen again. Next time, I'll whack his nuts off!"

"I see," Leo had said, her heart pounding. She took a deep breath, held her head high, and turned back to face the elevator door. "I completely understand." She got off the elevator a floor before she needed to and went directly to a phone to call building security. She never heard what happened to the woman, but she hoped the husband didn't ever accost her again.

Nowadays a hatchet sure wouldn't clear security.

Leo's key card granted her access, and she approached the dark-haired security guard sitting behind the desk. Her head was bent as she read something from a three-ring binder, but she looked up as Leo drew near. The name badge on her brand-new gray uniform top read: Charlotte Cardinal.

"Hello, I haven't gotten a chance to introduce myself. I'm Leona Reese."

The guard rose, awkward and shy, and reached out a hand. "Call me Charley. Just Charley. Nice to meet you."

"Well, Just Charley, you look like you're studying."

She looked down at the binder. "It's the SOP manual for security at Rentreau Plaza. I'm trying to make sure I understand all the protocols and proper procedures."

"Seems rather dry for a Saturday afternoon."

"It is. But I brought a nice murder mystery along, and I'll read my book later."

Charley grinned at her, and Leo wondered about her background. She had the black hair, square chin, and aquiline nose of a Native American, and yet, there was something different about her. "You haven't been here all that long."

"Nope. Only started three weeks ago."

"I've worked in this building a short while, too, off and on. I had some surgery in the middle of my assignment." She reached up self-consciously and touched the dark eye patch.

"I wondered if you'd had an injury."

"No, worse. Cancer."

Charley's face grew serious, and her dark eyes looked at Leo sympathetically. "For decades and decades my people have rarely had any problems with cancer, but lately things have changed. My granny's sister and another family friend only in her thirties have died from it. I'm convinced something toxic is loose in the environment, some sort of pollution is causing it."

"Your people?"

"Inuit. We're Inuit."

"Those relatives live here in the area?"

She shook her head. "Outside Juneau. In Alaska."

"You're a long way from Alaska, Charley. Have you lived here long?"

"My sister and her two kids moved here many years ago for a job, and now the boys are teenage hoodlums. My sister works swing shift, so I came down to help her get the boys back in line."

An honorable person was the impression that came to Leo, and she smiled. "That's very kind of you. I go into the juvenile detention centers, and I know how badly young men need guidance."

"In this case, they mostly needed a kick in their rear ends. They've shaped up. I don't think you'll be seeing them over at the JDC."

"That's good. You have a family, too?"

"No, never been married. No kids. You?"

"No kids for me either. My partner works in the Twin Cities. I'm assigned here temporarily and commuting on the weekends."

"Must be tough with the bad weather.'

"Yeah. I didn't make the drive last weekend, and it looks like I won't be going this weekend either." She took a deep breath, suddenly aware of how cold the entryway was. "Aren't you freezing here?"

"Nah. I've got a space heater under the desk if the icicles form, but I don't have much trouble. I'm Inuit. We're accustomed to much more chill than this."

"I can only imagine. Guess I better get back to work."

"You have a good day, Ms. Reese." She lowered herself into the chair.

"Oh, no, Just Charley. No need for formalities. I'm Just Leona— or Leo."

"Leo. Okay, works for me." Charley smiled again, and Leo headed for the elevator.

The upstairs was no warmer, but Paul Aitken's office was dark, which was a relief. She had no desire to run into him, even if she was on her own time. She was trying not to let it rankle that she wouldn't receive any salary for her extra hours, but that was the price she had to pay to stay with the BDC cases.

A glow of golden light shone out of the cubicle next to hers. Leaving her coat on, Leo set her valise on her desk and stood in the aisle between Thom's and Adam's work areas. Both men were bent over papers on their desks.

Thom looked up. "Hey, Leo." He wheeled a quarter-turn and came to his doorway.

"Your black eye looks worse," she said.

"I think one of the guys may have added to it last night."

"You ought to try wearing a helmet."

"What?" He laughed. "It's not football."

"Sure looks like it."

Finn came into the aisle and cleared his throat. She smiled brightly at him. "Hi, Adam."

Thom said, "Did you find out anything from the girlfriend?"

Leo shook her head. "Not a word. She's got two very angry, upset parents waiting for her to come out of her coma. And if Eddie Bolton hadn't died the other day, I have a hunch the Nichols girl's dad would have done him bodily harm."

"New suspect there?" Thom asked.

"He certainly has motive, but I don't think so. He's too over-whelmed to have organized a plan and carried it out in secret. I'll mention it to Clark. I'll bet they've already checked him out, though. Haven't they ID'd everyone who showed up on BDC video?"

"Yes."

"He was way too open about his desire to kill the kid. I'd bet a lot of money it's not him."

"Turning into a gambler, huh?" Thom said.

Before Leo could answer, Adam Finn interrupted. "I have some questions. Do you two have a moment?"

Thom said, "Sure."

"If you don't mind, come into the cubicle so we can consult the documents as we talk."

Leo moved to the far side of his space and stood by the cloth-covered cubicle wall. Tom rolled as close as he could to the side of the desk.

Adam pushed the keyboard tray in under the desk and dropped down in his chair. In addition to the computer on the right side of the desktop, there were stacks of computer printouts arranged all over the desk. Adam had written letters and numbers on the tops of the printouts in fat black marker, but Leo couldn't tell what any of the codes meant.

Adam picked up a three-inch-thick printout and fanned through several of the green-and-white-striped pages. "I'm not a certified accountant, but over time I've familiarized myself thoroughly with accounting practices and concepts." He stopped at a page that Leo saw contained red squiggles and question marks in the margins. "I've been going over spreadsheets and these dumps of expenses and income for the Benton Dowling Center."

"Aha," Thom said, "you've found something."

"Not so fast. I don't know what I've found, if anything. I've got to know some things first."

"Okay, shoot," Thom said.

"I'm not accustomed to or knowledgeable about anything to do with a facility like the Benton Dowling Center, and since the assistant administrator is now dead, the bookkeeping assistant wasn't as helpful as I'd like."

"Don't they have a whole accounting department," Leo asked, "or someone they farm out that task to?"

"No. Morton Milford was not only their administrator but also their de facto chief accountant."

Leo asked, "Isn't that a conflict of interest? Isn't there supposed to be checks and balances in administration and finance?"

"That's the general practice, and now without him or someone else who was well-versed in the facts, it's not been as easy to make sense of their accounting as I'd like."

Thom said, "Wait. What about the bookkeeper you mentioned?"

"He merely handled daily income and outgoing expenses. He wrote the checks, did the banking runs, and turned over the data to the chief accountant. He was basically useless."

"Could you go to the owner, Donald Robeson?"

"I called him, but he brushed me off. Said he knew next to nothing about the financial end and that Milford handled that angle. He did say he'd be getting someone new in there as soon as possible. Then he hung up on me."

Leo chuckled. "Yeah, he's a real sweetheart."

"Oh, I don't think so." Adam met her gaze, then must have comprehended she was kidding because he looked back down in haste. "I've carefully reviewed their books as best I can with what the bookkeeper provided. They've got the cost of maintaining the physical plant. They will have significant expenses for utilities, office supplies, insurance, property taxes, food, clothing and uniforms, medical supplies, consultant costs, and the like, all of which total some two-point-one million dollars."

"Okay," Thom said. He looked up at Leo, and she raised an eyebrow. He gave a subtle little shrug back.

Adam went on. "I've got accounts here showing they have a grand total of sixty-four staff, twelve of which are part-time. With everything from high-priced medical staff, social workers, administrators, counselors, and social workers to lower-paid secretarial, kitchen, and custodial personnel, they've got salary payouts totaling four-point-eight million dollars per year."

"Wow," Leo said, "that's a lot."

"Yes. So my first question concerns Social Security. I've got a contact who has clearance to access that federal database, and the numbers he gave me don't add up."

"How do you mean?" she asked. He frowned up at her. His face was pale, and somehow, he looked cold. She was still wearing her coat and she definitely felt the chill. "Adam, are you freezing?"

"Uh, well . . ." He blushed.

Thom said, "I'll let you have my space heater."

"That's okay. No need. Please don't bother." He blushed in embarrassment, as though admitting he was cold would diminish him in their eyes.

"For cripesake," Thom said. "It's tough to work when you're cold, and anyhow, I'm not using it."

Adam said, "If it's not too much trouble?"

"Not at all, bro." Thom backed out of the cubicle.

Leo said, "What doesn't add up in the paperwork?"

Thom returned with the space heater. "You can stick it under the desk, Leo. The plug-in is behind you."

After a bit of fumbling, the heater was on and cranked up. "Thanks," Adam said. "I appreciate it."

"Feels good to me, too," Leo said. "I might have to move in here with you."

Adam's face took on an alarmed expression, but he quickly composed himself. Leo had a blinding flash of the obvious. Adam was gay. Duh.

"All right." Adam focused on the printout for a moment. "You know how a certain percentage of your income up to a flat dollar amount of income is deducted for Social Security and Medicare?"

Leo said, "I think it's up over seven percent at the moment."

"Right. So why would the amounts deducted by the BDC be significantly lower than that percentage?"

"Oh, that's an easy answer," Thom said. "Salary over a certain amount per year is exempt. I can't remember the total, but it's like a hundred K."

"Except for the Medicare part doesn't have an exemption," Leo added. "Otherwise there's no maximum wage base for Medicare tax, but that deduction is only something like one-and-a-half percent."

Adam brought his thumb and forefinger to chin. "Hmm, it still doesn't add up. Out of all the staff, only the chief administrator and the assistant were paid over ninety-K. Even the psychiatrists on staff were paid less."

Leo said, "The psych docs probably consult on a part-time basis, so they wouldn't garner full-time salary and benefits. What else could it be?"

"I know," Thom said. "You also have to calculate in any health care expense accounts and stuff like deferred compensation, 401k contributions, or other fringe benefits normally excluded."

Adam shook his head slowly. "I did. I spent a couple hours going over every single employee, full- or part-time, and it doesn't make sense. And I can't help but think something is seriously off about the expenses as well."

"How so?" Thom asked.

"They're paying hefty fees for insurance and physical plant repair and upkeep. Apparently, they have a maintenance contract with an organization called Andiers Associates, and a variable monthly amount goes to some other place." He grabbed another printout and thumbed through it. "Turnbull Idaho, Ltd."

"Perhaps a mortgage?" Leo suggested.

"Could be. I can't follow up on that until Monday. So I'll set that aside and go on to the next query. What does it cost for each patient in the facility?"

Leo looked at Thom. "Can you answer that? I haven't been here long enough to have more than a general idea that it's spendy."

"We can check on Monday," Thom said, "but I can tell you the basics. Private facilities charge well over a thousand bucks a day for detox. I don't remember the exact amounts, but it's like thirteen or fourteen hundred bucks and sometimes a lot more, depending upon the services and level of privacy."

"Per *day?*" Adam asked.

"Yes. Per day. As soon as the medical aspect is introduced, even for hospital observation, the costs skyrocket. The most basic fourteen-, twenty-one-, and twenty-eight-day residential programs range between eight thousand and maybe as much as twenty thou."

Adam whistled. "Holy cow! I'm glad I'm not much of a drinker."

Thom said, "With all the outpatient costs, follow-up fees, and other types of treatment, it's not cheap. The BDC has a private endowment, and they go after public monies—medical assistance—wherever they can."

"Ahh," Adam said. "That must be who the offsite Benefits Bookkeeper is."

"Right. Some sort of trustee. So if a kid's parents in St. Louis County can't afford all of the fees but want their wayward youth to get CD treatment, they can ask for part of it to be paid by the endowment. In the case of someone like Eddie Bolton who was court-ordered into the program, the county pays."

"I see, and so—"

"But wait," Thom interrupted. "The county pays based upon the DRG, the diagnosis-related group, into which the patient has been classified. You know what that means?"

"Not exactly," Adam said.

"It'll make your eyes glaze over to go into too much detail, so let me say this. Each DRG is kind of like its own special category and is specific to each type of hospital or facility. The DRG represents the average cost of caring for a patient in that particular DRG classification."

"So it's an average of basic costs?" Adam asked.

Thom said, "Sort of. High-priced facilities with lots of overhead and lower-cost medical providers are lumped together, and somehow, through the magic of creative governmental mathematics, payment amounts are set. In general, facilities with patients receiving Med Assistance will benefit financially from shorter patient stays or stays that cost less than the DRG reimbursement amount."

"I get it. So when I look at the income end of the ledgers next, I'm going to see income from private pay, from the county, and from insurance companies."

Leo said, "And their private endowment may move funds into the mix periodically, too."

Adam sighed. "Thank God I'm not a CPA or an IRS auditor. I don't mind working books like this every so often, but I much prefer computers. I'll get back to work on it now. Maybe by Monday I can give you a full report."

Leo slipped out of her coat, finally too warm for the small cubicle. "You're not going to work the whole weekend."

"I might." Adam rose, and pushed his chair in. "That space heater sure does a good job."

"It was a present from my dear old mother," Thom said. "You're in a dead spot here ventilation-wise, so keep it as long as you want. The heating vent for this area is there by mine and Leo's offices, so it's never very bad over there."

As Thom rolled back, Adam stepped aside so Leo could pass by. "Hey, just curious," she said at the entryway, "what about Kryzinski? Will we see him today?"

Adam glanced away as he blushed. "I don't think so. In fact, he's gone . . . gone for the weekend."

"Back to the Cities?" Leo asked.

"No, he's an ice fisherman. I imagine as soon as the Milford service was over, he went off to wherever he goes. I've never actually worked with him before. I really don't know him. He's, uh, well, let's just say, a little rough around the edges. Just my first take opinion."

Leo gave him a big smile, hoping to communicate that she understood. "By the way, you know my sister."

"I do?"

"Kate Wallace."

He looked up at the ceiling for a brief moment. "Tall, dark-haired woman. Criminal Justice Ethics. She shared her notes with me once when I missed class due to a death in the family."

"That'd be Kate. She says hi."

He frowned slightly, squinting to look at Leo. Perhaps it crossed his mind that Kate looked nothing like her, but all he said was, "How nice. Please greet her in return from me."

He sat down stiffly and rubbed his hands together. Leo left him to his printouts and ledgers. With her coat slung over her arm, she paused in Thom's doorway.

"What's your plan, Thom?"

"Actually, I'm doing nursing home inspection paperwork now so I don't have to do it Monday. That frees me up a little."

"I should probably do the same thing with the cases I've gotten this week. I've hardly given them a glance. But to be honest, what I really want to do is go talk to Stevie Bolton."

"Go ahead."

"I don't think I better. Seems rude to show up on the day of the funeral. I'll wait until tomorrow or Monday."

"You're not heading down to the Cities?"

"I'm tired. By the time I got down there I'd have a couple hours, go to bed, then have to get up and get ready to truck back up here. Not a good use of time, especially since Daria's working. I think I'll go over to the JDC and talk to more of those kids."

Thom backed from his desk and rolled closer. In a low voice, he said, "Interesting what Finn is finding."

"It remains to be seen if irregularities actually exist."

"But if there were, it would go a long way toward explaining why somebody would kill the chief accountant."

Leo shook her head slowly. "Still leaves me wondering about Eddie Bolton."

"Maybe he was a nosy little bastard. He could have found some records to use for blackmail or heard or seen something he wasn't supposed to."

"That's a stretch. He hadn't been at the BDC for very long. I still get the feeling we're missing something."

"Keep digging, Leo. You'll find whatever it is."

# Chapter Eleven

Sunday morning dawned cold and clear. A scattering of snow had fallen overnight, but not enough to deter Leo from taking a trip over near Merritt Park where Eddie Bolton had lived with his aunt Phyllis and Stevie Bolton.

Though the road was clear, snow blanketed street signs, and the bright reflection off white surfaces glared in her eye. From Grand Avenue, she passed the turnoff for Denfield High School and kept going, looking for North Fortieth Avenue West. She wondered why a town would put two cardinal directions in a street address. North and West was total overkill.

Squinting against the light, she saw Thirty-Ninth and knew she'd gone too far. After a zig one way and a zag another, she saw Merritt Park. She was getting close. Children out in the park made snow figures and chased one another, tossing snowballs and shrieking. Had Eddie and Stevie Bolton played there when they were small? The Bolton house was only two blocks away.

The olive-green two-story house she parked in front of was nestled into a rise in the middle of seven other houses on one side of the street. She guessed they'd all been built in the 1930s or 1940s. Perfectly squared-off shrubs formed a wall along the front of the property line with only one break where cement stairs led up to the house. At the top of the stairs, Leo picked her way across an un-shoveled sidewalk to the front door and rang the bell.

So much time passed that Leo assumed no one was home. She opened her valise and pulled out a business card, but before she could write on it, she heard the working of a lock. The door creaked open.

A barefoot teenager in the doorway wore jeans and a baggy white t-shirt. His shaggy sandy-brown hair was so long in the front that it fell over his eyes. Leo had noticed this at the funeral. Stevie Bolton watched the world from behind a waterfall of hair shiny with grease.

He peered at her suspiciously. "Yeah?"

Leo introduced herself and asked if she could talk to him about Eddie.

"Why?" he asked. He shivered.

"Because you might possibly know him better than anyone, and I need all the information I can get to help figure out who hurt him."

"Thought you already talked to Gramma."

"I did, but I'd like to talk to you as well. Is Ms. Bolton home?"

"I think she's still on the phone. You can come in, I guess."

Leo stepped into a warm, stuffy entryway reeking of cigarette smoke. To the left was a hallway to the kitchen and stairs leading to the second floor. Stevie gave a toss of his head toward the right and followed Leo through a doorway into an enormous living room. Someone obviously put a lot of money into remodeling. Walls for two other rooms had been removed to form a spacious L-shaped area with gorgeous, gleaming hardwood floors. At one end of the L, two brown leather couches sat in front of a giant plasma TV mounted in the corner. In the center area, wingback chairs, a leather sofa, an Oriental rug, and three end tables were arranged into an attractive sitting area around an ornate coffee table with elaborate inlaid patterns. The other end of the L, nearest to Leo, contained a desk, five floor-to-ceiling bookshelves, and another Oriental rug. Curio cabinets sat in every available corner and against many of the walls.

None of this would have been particularly striking were it not for the fact that every free surface, shelf, windowsill, and curio cabinet contained hordes of knickknacks. Precious Moments, Snowbabies, scores of Swarovski crystal animals, LLadro and Hummel figures, Civil War soldiers, elaborate displays of little houses, Wizard of Oz plates, baby dolls and bride dolls and porcelain dolls, and an entire collection of Harry Potter figurines.

Leo looked back at Stevie. He rolled his eyes. "Don't look at me. I don't collect this stuff."

"It's really quite . . . remarkable."

"That's one way to put it. Grab a chair. I'll go get Gramma."

Leo perched on the edge of the leather sofa and set her valise next to her. Outside she saw light flakes of snow were falling again. On the sill of the casement window, eight colorful Samurai Warriors posed, each holding a sword or hefty knife out in front of them as if they were ready to leap off the sill and attack. They weren't quite a foot tall, and their bases kept them firmly on the sill, but Leo wondered how the curtains could ever be closed. She looked around the room at the other windows and didn't see how any of them could be closed up at night.

She checked her watch. How long had she been waiting? What was taking Phyllis Bolton so long?

A thumpity-thump noise came from the front hall. Someone descended the stairs in a hurry. Stevie came around the corner. Now he wore a pair of clunky tennis shoes. Leo thought if he grew into his large feet, he'd be quite tall.

"Gramma says to go ahead and get started without her. She's on the phone."

"I imagine she still has a lot of family and friends to console."

Stevie's face crinkled into an expression of disbelief. "Family? Friends? Ha. We don't have any of those."

"I saw an older gentleman at the funeral—"

"Uncle Nathan? He hardly counts. We never see him. My parents are dead. Eddie's parents are dead. Gramma doesn't have anybody. She's fighting with that dude at the funeral home."

"Is there a problem?"

"I guess. She thinks they overcharged her." He lowered himself into a wingback chair and listened while Leo went through the DHS rules and regs and set up her tape recorder.

"How old are you, Steven?"

"Almost seventeen. You can call me Stevie. Everybody does."

"What do you think happened to Eddie?"

Stevie folded his arms across his chest and sat silently for a few moments. "I guess I really don't know."

"When did you last talk to him?"

"I went Sunday with Gramma during visiting hours."

"How did he seem to you?

"Same as always."

"What does that mean? How was he the same?"

Stevie let out a sigh. "He was the same old Eddie. Full of it, you know?"

"In what way? Tell me about him."

Stevie wouldn't meet her eyes. He looked out the window and said, "Eddie looked out for number one. He had a one-track kind of mind, you know? When he wanted something, he went after it and almost always got it."

"Did that make it hard for you to get along?"

Stevie shrunk into the wingback, and his hair flopped down so she couldn't see his eyes at all. "He was, like, unstoppable. If he wanted something, he always got it."

"So you fought with him a lot?"

"Nah, I just let him have whatever. Wasn't worth the fight. He always won anyway."

"Can you give me an example?"

He paused. Leo didn't think Stevie was being uncooperative, but he was restrained, careful with his responses. She pegged him as an introvert who wouldn't have enjoyed his "uncle" Eddie much.

In a quiet voice, Stevie finally said, "I got into photography three years ago. I saved up my birthday and Christmas money to buy a good Nikon."

"I have a digital Nikon myself," Leo said.

"Yeah, I have a couple of those, too, but I mean a real camera. One that takes old-fashioned photographs."

"Oh, I see."

"Eddie took it. Dude went to school and burned through ten rolls of my film, then refused to give me back the camera until I developed the film."

"So you paid for the developing?"

"No, I did all the work myself."

"Developing the film?" she asked.

"Yeah. My gramma let me set up a darkroom in the basement bathroom."

"How did you learn how to set it up?"

"Internet."

"What about all the equipment?"

"Bought most of it used on eBay. I got the enlarger from a guy on Craigslist."

"Wow, that's impressive. You eventually got your camera back?"

"After I developed ten rolls of his loser photos. He took photos of cars in the parking lot, a bunch of shots with weird architecture angles, and pictures of girls' ass . . . ahhhh . . ." He clamped his mouth shut and blushed. "Don't get me wrong. Eddie did have a good side. Sometimes."

"Tell me about his good side."

So much time passed Leo wondered if Stevie was going to come up with a single incident. She was about to make a comment when Stevie cleared his throat. "There was this one time, see, I wanted to get on the yearbook staff, and this jerk said I couldn't."

"A teacher?"

"No, no, the dude was a senior last year. The president of the yearbook group. He's gone now. Graduated."

"What did this have to do with Eddie?"

"I don't know how Eddie heard Chuck blew me off, but next thing I knew, Chuck hunted me down at my locker. He was, like, totally weirded out. He told me I was on the yearbook staff and to report after school and booked outta there."

"Eddie had convinced him?"

Stevie sat up and swept his hair out of his eyes. "You could say that. More like he *made* him."

"Oh?"

"Oh, yeah. Chuck looked like he went a few rounds in the Mortal Kombat arena." Stevie bit his lip, and his face went pink. He ducked his head, and his hair covered his eyes again. "That's how I knew Eddie did sorta care about me."

"He'd never done anything like that for you before?"

"No. No, I guess not."

"Sounds like you had a difficult time growing up with Eddie. Was he hard to live with?"

"Lately, yeah. Delusions of—what do you call it?"

"Grandeur?"

"Yeah, whatever. He kept saying he was going to get his inheritance and get out of town. He hated living here. All they did was fight."

"They?"

"Yeah, him and Gramma. Fighting world war three, like, every other day." Stevie sat forward in the chair, head down, elbows on his knees.

"Did he have enemies?"

"Did he have friends is probably more the question."

Leo asked, "Did he?"

"Not really. He'd run with some guys for a while, then they'd all get pissed at him, and somebody'd get hurt, usually not Eddie."

From Leo's right a voice said, "Eddie didn't let anyone push him around."

Leo jumped. She hadn't seen or heard Phyllis Bolton sneak up on her blind side. For a moment, her heart beat extra hard. "Hello, Ms. Bolton," she choked out.

The woman looked haggard. Without any makeup, her face was pale and her eyes small and hard. The light blue flannel shirt she wore was rumpled, and her jeans bagged so much Leo wondered if she'd suddenly lost weight. One hand held a smoldering cigarette. With a sigh, she dropped into a wingback chair facing her grandson. "I don't stand on formalities. Remember, you can call me Phyllis." She took a drag and let out a stream of smoke.

Leo said, "Stevie was telling me Eddie had complicated relation-ships."

"He did. But that's no excuse for someone to kill him."

Leo could do no more than nod.

Despite Phyllis's fatigue level, she also sounded angry. "I've talked to the damn police and the damn administrator at that damn center, and nobody knows a goddamn thing." She wheezed and coughed.

"Are you okay, Phyllis?" Leo asked. "Maybe Stevie should get your oxygen for you?"

"No," she growled out. "I'd rather smoke." She met Leo's gaze. "I know what you're thinking, but how the hell do you think I got the emphysema? Yeah, yeah, I smoked all these years, and I'm not giving it up now."

Leo bit back a retort, instead saying, "I may be working for the Department of Human Services, but I don't actually insert myself into people's lives in that way. I'm here to find out once and for all what happened to your nephew, that's all."

"Right, right," Phyllis said as she waved the cigarette in the air. "I know that. What do you want to know?"

"Can you think of anyone who had it in for Eddie?"

Stevie said, "Who didn't?"

Phyllis pointed her cigarette at him and said, "You can just shut up now."

>■<

Leo dropped by her apartment to make lunch. She sat at the tiny kitchen table and looked out the window, thinking about the visit with the Boltons. She felt sorry for Stevie. Leo had thought she was building a bit of a rapport with him, but after his grandmother shut him down, he said very little. If she wanted to revisit any of his comments, she'd have to be in contact some other time, perhaps as he walked home from school. All she knew for sure was the kid was miserable. Likely he'd always been able to fly under the radar while his Uncle Eddie acted out, but now that Eddie was dead, would he be the focus of his grandmother's ire?

The business about the inheritance bothered her. Nobody had mentioned anything about Eddie Bolton coming into any money. Making a mental note to ask Gary Clark, she cleared her dishes, left them soaking in the sink, and decided to drive by the house where the BDC supervisor, Shelley Clifton, lived.

Lights shone through the front window, and a blue Chevy truck with a camper was backed up to the garage.

Yes! Leo thought. She went up to the end of the block, turned around, and parked the car in front. As she approached the house, someone emerged from the shadows behind the camper, her arms full of paper sacks. The woman wore clunky Sorel winter boots with her jeans tucked into them. Her pale blue winter jacket was zipped all the way to the top, but the hood wasn't up. Her tousled hair was ash blonde.

When the woman caught sight of Leo, she stopped and stared, taking in Leo's appearance from the eye patch down. She seemed to decide Leo was all right and said, "Hello?"

Before Leo could respond, a man in jeans, work boots, and a red flannel shirt burst out of the house and down the front stairs. When he saw Leo, he slowed down and shot a look at the woman, then glanced back and cautiously said, "Hey there."

Valise in hand, Leo said, "Are you Mister and Mrs. Clifton?"

The woman shivered, her untidy hair blowing sideways in the wind. "Yes, who are you?" She didn't say it unpleasantly, but she seemed tired and irritated. Leo quickly introduced herself and told them she had questions about the BDC, ending by saying, "Could I have a few minutes of your time, Mrs. Clifton?"

"I guess." She looked at her husband uncertainly. "I can finish clearing out the kitchen goods in a while, Dwight."

"Okay. I'll clean out the cab."

"Let's go inside." The woman headed toward the house. "It's still warming up, but it's a far sight better in there than out here."

Leo followed her into a foyer. The front door closed with a loud whumping noise. She heard the hum of the furnace, but it hadn't yet taken the chill out of the air. Straight ahead a hallway led to a kitchen. To her left was a stairway, and at the foot of it were piles of things: a red ski suit, battered brown grocery bags, a Coleman lantern, boots, a heap of laundry, and more, all in a big messy jumble, as though the Cliftons had pitched everything there willy-nilly. Shelley Clifton set the bags she carried next to the pile of laundry and shoved it all out of the way with her foot. Leo figured that was exactly what their unpacking method was: dump and shove and tidy up later.

To the right and down a stair, the foyer led into another room. Gesturing toward it, Mrs. Clifton said, "Let's go sit in the family room. It's warmer there."

Leo started to slip out of her ankle-high leather boots, but Shelley Clifton stopped her. "Don't bother. Your toes will turn to little ice cubes." She let out a giggle. "The carpet feels so stiff it might as well be frozen. Just come on."

Leo followed her down the stair into a room with a television, stereo system, jumbo-sized couch, and two recliners. The house smelled stale, like a faint odor of burned toast from days ago. Her hostess claimed a recliner. Leo set her valise on a coffee table and lowered herself to the edge of the sofa, which was so cold and rigid it sent waves of arctic ice through the wool of her pants. She ignored her discomfort. "I'm sorry to bother you on a Sunday, especially when you're only now getting back from—from being gone."

"We meant to return yesterday, but Dwight hadn't gotten a deer, so we stayed an extra day."

"Oh, hunting." A sport Leo never much cared for. "Where do you hunt?"

"Up in Ontario, over the border, on some property owned by friends of Dwight's. Slim pickings this year, I'll tell you. Dwight never did bag a deer."

"Do you and your husband have kids you have to pick up from somewhere?"

"Oh, no. No kids yet. It's only Dwight and me for a little while longer. Until recently I've been focused on my career, but I'm pregnant and due to give birth the first week of May."

"How nice. Congratulations."

"Thank you. So what's this all about? Something happened at work?"

"Yes, something serious, Mrs. Clifton."

"Please, call me Shelley."

"All right, Shelley. Last Tuesday there was a death at the BDC."

Shelley gasped. "One of the kids?"

Leo watched the other woman's face closely. "Yes."

"Oh, my God." She brought her fingers to her lips. "Who?"

"His name was Edward Bolton."

She gasped. "I know him! I remember him." She scooted back in the recliner. "He was an angry, troubled kid as so many of our patients can be. Was it a fight—him and another patient—or what?"

"Actually, no. There was foul play involved."

"What? Foul play?"

Shelley Clifton's frown appeared genuine. Her blue eyes bored into Leo's, waiting expectantly for more information.

"The police have ruled it a homicide, and that's why I'm here, wanting to get information to continue to investigate the death." She gestured toward her valise. "Could I tape your comments so I don't have to take notes?"

"Uh, well, yeah. I guess."

Leo quickly set up her tape recorder. Shelley Clifton sat with a worried look on her face. The front door opened, and Dwight Clifton came in gripping a rifle in each hand. He stomped his boots, then slipped out of them. "Hon, I'm going to put away the rifles and hop in the shower."

"Okay," she called out.

He scrambled over the pile of stuff at the foot of the stairs and clumped upwards. Leo heard him banging around above, then the distant sound of water running. She pushed the button to record and looked up at her interview subject. The woman's blue eyes were sharp under arched eyebrows. She wore no makeup, but her oval face was naturally pretty. Leo wondered if she had even hit thirty yet. Right now, with her features set in an expression of worry, she seemed very youthful, so Leo started with that as an icebreaker. "You're very young to be the supervising social worker at the BDC. You must be quite good at your job."

"I work hard. I'm good with people, and not to brag, but I'm a great trainer. The powers that be figured out my skills early on, and I've been nicely rewarded for being able to get staff up to speed quickly. Really, you have to be organized and patient, and most jobs go well. Can you tell me what happened to the Bolton kid?"

"He was poisoned."

"Poisoned. I didn't expect you to say that."

"Somehow he got hold of a flask containing liquor laced with poison."

"I don't understand. Drugs and alcohol aren't allowed in here, not even cigarettes. How was he poisoned?"

"Nobody knows yet. That's why I'm here."

"I'm not sure how I can help you. I don't know anything about it. When did you say he died?"

"Tuesday."

"We left the week before on Wednesday and we've been gone all this time. Dwight can verify I went north and have been with him all along. We were with other hunters as well and they can—"

"Shelley, you're not a suspect. I'm sure the police will talk to you, too, but I'm not here because you're in any kind of trouble. I have a lot more to explain, but first, please tell me everything you know about Eddie Bolton."

"Let's see, his primary counselor is Mike Seaver, secondary Fritz Sorenson. I did the initial intake, and although I didn't write it up this way, he displayed all the symptoms of antisocial personality disorder. He's young to have that diagnosis, but his behavior in treatment and out in the world was classic APD. Impulsive actions, deceit, excessive aggression, disregard for others' safety, chronically chaotic interactions with others. It was easy for me to see he lacked any feeling of guilt about his actions."

"A sociopath in the making, then."

"Already made, actually."

"That's what the father of the girl injured in the car wreck said."

"He was a real piece of work, a firebomb waiting to go off. We needed to do a lot more assessment to determine his level of sociopathic tendencies. Obviously, I wasn't there for that. I assumed the other social workers and the psychiatrist would work on the assessments in my absence. Have you spoken to them?"

"Oh, yes, but since you're the chief supervisor, I wanted to get some other background from you. Tell me about the primary counselor, Seaver."

"Mike? He's been there since shortly after I came on board, so that's eight years. He started as an aide, got his certificate, and worked into a CD counseling position. He shows up for work on time and usually manages a decent rapport with the kids."

"I know you may not want to say anything negative about your staff, but I need to know the big picture."

"Well, sometimes Mike tries to be a little too buddy-buddy. Several times I've discussed with him that he can't be so concerned about the kids liking him. Of course, it helps if they like and trust the counselors and teachers and social workers, but most of these youths need structure and firm rules. Overall, Mike has always been solidly competent. His direct supervisor rated him proficient on his last evaluation. That's not exceeding standards, but he does meet all the standards."

"And Fritz?"

"Fritz is new. He follows every rule, goes by the book in every case. He's still a little too afraid he's going to make a mistake, but he's coming along nicely. He'll relax as time goes on. We've yet to do anything more than a preliminary eval on him at this point, but I imagine he'll be proficient as well."

"Let's go back to Eddie Bolton. If he'd made it through the court-ordered treatment, how do you think he would have done?"

Shelley sighed and shook her head. "No way of knowing, but I would expect not very well. I've worked with so many of these kids, and some of those you expect to succeed go out there and screw up royally. Others you thought for sure would mess up their lives and do really awful things will pull themselves up by their bootstraps and succeed."

Leo unzipped her coat and noticed the house was several degrees warmer. She wasn't willing to take her coat off yet though. "Can you make an educated guess?"

"With APD and his utter lack of concern for others, Eddie's outlook was poor. At intake wasn't very upset that he'd nearly killed his girlfriend in a car wreck. He displayed no guilt and little concern for her. The sociopathic angle with him stuck out in a big way. Maybe I'm being too harsh. I only spent a couple hours with him, and when kids first arrive, they often do put up a front that's tougher and meaner than they really are. But Eddie Bolton stood out, and I remember his comments and attitude very clearly. He made a practice of manipulating and exploiting others. He hadn't even been on the ward three hours before he was menacing the other patients. He was only there a few days before I left on vacation, but I clearly saw his aggressive behavior. His addition to the unit made problems for the counselors and the teachers."

"So you wouldn't be surprised to hear that he coldcocked Mike Seaver?"

"Oh, no, really?" She leaned forward, elbows on her knees. "Is Mike okay?"

"I think so."

"From the little I saw, Eddie had power issues and obstinance toward authority, not to mention a lot of anger. Perhaps he would have been diagnosed as having oppositional defiance disorder and anti-social personality traits. His propensity for alcohol and drug use made his actions potentially lethal."

Leo heard a muffled clunk above her, and the sound of water stopped. "You paint a pretty grim picture, Shelley."

"Please, don't get me wrong, Ms. Reese. I have a great deal of hope for many of these kids. I wouldn't work in this field if I didn't. I've seen kid after kid turn his life around because of our treatment program. Sure, some of them come back. Recidivism is high with CD treatment, and some of them get into lives of crime and violence. But a surprising number of them, when faced with consequences and given new tools for making better choices, actually get their lives together."

"I'm glad to hear that."

Shelley's voice took on a fervent tone. "So many of them come from poverty, alcoholism, physical and emotional abuse. It's amazing more of them don't turn into axe-murderers. I have to tell you, it's a humbling thing to run into a young man clerking in a store or working at some event or other and have him come up and talk about his life. This happened to me a few weeks ago. My husband and I were hiking up near Gooseberry Falls and came upon three young men. I didn't recognize any of them, but as we passed on the trail, one of the guys called out my name. He'd been through treatment with us three years ago. Now he's a sophomore at UMD majoring in history and economics. He said he'd chosen not to drink, and he thanked me for being there for him."

Leo knew what she meant. Out on the street she, too, dealt with people, both young and old, who occasionally sought her out to thank her for helping them. It didn't happen often enough though. Cops who needed that kind of affirmation in order to do their jobs usually didn't last long.

Clifton slipped her arms out of her coat and leaned back against it. "It makes the hard days worthwhile when something like that happens. And wait! Before you ask another question. I want to tell you something else. More than twenty million people need treatment for chemical dependency each year. Do you know how many receive it?"

"No, I'm not familiar with those particular stats."

"Ten percent, if that. There may be close to a million teens across the country who need CD treatment, but because of the cost or due to the barriers the insurance companies erect, the majority of them don't get it. What's wrong with this country? Studies show that the cost of treatment, though I admit it's high, is significantly lower than the havoc these kids wreak on society. Pay now or pay ten or twenty times more later. Why do we choose the latter?"

She rose, stomped up the stair, and took her boots off in the foyer. She hung her coat in a closet and came back down to the family room. "I get worked up over this topic. I need a cup of tea. You want me to make you a cup?"

"No need to go to any trouble."

"Grab your tape recorder and let's go into the kitchen." Before Leo could respond, Shelley Clifton spun around, bounded up the one stair, cut through the foyer, and went down the hall to the right. Leo took her coat off and left it on the couch. She scooped up the tape recorder and followed.

The kitchen looked brand-new. The wallpaper was off-white and decorated with little bunches of strawberries and blueberries. The border at the ceiling was maroon and dark blue, and the accents throughout the kitchen—toaster cover, dish towels, chair cushions—were also red and blue. As she seated herself at a table, Leo saw there was a light smattering of dust on everything.

Shelley Clifton busied herself with mugs and the kettle and made small talk about what a big pain it was to unpack from a long camping trip. "I did get a lot of reading done," she said. "Some days I holed up in the camper with the heater, and Dwight and the guys went out for hours. It was restful." The teakettle whistled, and she turned off the burner and poured water into the two mugs. "I hope you like orange tea. That's all I've got at the moment."

"Yes, sounds great. Thank you."

She delivered the mugs to the table along with teaspoons and grabbed a sugar bowl from a counter. "Do you put milk in your tea—never mind. I don't have any."

"I don't, though, so no loss." Leo wrapped her hands around the mug and relished the warmth. The kitchen was cozier than the other room, and the spicy scent of the tea relaxed her in a way she hadn't felt all day.

"Back to work." Shelley pointed at the tape recorder. "We better stay on task before you run out of tape."

Leo smiled. She was starting to like this woman, and she felt like a traitor since she'd withheld the rest of the BDC story from her. "Let's talk about your job. Who reports to you?"

"Everyone in the treatment area. Not the schoolteachers or Mort and Mister Robeson's administrative staff, but I'm in charge of coordinating all the medical areas, treatment, and social work services. Myself and Sylvia Wentworth cover the chem dep program oversight, and I supervise the three daily shift supervisors and the two weekenders. They, in turn, directly manage the majority of staff. It's kind of a patchwork of who does what based on whatever the needs are at the time and who's got what skills."

"And you answer to?"

"Mort Milford."

Conscious of her verb tense, Leo asked, "How has Milford been as a boss?"

Shelley stirred her tea, pinned her spoon to the side of the cup, and took a sip. "He's hands-off and lets me do my job. He was there long before I was, and he's the one who trained me in." She set the mug down. "Mort's a funny guy—fastidious and persnickety. Keeps to himself. In all the years I've known him, I've never been to his house or anything, but he does a lot of volunteering in the community. Behind his stiff façade, he's a kindhearted man. So I don't know him well personally, but I respect his judgment. Not to tell tales out of school, but I have to say he's not all that good with people."

"I always wonder why certain personalities end up choosing people professions."

"Me, too. Why go through all the training to become a teacher or social worker—"

"Or a cop."

"Right. Why pick those fields if you don't enjoy relating to people, especially when they're in crisis? I'm not sure why Mort went into social work. He's quiet and introverted, and I don't think he likes people all that well. But he's a wizard when it comes to numbers and analysis. We went through a budgetary crisis at one point a few years ago. The state legislature cut funding to private facilities, and it looked like we were going out of business. He and Mister Robeson put their heads together and not only found some alternative sources of funding, but also streamlined operations."

"Were there layoffs?"

Shelley nodded. "We lost a total of six positions, but five of the six staff weren't very productive, and the sixth person got hired back after only a few weeks. We've been running a tight ship ever since."

"You mentioned alternative sources of funding?"

"A combination of grants and donations, I think. I didn't ask for the details. We got over the rough spot, and we've been doing fine ever since."

"Do you work closely with the owner, Mister Robeson?"

"Never. He's not in the office all that often, at least not when I am. Tends to work early mornings or late in the evening, so I don't see him much. I think he spends a lot of time glad-handing and beating the bushes for funding."

"What's he like as a person?"

"I have little to do with Mister Robeson. Mort handles pretty much everything having to do with the program. Mister Robeson is usually aloof, doesn't spend much time outside of his office. He's rarely seen anywhere in the facility except in his or Mort's office. He's pleasant whenever I do see him, though. He's always liked me, I think. I'm sure Mort gives him good reports because Mister Robeson has always treated me respectfully."

"Has anything seemed unusual around the BDC lately?"

"No," Shelley said, shaking her head. "Same stress level. Same procedures. No big changes or anything. It's been the same old thing. Say, we've ranged far afield. What does all this have to do with the poisoning of the Bolton kid? Was it possibly an accident?"

Leo hesitated, and suddenly the look Shelley Clifton gave her was penetrating. "What aren't you telling me, Ms. Reese? I've been completely forthcoming with you."

"Call me Leona."

"Leona, then. What else is going on?"

"Thursday, two days after Eddie Bolton's death, Morton Milford was found dead in his office."

Shelley's mouth dropped open. She pushed her tea away, and some of it slopped over the side and made a puddle for the mug to sit in. Her eyes blinked rapidly, and Leo watched the woman's face go through a series of contortions. Then she took a deep breath and looked up with fire in her eyes. "You've got a lot of nerve coming into my house, asking questions, and withholding information like that!"

Leo wanted to apologize, wanted to smooth things over, but she sat quietly. Shelley rose and went to the refrigerator. She reached up and took down a box of tissues. When she returned to the table and sank into the chair, her eyes were filled with tears. She used a tissue to blot them.

"What happened to Mort?"

"He was murdered."

"Oh, God." She couldn't stop the torrent of tears. "Mort's dead? I can't . . . I can't . . ." She pressed a tissue to her face and sat shaking for a moment.

"I'm sorry for the loss of your friend and colleague, Shelley. Very sorry."

"Who did it?"

"The police are working to find out. For now, the BDC is closed."

"Closed?" Now she met Leo's eyes, fear on her face.

"For the time being, all of the patients have been moved. Robeson is doing all he can to reopen as soon as possible. After two unsolved homicides, though, the program was deemed unsafe to continue until this is sorted out."

"Who would want to kill Mort?"

"I was hoping you might know."

Shelley plucked another tissue from the box and blew her nose. "How did he die?"

"He was strangled."

"Who the hell would do that to Mort?" Shelley closed her eyes and took a deep breath. After a moment, she sighed. Her face was red and her eyes sad, but Leo saw Shelley Clifton was not a woman who stayed rattled for long.

Leo said, "Let's back up again and consider. Has anything been different at the BDC lately?"

Shelley mopped up her spilled tea with a tissue. She took another wad of them out of the box, caught the last of the liquid, and rose to toss the soggy mess in the garbage under the sink. When she stood and turned back to Leo, she said, "Not a single thing comes to mind. Nothing. We've consistently had thirty to forty-five kids in-patient. Lots of misbehavior, but nothing homicidal. Only one person has quit lately."

"Who?"

"Chet Myers. He got married in September. He'd planned for months to move to Minneapolis with his bride. There was no surprise or problem there. He can't have anything to do with this. We've got a couple newer staff, brought on in the last three or four months."

"Angela Vang and Glenn Dorris."

"Right. Nothing remarkable there." Shelley sniffed and shook her head slowly for a good five seconds. "I'm sorry. I can't think of anything. Not a thing that would cause the deaths of two people. I wish I could. I very much wish I knew something."

She folded her arms over her chest as though she were suddenly chilled to the bone. Leo had started to sweat sometime earlier. Now that Shelley Clifton knew the details, she didn't think there was anything else she'd get out of her today. "I know this is terrible news to come home to."

"Yes, yes, it is. But I probably should thank you. When I show up at work tomorrow, I'll be emotionally prepared."

"I suspect you won't be there very long. You'll be talking to the police. They'll want to ask you a lot of the same questions I did, and then you'll likely be off work for a while."

She groaned. "I can't get over this. What a mess. I don't think I know anything to help, which is maddening. But I'll tell them what I can."

"And if you think of anything else, will you let me know?" Leo slid her business card across the table. Shelley didn't step over to pick it up, and it came to a stop next to a small drop of tea. Leo watched as the card absorbed the dot of liquid. It left a ragged tan stain on the edge of the card.

# Chapter Twelve

The first thing Thom said to Leo Monday morning when she stopped by his cubicle was, "Whoa, Leo, are you ever in big trouble with the detectives."

"What?"

"Just got off the phone with Brandtson."

"And?"

"He's pissed beyond compare."

"I'm beginning to think that guy has it in for me. What's his problem now?"

"From what I can tell, he's saying you compromised the investigation by talking to a witness yesterday."

"Oh, please. He must be talking about Shelley Clifton."

"I don't know. He hung up on me after making a few veiled threats. So you talked to her?"

"I did."

"What did you do? Stake out her house?"

"No, be real. I drove by, and she and her husband were arriving home from vacation. They'd been hunting up in Canada. She's been gone since before Eddie Bolton died."

"Any useful dirt?"

"Sorry. Not a thing that helps. She loves her job, got along well with Milford and Robeson, and was shocked to tears about Milford's death. She's not anywhere close to my size, so even if she had managed to sneak back to town, she couldn't have strangled Milford without help. I don't think she has anything to do with this."

"I'm sure the cops will check out all the angles. So what have we got now?"

"Big fat goose egg."

"That's what I was thinking."

She glanced back over her shoulder. "Where's Finn?"

"Not in yet. Neither is his partner, I mean, his *non*-partner."

Leo laughed and leaned in to say softly, "I wouldn't claim him either." She gave a toss of her head. "What about old Grumpy Guts?"

"Not a word to me. He's been working quietly in his office."

"Without even counting the Clifton interview and the funeral, the paperwork I did here and at home adds up to about five hours, so I'm going to offset that time by working on your case."

"Our case."

"It's *your* case officially."

"Whatever."

"Any news about Seaver?"

Thom shook his head. "Not that I've heard. I'm starting to think maybe you're right. Next spring some poor person is going to uncover his body in a snowdrift."

"I hope not."

"I was thinking about this case off and on all day yesterday, and something occurred to me. What if Eddie Bolton actually has nothing to do with this case? What if the flask wasn't supposed to end up anywhere he'd find it, and it was totally an accident that it did?"

"Good theory. The cops assumed the flask was hidden somewhere on the BDC premises, but he could have picked it up anywhere."

"He couldn't have hidden it in his pockets." Leo gestured at the pockets of her slacks. "The front pockets of the crappy jeans the kids are issued were cut out."

"What do you mean?"

"It's much better if they don't have deep pockets for anything dangerous, like knives or drugs. So they're cut out before they're issued to the patients."

"I didn't know that. But don't they have back pockets?"

"Right, but they're flat and not very big. A flask would have been visible. Even if he put it down his pants, it would have been noticeable. From what the witnesses all said, when Eddie left the cafeteria Tuesday morning, he had nothing on him."

"So he picked it up on the way or else found it in his room."

"One or the other, I guess," she said. "I keep wondering about William Cattrall. What if the poison was meant for him, and we're looking at this all wrong?"

"Who'd want William dead and what would he have to do with Milford and his death?"

"I don't know. I did some background checks on William and his family. His dad is a software designer. His mom works in real estate. They earn piles of dough."

"No wonder they're on a cruise."

"They make good money, but it's not like they're millionaires or anything. William is their only kid."

"He doesn't have a record," Thom said, "not one I recall."

"No. First offense for him. He's never been in any trouble, so his parents probably felt all right about leaving him with his best friend's family. They won't be back for another week, and I imagine this'll be a big surprise for them."

"What kind of parents ditch their kid for half a month and don't even give him a way to contact them? He doesn't belong in juvie, that's for sure."

"Does William go to Denfield High?"

Thom sifted through the files on his desk and pulled one out to open. "No. Duluth Central."

"Maybe we ought to go check him out with the principal and guidance counselors there. I want to do some further checking on Eddie and Stevie Bolton at Denfield, too."

"I'll hit Central if you hit Denfield."

"Deal."

Thom said, "I might stop and check on William, too. I liked the kid, and he seemed pretty lost."

"Back to the question of Eddie and the flask. If he picked it up on the way to his room, a whole new can of worms opens up. Finn said during the course of the three shifts, there can be as many as sixty staff and quite a few other service providers who frequent the building. If the flask was meant for anyone else, how do we ever sort that out? To make matters worse, what if one of the staff had the flask on hand to use elsewhere? What if the murder wasn't intended for anyone at the BDC and was meant as a special treat for some other poor sucker?"

"Jeez, Leo, you have a vivid imagination. I hadn't thought of it that way."

"We need to find out if the videotapes have given the cops any more details."

Thom said, "Those halls are all wired up. If Eddie stopped anywhere on the way to his room, there ought to be some indication on a tape."

"I'll call Clark this morning. I need to ask him about Seaver anyway. For all we know, maybe the cops do have him now and haven't mentioned it."

"If Brandtson's pissed enough, that could be true. Did you have some conflict with him you haven't told me about?"

"No. I don't know why he's on my case. If it weren't for Clark, we wouldn't know a damn thing about either of these cases. They expect us to keep them apprised, but the road doesn't go both ways."

"Brandtson plays his cards too close to his chest. That's not how Clark operates."

"Luckily. Otherwise we might never know anything." She checked her watch. "I better get busy. I'm leaving the Clifton tape with Tonya to transcribe, then I'll take a trip up to Denfield High. Along the way, I'll check in with Mike Seaver's grandmother again."

"Just to get our stories straight," Thom said, "if His Nastiness asks, where are you?"

"I got a complaint about an orderly at the Granger Group Home, so I'm going to swing by and get statements. I don't know how long it will take me, but I'm going there first."

"I'll wait for Kryzinski and Finn to show up and see what they know. In the meantime, I've got two deaths by natural causes at nursing homes, so I've got to issue that paperwork. Oh, and by the way, I forwarded you an e-mail from our Fearless Leader. He's issued a demand for the two agents and me to update him at four p.m. today."

"All right. Maybe I'll have something to share with you by then. Call me on the cell if you get any hot news, and I'll do the same. Otherwise, I'll be back in the early afternoon."

She left the Clifton tape for Tonya and returned to her cubicle to call Gary Clark, who sounded pleased to hear from her.

"Hi, Gary," she said. "I hear my head's on the chopping block."

"Nah, nothing that bad. Ben wanted to get to the Clifton woman first, that's all."

"I taped my interview and would be happy to dub a copy or hand over the transcript once it's typed."

"Do you think Clifton is involved in any way at all?"

"No, I don't. I don't believe she had a motive or opportunity. She seemed concerned about the Bolton death, but she was genuinely upset by Milford's passing."

"Send over the typed transcript as soon as you can, and if we want to listen to the tape, I'll let you know."

"How's it going with the BDC videotapes?"

"Slow."

"Thom and I were talking about the Bolton kid and wondering if he could have picked up the flask somewhere in the facility after leaving the cafeteria."

"Not a possibility. We're certain it was in his room. We think in the bathroom."

"How can you be sure?"

"We've got every step of his passage on tape except for a brief moment at a corner where he steps out of range for two seconds. He continued down the hall during those two seconds before coming back into camera range. We checked it out. On every camera, we can see him approach and walk away, and he's got nothing in his hands, nothing in his pockets."

"So much for that theory."

"We cops are nothing if not thorough. We found a damp indentation in the towels under the bathroom sink. We had the towels tested, and the substance was bourbon laced with potassium cyanide. The poisoned container had been stuck under the top towel."

"Aha! The towel man did it."

"I wish," Clark muttered ruefully. "We tracked the towels from the outside laundry provider to the delivery company to the loading area of the secure dock beside the kitchens. Dirty towels go out in big cloth bags and come back clean in smaller cloth bags. They're stacked on shelves, and the cleaners and janitors distribute them as needed."

"I suppose you've done the third degree on all those cleaners and janitors?"

"We've done complete background checks and interviews of all of the people who had access. The housekeeper who cleans the wing Bolton was in is a recent immigrant from Honduras. She's legal, but her language skills are still pretty rough. We got an interpreter and grilled her. She's got no motive. We checked her finances. Not a cent out of place for her or her husband. Dead end there."

"Could you determine when she last cleaned?"

"Oh, yeah. She mucks out the bathrooms in that wing on Tuesday, Thursday, and Saturday, generally starting around ten a.m. while the boys are out of their rooms. She's got Sunday and Monday off. She hadn't yet worked in that room on Tuesday. In fact, she hadn't even arrived at work yet."

"Okay, what about Seaver? He turn up yet?"

"Nope."

"Seems suspicious."

"Yup."

"Anything worth noting at either of the funerals?"

"Not a thing. The attendees all belonged there, and none of the cars in the area were suspicious. I will say one thing, I had no clue Morton Milford was such a civic treasure."

"In what way?"

"Through his temple, he was part of something called Justice Squared. Involved in lots of social justice initiatives. His main area was assisting the homeless and helping with coordination of food shelves. He was also a leader in his temple's B'nai B'rith Youth Organization. He served as a volunteer advisor for high school-age students."

"Is there a link there to any of the kids at the BDC? Any inappropriate relationships?"

"Leona! You're such a cynic. You're making me look like Polly Purebred. No, we haven't been able to connect a single Jewish kid with Milford and the BDC. There have, of course, been Jewish kids in the facility in the past, but none at the moment."

"Another dead end."

"Apparently. Far as I can tell, this guy was well-loved. We talked to scores of shocked grievers from Temple Israel. Milford's heavy church involvement behind the scenes made him a lot of friends. There were over eight hundred mourners at the memorial service."

"Wow, I hadn't heard that."

"We spent all weekend on follow-up. The Bolton funeral was a heck of a lot easier to handle."

"I bet."

"No leads, but I'll keep you posted. I still think our best lead is Seaver. I've got a hunch he's the one. Something funky was going on at the BDC, and he must have been in the thick of it. I wish we could nail it down."

"I know you and Brandtson are probably doing the same, but our BCA guys are sifting through financial records, which might tell tales. I'll let you know if we find anything."

"Maybe we could meet for a drink after work and swap details."

Leo hesitated. She didn't want to alienate Gary Clark, but how was she to put a stop to his interest in her? She weaseled out and said, "I think Thom will have more details to share with you. Our boss made him point man on this case. I'm helping on the side."

"Oh, I see."

"I'll update Thom and have him call you later today, all right? I have to run now. Later."

She hung up the phone and sat for a moment. Clark seemed like a decent enough guy. Why would he be chasing her skirts? She closed her eyes, imagining how she looked in the eye patch. Why was he even interested?

She pulled her cell from her valise, dialed Daria, and got her voicemail. "Hey, Daria. Sorry I missed you. Are you at your conference yet? I've got a busy day ahead. I hope yours goes well." She stopped, feeling an unexpected sadness sweep over her. "I miss you. Maybe call me tonight when you get a break. Call even if it's late. I'll be up. Love you."

She snapped the phone shut and dropped it back into the valise with a sigh. Onward and upward, she thought. Granger Home, here I come.

Leo got the visit to the group home out of the way first, discovering that the complaint wasn't exactly what the intake form indicated at all. It wasn't an orderly against whom the complaint was lodged but a fellow resident. A mentally ill woman had confused a bossy and belligerent patient with the people in charge and secretly called to complain. The workers at the home had already figured out what was going on and moved the complainant to the second floor, away from the woman who'd been bothering her. Three short interviews later, Leo was finished and only needed to write up the paperwork to close the case.

She got in the car and cranked up the heat. Delicate fluffy flakes of snow fell. They hit the windshield fully formed, but in the space of a couple seconds, the fragile flakes disintegrated, becoming slushy, dime-sized smudges. She turned on the wipers, swept it all away, and pulled away from the curb.

The narrow street hadn't been plowed, so she drove through furrows of snow four inches deep. At the stop sign, the car slid, and her stomach dropped. She pumped the brakes and got the Corolla under control. Last thing she wanted was to skid out to the middle of the intersection into traffic. She turned carefully onto a plowed street and headed for the high school.

After the school secretary sent a student runner out with a message, Leo sat for fifteen minutes in a warm, stuffy waiting area before the vice principal returned to the office. He was easily seven feet tall and dressed in a worn black suit and black tennis shoes. The top of his head was shiny bald, but a lot of thick, wiry gray hair puffed out from the sides and back of his head, giving him the appearance of Bozo the Clown in monochrome.

"I'm Vice Principal Hal Dexter." His voice echoed, as though it were coming from a deep well rather than from high over her head. "Can I help you, miss?"

She rose. "I'm Leona Reese from the State Department of Human Services." He insisted on seeing her ID, and he kept surreptitiously looking her over. She wondered if the forest green pantsuit she wore met his approval. Did he think it clashed with her navy-blue eye patch? When he handed back her ID, she said, "I'm here about Edward and Steven Bolton."

Bushy gray eyebrows raised, and his face took on an expression of alarm. "You have been informed that Edward Bolton has passed away?"

"Oh, yes. That's why I'm here. I need to speak to you about his character as well as Steven's situation."

"Come into my office."

Leo followed him into a small room made all the tighter by the huge desk sitting in the center. The mammoth wood desk was hiked up in the air with four-by-four blocks under each leg. He gestured for her to sit in one of the chairs facing the desk, and he sat in a wooden swivel chair. She felt like a three-year-old. He sat up so high, and her chair put her so far below him she was pretty sure she could count his nose hairs. She held back a snicker and forced her face into serious mode. "So, Mister Dexter, we're trying to figure out who had it in for Edward Bolton."

"I've already talked to the police. So has the principal. They've talked to teachers and guidance counselors as well. I gave them free run of the place. We're all talked out."

"Please don't say that. It's very important to get this sorted out. We have to punish whoever is responsible for the young man's death."

"I'll tell you who's responsible."

"Who?" She sat forward in her chair.

"Eddie Bolton." When she frowned, he nodded, dropping his chin nearly to his chest over and over. Leo watched the slow bobbing, wondering if Mister Dexter knew how bizarre he looked. Did he do that with the kids he disciplined? She wasn't sure how anyone could take him seriously.

"That kid brought this upon himself with his actions. Are you familiar with the Law of Karma?"

"You mean what goes around comes around? That concept?"

"Ahem, well, in part. The Law of Karma is central to religions originating in India. Hinduism and Buddhism, for instance, adhere to the principle. Karma is made up of all that a young man has done, is currently doing, and will do. It affects the individual and all the people with whom he comes in contact. Eddie Bolton's accumulated Karma—the effects of all his misguided, misbegotten decisions—eventually caught up with him. Every action he took left a trace of Karmic residue, and that residue finally built up to a point with lethal consequences."

Leo didn't quite know what to say. She hadn't expected a dissertation on kismet and cosmic principles, but she felt if he was to cooperate with her, she'd have to humor him. "I spoke to the parents of his girlfriend, Kimberly Nichols."

"Now that situation is such a shame. What a bright and talented girl like Kimberly saw in that hellion is beyond me. Did her parents tell you she tested in the upper ten percentile on her college entrance exams? The world was her oyster until the residue from that miscreant rubbed off on her."

"Mister Dexter, could you tell me what exactly Eddie Bolton did to merit the level of antipathy you feel for him?"

He took a deep breath and cleared his throat. "You name it, he did it. Set fires, beat up other students, petty vandalism, threats, sexual harassment. Whatever he wanted to do, he did it. His level of violence was quite frightening."

"Why couldn't he be suspended—or expelled—from school?"

Dexter shook his head. "That's the problem. He always had an alibi, an excuse, or someone to lie for him. Sometimes I could tell he was compelling other students to back him up, but I was unable to get them to recant. He could be charming. Once he persuaded a group of underclass girls and boys to get up on the roof and moon the incoming school buses."

Leo couldn't contain a half-smile.

"Yes, it sounds so innocuous, so juvenile and harmless, but Ms. Reese, it wasn't. That sort of ploy is symptomatic of the type of power he regularly exerted to hurt or humiliate fellow students. He managed to exert an unbelievable level of influence over the young people here, and we adults were helpless to stop it. I *knew* what he was doing, but I wasn't able to prove it. These days, an administrator has to do a lot of paperwork, and evidence of misdeeds must be proven conclusively. I was able to suspend him a few times but never expel. It's a shame. Perhaps if I'd been successful, Kimberly Nichols wouldn't be languishing in the hospital."

"So who would want him dead?"

"Let's see." He raised a huge hand and counted off the classifications. "Dozens of the students, most of the teachers, every single custodian, and any bus driver he ever rode with. Oh, and all the lunch ladies. He was particularly rude to them."

"I was led to believe he was rather incorrigible, but you make him sound like a mass murderer."

"It was only a matter of time, Ms. Reese. A matter of time."

"What about his cousin, Steven?"

"An entirely different personality there. Steven is quiet and shy. He's not a bad student, but he's not the best either. I can check, but I'm under the impression he earns solid B grades. He's always stood up for Eddie, but sometimes I think he's been a little ashamed of Eddie's actions."

"So they weren't close?"

"Hard to say. Eddie often arrived at school with Steven in tow. Once Eddie got a car, they rode together. But when they got into the building, they parted company. Eddie was a senior. Steven is a sophomore."

"But they're less than a year apart in age."

"I'm not sure whether Steven got left back sometime in the past or if his parents decided to hold him another year for kindergarten. Perhaps his birthday is a few days before the October cut-off date. A lot of parents force immature kids into kindergarten to save on daycare. Maybe that didn't happen with him. Look, miss, I've told everything I know to the police. Everyone has. What more can we tell you?"

"Good question." Leona didn't know what direction to go, so she rose. "Perhaps I could speak with Steven Bolton?"

Dexter unfolded himself from his chair and towered over her. "Excuse me for a moment."

He went out to the main office. From where Leo stood in the doorway, she couldn't make out what he whispered to one of the secretaries, but the woman shook her head. Dexter covered the twenty feet between him and Leona in five long strides looking like a strangely upright water-skeeter.

"I'm sorry but you can't speak to Steven today. He's out ill. It's just as well. I'd have had to contact his guardian to get permission anyway."

His voice had an odd tone to it, as though he was relieved not to have to contact Phyllis Bolton. Leo debated asking why, but then decided to hold off. She reached out, glad Hal Dexter would have to find her hand and not the other way around. "I know you're busy, so I appreciate you taking the time. If you think of anything else I should know, please don't hesitate to call. Thank you for your help, Mister Dexter."

"You're welcome." He let go of her hand, and she moved to the door. He looked like he wanted to say something else but thought better of it. She had the distinct impression it would have been something along the lines of "Good luck finding the murderer so we can all pin a medal on him."

➤ ■ ◄

Leo knocked on Mike Seaver's door and waited. When the door opened a crack, she looked through the glass of the screen door and said, "Mrs. Hardaway? Remember me?"

"Well, of course." The door whipped open, revealing Dorothy Hardaway in a dark purple pantsuit and the same pink slippers Leo had seen during the last visit. "Ms. Keen, was it?"

"Reese. Leona Reese."

"Yes, that's right. Have you brought me news about Mike?"

Her face looked so hopeful Leo hated to have to answer no. She shook her head. "I was hoping you had news for me."

Dorothy Hardaway bit her lip. "I have to tell you I'm getting plumb worried. Mike doesn't pull vanishing acts like this. It's not like him."

"Did you keep my card?"

"Yes, I did."

"If he shows up, please have him contact me. And why don't you give me your phone number. If I hear anything at all, I'll give you a call." Leo took out a business card, wrote down the number Dorothy Hardaway gave her, and tucked it in her coat. She already had the number written down back at the office, but she thought asking for it would make the older woman feel better.

Back on the road she puzzled over Seaver's disappearance. He had been very clear about wanting to keep his job. Although he was initially rude, when it came down to giving her information, he'd been mostly helpful, though she didn't believe he'd told her everything, and the information from William Cattrall confirmed that. Still, it was a long way from breaking facility rules and providing a few select boys with cigarettes to committing a murder.

# Chapter Thirteen

Immersed in the report she was typing, Leo didn't hear her name called until Tonya was in her doorway. "Sorry to bug you, Leo, but I've got a lady on the phone who needs to talk to you. She says it's about the Milford case."

"Put her through to Thom's voicemail."

"I already tried that, but she's insistent. She only wants to talk to you."

"All right. I'll take it."

Tonya disappeared and soon the phone rang. Leo hardly got a chance to identify herself before she heard a whispery voice.

"Ms. Reese, I'm the daughter of Mister Milford. I need to see you."

Leo fumbled through her notes, phone clenched between her ear and shoulder. She found the pages from the Milford interview. "Traci? Traci Francisco?"

"I'm Morton's daughter."

"Ms. Francisco, I'm not exactly assigned to this case. You need to talk to—"

"Please, no. I need to speak to a woman. I'd like to give you some information about my father that you simply must know. But I don't want to talk to a man."

I knew it, Leo thought. Something about Milford *was* off. She asked her to come into the office and started to give her the address.

"I can't," the woman interrupted. "I don't have a ride. But I'll be here in town at the Andresen Arms for a short while longer, you know, up the hill from Division?"

"In the row of historic apartment houses?"

"That's it. The street parking is bad, but there'll be spaces in the lot on the right."

Leo took down the number. "I can zip over now. I'll be there in a few minutes."

"Thanks." The line went dead.

Tonya appeared in the doorway again. "Do you know when Thom will be back?"

"No idea. I'm not sure which leads he's following right now." She shrugged into her coat. "I'm going up to meet a witness for him who's only in town for a little bit longer. Tell him Morton Milford's daughter, Traci Francisco, has some vital information for us, and I went to get it. If he gets back anytime soon, have him meet me at the Andresen Arms. Otherwise, tell him I'll meet him back here no later than four." Tonya wrote down the address, and Leo hastened off.

The sky was full of leaden clouds. Any bits of sun that got through were reflected brightly on the fresh snow. Leo donned her sunglasses, which fit oddly on the left side because of the strap for the eye patch. She jerked at the frames, twisted them one way, then the other, and gave up in frustration. No matter what she did, they weren't going to sit on her nose properly. She was sick of the damn patch and couldn't wait to get rid of it.

She slowed the rental car near the entrance to the parking lot's uphill driveway. The apartment houses on either side were built on top of a slope, and an ice-encrusted incline, about fifteen feet long, eased up to the lot. Before she could make the turn, a public works truck with a giant orange plow attached to the front came down the incline.

What the hell was it doing up there? Fuming, she backed up to give it room to turn in front of her. The vehicle lumbered down the street like a giant orange elephant, clots of snow spitting out from under its massive wheels.

She goosed the gas and went up the incline. The city crew had pushed a huge mound of snow to the left. The monstrous, whale-sized wall was so high it blocked the view of the ground floor apartment windows. With so much snow piled up, the lot was tight. The car's rear end fishtailed on a slick patch of ice. At the far end of the lot sat the only other vehicle, and she was glad it wasn't near enough for her to slide into.

She backed into a slot next to the other building and sat feeling reluctant to get out of the cozy car. She closed her eyes and let a little wave of lethargy pass over her. After a moment, she gathered up her valise and looked at the swell of snow ahead. There was a space to the far left barely enough room for a person to squeeze past. Assuming it led to the path to the apartment's front door, she exited into the chilly air and headed for the gap. She slid her boot forward, keeping her ungloved hand on the side of the car for balance. The plow had scraped away inches of snow, leaving only the hardened glaze from the sleet a few nights previous. She picked her steps wisely, with short, careful strides.

The wind was sharp, and she smelled something yeasty, like bread baking. She lifted her nose to sniff and promptly slipped. Recovering her balance in the middle of the lot, she heard the rev of an engine. The dirt-brown car from the other end of the lot pulled out and turned toward her. Leo expected it to wait for her to pass. Instead, the driver hit the gas.

She didn't have time to think. Instinct kicked in and she leapt forward. Her right boot heel twisted, but she managed to take another step. She glanced to the side and saw the car's grill coming at her, dirty with splotches of mud.

She let out a shriek, dropped her valise and dove out of the way. Something hard as a hammer blow struck her right calf. A white-hot current of pain exploded up her leg, seething and burning like a fire. She spun. Skidded into the huge drift on her butt. Piles of snow from the top shifted and crumbled down upon her. She struggled to sit up, snow in her one good eye.

An engine roared. She heard gears grinding and tried to rise. When she put weight on her right leg, she slipped in pain onto the icy ground. Frantic, she used her other knee to push forward, her hands grappling for purchase in the tall snowbank. She might be safe if she could get over the pile of plowed snow and slide to the other side. She got to her feet, dragging her useless leg behind her. Slipped. Fell. Cracked her elbow against frozen ground. She rolled and looked over her left shoulder.

The brown car backed up. They're going to get a run at me, Leo thought. Oh, my God.

Her heart beat so loud, it sounded like she was inside a bass drum. "Stop!" she screamed. She squinted, trying to see who was behind the wheel. With renewed energy, she rose, teetering on her sore leg. No strength to push off, but she tried anyway. Grabbed at snow. Pushed up. Beat helplessly at the dense mound.

I'm going to die here and never even know who's in that car.

She staggered along the edge of the snowbank, hastening for the gap, hoping to get around it in time.

Wheels spun and shrieked. The brown vehicle lurched forward. Leo slipped and fell forward, her knee hitting the sheet of ice with a cracking sound. It hurt too much to crawl. She slid sideways and landed on her butt. Using her elbows and one good heel, she struggled like a backstroking crab until her head came in contact with the plowed mountain of snow.

Through a shower of flakes, she saw a shiny white sail off to her right. It looked like an enormous ghost frigate making its way on an ice-encrusted sea. Cutting through the lot like a windjammer, it sped to the center and intercepted the brown car. When the brown sedan struck the white nose, the ground shook. Leo saw sparks. A shrieking, grating sound rent the silence.

The car and the broad-sided white savior ship slid toward her, coming fast. With her back against the frigid pile of snow, she had nowhere to go and knew she'd be crushed. Choking in a last breath, she pushed away one more time, awaiting a collision. As the pile of conjoined metal glided toward her, she looked up at a porthole in the ship and met desperate brown eyes.

Thom.

The shifting, sliding mass of brown and white metal slowed and came to a rest, but not before catching up to her and pressing her farther into the snowbank than she could have forced herself.

Blocked in, wet rubber against her face, she found she was pushing at a tire in front of her chest. The plastic of a silver hubcap was solid against her jacket. The smell of oil and exhaust wafted over her, and she heard a whirring sound. A porthole opened, and Thom's head poked out directly above her. "Leo!" Thom's voice was frantic. "Leo! Can you hear me?"

She groaned.

"Can you get out? Shit! I'm blocked in. I can't help you."

With a gasp, she wriggled to the right and managed to free herself from the compressed space, but not before showering down a new load of snow on her head and back. At eye level, a door slid to the side, revealing a dark opening. She reached. Grabbed the edge and used her good leg to lever herself up and forward, into the opening.

"Leo!" he called out.

"I'm okay," she panted. "I'm all right." Face pressed against the damp rubber matting on the floor, she clutched the metal support of the passenger's seat inside Thom's van.

"Get your legs in. Gotta close the slider."

Her leg ached. She pulled it toward her and groaned again. Tears blurred her vision. She gulped in air, realizing she was safe in the hold of this strange sailing ship. When Thom reversed and separated from the other car, it sounded like the shriek of seagulls.

She closed her good eye for a moment and lay curled in a fetal position, waiting to catch her breath.

Wham!

The van jerked and slid to the side. "Whoa!" Thom hollered.

"What?" With difficulty, Leo clambered to her knees and looked out the van's side window. The driver of the brown car was now backing away for another go at them. The bleak afternoon sun shone down upon the car's front window, and Leo couldn't see inside. All she could make out in the windshield's reflection was a strange web from the trees along the west side of the lot.

"Hold on!" Thom wrenched the wheel and hit the gas with the hand throttle. Leo was thrown back and landed with a jerk, her shoulder blades thrust hard against the rear seats. Through gritted teeth, Thom said, "Get a seatbelt on, Leo."

She almost said, "Aye, aye," but saved her energy for pulling herself up into the rear bench seat. The material of the seat cushion was rough against her cold hands and the belt mechanism awkward. Thom put the van in reverse, and she managed to get turned around with the shoulder belt over her wet jacket. As it clicked across her, Thom grabbed the headrest of the passenger seat next to him, looked over his shoulder, and gazed past her, out the rear window. "Hold on!" He backed up and turned, smashed into the snowbank. The brown car collided with his left quarter-panel, bounced off, and weaved out of control toward Leo's rental car. The Toyota took the brunt of the collision on the driver's side, leaving the vehicle horribly dented.

The headrest felt like a rock against the back of Leo's head. Thom slapped the van into drive. The engine whined. The tires spun, then grabbed purchase. The brown car slid into them again, and Leo reeled forward.

Thom turned aside and revved the engine again. "C'mon, you bastard! Do it!"

The van shot forward. Leo heard a horrible scraping noise and felt a shuddering vibration next to her left shoulder. Thom forced the van past the brown car.

And then they were free.

When the van's right tire hit the entrance incline, they tilted like a speedboat in a quick turn. There was nothing in front of her for Leo to grab. She reached to the side and held onto the bench seat and gripped the seatbelt across her chest with her other hand.

"Hang on!" Thom shouted.

The tail end of the van hit bottom. They shot out into the street. She didn't know how Thom did it, but somehow, he hit the gas and brakes at the same time. The rear end fishtailed around. Suddenly they were rolling south in calm waters. She took a deep breath.

He looked in the rearview mirror, eyes alarmed. "Leo?"

"I'm okay."

"Are they following us?"

She swiveled around and gazed out the fog-encrusted back window. The street was empty save for parked cars. No cars exited from the lot. "No. Not yet anyway. They? Was there more than one? Did you see them?"

"No. I don't know how many there were. Couldn't tell. Too busy trying to keep that fuckin' Ford from running you over."

"Turn around. We have to go back and find out who they are."

"Are you kidding?"

"No, I'm not. They're no match for your van. It's big enough to protect us. Go back."

"It's already cracked up. I'm not going back."

"We need to find out who that was. Why did they target me?"

She looked behind again. Several cars followed now, but none of them were brown and damaged.

"It's too chancy," he said.

"Dammit," she said in a low gruff voice. She sat back, feeling a sense of unreality pass through her. "You saved my life, Thom."

"That was close. Way too close."

She reached up and touched the patch on her eye. She was amazed how throughout the entire attack, somehow the patch stayed in place. She unclicked her seatbelt. Bent forward, she limped her way to the front of the van and belted herself into the passenger seat next to Thom. "I don't understand. What the hell was that crazy attack all about?"

Thom shot her a look. "You tell me."

"How would I know?" She looked out the windshield, searching for brown sedans, but all they passed were SUVs and trucks. "Why are you here? How did you know to come?"

"Tonya left me the message about Traci Francisco. I talked to her husband this morning. She had her baby."

"Who had a baby?"

Thom let out a long breath. "Traci Francisco, now Traci Spencer. She lives in Houston and was nine months pregnant, which is why she didn't come to her birth father's funeral. I wondered about that, so I called and left a message. Her husband called back today."

"Oh, God," Leo said, realization dawning. "So she's not the one who called me."

"Couldn't have been."

"Who then?"

"Got no clue, but I knew something was up, so I thought I'd better follow you. Good thing I did."

"No kidding." The enormity of the situation washed over her, and Leo felt light-headed. Fear and rage came together, threaded into an emotion so strong it darkened her vision to red. Her body went cold, and her throat clogged, giving her ripples of nausea. She thanked God she was seated. She didn't think her legs would be strong enough to support her.

Was it possible someone had purposely tried to kill her? Of all the times not to have a gun, although even if she were carrying, it would probably have been in her valise, so she wouldn't have been able to get at it anyway.

Thom slammed on the brakes at the stop sign and wrenched the wheel to the left to head down the hill toward the lake. "We have to call the police. Got your phone?"

She shook her head. "It's in my valise. Probably crushed back there in the lot."

He fished around in his coat pocket and handed her his, then careened around the corner onto Highway 61 and accelerated.

She sat holding the phone, wondering how badly she needed medical attention. Her knee screamed in pain. Her calf felt like it had a permanent charley horse, and her shoulder, hip, and ribs hurt enough that she knew she was badly bruised.

"You look like a drowned rat. Oh my God, do you have blood on your forehead?"

Leo touched her temple and looked at her fingers. "Can't be too bad. It's not bleeding much."

"You could have a concussion. Or worse." Thom reached for the center controls and turned up the heat.

"I don't feel cold. Don't worry."

"I'm taking you directly to the ER."

Alarmed, she said, "I think I'm fine. Really."

"Jesus, Leo! They hit you. I think the van clipped you, too. For a moment there, I thought I'd run over you completely. I was sure you were crushed under the wheels. You need to be checked out."

She looked at his pale face and saw beads of sweat on his forehead, then looked away. Trembling a little, she pressed her feet against the car mat and rolled her shoulders. With the phone in her lap, she shook out her hands.

"I think I'm fine, Thom. A little beat up, but okay." Fear was an incredibly effective anesthetic. Her pulse still pounded, and she felt a rush of power brought on more by relief than anything. "Why don't you pull over up ahead at the next gas station. I'll get out and move around a little to see."

He glanced at her, then looked away. "Are you absolutely nuts?"

"What?"

"This is serious. It's attempted murder."

# Chapter Fourteen

Leo thought far too much attention was paid to her at the emergency room. The minute the police arrived, she suddenly became a priority patient and was whisked off for treatment. After an initial look-see by an ER nurse, she was handed a surprisingly roomy gown to change into while Thom talked to the cops out in the waiting area.

She sat on the end of an examining table and catalogued her bruises. Half an hour hadn't even passed since the attack, and already her knee was turning purple. She couldn't flex her ankle, and her calf was bruised badly. She figured her whole backside would have to be scraped and covered with contusions. Her ribs hurt from flopping up into Thom's van. Really, she knew she was a mess.

But she also felt embarrassed. She was a cop, for crapsake, and how could she have been caught so unaware? Trapped in the lot, surrounded by huge piles of snow—how ridiculous was that? If the attacker had succeeded in killing her, she could just see the headlines: *Police officer crushed in snowbank.*

It'd be funny if it wasn't so damn appalling.

When she undressed, she found her cell phone. She'd thought it was in her valise, but she'd zipped it into her coat pocket. She marveled that it hadn't taken any damage.

With a sigh, she hunted for the number for the car rental place. At this rate she was going to have to put them on speed dial. The man she talked to didn't sound surprised about her accident. She asked if this happened often, and he told her that people cracked up their rentals way more frequently than you'd expect, especially in the winter. She had to pull rank as a police officer to get him to deliver a new vehicle to her apartment. He made arrangements reluctantly and told her a lot of paperwork would be generated.

He didn't know the half of it. She'd been working when the attack occurred. Her insurance wasn't responsible. The county should be. She didn't look forward to submitting that claim to Paul Aitken.

The hospital was overly warm, so when a policeman called out and entered the curtained cubicle, he and his partner were sweating in their winter wear. She didn't know either of the earnest young beat cops. They were very polite as they took down notes. Had she seen a face? Did she notice a license number? Had she ever seen the car before? And on and on. She was angry she couldn't help with anything other than the color and make of the vehicle.

"We'll get someone over to the site," the officer named Hanson said. "Maybe there'll be some evidence left behind that will help."

"Please find my leather bag there," she said. "Everything in it will probably be crushed, but I'd like it back. I need my work files. In fact, they contain private information about clients, so recover them if you can."

Hanson nodded as he made another note. "We'll get back to you on that." He took down her home and work phone numbers and they left.

Before the curtain even stopped moving, Thom wheeled up and stuck his head in. "Are you decent?"

She let out a huff and tucked the gown tighter under her thighs.

He rolled in another foot and slung the curtain behind him. "That was scary as hell."

"Tell me about it. I think I'm perfectly okay though, just banged up a little."

"A little?" He laughed. "Do I need to repeat how many ways you could have been killed?"

"I know, I know. I'm embarrassed enough to be caught that way. I'm thankful I wasn't seriously injured and then laid up here in the hospital."

"Go with the flow. It's work comp anyway, so you don't have to pay for it. I called our Fearful Leader."

"Please tell me he's not coming up here."

"He's not, but I had to do some fancy dancing, and you know how hard that is for me, to keep from explaining why you were at the location."

"If he asks, tell him the witness would only speak to a woman."

"Is that the truth?"

"Yes."

"So whoever tried to kill you has a female accomplice."

"What if a woman was in the car?"

"You saw a woman?"

"No, I couldn't see a thing. I realize this sounds sexist, but what are the odds a man would drive a car that way? Despite the snow and ice, if I had been behind the wheel, or if you had, we'd have handled the car a lot better than that. I believe the occupant was a really bad female driver. I think the same person who called me was probably the one in the car."

"You've got a point. We can be thankful she didn't have better skills. But why target you?"

"Something has happened in the investigation to set somebody off. I talked to Shelley Clifton." She paused. "But I don't see how she could have anything to do with this. Phyllis Bolton is another story, Thom. I've got a bad feeling about her. If she heard some of my conversation with her grandson this afternoon, it could have set her off."

"She's old. Sickly."

"She smokes like a chimney. She only uses the oxygen tank sporadically. I don't know how she got the tank prescribed, but she was a lot sicklier the first day I met her than she's ever been since. What if *she* killed her own nephew? Dragging that metal tank into the BDC would have set off the metal detector, and we saw how thorough the nitwit is at the security check. She could have brought in the metal flask herself and never been suspected."

"Surely they'd check her."

"Oh, you mean the way Serena and Charley check you when you go through security at the office?"

"That's different. They know me."

"Ding-dong Richland probably *thinks* he knows Phyllis Bolton, too. She doesn't look very threatening, especially hauling that tank with her."

"But why? What's her motive?"

"Stevie Bolton said Eddie and Phyllis had been fighting about his inheritance."

"What inheritance?"

"That's what I wanted to ask the kid, but Phyllis came along and shut him up. There's more to this than we've been told or that the cops know."

"She'd kill her own nephew to get his money? How much are we talking about?"

"I don't know, but we need to find out."

Thom shook his head slowly. "It doesn't square up. Maybe she's not as sickly as she lets on, but still, no way she could've killed Mort Milford. He wasn't a very big guy, but she couldn't have choked him to death."

"Could be why the method of death is so different, Thom. Two completely different methods, so what if there are two different killers?"

"Back to motive again, Leo. Who would kill Milford and why?"

"Let's go back to the office and talk to Adam Finn. There has to be something more about the BDC that we don't know."

"First you have to be checked out and cleared."

"Right. Thanks for not letting me forget that."

➤■◀

As Thom cooled his wheels in the waiting room, he pondered about what Leo had suggested. Was it possible that two murderers were in on this? The idea made some sense. He wondered if Clark and Brandtson had considered the likelihood. And were they operating independently or in league with one another?.

His phone rang. He pulled it from the breast pocket of his suit and didn't recognize the number displayed.

Someone cleared his throat. "This is William Cattrall. You said I could call any time I had more information."

"Yeah, good to hear from you. Did you get the gum and candy I left for you at the JDC."

"Uh-huh, but that's not why I called."

"What's up?"

"Uh ... well ..."

Thom waited out the hesitations.

"I don't like to be a narc or anything, but this is bad and it's bugging me. I can't let it go. I didn't do it. You need to know that. But—but, well, I did watch."

"Okay, I understand, William. Go on."

"The day Mister Milford was killed, a little more happened after I saw Mike in the hall. I didn't tell you everything. When we got out of math, Speed and Mouse grabbed me and dragged me off to find Mike. He was real mad at us. Mouse insisted he take us outside for a smoke. I don't know why Mike agreed. Why didn't he say no?"

Thom waited. He heard anguish in the kid's voice, and he wanted to assure William, but what assurances could he make until he knew the full story?

"When we got out back, they jumped him. Beat him all to shit. I didn't hit him. I swear! I didn't touch him. But I didn't stop 'em either. They kept saying, 'That's for Eddie' and calling him asshole and worse."

"Whoa, I can see how this has been bothering you, William. What happened to Mike?"

"He tried to get away. They were on him like wild dogs, punching and kicking. He kept falling down on the ice, and then pretty soon he didn't get up anymore. They rolled him down this little hill back there. Out of sight. I—God—I figured he was dead, so what was the point of telling." His voice broke on the last word, but he drew in a breath. "I should have told sooner. I'm sorry."

"It's okay. I'm glad you told me now. I'll go check it out and call you back."

"I'm using the facility phone. I don't know if you can call me."

"I'll get word to you one way or another as soon as I can. I promise."

Thom got off the phone and sat for a moment. What were the odds of three murders in three days committed by three different parties? It strained credulity. He dialed Gary Clark's number and was relieved when the detective picked up. When Thom explained what he'd learned, Clark got off the phone fast.

A few minutes later, Leo came limping out, escorted by a nurse. Thom said, "Hurry up! I think we might have found Mike Seaver."

"No kidding?" Leo asked.

The nurse said, "Sir, she's got some paperwork to sign."

"I'll go get the van and pull it around," Thom said, "and meet you out front."

Leo nodded, her face pale. Thom didn't think she looked very good, but she was a trouper. They were letting her go, so she must be all right.

>■<

At the BDC, Leo got out of Thom's van feeling a second wind. Every part of her body ached, and she hadn't had a chance yet to pick up the painkillers the ER doctor prescribed, but she wasn't going to let a little discomfort stop her.

Two cop cruisers and a sheriff's unmarked car waited in the BDC parking lot along with a couple other vehicles. She and Thom followed the snowy sidewalk, much of which was icy from all the boot prints packing it down. They ran out of sidewalk in the back where delivery trucks unloaded onto a dock. Thom was able to roll farther on snowy blacktop, but he was stymied at the edge of the lot where snow had been pushed into high piles.

A Saint Louis County deputy stood with his back to Leo. Down an incline she saw a couple of uniformed police moving around, and she recognized Gary Clark's brown corduroy suit jacket. She shivered, wondering how he could stand the cold without an overcoat.

Behind the BDC, snow from the kitchen door out to the line of trees was packed down here and there. Someone had walked over it regularly. Leo took the same track the police made, not deviating from the path in case evidence was buried in the snow.

"Hey," she called out to the deputy.

"You can't be here, ma'am." He raised a hand and came toward her.

"Hampstead!" Gary Clark gestured at Leo. "Go ahead and let her through."

The deputy didn't look any too happy, but he stepped aside.

Leo dug her heels in and carefully picked her way down the slope. Nothing looked out of the ordinary, but then again, several inches of snow had fallen since the previous Wednesday. "Did you find him?" she asked Clark.

"No."

Two cops came out of the woods, pausing periodically to kick at buried stumps.

Clark said, "We did find some blood up near the kitchen door. There may be more blood covered over. He's not here in the immediate vicinity though."

"Maybe he crawled way out into the woods."

"He'd have had to be out of his head to do that. Ben's interviewing the witness and called me a bit ago with an update. The Cattrall kid said he and the other two douche bags split right away. They didn't stick around to see what happened to Seaver. Even injured, the guy should have made for the kitchen door."

"Or for his vehicle," Leo said. "Maybe that's why you never found his car. Maybe he staggered over to the lot and drove away."

"We'll get some Search and Rescue people out here, but my feeling is the guy took a beating and didn't die."

"Will you call me and let me know if you find him?"

"You bet." He smiled at her, an extra cheery expression on his face, and Leo wanted to groan. He was going to ask her out before too long. She could tell.

On the way back to the van, she filled in Thom, and he had the same impression she had. "Nobody would crawl out to the woods to die," he said. "They'd seek warmth and maybe medical care. If he was that out of his mind, they'd have found him nearby."

Dusk had gradually arrived. The clouds above were dark and ominous, threatening more snow by morning. Leo shivered. She wanted to go back to the Bolton house and talk to Phyllis Bolton. She remembered she hadn't told Gary Clark about her suspicions, though. Did he even know someone tried to run her down? Maybe news in the Duluth PD traveled slowly. He was damn busy at the moment. She'd call him in the morning.

Leo settled into Thom's crumpled van and felt a wave of exhaustion hit her. She regretted being cavalier about painkillers, but if she felt worse in the morning, she'd call the pharmacy and get the prescription after all.

# Chapter Fifteen

In Leo's world, she most often got bad news at home in one of three ways: her sister texted her; someone left a message on the answering machine, usually while she was in the bathroom; or she was awakened by the phone from a dead sleep at midnight. The latter occurred this time. Leo was curled up, dreaming of Daria strolling with her on a sandy beach, when suddenly she saw a metal detector, and they had to walk through it. A giant gerbil waved a wand upward, and an alarm sounded. Down with the wand—and the alarm stopped. Up—the alarm went off again . . . down . . .

She woke up with a start and grabbed the house phone. A man spoke fast, with a lot of noise in the background. Leo couldn't understand what he was saying. "Excuse me? Who is this?"

"Leona, it's Quinn Fontaine. Contract manager at Daria's law office. Remember me from last year's Christmas party? I work with Daria."

She threw the covers off, sat up, and swung her legs over the side of the bed. "Yes, Quinn. I remember you. I'm sorry. I wasn't awake."

"No, I'm the one who's sorry. I wouldn't have called if it wasn't important. Listen, Daria was in a—well, an altercation tonight at the conference."

"What!" Fully awake now, Leo stepped down to the cold floor, painfully aware of how sore her knee and calf were. She fumbled around for the light. In a short burst of breathlessness, she said, "What happened?"

"She was knocked unconscious in a—you know, like I said, in an altercation."

"Oh, my God. Is she all right? Where is she?"

"I'm not too far behind the ambulance on the way over to United Hospital. I thought you would want to know she's been injured. It's probably not life-threatening."

"*Probably?* You don't know?"

"Well, she was out for several minutes, briefly woke up disoriented, and passed out again. And you know how paramedics are. They don't tell you anything."

"Okay, I'm on my way. Did you say United?"

As he gave her general directions, Leo hurried to the walk-in closet and grabbed a pair of jeans. She tucked the phone under her chin, got out of flannel pajama bottoms, and tried to step into the Levis, which made her stumble. She threw the jeans at the bed and went to the dresser to pull out clean underwear, a bra, socks, and a t-shirt.

"I'll be there in something over two hours, Quinn. If she wakes up, tell her I'm on my way."

"Will do. Give me your cell number, and I'll call if there's any need to update you."

She recited the number and signed off, feeling panicky. Where was her cell phone? She found it on the bedside table and stuck it in a pocket along with a wad of cash. She finished dressing and grabbed her house keys along with the set the rental guy had delivered. At least this time she had keyless entry. When she opened the hall closet to get a warm coat, she remembered the mess inside. She snatched up the first winter jacket she saw and limped for the rental car.

The night sky was extra-dark with clouds obscuring the moon. Cold snowflakes slid down the back of her neck. She ducked her head to keep the moisture off her face, ripped open the car door, and jumped into the unfamiliar vehicle. She didn't even know what color it was—blue? Green? Something dark. She backed out of the driveway without even looking in the rearview mirror, and when she finally did glance at it, she gasped. In her haste, she'd forgotten an eye patch. She slammed on the brakes and dug around in the jacket pockets, thanking God when she found a spare one in a baggie. With quaking hands, she fit it over her head, adjusted it, and resumed backing up.

She was ten minutes down the road before she stopped shivering. That was, in part, because the heat kicked in and flooded her ankles with warmth, but some of it had to do with the way driving always calmed her. She focused on the road, on the street signs, and then accelerated onto the I-35 freeway, pushing the pedal to the metal all the way up the hill, past Thompson Park, and down the long, dark road to Saint Paul. She didn't want to get stopped by a cop for speeding, but she set the cruise control for nine miles over the speed limit and flew.

At half past twelve, little traffic surrounded her. She hoped the 160-mile drive stayed that way. She turned on the radio. The "Late Night at the Seventies" program played the tail end of The Eagles' "Desperado" and then segued into Fleetwood Mac's "Landslide."

Instead of calming her down, the oldies made her edgy, so she clicked off the radio.

With a start, she recalled that she hadn't checked her cell phone battery. One-handed, she groped in her pocket to find it and plugged the cell into the charger. In the bright LED light, she saw the message readout was blank, so nobody had called. She didn't know if she should be relieved or not.

She found the speed-dial entry for her sister's cell phone. Kate answered on the second ring before Leo even had the earbud situated. "Kate, are you on duty?"

"And hello to you, too, big sister. What are you doing up so late?"

"Oh, God . . ."

"What?" Kate's voice was tinged with alarm. "Is it mom again?"

"No. Daria got hurt at a conference there in Saint Paul. She's been taken to United Hospital."

"Oh, no. What happened? Where are you?"

"In the car. On the way. Would you check?"

"Yeah, we'll swing by the hospital. I'll call you back in twenty."

Leo didn't even have a chance to say goodbye. Kate clicked off, so all Leo could do was continue along down the dark and windy road, wondering, worrying.

What would life be like without Daria? Something far too large for her throat to contain pressed up from Leo's lungs and into a place somewhere in the vicinity of the back of her mouth. She told herself not to get all worked up. It might be nothing—some small thing. A minor concussion, maybe. Leo thought about Daria's beauty. She prayed nothing happened to mar her face. They already had someone in the family with seriously marred looks.

She glanced in the rearview mirror. Even in the low light, she saw her unruly hair and that damn patch, so she turned the mirror away. She concentrated out in front of the rental car, as far as her headlights revealed, as if that would take her into Saint Paul a little bit faster.

Ten minutes elapsed, and she was more nervous by the minute. As she passed the exit for Barnum and Hanging Horn Lake, the phone buzzed. She hit the button, not knowing if it would be Kate or Quinn Fontaine.

"Leo." Kate sounded calm and confident. "I'm in the ER now. She's going to be fine. Concussion, some other slight injuries. They'll keep her for observation, probably let her go in the morning."

Relief flooded through Leo's body, though her aches and pains amplified then instead of reducing. She felt tears and pressed them back. "What happened?"

Kate hesitated. "Sorry. No time. Gotta get back on patrol. I'm off at two. I'll meet you here at the hospital after."

She hung up.

Leo wanted to kill her. As soon as she caught up with Kate, she planned to kick her ass. Then again, she felt so grateful to have news—any information at all—that she might just give Kate a great big hug instead.

The clock on the dash showed the time was two minutes after one. She turned on the radio and heard the melodic guitar for a very ancient song, "Goodbye Again," by John Denver. Her mother had liked it. Leo left it on just to hear the singer's smooth voice.

Later, Leo wouldn't say the drive was the longest of her life. That honor remained with a frenzied ambulance ride she had taken as a twelve-year-old when her mother first collapsed. At least for that one, she was so busy trying to keep her mother calm she didn't have time to think. For this simple trip down to the capitol city, though, all she did was fret.

When she drew near, she didn't believe she'd ever been so happy to see the Twin Cities skyline. She drove right to the hospital, which was nestled in the shadow of the Saint Paul Cathedral. She took that as a good omen and sent a silent prayer to the church's namesake.

One thing nice about downtown at 2:30 a.m. was no problems parking. She grabbed a street slot and entered through the ER door, only to discover Daria had already been moved to a room. A nurse told her how to find the elevators, and she managed to make her way through the horrid maze. The first person she saw was Kate in her civvies, arms folded across her chest, leaning against the wall near a fire extinguisher. She pushed off, came to Leo, and opened her arms to give her a huge hug.

Kate Wallace had very little in common with her foster sister in the way of looks. Kate liked to joke that Leo was every straight guy's dream girl: tall, slender, with laughing blue eyes and beautiful shiny dark hair. Black Irish with a lovely peaches-and-cream complexion. Meanwhile Leo joked that Kate must be every lesbian's nightmare girl. She, too, had blue eyes with a hint of green in the right light, but her hair was as light as Leo's was dark. While Kate kept growing taller and more willowy until she was in college, Leo stopped long before graduating from high school and ended up nowhere near as tall. Kate stood a couple inches shy of six feet, and the few times she ever wore a dress, she was a knockout. Leo's shoulders were a bit broader than Kate's, giving her an advantage in pickup football and other strength-based sports, but Kate could play basketball like nobody's business. She'd always been a great athlete.

Leo knew plenty of guys who simply would not believe her femme sister was a cop, much less a lesbian.

"Where is she?" Leo asked into her sister's shoulder.

"She's fine. Don't worry. She's okay."

"Where's room 308?" Leo looked down the hall and saw 312. She craned her neck to try to locate 308. "Come on."

"Wait, Leo."

Leo grabbed Kate's forearm and pulled her along. Kate jerked her arm away. "Leo!" She glanced around, obviously concerned she'd been too loud. She stepped closer. "We need to talk. I need to tell you—"

Leo didn't want to wait a moment longer. She twisted away, rushed to the room, and blasted into the partly closed door.

What she saw took her breath away.

Daria lay face up on the hospital bed, her eyes closed, and a bandage around her forehead. Her eye was blackened and her lip split. Her face and jaw looked puffy.

Next to the bed, on her left, a figure had pulled a chair up close. A blonde head lay on the side of the bed with one hand resting on Daria's chest. Even in sleep Leo's lover held his hand tight to her breast.

Leo heard Kate behind her in the doorway, and then she was jerked back into the hall.

"Jeez, Leo. Don't you ever listen? Shit!"

Leo spun around and saw that Kate was embarrassed. "What's going on? Who the hell is she?"

Kate pulled her down the hall to a lounge furnished with two loveseats and a bunch of crappy plastic chairs. She pushed Leo toward a loveseat and paced in front of it for a moment, then threw herself onto the cushion next to Leo.

Leo was not an investigator for nothing. Already some unpleasant possibilities were occurring in the back of her mind, but she waited for Kate to speak.

"I talked to the work guys who came in with Daria, and here's the story. That woman in there," Kate pointed at the door, "and Daria— well, they're more than friends. The woman's husband busted in at the conference hotel, went to the after-hours lounge, and beat the hell out of Daria. I guess Daria got some licks in, too, because the husband was also treated, but he was released a while ago."

Leo sat back on the couch in shock. Kate kept talking, but over the rushing in her ears, Leo didn't hear it all. Part of her wanted to march back into the hospital room, grab the other woman, and throw her out the window. The other part wanted to slink away and lick this brand-new gaping wound in privacy.

". . . and stay the night, okay? Leo! Earth to Leo."

"What?"

"Let's go now. Sleep over at our place, and we'll come back in the morning and deal with Daria."

Leo was torn. How could she walk away from Daria and leave her in the clutches of some adulteress? But what else was she supposed to do? She felt exactly like she had in the eye specialist's office when the doctor explained they couldn't save her eye.

"I could drive home and sleep at the house."

"No. You should be around other people." Leo didn't bring up the fact that she'd be around a household of slumberers. She felt so deflated she rose and let Kate lead her to the elevator and out the door of the hospital.

The Saint Paul Cathedral loomed up, its tall spire and dome visible in silhouette against the dark night sky. Saint Paul had been no help at all to her tonight, but then again, she'd never found comfort from the church in the past, so why should she now?

Leo slept fitfully for a couple hours on the couch at Kate and Susie's house. They offered her one of the kids' beds, but she didn't want to chance waking the little ones, especially since she knew she was going to toss and turn anyway.

At five a.m. she went into the kitchen and made a pot of tea, then called the office and left a voice message with Paul Aitken's assistant, the woman she reported absences to at Rentreau Plaza. She said she wouldn't be in but didn't go into details, then left brief messages on Thom and Tonya's voicemails.

She needed to talk to Daria.

Kate had lent her an over-size t-shirt to sleep in and given her another shirt, socks, clean underwear. She thought about all those years her little sister had borrowed her clothes. It was about time she paid Leo back. She scratched out a thank you note, hung it from the metal clip on the fridge, and went out to the car.

The hospital was surprisingly lively at half past five. Nurses and orderlies moved through the halls, stopping at various stations, popping in and out of patient's rooms. When Leo got to Daria's wing, a tired-looking nurse stopped her and asked if she needed help.

"I'm here to see Daria Emerson in 308."

"All right, dear." She headed off in the other direction, and Leo went to Daria's room.

She didn't know what she expected, but it wasn't to see the little blonde-haired slip of a thing was now curled up on the hospital bed next to Leo's partner. Daria held her protectively, as though the tiny woman were the injured one and not Daria.

Leo stood in the doorway in her borrowed clothes feeling like the giant pit in *Indiana Jones and The Temple of Doom* had opened up in the floor before her. Every impulse told her to run. She might have—except for the shock. People often say in terrible situations their lives flash before their eyes, but in this case, Leo could think only of a stunned, numbing death as she fell down the pit into hell.

She would have turned to leave, but Daria chose that moment to open her eyes. It took a moment before she found Leo, and as her eyes took on comprehension, Leo looked for some outward sign of shame. There was none. Daria shook her companion, who woke up, mumbling groggily. Daria whispered something to her, and the woman slid off the bed, straightened the slinky, satiny dress she wore, and picked up her shoes from the floor. She tiptoed past Leo in her pantyhose and rumpled outfit, never once lifting her eyes. Leo recognized her from Daria's office. She didn't know her job title, but she wasn't one of the lawyers.

"Hello, Leo." Daria's voice was scratchy, and the hoarseness didn't go away as she kept talking. "I am so sorry. You don't know how sorry I am about how this went down."

Leo didn't answer her at first as she moved closer to the bed. She stopped near the foot, along the side. Something metal pressed into her sore knee, serving to ground her. "I thought you were dead."

Daria shook her head and gave her handsome lopsided grin that always made Leo want to kiss the corner of her lip. "No, luckily for me, he concentrated on my head, the toughest part of me."

Such an attractive woman, so full of life. How could she do this? Never in a million years would she imagine Daria would betray her. Leo looked at her askance with her one good eye. "Why?"

Daria knew what she meant. She crossed her arms over her chest and looked down at the thin hospital blanket. "Sometimes things just happen. I'm not saying what you and I have isn't good—"

"Isn't? Or wasn't?" Through her sense of shock and sorrow, a new emotion bloomed forth. Heat—lots of red, explosive heat. The inferno burned up from the soles of her feet to the top of her head. "Is it over with us? Or with her?"

Daria looked confused. "Nothing needs to change, you know. Things can be the same and—

"You—you—" She turned and stomped out of the room. Daria called out but didn't come after her. Little Miss Curly Blonde stood in the hallway, leaning against the wall with her slingback shoes in her dainty hands. Before Leo could kill her, the woman scurried across the expanse of tile and into room 308. Leo looked back at the door as it slowly closed, fighting tears with all her might.

→■←

Leo had never thought about the fact that even without one eye, both sets of tear ducts continue to function unless, of course, part of the eyelids are also destroyed. Both of Leo's ducts worked fine, and as she wheeled the car out of the parking lot, the black patch was rapidly soaking. Other patches had gotten damp from a stray tear a couple of times before, but not like this. Before she even got out of downtown Saint Paul, she pulled to the curb and sat for some time with her arms on the steering wheel and her forehead in her hands.

My beautiful girl, oh, she of the ethical gray world. A double major in philosophy and business followed by law school equipped Daria well for the cutthroat world of private practice. She could talk her way into or out of any situation, and with her charm, both men and women lined up to work with her, play golf or tennis, and to bask in the glow of her powerful personality. She'd make a great politician, especially since she had the knack for telling people what they wanted to hear. Always the relativist, always asking, "But what if," always looking at both—or all—sides of every single situation and rarely committing. When faced with the horns of a dilemma, Daria always seemed to think she could have both horns.

Not this time, Leo thought. I am not a horn.

She lifted her head and looked around to find she was parked along the street across from Marshall Field's. Next to her, the windows of the drugstore were dark. She was surprised to see three people walking on the wide brick promenade between the pharmacy and Bruegger's Bagels. She would expect to see pigeons running along the ground pecking at bits of food, but at six a.m. who were these people out and about in downtown Saint Paul? A lone man in a raincoat, carrying a briefcase and clutching a newspaper to his chest, came down the street. He passed the closed Candyland store and ducked into the bagel shop.

That settled it. She wiped her face with a tissue and got out. Thirty paces later she was in the bagel shop ordering a large coffee and a blueberry bagel with cream cheese. She didn't think she'd be able to eat much but was surprised at her stomach's sudden growling. She took her tray to a table in the corner and sank into a chair. Even though the place was warm and moist, she felt cold clear through. She ate half the bagel, not thinking about anything at all.

The ring of her cell phone brought her back to reality. She expected it to be Daria, but Kate's phone number showed up on the tiny screen. "Kate?"

"Hey, this is Susie."

"What are you doing up so early?" Kate was, no doubt, still crashed in bed.

"Checking on you. What's up?"

Leo had always felt comfortable talking to her sister's lover. Susie was more like family than some of the Wallace family. But right now, Leo had little to say. "Not much. Daria will be released today, I guess."

"Anything we can do to help? Do you need to stay here?"

"No, I don't think so. I'm heading back to Duluth now."

"Oh."

Leo knew Susie was no dummy, but she was also not one to pry. Still, after being awakened in the middle of the night, she deserved some explanation. Leo steeled herself to say the words. "It looks like it's over between Daria and me."

Susie's rapid intake of breath made her want to cry. "Are you sure, Leo? You're not going to do anything rash now, are you?"

Leo very nearly laughed out loud, but bitterness won over. She was never anything close to rash. In fact, she'd already decided what to do for the rest of the day, and it was anything but rash.

"Do you need anything?" Susie asked. "Will you be all right?"

"Yup. I'm fine. Tell Kate if she wants to reach me, I'll be at work this afternoon."

They ended the call, and Leo finished her bagel. When she rose to throw away the wrapper, she found a newspaper on top of the garbage can. The man in the candid photo below the fold on the front page looked familiar. The news item was titled, *Duluth detectives stumped by disappearance of chief witness.* She scanned the article. Mike Seaver was the man in the picture though much younger, more handsome, definitely alive.

She'd had no idea the story had made its way down to the Twin Cities. That's what she got for being so focused and not paying attention to what was going on around her. She thought her inattention was true about her work and now with her personal life. What a fool she was.

Carrying the remaining hot coffee outside, she stood in the chilly air feeling numb emotionally and physically. She watched the traffic light turn from green to red and back, despite the fact that no traffic came up the street. Even the streetlights were on autopilot. Perhaps autopilot wasn't so bad after all.

She got into the rental car, which she noted was medium blue and a late model Ford Taurus. She consciously added the fact to her memory bank so she'd be able to find the car again in a busy parking lot and started the engine. Soon, commuters would be pouring into the Twin Cities, and the traffic heading north ought to be light. She could drive to the apartment, change clothes, and be at her office in less than three hours. With a little luck, she might not even be all that late.

The Rentreau Plaza parking lot was nearly full, but when Leo got into the office, Thom, Adam Finn, and Mel Kryzinski were nowhere to be found. Even Tonya was gone. She thought of Thom and wondered if he'd hear about Daria's little "altercation." The public safety conference Daria attended included many law enforcement officers, and the grapevine was a hugely efficient method of news proliferation, though, unfortunately, much of what was disseminated was inaccurate. The Duluth office didn't always get information quickly, but eventually the scuttlebutt tended to arrive. How long would it take before the place was buzzing?

During the drive, Leo conveniently managed to push the issues about Daria to the back of her mind, but now they returned, front and center. What the hell could she do? More important, what would *Daria* do? Was she planning to leave Leo? She couldn't possibly expect her to look the other way while she had a mistress on the side!

Without taking off her coat, Leo leaned down and dialed Daria's cell from the office phone. When she picked up, it sounded like she was in a wind tunnel. "Daria!" She didn't care if any of the other workers on the floor heard her.

"Leo?"

"Where are you and what the hell is going on?"

"I'm in a taxi on I-94 heading home."

"What about your little dolly?"

Daria was silent a moment, Leo hoped because she was thinking of how to apologize. Instead she cleared her throat. "She's here, too."

That knocked the wind out of Leo. She rolled out the office chair and sank down in it. "So what's it going to be, Daria? Her or me?"

"I'm going to her apartment tonight to think it over."

Leo was momentarily speechless. "Her apartment! You must be kidding." She couldn't take any more and slammed down the phone. All around her was quiet. She didn't hear the usual low murmur of voices for a few seconds, and then a phone rang somewhere to the front of the office. Gradually the normal sounds of drawers opening, printers spitting out paper, and people talking started up again.

Well, crap, she thought. Now everyone knew.

She turned to look out the window, unable to fight back the tears. At this point, she no longer cared. Her lack of sleep and functioning on adrenaline for so long combined to make her feel like she was in some sort of strange aura, as though she was of this world, but not quite in it. She felt ancient, like an enervated old woman. Coming in to work was a stupid plan. What had she been thinking?

She picked up the phone and called Tonya's cell. "I hope I'm not interrupting?"

"Oh, no. I'm getting coffee at the café. I'll be back shortly. You want one?"

"I don't think so. Thanks for offering. Is there anything I should know? Any message or faxed stuff?"

"Nope. Nothing this morning so far. Except, well," Tonya lowered her voice, "some gossip is going around. If it's true, then I'm sorry. Please let me know if I can do anything."

"You mean like kill my partner for me?"

Tonya hesitated. "I can't do anything that would get in the way of completing my college degree."

Leo laughed. "That would definitely interfere. No, I don't think anything can be done, but thanks for asking. You're probably the only person in the building with enough class to be straight-up with me. Will you buzz me on the cell if you get anything related to the BDC case before the end of the day? I'm going home."

At the apartment, Leo made sure her cell phone ringer was on. She set it on the nightstand and stood staring at the rumpled bed. She hadn't had time to make it when she flew out in a panic in the middle of the night, and everything was in disarray. The bedside lamp lay on its side, her pajamas were wadded up in the middle of the shabby area rug. She thought of her bedroom at home, the room she'd shared with Daria. The king-size bed had a wonderful mattress, and the maroon and dark blue accents throughout the bedroom were homey and soothing. They'd bought matching mahogany chests of drawers, two valet chairs, and remodeled the giant walk-in closet. Would she ever sleep there again?

She stepped to the dirty apartment window looking out on the partly cloudy afternoon. She was far enough up the hill to be able to see Lake Superior, a broad expanse of gray-blue water beyond the line of houses on the bluff. From this vantage point, several miles of the arc of the shoreline were visible to her. Far off, nearly to the horizon, the outline of a tiny ship—probably an ore boat—traveled south and toward the Duluth harbor.

She turned away, unwilling to look any longer at the frozen scene below. She, too, felt frozen, and though she wished she could decide what to do, she still had too many questions. Was this a temporary midlife crisis for Daria? Was she leaving? Better question: would Leo leave her? She imagined herself putting all of Daria's clothes in garbage bags, lighting them on fire, and throwing them off the balcony of their Kenwood home in Minneapolis. It was a tantalizing thought.

But fatigue won out over revenge.

A bone-deep, heartsick exhaustion hit her as she undressed and got into bed. She'd never been both so physically sore and emotionally distraught in her whole life, not even when her mother was dying. At least then her body had been strong. Right now, she felt so weak and sore, she couldn't trust her body to hold her up any longer.

She couldn't stop thinking of Daria, probably off wining and dining her new woman, the little blonde with the Shirley Temple curls. Leo had never even looked into her eyes. She didn't want to see her face. All she wanted now was sleep.

# Chapter Sixteen

Leo's cell phone rang, jerking her out of a deep sleep. She was slow to sit up, but by the time she got the device to her ear, she was awake.

"I hope I'm not bothering you," Thom said. "Tonya said you wanted an update."

Leo had no idea what time it was. She didn't feel sharp, but she wasn't groggy. The display on the cell told her it was almost five p.m. She'd slept about six hours.

"I'm glad you called. What's happened? Did they find Seaver?"

"No sign of him yet. No sign of Paul either. He's been out of the office all day. Tonya said he got a call from someone at the capitol, and he's been gone ever since."

"Rats fleeing a sinking ship?"

Thom chuckled. "We can only hope. Mel Kryzinski interviewed those little miscreants, Speed and Mouse, real names John Karn and Russell Low. He said he scared the hell out of them. They admitted to the attack on Mike Seaver, but they swore they did it to avenge Eddie Bolton and they had nothing to do with the kid's death, said they idolized him. Kryzinski thinks they're telling the truth. They didn't kill Milford. Only one murder charge for them if Seaver ends up dead."

"What about the BDC—oh, crap. I never called Clark to tell him about—"

"Don't worry. I told him all about Christine, the Stephen King car that tried to kill you."

"Did you share our theory about Phyllis Bolton?"

"I did, but he's so busy hunting for Mike Seaver he didn't seem to take it in at all. Seaver is still their prime suspect. He has motive for killing both Milford and the kid."

"What should we do next?"

Thom didn't answer for a moment. "Our job is to make a ruling about the BDC."

"You mean, *your* job is to make that decision."

"Officially, it's my job, but realistically, it's *our* call. As far as I can tell, we can't reopen the BDC any time soon. I know Aitken will be pissed to hear my assessment. That is, if he ever comes back. Maybe they've sent him to Siberia."

"I don't know about you, but I still want to figure out who killed these people? And why try to run me over?"

"Again, we're on the same track. That's why I was thinking you and I and Adam could get together over some food and run the case. He's got some new information to share. Aitken can't fire us for consulting with one another after work hours."

"You got that right."

"Oh, and one other positive thing has happened." He paused.

"Yes? Something positive?"

"The Nichols girl has awakened, and it looks like she may be okay. She's still physically a mess, but her brain doesn't seem to be damaged too badly after all."

"Thank God for that. I'm so glad to hear it."

"Okay, then. Get going so you can meet us for supper in an hour at the Pickwick down on Superior. We can talk more then."

"All right."

"And Leo?"

"Yeah?"

"I heard you've had some upheaval in your personal life. If you want to talk about it, I hope you will."

"Right. Okay. Thanks, Thom." Her face burned. Though she was grateful he'd acknowledged the situation, she was relieved he'd done it by telephone instead of face-to-face. "See you in an hour."

➤■◄

While vacationing over the years, Leo and Daria had often driven past the Pickwick Restaurant many times but never had the occasion to go in. She didn't find parking nearby and had to hoof it back along a snowy sidewalk. Night was falling, and the last light of the day was seeping away like Leo's energy. By the time she reached the entrance, she was cold and tired.

Inside, she was surprised to see old English décor, tall ceilings, giant globed chandeliers, and all the highly burnished wood. The warmth revived her a little, and she found Adam and Thom in the old-fashioned, 1920s dining room. They sat at a good-sized table, a quarter of which contained a stack of agency files. Sliding into a chair, she greeted them and noted the guys were already on their second beer.

Thom said, "You're looking a little more rested and a lot less beat up than yesterday."

"Thanks. I'm seriously short on sleep, but that'll pass." She picked up a menu.

Adam said, "Every time I come through here, I get the Walleye. It's truly the most exquisite fish I've ever eaten."

"I'm a steak man myself," Thom said. "I hardly ever have it and their charcoal broiler does amazing things. Give me a loaded baked potato and a fine liqueur and I'm in heaven."

Leo grinned. "Why do I feel like I've fallen into an episode of *Queer Eye for the Straight Guy?*"

Adam's face took on a shocked expression, but Thom roared with laughter. "Adam, you gonna let her get away with that? Or is there advice you'd like to dispense to me?"

Leo thought Adam looked like he'd swallowed his tongue, and she had to grin. Did the guy really think he was flying under the radar? She patted his arm. "Pay no attention to us. Thom in particular likes to tease, and I'm so tired that you can't count on me to protect you."

The waitress appeared and Leo ordered a Seven & Seven. She didn't drink often, but tonight, after all she'd been through in the last twenty-four hours, she decided to splurge. They each placed their dinner orders and sat back to talk.

"Before we get serious and start opening files," Thom said as he reached behind his chair and rooted in his backpack, "I want to make sure you get this back." He handed Leo her valise. "Clark brought your bag over to the office this afternoon. I think he was disappointed you weren't there to receive it directly from him."

One of the buckles was missing, and the leather was scraped badly on one side, but it was still in one piece. The contents inside were another story.

Thom said, "I almost dumped out the five thousand pieces of broken plastic, but I didn't know if there was anything private in there, so I refrained."

Thom wasn't kidding about the pieces of plastic. The cassette tape cases and tape recorder had been reduced to plastic shards. The file folders were intact, but things like her ChapStick and mint box were flattened.

She pulled out her wallet and examined it. None of the money was gone. "I guess the assailant didn't stop long enough to get out and swipe anything." Leo returned the wallet and removed the case files, then closed the remaining buckle and set the valise under her chair. She felt a twinge of anger. The bag was a present from her foster father when she graduated from college. Dad Wallace spent good money on it, and to see it so beat up and bedraggled made her heart hurt.

When their meals arrived, they spent quite a bit of time on small talk. She was shocked to learn Adam Finn was thirty-six years old. She'd pegged him a decade younger.

Once their plates were cleared, Thom rearranged the table so Adam could lay out files.

Leo observed Adam's hands as he sorted through the paperwork. Large palms with long, tapered fingers, and his nails were professionally manicured. He wore a ring on his left hand, an ornate silver band with a pattern. She wondered about him, about his life. How long had he been partnered? What was it like to be gay in an alpha-male-dominated profession?

Adam slid a piece of paper to each of them. "That's a summary of my findings. Over eight million dollars made its way through the BDC coffers last year. Through October this year, it's up to six-point-four million dollars. As far as I can see, anywhere from twenty to forty boys are in residence during any given month. Tracking the funds disbursed by the state and insurance companies was difficult, but I was still able to determine incoming funds far exceed the expected levels, given census and expenses."

Thom said, "In English?"

"They're cooking the books?" Leo asked.

"Precisely." Adam sat back.

"Okay, this is big," Thom said as he pulled out his phone. "Let me give Clark and Brandtson a quick call."

"Wait," Adam said, "there's a lot more."

Thom said, "I want to get him over here, if possible." He rolled back from the table.

Leo wasn't surprised about discovering improprieties. She wouldn't have been surprised if there'd been widespread embezzlement either. Murder, however, seemed extreme, but people went to great lengths to hide their secrets. "I always thought Robeson was suspicious. He wanted to get rid of us in the worst way. Has he been squirreling away huge sums?"

"No," Adam said. "That's what's strange. Neither Robeson nor Milford have unusual financials, though they could have been receiving cash. If they are, they're not depositing it in their accounts.

They both receive substantial salaries, definitely on the upper end of a proper income range for that sort of job."

Thom tucked his phone in his breast pocket and resituated his chair at the table. "Clark was just leaving the station. He's going to stop by to talk with us."

Adam pointed to the printouts in front of Thom and Leo. "Many line items appear suspicious to me. Look at the vendors I noted."

Leo saw a list of names: Wilmouth Catering, Speedy Suds, HRN Cleaning, Carlson Laundry, and several more. "Doesn't the BDC do food prep and cleaning in-house?" she asked. "I mean, the laundry they send out, but why is there a three-hundred-thousand-dollar payment to a catering company?"

Thom said, "Maybe they had a fund-raiser?"

Adam shook his head. "I inquired about that. They do have fund-raisers, but nothing requiring more than a few hundred dollars in expenses. I looked further into these companies and researched them to their origins. Took me the better part of a day. To make a long story short, all of them are owned by shell companies that ultimately trace back to one Everett Robeson."

Leo gasped. "No kidding?"

"I would never kid about this."

"I know, Adam. But—but it's Everyday Everett. You know, the guy on TV?"

"I don't watch TV."

Leo knew she was gawking, but she couldn't stop herself. What kind of person didn't watch TV? At all? She shook herself. Back to the case. "Money laundering," she said. "That's the only thing that makes sense."

"My thoughts exactly." Adam closed a folder. "I'll spare you the recitation of further details which I'll surely have to provide to your superior, but the bottom line is the BDC has been receiving funds and allocating them to services that don't exist. They appear to be in violation of several state laws, not to mention some federal ones since two of these vendors are located in Wisconsin."

Thom knocked on the table. "Forgive me for asking dumb questions, but where do the funds come from? And how do they get into the BDC accounts?"

"I am unable to discern the source of the funds, but it appears BDC personnel frequently make deposits of several thousand dollars in cash at a time, along with checks and money orders. These funds go to three different banks. They also receive electronic fund transfers from the state Medical Assistance program, from insurance companies, and from other governmental sources. The accounting is complicated, and a high volume of payments is expended daily."

Thom said, "Aren't transactions over ten thousand bucks red-flagged by the feds?"

"Yes, but they seem to avoid exceeding that threshold much of the time."

Leo asked, "How do they explain the huge amounts of cash flying around then?"

"As far as I can tell, no explanation has ever been asked for. I went back two years, and it's always been this way with nary an inquiry. A thorough forensic accounting needs to be done back to the inception of the business."

"When I spoke to Shelly Clifton, she talked about a time when the BDC almost went under. She thought Robeson and Milford secured grants. I'll bet they secured a special arrangement with some shady organization."

Thom said, "I can spin a lot of reasons for Milford's death now that we know this."

Leo didn't see anyone on her right and was startled when Gary Clark slid into the chair next to her. "Oh, hi," she mumbled lamely.

"Hello, Leona." He looked at her with such hopefulness that she shifted to the side, then made herself sit still.

Thom said, "Holy shit, Clark, tell me you don't believe what Adam's come up with."

"Excuse me," Leo said. She rose and scooted off toward the restroom, grateful to get away. The case had her feeling a tiny bit of exhilaration, but behind the shot of temporary energy, she knew she was holding back a wall of other emotions. How did people function when their personal lives imploded? It had been bad enough when she'd gotten the news about the cancer in her eye. At least Daria was with her through that horror show. But now, everything was a muddle. Daria had defected, like some sort of Russian spy, off doing devious things and then escaping, only to leave everyone in her wake in a state of shock and confusion.

She washed and dried her hands and adjusted her eye patch. An old proverb came to her: *There are none so blind as those who will not see.* Had she been in denial about Daria's duplicity? Should she have seen this coming? She didn't want to think about it. Everything about her situation stank to high heaven. Stinking to high heaven? That reminded her of something. She stood gaping in the mirror for a moment.

Steeling herself, she took a deep breath and exited the ladies' room determined not to think about her personal situation. Focus, she thought. I can focus.

Clark was on his feet, gripping the back of a chair and speaking excitedly. She heard him say "How come my people didn't come up with any of this?"

"Don't blame your staff," Adam Finn said. "The BDC did a very good job burying the details. Even I didn't notice irregularities at first."

She approached, and when Clark caught sight of her, some of his excitement deflated. "Gotta run." He smiled nervously and shoved the chair up to the table. "I think another interview with Robeson is called for. I'll get back to you guys about what he says." He strode off so quickly that he nearly ran into a waitress carrying a full tray.

Leo looked at the two men at the table as she seated herself. "What was that all about?"

"I hope you don't mind," Thom said, "but Gary Clark is an idiot. He had no clue you're gay, so I found a chance to squeeze in that little fact."

"I don't know whether to thank you or clobber you with the table's centerpiece."

Adam blushed. "He asked us if we'd get a read on you, to see how he might go about asking you out."

"Oh. I see. Guess you saved me some embarrassment then."

Thom held up a hand. "Don't just thank us. You can show your gratitude by buying us another round."

Adam said, "Not me. Two beers is my limit on a work night. Besides, I think we've determined the scope of your report. Without even giving consideration to the murders, it's clear the BDC must be closed for financial irregularities."

"You're right." Leo sat thinking for a moment. "Thom, you said something Wednesday about living life at fart level."

He laughed. "Guilty as charged."

"Remember the day of Milford's murder, when we were waiting with the receptionist?"

"Yeah?"

"You said something about the lobby smelling like crap."

"Uh huh. Literally. It did."

She closed her eyes and imagined the reception area: Lizzie crying, Robeson's angry face. When she opened her eyes and gazed at Thom with her one good eye, she wasn't quite sure how to explain her hunch. "I took a domestic disturbance call a few years ago where neighbors reported a screaming fight. When we got to the apartment, an old woman and her granddaughter were having it out. My partner and I separated them. The grandma was red-faced and totally freaked out, shaking and babbling, and then she got this wide-eyed weird look and started to fall forward. I grabbed her under the arms and got my knee between her legs to try to control her descent. Dead weight is amazingly heavy. I about fell over. I didn't realize it, but as I helped her to the ground, she was dying. Her bowels opened up, and whoops!—everything let loose. You can bet that was one pair of uniform pants I changed out of. Pronto."

Adam looked like he wanted to throw up, but Thom frowned, listening intently.

Leo said, "Do you remember the next time we saw Robeson, how he'd changed clothes?"

"Yes, into scrubs," Thom said. "No way that guy would ever wear scrubs unless he was forced to."

"I think Robeson killed Milford. That's exactly what would have happened to Milford as he was choked to death."

Excited, Thom said, "Wonder what happened to his suit?" He fumbled for his phone again. "Too bad Clark booked out of here so fast. I'm going to call him again." He rolled his chair back and stabbed away at his phone.

Leo turned to Finn. "You look thoroughly disgusted."

"That's why I left police work and moved to the BCA. The first time someone vomited on me, I very nearly passed out."

Given his temperament, Leo thought Finn had chosen an odd profession, a rough-and-tumble job requiring quite a bit of intestinal fortitude. "Why did you go into police work to begin with?" she asked.

He cleared his throat and looked away. "My brother was murdered when I was young."

"A drive-by?"

"No. He was taken, then found dead two weeks later."

"Oh my God, I had no idea, Adam. How old was he?"

Adam couldn't meet her eyes. "Twelve. I was nine."

"Did they catch the kidnapper?"

"No. I've had a lifelong desire to find out who killed Tony, so therefore here I am." He raised his chin and gazed at her evenly.

She wanted to ask a whole string of questions about his brother's case, but Adam set some bills on the table, neatly folded his cloth napkin, and scooted back his chair to rise. "I'll check in with your superior tomorrow and find out whether he wishes me to do any more analysis, but I suspect I'll be sent home."

Thom set his phone on the table. "Okay, Clark's updated. You leaving, Secret Agent Man?"

"Yes." Adam smiled, and it transformed his face. "Nice to meet you both."

"Thank you for all of the insight, Adam," Leo said. "You've done great work and also been a wonder to work with."

He shook their hands and bid them goodbye, and after he left, Leo exhaled a deep breath.

Thom said, "I guess we're off the hook now for the BDC case. I can fill out the paperwork and be done with it."

"But who killed Eddie Bolton?"

"If it wasn't Robeson or Seaver, then I think you're on to something regarding his grandmother."

"Did you mention our theory to Clark?"

"Before I delivered the bad news that he wouldn't ever be creating a Love Shack with you, I did tell him we suspected Phyllis."

"Lucky you're sitting across the table there, Thoreson. I'd like to hit you, you know."

"Who, me? Little old me?"

"Yeah, you. Go ahead and play the innocent."

"Clark was skeptical about Phyllis Bolton. The cops still think Seaver is the key."

"I hope they find him eventually. I don't know why Robeson would have done anything to Seaver, but I suppose it's possible he knew something or saw something. He also could have killed Eddie. The kitchen door access made it easy."

"It's anybody's guess," Thom said. "Why don't we head home and figure it out tomorrow?"

# Chapter Seventeen

When Leo arrived at the office in the morning, she found Paul Aitken on a rampage. He was yelling something about the copy machine at Tonya, but when he caught sight of Leo, he stomped over and shook his finger in her face.

"You've caused nothing but trouble ever since you got here!"

With a sigh, Leo slipped out of her coat. "I'm sorry to hear you say that, sir." No way did she have the energy to deal with him. She stepped into her cubicle, set her banged-up valise on the desk, and hung up her coat. She slid open a desk drawer and moved the valise there. The .38 caliber off-duty weapon she'd brought with her made a thumping sound against the metal. No way was she going to get caught in a parking lot or anywhere else now without some firepower to protect herself.

Aitken followed her. "I ought to terminate you. I ought to get you blackballed from ever working in law enforcement in Minnesota. I should—"

A massive hand clamped down on Aitken's shoulder. The boss's eyes widened before he was jerked out of her cubicle doorway. A deep voice said, "Is that any way to talk to a lady?"

"Hey, take your hands off me," Aitken said. He stepped back into Leo's view, and now she saw Mel Kryzinski standing out there, a briefcase in one hand.

Kryzinski's craggy face had turned red. His suit was rumpled, but his hair was neatly combed, and his tie squared off. "Pardon me for interfering, Mister Aitken, but I think you'd better go back to your office before you say or do something you'll regret."

Aitken scampered away like a whipped dog confronting the pack's true alpha male.

"What's that guy's problem?" Kryzinski said in his deep, raspy voice. "What an asshole."

"Yeah, I don't know, and I'm not sure if you've made it better or worse for me."

"I don't envy you." He looked her up and down. "That guy's got a problem with women."

From what Kate confided, Leo didn't think Kryzinski could brag about any great skills with the opposite sex either, but she kept her mouth shut.

He said, "Finn and I are driving back to the Cities. He's meeting me here. Thought I'd come by and hand over my notes. I recorded a lot of details that may be relevant to your case."

"Did you happen to do any checking on Phyllis Bolton?"

"Quite a bit. Enough to be able to say that broad is a real piece of work. I don't think she's ever held a job. Couldn't find any evidence of it anyway, and I ran wage-matches way back to check her work history."

"Did you happen to look into her vehicle history?"

"She's got a fairly new SUV and a couple other older cars. Why?"

"I thought maybe she was the one who tried to run me over."

"She sure could've been. She's batshit insane, you know."

"Why do you say that?"

"Wouldn't you be crazy, too, if you had her past and family circumstances?"

"Come sit down." She invited him into her cubicle and cleared files off her visitor's chair. "Tell me what you've found out about her."

"You can probably read most of this in my notes."

"If you've got a minute, it'd be nice to get it direct from you so I can ask questions."

He lowered his bulky frame into the chair, and her cubicle suddenly seemed very small. The dank smell of some sort of men's cologne wafted her way and made her stomach turn. She was glad she'd skipped breakfast.

Kryzinski opened up his briefcase and pulled out a file. "Here's the skinny on the old bat. Her mother died of cancer when Phyllis Bolton was eight. Her father remarried a couple years later. Phyllis didn't like her stepmother. She got pregnant by a kid from the poor side of town named Robby Parklin who she thought would marry her. The Boltons had a lot of money, though, and it's likely the father paid off this Parklin. The kid disappeared. He dumped her, deserted the kid, and moved away."

"Unless she did away with him herself."

"Well, there is that. I wouldn't put it past her," Kryzinski said. "She gave birth to a daughter before she turned nineteen. The parents were pissed as hell."

"How did you find all this out?"

"The uncle. Duffin . . .uh . . ." He opened his file and scanned a page. "Nathan Duffin. He had plenty to say about what a creep-show his niece is. Her older brother, Edward, was the good son. Duffin actually called Phyllis a bad seed."

Leo remembered the elderly man at Eddie Bolton's funeral. "He must be on Phyllis's mother's side?"

"Yup. Mother's brother. Duffin was fuzzy on dates, but he knew a lot of details and the kind of dirt you don't find in reports. The family owned a house in Minneapolis and the place here in Duluth. They also had a time-share in Hawaii. When the kid—" he thumbed through a couple of pages "—Kayla was her name. When she was a little tyke, not in school yet, Phyllis's father and stepmother died of smoke inhalation. Their Minneapolis house burned, supposedly careless smoking. Phyllis and her daughter got out."

"She never mentioned any of this to me."

"Of course not."

"So she hasn't gotten a job all these years because of the family fortune?"

"Gets complicated there. She took over the Duluth house, but her parents only left her a small bequest and a monthly allowance for Kayla that Phyllis's older brother controlled. He's the one who inherited the bulk of the estate."

"How much older was he?"

"Four years. He lived in the Twin Cities and was a successful businessman who owned accounting businesses. Duffin said the brother and Phyllis fought like cats and dogs, especially after Kayla became a druggie in high school. She ran away from home multiple times, then finally disappeared for a while. When she came back, she'd given birth to a kid."

"Stevie Bolton. Phyllis did tell me about that."

"This Kayla split pretty often, leaving the baby with the Bolton woman. Then one day she didn't come home. She OD'd when the baby wasn't even a year old. Nobody knew who the father was. Authorities awarded the baby to Phyllis, and she took custody."

"Hey." Thom wheeled into the doorway, followed by Adam Finn. "Can anybody join your little tea party?"

"Sure," Leo said, "but it'll be tight."

"We'll huddle for warmth," Thom said. He gazed back at Adam, who was blushing furiously. Leo wondered how the guy had made it through thirty-six years of life—and police academy—if he was so easily embarrassed.

Leo summarized what Kryzinski had already told her, and the grizzled agent went on. "Edward, the brother, didn't get involved seriously with anyone until age forty when he married a real daredevil of a wife, twelve years his junior. Her name was Lindy, nickname Lucky Lindy. She wasn't so lucky in the baby production department, but after a few years they finally produced a child. Then she goes off and gets killed in a freak hang-gliding accident when Eddie, the kid, was two."

Thom said, "Now we know where Eddie Bolton got his daredevil attitude."

Kryzinski said, "Not sure where he got the anti-social personality, though. Duffin said the dead kid resembled his aunt more than his father. As for Eddie Junior's mother, Duffin didn't seem to know much about her except that she didn't come from much family. After Lucky Lindy's luck ran out, Edward Senior made his sister the guardian if anything happened to him. Like I said, Duffin was fuzzy on dates, but a while later Edward got serious about another woman, a business associate, and was planning to ask her to marry him. One night when the kid was at a sleepover, Edward got a call and left the house. He was run down in front of his own place."

"Who was the call from?" Leo asked.

"I asked that, too. Duffin said the cops could never determine who made the call or what it was about, only that it came from a pay phone a few blocks away."

Leo said, "I'm starting to see a pattern here."

"I have to agree with Leo," Thom said. "Let me guess. When the brother died, Phyllis got control of the estate."

"Bingo," Kryzinski said. "What I wonder is how long the money lasted. The uncle said Phyllis is a spender with no restraint. Buys whatever the hell she wants whenever she wants it. Her money issues were why the elder Boltons didn't want Phyllis to inherit directly. Duffin said his bro-in-law knew she'd squander it all."

Adam Finn said, "I pulled financials on practically everyone. To the best of my recollection, Phyllis Bolton has only a few thousand dollars in her bank accounts."

"But there are two estates here," Leo said. "Phyllis's parents' money is one source, and Stevie Bolton referred to Eddie's inheritance. Edward, Senior, no doubt left his funds in a trust or with a trustee. He must have made some sort of arrangements."

Thom said, "I'll find out, Leo. I can call the probate people in Hennepin County and get the scoop. What I want to know, Mel, is how'd you get all this info out of the uncle?"

"Followed him to a neighborhood bar. The old man has a real taste for Maker's Mark. I spent a little more than I'd intended, but he sure gave me the background. After he had a few, he admitted he always thought Phyllis had set the fire to kill her father and stepmother, but he couldn't prove it. Pretty sick situation."

"I'll say." Leo shook her head slowly. "First the parents, then the brother, now the nephew. All suspicious deaths. How come Duffin's still alive?"

"He hasn't got a pot to piss in," Kryzinski said. "If he dies, his pension and Social Security stop. He lives at a senior high-rise, and he's made sure not to let his niece know his bank account balance, which isn't very hefty. In Phyllis Bolton's world, he's not worth killing."

Two hours later, Leo sat in her cubicle in a funk. Thom had reached his contact at Hennepin County, and he hoped to have the probate records by end of day, so they waited.

Without much energy, Leo worked at the computer, going through reports and prioritizing what needed to be investigated. Periodically she stopped and marveled about how screwed up her life was. Everything seemed completely surreal, and yet here she was, dealing with intake as if it were just another day.

Her cell phone rang, and when she saw who was calling, she felt like she was sinking through freezing water. She clicked it on and said, "Hello, Daria."

"Hi." Silence.

"You called. What is it you want?"

Daria said, "This is the hardest phone call I've ever made." Silence again.

Leo was tempted to ask if they were finished, but she wanted to hear it from her lover's lips. Why should Leo have to do all the work? She waited.

"I'm sorry," Daria mumbled. "Really. I'm very sorry."

Motion to her left caught Leo's eye. She shifted to see Tonya standing in the doorway waving a white slip of paper. "I have to go. We'll talk about this another time."

"But—"

Feeling a combination of rage and hopelessness, Leo disconnected. She swallowed and took a deep breath before turning toward the entryway. "Tonya, did you get your Con Law grade yet?"

"It's all good. I passed. But I'm not here to talk about that. The principal from Denfield High School called and said he urgently needs to talk to you. Said it was an emergency. Here's his number."

"Okay, seems like everyone's on fire today."

Tonya said, "You have no idea."

Leo dialed and waited for a secretary to transfer the call. When Hal Dexter droned his name into the phone, she realized she'd recognize his voice anywhere.

"Ms. Reese, we've had an incident here at the school, something I thought you should be apprised of."

"Stevie Bolton was injured?"

"No. He sent out a text to a number of students earlier this week, which one of them has only now brought to my attention. Better late than never. Let me read it to you. *Thanks for being my friend. Wish things had been different.* Of course that's all abbreviated with a TX for thanks and the numeral 4 instead of the word, and—"

"Mister Dexter, where is Stevie now?"

"I don't know. The kid hasn't been at school all week. Do you think—"

"Call the police and report this right away. I'll get back to you."

She hung up the phone and rose. "Thom, are you over there?"

"Yeah?"

"Trouble in River City. I've got a bad feeling. Let's get over to Phyllis Bolton's house."

Leo jerked the wheel to the left, then back. She hit the gas, and her rental car fishtailed around a slow-moving Escalade that had strayed into her lane.

"Holy crap, Leo," Thom said. He put a hand out to the dashboard. "You almost hit that guy."

"But I didn't."

"I wish my van wasn't in the shop."

"Quit your bellyaching. I've been driving cruisers like this Taurus for years." Adrenaline raced through her veins, and she felt a familiar excitement she hadn't experienced since the last time she was on patrol. At the same time, she was trying to ignore a feeling of dread. Something bad was going on with Stevie Bolton. Would they be too late?

She said, "Call Clark and Brandtson again."

"Got 'em on speed dial," Thom said, phone to his ear.

She pulled off the freeway and whizzed down the exit ramp.

"No luck. They're not picking up."

Leo slowed at the light. Too much traffic rolled through the intersection to allow her to make the turn until the light changed. When she got the green, she hit the gas.

"Jesus, Leo, I sure hope you can see well enough to get us there."

"You keep an eye out."

"Jokes during this rough time?"

"I didn't mean it that way. Just warn me if you see anything."

He shouted, "Pedestrian on the corner."

She honked the horn. The woman jerked to a stop without stepping into the street. "Last time we did this, Thom, you were driving. Seems like only yesterday it was my life in your hands."

"And I got you there safe and sound. All by yourself you managed to get yourself sent to the ER."

"No way. The person in the brown car had more to do with it than I did."

"Try to avoid needing the ER this time, okay?"

"My sentiments exactly," she said grimly. She turned onto the street where the Boltons lived. "I was hoping the cops would be here by now." She parked, reached into her valise, and was out of the car before Thom could wrestle his chair out of the backseat.

"Wait, Leo," he called out. But she was already halfway up the stairs and not about to go back. She looked around—no ramp. She was on her own. Pressing her .38 next to her leg, she went to the front door and knocked. Nobody answered. She tried the doorknob. Locked.

Back down the stairs. She glanced down toward Thom. He held the phone to his ear, then raised a finger in the air and mouthed, "Wait."

She shook her head and moved toward the side yard. Moving carefully on the icy sidewalk, she made her way around back. An odd smell came on the wind but was gone in a fleeting moment.

Tall shrubs on three sides made the backyard seem private, but the yard was built into a bluff so the neighbors behind the Bolton house were up above enough to have a bird's eye view into the house.

Leo scanned the neighbor's house and yard. The lights were out, and the place looked vacant.

She edged along the sidewalk, avoiding ice. Someone had cleared snow off the patio, but a two-foot-high stack sat on top of a jumbo-sized gas grill. She smelled that scent again and thought it must be from the grill.

The sliding glass door was open. Leo saw a green-clad leg, but the rest of the person was still out of sight inside the house.

Leo called out, "Mrs. Bolton?"

The figure stepped out onto the patio. Phyllis Bolton held a white square thing in one hand and something in the other hand that Leo thought looked like an electric toothbrush. Leo squinted, trying to identify the objects the woman held, then it clicked. Phyllis held a metal can upside down. Some sort of liquid was dripping out of it.

"Don't come any closer!" Phyllis held up the toothbrush and moved her thumb against it. A flame of fire came out the end.

Oh, Leo thought. A picnic fire-starter. The odd smell wafted her way again, and she recognized it as some sort of accelerant. Not gasoline, but something else sharp and bitter-smelling.

"Where's Stevie?" Leo asked. "I came to ask him a couple of questions about Eddie."

"Stevie's gone."

"He's out of the house?"

"He's . . . he's gone."

"Phyllis, please put down the lighter, okay? I'd really like to talk to you."

She didn't answer. Leo saw her chest rise and fall rapidly. Little gusts of smoke from the cold came out of her mouth. She tossed the metal can aside and grasped the fire-starter in both hands, gazing at the flame. She was dressed in olive green pants, black boots, and a long tan jacket with fuzzy fake fur around the bottom and the wrists. One awkward move and she could set that fur on fire.

"Phyllis. Phyllis," Leo said in a louder voice, "snap out of it. Turn off the lighter." Leo tightened her grip on the handgun behind her back and slowly took a step.

"Stop right there! Don't come any closer." She held up the lighter.

"Listen to me, Phyllis. You don't have to do this. You shouldn't do this. It won't help. I know how much you need Eddie's funds, but this isn't the way to get them."

"They're not Eddie's funds. They weren't my brother's either. They're *mine*. Do you understand? Mine."

"Let me make sure you get that money. I can help you. Turn off the lighter and talk with me."

The expression on Phyllis Bolton's face looked conflicted. She gazed through the flame at Leo and met her eyes. She took her finger off the button, and the flame went out. "How can you help me?"

Leo took a step.

"No!" She gestured wildly with the lighter. "Stay exactly where you are, or I'll light it up."

"Okay, okay." Leo felt sweat on her exposed neck and forehead. The air was so cold her skin felt like it was freezing. She had to do something. But what? Where were the cops? Wasn't anyone coming?

Leo took a long shot. "When Eddie was admitted to the BDC, he filled out some paperwork."

"What paperwork?"

"A lot of questions about his life and circumstances. He signed a paper saying he wanted to leave his worldly possessions to Stevie."

She stomped her foot. "That little son of a bitch."

"He wasn't much of a sharer, was he?"

"He sure as hell wasn't."

"But Stevie is a sharer. Stevie wants you to be happy. He'll share with you. He'll be fair."

"Stevie can't keep his lousy mouth shut."

Leo heard the words. *Stevie can't . . .* not *Stevie couldn't.* Present, not past tense. Was he still alive? Or was he "gone" as Phyllis had said?

"Come with me, Phyllis. Let's go see a lawyer to assert your rights. I'll help you."

A strange smile started on her lips and grew to a malevolent-looking sneer. "Lawyers? Fucking lawyers? All they've done is screw me over and charge me for their pleasure."

"I know how that is." With her free hand, Leo pointed to her eye patch. "I'm up to my eyeballs in lawyers myself. But sometimes they can help us."

For a moment she thought she'd gotten through, that the crisis could be averted. Leo opened her mouth to speak, but Phyllis's eyes narrowed, and her head went down. Click-click-click.

Leo saw the lighter flare. She screamed, "No!" and brought her gun around, but it felt like slow motion. Too slow, way too slow.

Phyllis Bolton laughed as she pointed the fire-starter toward the doorway. A single gunshot rang out, and Phyllis Bolton fell.

"Oh . . . my . . . God," Leo whispered. She stared wide-eyed at the barrel of her gun. She could swear she hadn't pulled the trigger.

Leo ran forward, ready to stamp out any fire, but the lighter must have extinguished before it hit the accelerant. It lay on the ground, still looking remarkably similar to an electric toothbrush.

Phyllis rolled into a fetal position and made mewling sounds. Leo watched as bright red blood leaked onto the icy patio. She stood, frozen in place with cold winter wind blowing in her hair and couldn't bring herself to kneel down and administer first aid. Instead, the face of a shy teenager came to mind, and Leo turned to enter the house. She had to find him and determine if he was dead or alive.

And then she heard shouts. Someone grabbed her and pulled her aside. Men in black SWAT outfits shoved past. A Duluth police officer handcuffed Phyllis Bolton as she screamed in pain.

The whole yard was crammed full of cops and medics and people stringing yellow crime scene tape.

Spooked and angry, Leo said, "What the hell took you so long!"

# Chapter Eighteen

Gary Clark was the first person to address her. "Leo? Leo, come with me." He tugged at her sleeve and pulled her around the corner of the house. She slipped once, but he grabbed her elbow and held her upright. They stopped a ways down the path by the house's bay window.

She took a big gulp of air. "It took you long enough to get here."

"Yeah, but you did a great job keeping her distracted while we set up. You almost talked her down, too. Maybe you have a future in hostage negotiations."

She looked at her gun again. "For a minute there, I thought I shot her."

"Nope. Sniper. If it weren't for you, he wouldn't have been able to get in position in time. You did good out there."

She tucked the weapon into her coat pocket. "What about Stevie Bolton? We need to get him—"

"Not possible. The house is a powder keg. One spark and it could go up in smoke. The fire department cut the power, and SWAT'll bring out the bod—the kid momentarily."

"The body? You know he's dead already?"

"No-no-no-no, I don't. I misspoke." He reached over awkwardly and patted her upper arm. "He may be dead. He might not be. We'll find out."

As if answering Leo's question, paramedics came hustling around the corner navigating a cot between them. She and Clark stepped off the sidewalk to let them pass. Leo thought for a moment that they might have Phyllis Bolton, but the pale face staring blankly toward the heavens had long straggly dark hair.

Leo put a hand to her mouth and watched them navigate the stairs. "She killed him, too."

"Maybe not. See how they're rushing?"

"That's true." She'd been to countless crime scenes, and if someone was dead, the medics didn't shake a leg like those two were. "Did you arrest Donald Robeson?"

"We did. That's why I didn't get Thom's calls right away. Got him, then his brother. Who'd ever guess Everyday Everett was transporting illegal drugs in his RVs? He's been using his brother to launder the proceeds through the BDC for years. Everett isn't talking, but Robeson is singing like a bird, trying to get the murder charge reduced."

"Don't even tell me about that. I hate it when crooks get reduced sentences for 'cooperating' on other offenses they're involved in. Why did he kill Milford?"

"Believe it or not, Milford, a/k/a Mister Upstanding Citizen, was the one who cooked the books, but he saw the writing on the wall and was going to turn in Robeson and himself. Robeson couldn't let that happen. Says he snapped and killed him in a fit of rage."

"Hardly. He's going to have a hard time explaining how come he adjusted the cameras in advance. Sounds like premeditation to me."

"We also found Mike Seaver."

"Dead?"

"Nope, hiding out in a sleazy motel down in Minneapolis. He thought he'd killed Morton Milford."

"Is there no one who takes responsibility for their actions?"

"Not often in our line of work. Look, I'm going to be busy for several hours as you can expect, but I want to talk to you and Thom at length. I need to take a statement from you later tonight. Will you be available?"

"Of course."

"You'll want to get out of here before the media swarms us. The governor will be apoplectic when he finds out his brother-in-law has been arrested."

"Right. I'm going to the hospital to get an update about the boy's condition."

"Okay. I'll call your cell in a few hours so you and Thom can meet me and Ben at the station." He gave her a crooked smile and headed off toward the backyard.

She couldn't help herself. She stepped into the snow piled beside the house and up to the big window. Cupping her hands around her face, she squinted to view the inside. What she saw shocked her. She stumbled back and hastened down to the street.

Thom had obviously been rolling back and forth like a mad man. "It's about time you came back. This has been the worst ten minutes of my life. What the hell happened?"

"Get in the car."

"I heard a gunshot."

"I'm freezing. You must be, too. Let's get in the car. We need to get you out of here."

On the way to the hospital, Leo described what happened. Thom interrupted often to ask questions. When she got to the end of her recitation, he said, "She's a serial killer, Leo. Unbelievable."

"And one sick puppy, too. You won't believe what I saw through the window."

"What? Blood on the walls? Dead bodies? What?"

"Every single knickknack and figurine was gone."

"Huh?"

"When I went to talk to Stevie, the entire living room and sitting room was jam-packed full of shelves and surfaces covered with collectibles." She glanced at Thom, who looked completely befuddled, then returned her gaze to the road. "There had to be two hundred, maybe three hundred knickknacks in there."

"And they weren't there anymore?"

"No, Thom. She took the time to pack them up and remove every single one before dumping accelerant all over to burn down the house with her own flesh and blood in there."

"Holy shit, that's cruel."

All Leo could do was shake her head.

Thom's phone trilled. He pulled it from his coat pocket to check his text messages. "Oh, it's here, the probate information. My buddy says, 'Paperwork attached plus police report for Bolton death. You owe me.' Damn, I probably do." He was silent for a few moments as he read.

Leo entered the hospital ramp and looked for a parking spot.

"You won't believe this, Leo. Do you know how Phyllis Bolton's brother died?"

"I think Phyllis told me a car accident."

"That's the understatement of the new millennium. He was hit by a car multiple times. Whoever ran him over backed up and flattened him at least twice more. Murder by car." He socked her in the arm.

"Ouch. I have a bruise there."

"You're lucky to be alive because here's the question of the day. Where have we seen that car crusher M.O. before?"

"Yeah, yeah, rub it in." She parked in a slot. Despite the heater running the whole time they'd been driving, she was cold to the bone. "That is one sick woman. I feel like a terrible cop. I couldn't even bring myself to give her first aid."

"You weren't acting in your capacity as a cop. You're off the hook on that one." Thom's cell rang again. "You can go on without me."

"Are you kidding? The heater finally kicked in and I'm thawing."

Thom held up a finger and answered the phone.

Leo let out a sigh and relaxed for what felt like the first time in hours. Her whole body hurt, and the cold could only be blamed for a small part of the pain. She looked in the rearview mirror and saw a bruise coming up on her brow and another on her chin. The bruises and contusions from her Xtreme Sports Event of Car versus Human were starting to show themselves.

Thom said, "That's great news, William. Thank you for letting me know." He glanced at Leo.

She whispered, "Cattrall?" and Thom nodded.

"You still have my card, right? Yeah, keep it. If you need advice or a listening ear, call me. I mean it. Okay?"

Thom said goodbye and put away his cell phone. "The Cattrall kid's going to be okay. He's in temporary foster care, but he said the people are nice and are feeding him well. His parents cut short their travels and are heading home."

"I bet William is relieved. He wasn't cut out for juvie or detox or any of this."

"No, you're right. But he found out he's tougher than he thought he was. It's also a good sign that he reached out to me."

"He's called before?"

"Yup. Just needed a little moral support."

"Doesn't everybody?" she asked.

"Personally, I go for the immoral support."

"Yeah, you would."

Leo reluctantly shut off the engine and limped through the cold air into the hospital. They were told Phyllis Bolton was in surgery. Stevie Bolton, however, was in recovery. The doctors pumped his stomach and saved his life.

"Poison?" Leo asked the nurse.

The woman hesitated, so Leo took out her state ID. Once she saw the identification, the nurse said, "We think he consumed an overdose of barbiturates. The stomach contents have been sent to toxicology."

"Thank you. Can we see him?"

"It'll likely be quite some time before he's lucid. He still has a lot of the drug in his bloodstream, but once that clears, he'll wake up. I'll come get you then."

➤■◄

Two hours later the doctors emerged from the OR to report Phyllis Bolton had made it through surgery. She'd taken a shot to the stomach, but they were able to get the bullet out, stop the internal bleeding, and stitch her up.

"Only the good die young," Thom said. "The evil people just keep right on living and sucking the life out of society."

"At least it sounds like Stevie's going to make it," Leo said.

"Not sure what'll happen to him. He doesn't have much family."

"Maybe his great-uncle can ease him through the last of his high school years."

➤■◄

They waited another hour. When the nurse came out to see them, Leo assumed Stevie was awake and ready for an interview. She rose, but the nurse held up a hand. "The grandmother would like to see you."

"Me?"

"Yes. Only you. Follow me." She turned to leave.

Leo met Thom's eyes and shrugged. "If they come about Stevie, go talk to him, okay?

Thom nodded.

The space where Leo was escorted was an open ICU bay. Leo couldn't even count how many tubes and lines and monitors were attached to Phyllis Bolton. She stopped at the foot of the bed, not wanting to get any closer. Hair swept back and swathed in blankets, the woman looked harmless and vulnerable. Then her eyes opened, glittering and wild. Leo was reminded of how small but utterly deadly many snakes were.

"I . . . need . . . a cigarette." The voice was soft and raspy.

Leo said, "I can't help you there."

The glittering eyes looked Leo over as though she were prey. "Did the . . . house burn?"

"No."

"Stevie?"

"Alive."

She closed her eyes. "Damn kid."

Leo moved around to the side of the bed. "Why, Phyllis? Why hurt him?"

Phyllis opened her eyes but pressed her lips together, clearly unwilling to answer.

Leo said, "I can almost understand why you poisoned Eddie. But I don't see why you'd hurt Stevie."

"Stevie . . . never kept his damn mouth shut."

"You took a big chance when you brought the flask to the BDC."

Phyllis responded by glaring at her.

"I'm curious. What if the other boy, Eddie's roommate, William, had found the flask? What if the wrong boy died?"

The tiniest wisp of a smile graced Phyllis's lips. "If I did . . . what you claim . . . 'course I *didn't* . . . but if I *had,* then I would've . . . hoped they'd drink . . . together."

"But the other kid had nothing to do with any of this. He was innocent."

"Not really. He was . . . locked up. Did something wrong . . . to get there." Phyllis let out a sigh, then yawned. "So tired."

Leo didn't know why she was wasting her time. She stepped back, but before she could leave, the other woman lifted her head from the pillow.

"You said you'd . . . help me."

"What do you want help with?"

"Lawyer."

"A criminal lawyer will be appointed for you if you can't afford one."

"No. To get my money."

"What money?"

"My money . . . from Edward . . . that's mine."

"There isn't a snowball's chance in hell that you'll see a dime of those funds, Mrs. Bolton. And where you're going, you won't have an inch of space for your collectibles either."

An expression of alarm flitted across Phyllis's face, but the drugs must have been working. Her eyes rolled back into her head. Though she mumbled several more words, Leo couldn't understand anything she said. Just as well, she thought. Every word the woman expressed was a selfish demand or a cruel lie.

Out in the waiting room, she sat down, wondering where Thom had gone. He came wheeling up a few minutes later.

"The kid's okay," he said. "She locked him in the basement for the last few days."

"He knew she was going to kill him?"

"Yeah, and he's pretty broken up about that."

"Lucky he sent out the text."

"She took his phone away after that. I asked him why he didn't dial 9-1-1. He said he couldn't rat out his grandma and he hoped she'd change her mind."

"Poor, poor kid." Leo closed her eyes and leaned her head against the wall behind her. "This has been the longest several days of my life."

"I bet. But you've still got your feet on the ground. Show me a man with both feet on the ground, and I'll show you a man who can't put on his pants."

She stifled a chuckle. "What the hell? I thought we had a very clear agreement."

"Ah, yes, we did. For the length of the case. But methinks the case is over, so it's back to my regularly scheduled programming."

She let out a groan. "God save me."

Thom's phone rang. Leo half-listened to his responses. He said, "Okay, we'll be there in fifteen," and clicked off the phone.

Eyes still closed, she said, "Clark and Brandtson?"

"No, it's a case. A suspicious death in a nursing home."

"Another case?"

"There's always another case, Leo. Isn't that a comforting thought? You'll never run out of work to do, you'll always be busy, and you'll always have me to educate you in the ways of the world."

She rose and followed him down the hall.

"For instance," he called over his shoulder, "do you know why eye doctors live to such a ripe old age?"

She didn't dignify his question with a response, but he called back gleefully, "Because they dilate!"

"Oh, please," she muttered, "someone make him stop."

"Come on, Ms. Tough Cop. Race you to the car."

He took off, wheeling as fast as he could make the chair go. Leo was tempted to try to catch up, but she was far too weary. Besides, it looked like it might be a long night. They had this new investigation, and at some point, police interviews about today's events must be done. At least it kept her mind occupied, and right now, she thought that was the best thing for her.

Another case, she thought. Always another case. Thank God.

# About The Author

Lori L. Lake is the author of over a dozen novels and two short story collections. She's edited four anthologies, including *Lesbians on the Loose* with Jessie Chandler, which won a Golden Crown Literary "Goldie" Award. Her short work is featured in over a dozen anthologies including *The Silence of the Loons, Time's Rainbow, Once Upon a Crime, Silence of the Loons,* and *Women of the Mean Streets.*

Lori facilitates the Portland Lesbian Writers Group and is known for sharing writing craft resources. She is especially fond of teaching about crime fiction, short stories, and the craft of creating novels. In her spare time, she runs a small publishing house called Launch Point Press and administers the Alice B. Reader Appreciation Awards.

Right at the edge of Portland, Oregon, Lori lives in the Fortress of Solitude/Sanctuary of Solace where she spends time reading, writing, editing, playing guitar, adoring pop and oldies music, painting and coloring, photographing nature, and enjoying the exploits of her multitude of nieces and nephews.

You can find out more about her at:
http://www.LoriLLake.com

*9781633040168*